# The
# Phoenix
# Unchained

# The Phoenix Unchained

## Book One of The Enduring Flame

# Mercedes Lackey and James Mallory

A TOM DOHERTY ASSOCIATES BOOK    *New York*

THE PHOENIX UNCHAINED: BOOK ONE OF THE ENDURING FLAME

Copyright © 2007 by Mercedes Lackey and James Mallory

A Tor Book
Published by Tom Doherty Associates, LLC
175 Fifth Avenue
New York, NY 10010

www.tor.com

Tor® is a registered trademark of Tom Doherty Associates, LLC.

Library of Congress Cataloging-in-Publication Data

Lackey, Mercedes.
    The phoenix unchained / Mercedes Lackey and James Mallory.—1st ed.
      p. cm.—(The enduring flame ; bk. 1)
    "A Tom Doherty Associates book."
    ISBN-13: 978-0-7653-1593-9
    ISBN-10: 0-7653-1593-9
    1. Magic—Fiction. 2. Magicians—Fiction. 3. Elves—Fiction. I. Mallory, James. II. Title.
    PS3562.A246P5 2007
    813'.54—dc22

                                                                    2007019647

First Edition: October 2007

Printed in the United States of America

0  9  8  7  6  5  4  3  2  1

TO DIOGENES, MY CONSTANT COMPANION

—JM

# The Phoenix Unchained

# One

## The Flower Festival

IT WAS FESTIVAL Sennight in Armethalieh, and even though spring was sennights away, the entire city was garlanded in flowers of every kind. The City's greenhouses were always kept busy for moonturns in anticipation of the demand, for what was the anniversary of the Great Flowering without flowers?

Though the City streets were still crusted with the remains of a late snow—it was barely Kindling, and the only flowers to be seen in the natural world were snowdrops and a few hardy early daffodils—every house on the street was garlanded in evergreen swags and bright glass and metal flowers. Even the lampposts had been decorated. Indoors, where it was warmer, every home's Lightshrine was filled with flowers dedicated to the Blessed Saint Idalia and her brother Kellen the Poor Orphan Boy, who had broken the power of the Endarkened over ten centuries before.

When he'd been a baby, Harrier Gillain had been sure that all this celebration was entirely for him. After all, he'd been born during Festival Sennight, and his Naming Day was the first day of Festival. His three older brothers had been happy to contribute to his confusion for as long as possible, assuring him that yes, indeed, the City-wide celebration was entirely for him, and certainly it all meant that he would grow up to be a great Wildmage, perhaps even a Knight-Mage like Kellen the Poor Orphan Boy.

Even as a baby, Harrier had found that hard to believe. Everyone knew that Knight-Mages belonged to the Time of Legend. You might as well hope to see a dragon or an Elf. And while everyone knew that they were both as real as Wildmages, it was also true that they'd withdrawn to the lands far to the East only a century or two after the Great Flowering. Harrier had more chance of meeting a Wildmage, and he had about as much chance of that as he had of . . . well, of becoming the Chief Magistrate of Armethalieh, Highest of the Nine.

But that was something he'd actually stopped thinking about a very long time ago. These days, Harrier knew exactly how his future would go. Once he'd finished his schooling, he would do exactly as his father had done, and his father, and his father, for more generations than Harrier could count. He would do just as his brothers had already done, and go to work for their father, Antarans Gillain, the Harbormaster of Armethalieh.

His eldest brother Eugens worked in the Customs House. His second-eldest brother Carault was apprenticed to a captain who plied a packet (one in which Antarans Gillain owned shares) between the Harbor and the Out Islands; some day, Carault vowed, he would earn his Sea Mastery and captain a Deep Voyager to the Selken Lands at the far side of Great Ocean.

And then there was Brelt.

Harrier sighed.

Brelt was twenty—three years older than Harrier—and the

Gillains had thought that he would be their last child. Everything would have worked out very well if he had been, for that would have meant one for the sea, one for the land—in this case, the Customs House—and the youngest child to follow in his father's footsteps and be trained up to assume his position, as was the tradition in the Gillain family. Brelt Gillain absolutely loved everything to do with the work of being Harbormaster: the details, the diplomacy, the need to have the customs and rules not only of Armethalieh the Golden, but of every land she traded with, constantly at the forefront of his mind.

But then Harrier had been born. And later this year, when Harrier graduated Armethalieh Normal School, he would come to work as Apprentice Harbormaster, and Brelt would move over to the Customs House to begin an apprenticeship under Eugens. It really didn't seem fair. But as Brelt had told Harrier cheerfully, Harrier was even *less* suited to the Customs House than he was to being Apprentice Harbormaster. Brelt assured him he would be happy enough in the Customs House. Much of the work was similar, after all.

Harrier knew that Brelt was right. And both of them loved the Port and the Docks—they'd grown up there, having been brought to work by their father from the time either of them could walk. It was just that Harrier knew, deep down inside, that Brelt had the potential to be a far better Harbormaster than he would ever be. Brelt was glib and diplomatic, and always knew the right thing to say.

Harrier? Well, even Harrier's best friends called him stubborn.

*But Da is a good man, and a smart man. He'll do what's best for the City. If I am a hopeless apprentice, why, he'll see that. He'll have Brelt back out of the Customs House so fast it'll steal the wind from the sails of every ship from here to the Out Islands. And then . . .*

What then? Harrier certainly couldn't take Brelt's place in the Customs House.

*Well, Da will think of something. And today's too fine a day to worry about something that's moonturns and moonturns away. Not with a whole sennight of holiday from lessons, and me with a day of liberty from chores.*

In fact, Harrier not only had a day of liberty, he had a day of exile, since he'd been strictly banished from his own home, forbidden to return before Evensong Bells. His mother had assured him that the preparations for his Naming Day party would proceed much more smoothly in his absence. And so, as he often did, Harrier went seeking his best friend to share his rare day of freedom with.

HARRIER'S household rose at First Dawn Bells—even though his father, as Portmaster, was one of the most important men in the City, Antarans Gillain's family still kept Tradesmen's hours. Harrier knew that in contrast to his family's habits, most of the rest of the City—especially the Nobility—preferred to lie abed and miss the best part of the day. But even though the Rolforts were members of the Nobility—*minor* nobility, Tiercel always corrected him, whenever he mentioned it—the Rolfort household stirred to wakefulness only a bell after Harrier's did, for even during Festival Sennight, when the Port was quiet, and many of the shops were closed, the administration of the City must go on. As he headed in the direction of the Rolfort townhouse, only two Bells after his own awakening, Harrier was confident he would not only find them all awake, but that Lord Rolfort would already have departed for the day to his duties in Chief Magistrate Vaunnel's office.

When Harrier reached his destination, he took a moment to admire the Festival Sennight decorations that bedecked the front of the Rolfort townhouse before entering the small neat courtyard. The great stone unicorns at the gates had been garlanded with evergreen wreaths studded with the traditional glass flowers. His nurse used to tell him wondertales about the Time of Mages, when all the statues in Armethalieh were alive, and could walk and talk. It was a pretty story, though he'd long since outgrown wondertales. He didn't believe it, anyway. Not even a Wildmage could bring stone to life. But the stone unicorns with their garlands were pretty enough.

In the little courtyard between the unicorns and the front door, tall evergreens in pots had been brought from the back garden and arranged in front of the pillars. Each one had been carefully garlanded with brilliant glittering swags of tinsel—Harrier recognized Hevnade's work; the eldest of Tiercel's four sisters was always the one who took charge of the Festival Sennight decorations. Under her direction, the little courtyard of the Rolfort townhouse had been turned into a spring forest in full magical bloom.

Over the door of the house itself, a representation of the Eternal Light had been hung, its golden rays sparkling in the early morning sun. More garlands of green framed the door itself and, as a final touch, an enormous wreath was attached to the door, the evergreen interwoven with sweet-scented herbs and bright berries. With only a little difficulty, Harrier located the door knocker in the midst of it—a large brass object in the shape of a cheerful, fat-bellied Faun—and knocked loudly.

"I knew it would be you!" Doreses said, opening the door. She was the second-youngest of Tiercel's sisters, claiming the door-duty today because, like most of the noble households of the City, the Rolforts had given their servants the day off. "You spend more time here than in your own home."

Harrier didn't bother to dignify the gibe with a response. Instead, he focused his attention on the squirming bundle in her arms. "And how is the man of the house today?" he teased.

"*You* hold him," Doreses said promptly, depositing baby Priadan unceremoniously into Harrier's arms and walking off.

There was a moment of chaos while Harrier juggled his giggling kicking burden—fortunately he was already an uncle several times over, and not in the least afraid of babies—before settling his unexpected charge securely in the crook of his arm and kicking the door shut with a backward jab of his boot.

Priadan's birth, just a bit over a year ago, had come as a great surprise to the Rolforts, for after Brodana's birth, the Healers had told Lady Rolfort that there would be no more children, and that had been eight years ago. With five children—and four of them girls—the Rolfort family had seemed entirely complete. Priadan had come as a complete surprise to everyone.

But a *good* surprise, as Tiercel—the eldest—insisted. It gave his younger sisters something to fuss over. And—as he told Harrier—he no longer had to worry about being the only one to carry on the Rolfort family name. Though as Priadan was only a little over a year old, it would be quite some time before they could expect much from him. With the baby in his arm, Harrier followed the familiar path to the breakfast room.

The family was still gathered around the table: Lady Rolfort, her four daughters—ranging in age from fourteen to eight, and all completely beneath Harrier's notice—and their elder brother, Tiercel.

Theirs might have seemed an unlikely friendship. Harrier was the sturdy bluff son of the Harbormaster of Armethalieh. Tiercel was the son of a member of the minor Nobility, destined, as generations of his family before him had been, for a secretaryship on an administrative council as soon as he had completed his schooling. But the boys had been inseparable since the day they had met. It was one of Harrier's first vivid memories. He'd been three years old.

⤳

THE day was bright and warm. Harrier Gillain sat outside his Da's office, watching the sun sparkle on the water of Armethalieh Harbor. He was filled with pride that his Da trusted him to play out here all by himself and not go wandering off. But he knew perfectly well that the Docks were a dangerous place for little boys, and Da had told him exactly where to stay. He concentrated on his wooden ships, racing them against each other over the wooden planks. Suddenly his eye was caught by a flash of movement. A little boy had come running out the back door of the Harbormaster's Office, and he was running down the wharf toward the water just as fast as he could go.

"Hey!"

The little boy didn't stop. He ran all the way to the end of the wharf, and Harrier was sure a grownup would appear, but no one did. That was wrong. He wasn't allowed out on the wharf at all unless Carault or Eugens or a grownup was with him.

"Hey!" he yelled again, setting down his wooden ship and getting to his feet. What should he do? There didn't seem to be any grownups around, and the little boy with the white hair was teetering on the edge of the wharf. In another minute he'd fall into the water, and while Harrier didn't quite believe his older brothers' tales of boy-eating sea monsters lurking in the water, he certainly believed his Da's stern warnings that little boys must not, on any account, go down to the edge of the wharf.

He got to his feet and ran toward the other boy.

He reached the end of the planks just about the time the stranger had decided to lie down on his stomach and squirm out as far as he could in order to see what he could see. And then wriggle out just a little farther. And then a little farther still. And just as he was slipping into the water, Harrier managed to grab his ankle.

And hold on, just long enough, for his Da and the boy's nurse to get there.

And that was how Harrier Gillain met Tiercel Rolfort.

It was the first time he saved the younger boy from trouble, but not the last, for Tiercel possessed an abiding curiosity about, well, everything, as well as a conviction that nothing could possibly go wrong during his explorations—a conviction that Harrier had disproven more than once down through the intervening years.

~

"HARRIER." Tiercel looked up as he entered the room, blue eyes glinting with amusement. "Is it Evensong Bells already? Come to escort us to your Naming Day party?"

"Cast out of my own home so they can prepare for it in peace, as you know perfectly well," Harrier answered cheerfully. "So I thought I'd come and bother you instead."

"You know you're always welcome here," Lady Rolfort said kindly from her place at the head of the table. "Especially as you're so good as to take over those duties that Doreses seems to feel are too much for her."

"Mama!" Doreses protested. "He *asked* to hold the baby!"

Lady Rolfort simply held out her arms, and Harrier crossed the room and deposited Priadan into them. The toddler promptly squirmed to get down from his mother's lap, taking an unsteady step before sitting down with a thump on the gently-worn carpet.

"Thank you, Gentle'dy," Harrier said politely.

"Have some tea, Har," Tiercel said. "And I'm sure you wouldn't mind another breakfast."

Harrier grinned. There were some advantages to visiting a Noble household. Breakfast in his own home had been almost two bells ago, and he had no objection at all to another one. He collected a clean plate and cup from the sideboard, helping himself from the wide variety of dishes laid out upon the sideboard before seating himself beside Tiercel.

As he ate, he made polite conversation with Lady Rolfort, assuring her that his mother looked forward to seeing them all this evening at the party (which was certainly true) and telling her anything he knew of the Port gossip that he thought might interest her.

"You begin your Apprenticeship this summer, don't you?" Lady Rolfort asked.

"Yes, Gentle'dy. As soon as I graduate from the Normal. Of course, Tyr has a much grander future before him."

Tiercel kicked him under the table.

Lady Rolfort smiled. "University. You really must choose a course of study, Tiercel. You shouldn't leave it till the last instant."

Tiercel ducked his head. "No, Mama. I promise. I'll choose something soon."

Lady Rolfort laughed. "He has been saying that for the past year, of course! But I am certain that whatever you choose, it will be perfectly suitable. And now, since I am also certain that Harrier did not come here to spend the day indoors with you, why don't the two of you run along? Just be certain to be back here no later than Second Afternoon Bells, so you have plenty of time to wash and dress for the evening."

"Are you sure, Mama?" Tiercel said, gesturing at his sisters. "I mean—"

"I am quite certain that I can keep four girls occupied for the day," Lady Rolfort said firmly. "And if I don't decide to sell them to the Selken Traders, I might even take them to see the Festival Fair later."

The squeals of "Oh Mama" and "Yes, please" were quite loud and shrill enough to make Harrier want to cover his ears—and to be grateful that his nieces were not old enough to be quite so— enthusiastic.

❧

THE two boys stood in the courtyard of the Rolfort townhouse. But despite a pocket jingling with silver unicorns and copper demi-suns—more money than most boys his age saw in a moonturn— Tiercel's mood was somber.

"I don't see why Mama is so convinced I will somehow figure out what it is I want to study at Armethalieh University between now and Harvest moonturn," Tiercel said, sounding uncharacteristically glum.

"Well, it hardly matters what you study, does it?" Harrier answered bluntly. "It's not as if they teach anything *practical* at University."

"Why does everything have to be *practical* with you?" his friend retorted.

"See how far you get when things aren't. I like things I can see, hear, feel, and touch," Harrier said firmly.

"You always have," Tiercel responded with a smile. "So, we have time and money. Where shall we go?"

"The harbor?" Harrier suggested, as the two friends walked off down the street.

If the City was grandly decorated for Festival, then the Port was even more grandly decorated, for it was there, according to legend, that the unicorns had run across the water to save the City. Every ship in Port flew a unicorn pennant at Festival time, and competed to see which ship could produce the most elaborate unicorn decoration upon its bow.

"We always go to the harbor," Tiercel said dismissively. "We could go to Temple Square."

"The Great Library? *Bor*-ring," Harrier sing-songed. "And *you* always go to the Library."

"The University? The grounds are decorated for the Festival," Tiercel suggested.

Harrier took a deep breath and huffed it out in a snort of exasperation. "You'll see enough of it come autumn, won't you?"

"I suppose," Tiercel agreed.

It had been three years since the two boys had attended the same school. Those bound for University transferred to the Preparatory School at thirteen, to spend three years there before entering University at sixteen. Those who were going into Apprenticeships stayed at the Normal School until the end of the school year in their seventeenth year, and then signed Articles with a Master in their field.

As they argued amiably over all the places they *could* go, their steps took them from the streets of the Noble Quarter and into the Tradesman's District, which bordered it. Here the streets were busier, even on the first day of Festival.

Suddenly a shower of snow rained down on them from above. Harrier—who had gotten most of it down his collar, hopped and swore, looking around for his attacker. Tiercel danced out of reach of his frantic thrashings, laughing and pointing upward. Harrier looked in the indicated direction. On a second floor ledge, an industrious Brownie housewife was sweeping away at the snow with a tiny broom. Tiercel waved up at her, and the little creature paused in her labors to wave back before continuing to sweep the ledge free of snow.

Brownies were one of the few Otherfolk races who had elected to remain among humans when most of the Otherfolk—at least the ones that people could see—had gone Eastward with the Elves. Their lives and ways were a mirror of the humans they so closely resembled, and it was said that to have a Brownie family living in the walls of one's house brought luck. Both the Rolforts and the Gillains had had Brownie families—perhaps even the same set of Brownies—living with them for as far back as their family records stretched.

"She could have picked a better time," Harrier grumbled, still shaking himself free of snow, and skipping back to dodge a fresh shower of it. "It's Festival. Nobody works on Festival."

"Brownies do," Tiercel said inarguably. He stepped out into the street, motioning for Harrier to follow. "Did you know that there didn't used to be Brownies in Armethalieh?"

Harrier snorted. "I suppose that next you'll be telling me that there didn't used to be *Centaurs* in Armethalieh," he said, grabbing the collar of Tiercel's cloak and hauling him back onto the walk-way, out of the path of a troop of Centaurs who were trotting up the street in the other direction. This particular troop had undoubtedly come for Festival Fair; by the end of the sennight the

City would be jammed with visitors from all the Nine Cities, and there wouldn't be a bed to be had in a hostel from here to Nerendale. While every city had its own Festival, the one in Armethalieh was the oldest and best.

⁂

BY unspoken consent, the boys were heading toward the main Garden Park at the center of the City. The Festival Fair would already be underway there—singers and dancers and storytellers, games of skill and chance, and—later in the day—a dozen different retellings of the events that Festival celebrated, enacted by live actors, carved puppets, and even trained dogs. Festival Fair had something for every taste.

"Do you suppose it all happened the way they say it did in the wondertales?" Tiercel asked idly as they walked. "With the dragons and the unicorns and the Elves?"

It was the same question Tiercel had asked—in one form or another—every Festival Fair for as long as Harrier had known him, and every year Harrier gave him pretty much the same answer. "Well," Harrier said, "the Wildmages say that it did. The Elves came and rescued us and helped us destroy the Endarkened forever. And then they all went away to live far, far away—oh, not the Wildmages, of course. Just the rest of them." He was never quite sure whether Tiercel forgot the answer from year to year or it just didn't satisfy him.

"Well, yes. I saw a Wildmage once. At least, Mama did. She took me to Sentarshadeen when I was a baby, and so sick that the Healers couldn't do anything for me, and there was a Wildmage there, and he did actual magic and healed me—"

"Tyr, you *never* get tired of telling that story."

"Well, it *happened*."

"And your point?"

"Just that I'm wondering if all the rest of it is just as true? About

Jermayan Dragon-rider and Kellen the Poor Orphan Boy who became a Knight-Mage, and the Silver Eagle that got turned into a woman and became the Blessed Saint Idalia and killed the Queen of the Endarkened. That stuff."

"How should *I* know? You're the one who's always got his head stuck in a musty old book. Anyway, it happened about a million years ago."

"Well, if the priests in the Temple are right, it happened one thousand and eight years ago this sennight."

"Too much information, Tyr."

Maybe Tiercel ought to become the next Harbormaster, Harrier mused. Because anybody who could remember all the things that Tyr was always telling him about could certainly remember the catalogue of Ships In Port and all the Customs regulations, too.

Of course, that didn't mean that Harrier wanted to spend the rest of his life doing what Tiercel was going to be doing when he graduated University in four years, even if he'd been smart enough to get into University in the first place. No, he liked his life just the way it was.

More or less.

TIERCEL Rolfort regarded his friend with an indulgent expression, doing his best not to grin.

He loved teasing Harrier.

He just wished, sometimes, that Harrier would stop pretending he was *dumb*. Because Tiercel knew perfectly well that Harrier wasn't. He was going to be Harbormaster some day, and the Harbormaster was the second most important person in Armethalieh. Tiercel's father had said, over and over, "stupid men might gain power, but they never hold it." Harrier's family had been Harbormasters in Armethalieh for centuries—and not only had the post passed down in the family in an unbroken line, but the City had prospered.

In a way—though he'd never say something like that to Harrier of course—Tiercel envied his friend. Harrier had always known exactly what his future would hold, and he'd always seemed happy with it. He loved the Port and the Docks. He was prepared for his future.

Tiercel had no idea what he wanted to do with his life. He knew what he *was* going to do with his life, of course. He was going to University.

Harrier was right about one thing. It really didn't matter what Tiercel studied there. It wasn't like an Apprenticeship, preparing him for his future trade. It was to lend him polish and sophistication and culture, so that when he joined the ranks of the other minor nobles and high-ranking Tradeborn who served in the secretaryships and clerkships and consular posts that did the work that kept the City running, he would be among friends.

Friends who shared his interests.

Only he didn't think that was going to happen.

It wasn't that Tiercel Rolfort was a shunned outcast. People liked him. He made friends quickly and easily. Only . . . not close friends. He liked helping people, and he liked solving problems, and over the years, those around him had naturally developed the habit of coming to him with their problems. But once the problem was solved, they sort of . . . drifted away again.

All but Harrier. Tiercel shrugged inwardly.

From the moment they'd met, the two boys had been allies. It didn't matter what harebrained scheme it was—Harrier's plan to sail a small boat to the Out Islands; Tiercel's plan to explore the City sewers to discover evidence of the City's ancient past—each had willingly fallen in with the other's plans. There could not have been two boys more un-alike in every way: Tiercel slender and blond, blue-eyed and fair; and Harrier, ruddy and red-headed and stocky, with eyes that went from brown to green depending on his mood. When they were *entirely* green, Tiercel had long-since learned, it was best to be quiet and careful around his friend, for

Harrier was capable of losing his temper completely, and when he did, it was a very bad thing for all concerned.

But their friendship seemed to be built as much upon their differences as upon any ways in which they were alike—and in fact, the further they had gotten from boyhood, the fewer of those there had been. Harrier was interested in things he could see and touch, and the only problems that held his interest at all were ones he could see a quick solution to.

Tiercel liked puzzles and problems and mysteries, the more peculiar the better. He liked solving them, of course—the problems his age-mates brought to him could almost always be solved, once you knew all the elements—but the problems he liked best were the ones that didn't really seem to have any solution.

*Why* had the Elves gone away, for example? They didn't dislike humans. His schoolmasters taught that the Elves had lived among humans for centuries after the defeat of the Endarkened and helped them rebuild everything that the Endarkened had destroyed. In fact, all of the Nine Cities were built in places that the Elves had once had cities.

So why had the Elves left? No one seemed to really care. It was such a long time ago, after all.

Maybe somebody at the University knew. He supposed he could ask the professors once he got there, though what he'd do with the information once he had it, he wasn't exactly sure.

"Look!" Harrier said excitedly, breaking into his reverie. "I can see the Fair! And look! They're setting up the Flower Wheel! Oh, Tyr, it's even taller than last year! We've *got* to ride that!"

Tiercel gulped and nodded. He hated heights.

‹❧›

SEVERAL bells later the two overstuffed and nearly exhausted teenagers wended their way homeward, having spent a glorious day sampling all the pleasures that Festival Fair could offer. Harrier had ridden the Flower Wheel three times to Tiercel's once—once was enough, in Tiercel's opinion—and both boys had gorged themselves on highly-spiced meat pies and sweet pastries, despite the enormous feast that was to come this evening as part of Harrier's Naming Day celebration. Harrier had won several fairings at the games of skill—he'd given them to Tiercel to present to his sisters—they'd rented skates and taken a turn around the small ice rink, and had watched several different historical plays, including The Sacrifice of the Blessed Saint Idalia (a favorite of both of theirs, as it had both Endarkened and a dragon) and one showing the day when the Wildmages and the unicorns came to Kellen the Poor Orphan Boy as he stood shivering in rags in the snow, cast out by his family, and gave him his enchanted sword and told him he was the Knight-Mage destined to unite all the Armies of the Light against the Darkness.

(*"If a bunch of people came to me and said something like that,"* Harrier had said, *"I'd laugh in their faces. Then I'd run."*

*"No you wouldn't,"* Tiercel had answered. *"Not if it was Wildmages. And unicorns."*

*Harrier hadn't answered. Tiercel was right, of course. But Tiercel had known he wanted to disagree.*)

But now their day of liberty was at an end. As they reached the top of Tiercel's street, Evensong Bells began to ring out.

"Oh, Light, I'm late!" Tiercel groaned.

"Not yet," his friend assured him cheerfully. "But you're about to be."

Harrier watched for a moment as Tiercel headed for the Rolfort townhouse at a dead run, cloak and tunic flapping, then turned and made for his own door in a no-more-sedate fashion.

# Two

## A Naming Day Gift

**B**Y THE MIDDLE of First Night Bells, Harrier's Naming Day party was well underway. As befit a party commemorating the Seventeenth Naming Day of one of the sons of the Harbormaster of Armethalieh, the event was not only well-attended by friends of the family, but visited by those who wished Antarans Gillain to think well of them over the year to come. Fortunately those visitors came early and stayed only briefly, and by the time a few chimes had passed, the party was what it ought to be: a celebration held by family and attended by friends.

*Where will we all be this time next year?* Tiercel wondered. He was standing in a corner, attempting—so far successfully—to avoid the dancing. Harrier was not so lucky; at the moment he was out in the middle of the Gillains' main parlor—converted for the evening to a dancing floor—getting ready to dance with Tiercel's sister Hevnade while Goodlady Divigana, Harrier's mother, looked on indulgently.

Tiercel knew that there'd once been some talk of a match between the two, but the days when families did anything but advise their children on whom they should marry were long gone. This was hardly the Time of Mages. And Hevnade was barely fourteen.

*Next year . . .*

The glum mood he'd been fighting—mostly successfully—since he'd awoken this morning to the ring of the Festival Day carillon returned full-force. This was the last year he'd see much of Harrier at all. Next year Harrier would be far too busy with his duties as Apprentice Harbormaster to have any time for his old friend.

And he? Well, he'd be at University. Papa said you had to study hard there.

And after that?

Oh, maybe someday he'd win one of the coveted City Magistrateships. Magistrates spent their whole day solving other people's problems. That would be nice. Tiercel tried to work up an interest in his future.

"*There* you are, Tiercel! This is no night to be hiding in corners! Come and dance!"

"Oh, Mama, I don't—"

"Come and dance," his mother said firmly, taking him by the elbow and leading him out from behind the ornamental garland behind which he'd been—fairly successfully until now—hiding. Ignoring his half-voiced protests, she conducted him out toward the dancing floor. "They're making up a set, and we don't want to delay them."

But just as the dancers were about to begin—he was paired up with Brelt's wife, Meroine, to his relief: she was a good dancer, and would get him through the elaborate figures without disaster— there was a sudden disturbance in the doorway.

"What? Starting without me? Now, I call that rude!"

"*Alfrin!*" Divigana cried in delighted surprise.

"Now, little sister, how could you possibly think I'd miss my little nephew's Naming Day? After all he's—what? Eight? Nine?" the eccentrically-dressed stranger roared cheerfully, swooping Divigana off her feet and swinging her around as if she weighed nothing at all.

"Seventeen, Uncle Alfrin," Harrier said resignedly, stepping forward.

His uncle regarded him in disbelief. "Surely I haven't been gone that long," he muttered.

"Surely you have," his sister said firmly. "It was supposed to be only a *short* trip to the Selken Isles."

"Ah, but Divvy, once I was there, the stories I heard! There is a land—far to the west of the Isles—where, so they say, there are people with skin the color of the night sky. And others with the wings of birds! They say there's a country where dogs and horses can talk, and the people go about without any clothes at all, and do exactly what the beasts tell them. They say—"

"And did you see any of that, Alfrin?" Divigana interrupted, sounding indulgent.

"Well, no," her brother admitted. "But I saw wonders enough. "Why, let me tell you about the time our ship was attacked by pirates—sunk, too—and if not for a great warm-blooded fish that swam up out of the depths and carried me to safe haven, I wouldn't be here to tell you about it."

Divigana wrinkled her nose doubtfully.

"I swear by the Wild Magic, it's all true," her brother said virtuously. "It carried me to an island where the people use the creatures to herd their livestock, just as we do with dogs."

"Their sheep must get very wet," Antarans commented disbelievingly. "But come, let me get you something to drink. And then you can tell us all why you aren't still there."

"As to that, there were no books, of course," Alfrin said virtuously. "And speaking of books, it's a poor guest I'd be if I came all this way and forgot young Harrier's Naming Day present. I have it right here."

He delved deep into one of the enormous pockets of his gaudy traveling cloak and pulled out a gaily-wrapped parcel, thrusting it at Harrier and regarding him expectantly.

Watching his friend's face, Tiercel's heart sank in sympathy. It was obviously a book, and Harrier had little use for books. Tiercel's own present to Harrier had been a detailed and elaborate model of a full-rigged Selken sailing carrel, one that he knew Harrier had been admiring in the modelmaker's window for moonturns.

But Harrier opened it and exclaimed politely over the book just as if it were something he'd been hoping to receive all year. Tiercel craned closer, trying to get a glimpse of the title.

It was certainly not a new book. The dusty blue velvet binding was worn to threadbare shininess with age, and only the fact that the title was composed of metal letters fixed somehow into the cover of the book rendered it legible at all. A *Compendium of Ancient Myth and Legend, Compiled from the Histories of the City*. But if the letters had ever been gilded, the gilding had worn off long ago, and they were now simply black with tarnish and age.

"You're no better a liar now than you were at six, Harrier Gillain," his uncle said with fond irritation. "You'd rather have a new pair of boots, or a fine cloak, or whatever shiny new distraction entertains the young this season. But I assure you, there are more wonders to be found in this book than in all of Armethalieh, if you'll only take a moment to look. And isn't this the season above all others when we should contemplate the marvels of the past? Those days when magic and wonders filled the land and things were never as they seemed? I promise you, the world is wider than your silly little harbor with its silly little ships."

"Well, without our silly little harbor and its silly little ships, you'd hardly have a place to sail away from and back to, would you, Alfrin?" Antarans said, a bit sharply.

"Is it about magic?" Harrier asked doubtfully.

"That and more," Alfrin said grandly. "And I look forward to hearing what you think of it," he told his nephew meaningfully.

Tiercel saw Harrier do his best to repress a sigh.

At last Divigana was able to lead her brother toward the sideboard filled with good things to eat and drink, helping him off with his cloak as she did so.

"Don't worry, Har," Tiercel said. "I'll read it for you and tell you what's in it. I'm sure he won't ask too many questions."

Harrier shot Tiercel a grateful look, but in fact it was as much curiosity as friendship that prompted Tiercel's offer. The book looked interesting.

"He probably won't be here long enough to ask any at all," Harrier said with a relieved grin, promptly handing the book to Tiercel. "I can't even remember the last time Uncle Alfrin came back to Armethalieh. He's always off traveling somewhere. We've gotten some pretty strange presents over the years, though."

Tiercel grinned back. He remembered those. Most of them had wound up in the Gillain attic, like the giant stuffed lizard and the musical clock. Some had been pretty but baffling, like the set of glass fish that whistled when you put them out in the rain. And some, Harrier's parents had never let their youngest child see at all.

⁓

THE party broke up rather later than it might otherwise have done. For the rest of the evening, Alfrin Auvalen had been the center of attention, telling amazing tales of his adventures and dancing with every woman there. Tiercel had been fascinated. It wasn't, of course, that he actually wanted to *go* anywhere. He was perfectly content with life in Armethalieh. But he loved hearing stories of exotic places. And when the Rolforts left that evening, Harrier's Naming Day present was tucked firmly under Tiercel's arm.

❧

FOR the next several days, the *Compendium of Ancient Myth and Legend* languished in Tiercel's study unread, as Festival was a very busy time of year for everyone in Armethalieh. For the Rolfort family, there were parties to be present at, shrines to visit, commemorative ceremonies to attend at the Great Temple of the Light and the Magistrate's Palace, and, of course, Tiercel's studies, which could not be neglected even over Festival holiday. He'd only gotten a couple of opportunities to glance into it—it was a very thick book, and quite old—but it looked very promising, with pictures of unicorns, Otherfolk, and men in grey robes with *very* odd hats.

He saw little of Harrier during that time, because of course, even if school was not in session, that hardly meant that the Harbormaster's son had nothing to do, either. Harrier was at the Port from Second Dawn Bells till Evensong Bells, just as a good going-to-be Apprentice Harbormaster should be. But at last, as Festival Sennight drew to a close, Tiercel finally found the time to fulfill his promise to Harrier. He would treat reading Harrier's book just as if it were a school project, taking notes and writing a report and everything, so that just in case Alfrin Auvalen *did* ask Harrier about his Naming Day present, Harrier would be able to answer all his questions.

❧

IT was a damp dull day. A steady soaking rain pounded the streets of the City, washing away the last of the early spring snow and muting the carillons so that—if not for the clocks—it would be almost impossible to tell the passing of one bell from the next. Tiercel took the *Compendium* off to the window seat in a corner of his study and settled down to read.

*"Those days when magic and wonders filled the land and things were never as they seemed"* indeed. The title called the book "Myth and Legend," but it almost seemed to be history. Ancient history.

Tiercel had never really had the opportunity to read a lot of Ancient History. There weren't really very many books on it in the General Section of the Great Library. Oh, there were the traditional tales of the Great Flowering and the Blessed Saint Idalia, but they were so skimpy on details that he'd just skimmed them. They raised more questions than they answered, and nobody seemed to have the answers. Instead, he'd read books on Literature, Geography, Botany— even slightly-more-recent history (the kind that people could actually prove had happened). These were all courses taught in Preparatory School, and all subjects he'd dabbled in on his own time. He'd learned a lot, but it had frustrated him, too, because none of them had ever really engaged his interests. At heart, Tiercel had begun to wonder if he was nothing more than a dabbler. A dilettante. Light-minded.

But the *Compendium*—which said in the front that it contained excerpts from something else called A *History of The City In Six Volumes*—talked about the Time of Mages not only in more detail than any book Tiercel had ever run across before, but it spoke as if whoever had written it had actually been there and understood *why* those things had happened.

*"In that time, all Otherfolk and Other Races were Banished beyond the Bounds of the lands claimed for the City of Armethalieh, for the High Mages saw them as a rebuke to the power of the High Magick."*

High Magick? What was that?

*"Thus, when King Andoreniel of the Elves invoked the Ancient Treaty and called the humans to fight for the Light against the Endarkened—then called Demons—the High Mages refused to fight, or to allow their subjects to fight. It was only when they at last came to understand that they had been the first victims of the Endarkened in the Third War Against the Light—"*

Third War? There'd been others?

*"—that the High Mages were at last brought to set aside a thousand years of fear and prejudice and blend their power once more with the Wildmages and their ancient Allies of the Light to defeat the Endarkened."*

There was more, though not much more about the Third War—the war Tiercel had thought of all his life as the *only* war. The rest of that chapter talked about the High Mages from before the war.

And that was fascinating enough.

⤚⫸⤙

TIERCEL Rolfort had grown up in a world with magic.

Of course, you almost never saw it, but everyone knew it was there. Pretty much like Wildmages; everyone knew that *they* were there, but a person could go their whole life without seeing one—or knowing that they'd seen one, at least—because it wasn't like a Wildmage to announce his or her presence unless it was absolutely vital to the task at hand. And—according to the stories—they often swore the people they helped to secrecy.

And certainly he'd grown up in a world full of Otherfolk. Fauns and Centaurs and Brownies at least, and Harrier swore that there were merfolk in the deep ocean and Selkies on some of the more secluded Out Islands, though they hardly counted as magic.

And everyone knew that far to the East was the Kingdom of the Elves, and that even though the Elves had no magic, they shared their land with numberless races that did: unicorns and dryads and dragons and the Light knew what else. But this was something else entirely. If Tiercel was reading this book properly, once, long ago, there'd been another kind of magic besides the Wild Magic. A kind that you could, well, *learn*. The way you learned Maths or Geography or dancing. Something called High Magick.

And that—not the Wild Magic—had been what the High Mages who had ruled the City in the Time of Mages had practiced. They'd ruled Armethalieh for a thousand years before the Great Flowering.

Knowing that, realizing that, gave Tiercel an unsettled feeling, like standing in a room and suddenly realizing that it was twice as big as he'd thought it was. Of course he'd heard of the Time of Mages, and of course he'd known that the world didn't just *start* on the day of the Great Flowering, but for the book in his hands to speak so casually of events that took place so many years before that, well . . .

It was fascinating.

He wondered if anyone, anywhere, still knew anything at all about the High Magick.

ON his next free afternoon, Tiercel went down to the Great Library. The Library had always been one of his favorite places in the City. First his nurse, then his tutor, had brought him here, introducing him to the wonders of a building filled with books on every subject there was.

Though the Great Library had been rebuilt and expanded many times over the centuries, parts of it were as old as the City itself. When the "new wing" had been added a few centuries ago, it had been at about the same time the old City walls were being taken down, and several sections of the wall had been incorporated into the new wing, blending old and then-new together. Tiercel liked to go into the New Wing just to admire the brightly glazed and ornamented stones. The ancient Armethaliehans must have loved beauty above all things if they'd surrounded their city with such a highly-decorated wall.

On most days he wandered aimlessly through the library galleries, seeing what was new and then visiting the sections that held his favorite subjects. Today, however, he didn't dawdle. He was on a mission: research. Quickly he sought out Master Cansel.

Master Cansel was the Chief Librarian of the Great Library, and ordinarily he would have little time for someone Tiercel's age, but Tiercel's persistence in seeking out books far beyond those one of his years would normally be interested in had long ago piqued Master Cansel's interest, and the two of them, the aged scholar and the young student, had become friends. Master Cansel often said it was a great pity that Tiercel was bound for a clerkship, for he would have made an excellent librarian, and more than once Tiercel had been tempted to agree with him.

"I'm looking for some books on history, Master Cansel. Really ancient history. From before the Great Flowering. I'm wondering if you have—" Tiercel pulled a scrap of paper out of his pocket and consulted his notes "—a copy of something called *A History of The City?* It's in six volumes. It's supposed to be from then."

Master Cansel looked puzzled for a moment, then smiled. "You're interested in pre-Flowering History, Tiercel? Have you decided to study that at University?"

"I, um, well, I'm not sure. I think so. But I thought I'd read some of it now to make sure."

Master Cansel smiled indulgently. "Well, we do have some, of course. There's not much call for the books in the general collection. Let me get you a pass, and we'll go down to the closed shelves."

A few minutes later, with his new pass hung securely around his neck, Tiercel accompanied Master Cansel into the Closed Collection. The rooms were completely dark.

"This is the Old Building," Master Cansel said, holding his lantern up high. "As you'll note, there are no windows here. Scholars believe that in the Time of Mages, the building was kept lit by Coldfire, though no one is quite sure why anyone would waste magic in lighting a building."

"Armethalieh was the City of Mages," Tiercel said.

Cansel smiled. "I see you've already been doing a bit of reading. Yes, so they say. But it's hard to imagine that Wildmages would have been so wasteful. Of course, it is certainly fortunate that they spent so much time preserving the books. They're in better condition than many published only decades ago."

*Not Wildmages*, Tiercel thought to himself. *High Mages.*

As they entered the main room, Cansel stopped to light several lanterns that hung from brackets on the walls. As their flames grew and steadied, they provided enough light to allow Tiercel to see that the entire room was filled with books. Along one wall, directly under the lanterns, were several small desks.

"When the scholars from the University come here to do research, of course we light more of the lamps," Cansel said. "But this should be enough light for you to find a few books to read. Come, let's see if we can find that *History* for you."

❧

A moonturn and a half later, Kindling had given way to true Spring. As Tiercel exited the Great Temple of the Light one Light-Day morning, he was surprised to see Harrier waiting for him at the foot of the steps.

There were many Temples to the Light in Armethalieh; the Gillains attended Light-Day at the one near the Port, where the main Light-Day service was held much earlier in the morning than at the Great Temple in the center of the City. Harrier had obviously already been and gone to Light-Day Litany; he'd changed from his Light-Day best back into his everyday clothes.

"Tyr!" he cried as he spotted Tiercel standing with his family in the press of the crowd. Harrier shouldered his way through the press of Light-Day worshipers clustered in front of the Temple steps, and—obviously too excited to make his polite greetings to Tiercel's parents and sisters, began talking at once. "A ship came in—late last night—and they swear it was attacked by a *kraken*. Come and see!"

Lord Rolfort cleared his throat meaningfully and Harrier flushed at his own rudeness, hastily greeting Lord and Lady Rolfort and Tiercel's four younger sisters, who giggled at his discomfiture until Lady Rolfort regarded them sternly in turn.

"I'll come," Tiercel said hastily. "In a bell. Or two."

~

A chime less than two bells later, Tiercel arrived at the Port. It didn't matter that this was Light-Day; the business of the Port must go on. Ships could not be asked to stand out in the Harbor and wait until the next day to dock, after all, so he was not in the least surprised to find Harrier waiting for him at the Portmaster's office.

"So," he said, sticking his head in the doorway. "About this ship?"

Harrier looked up from a table in the doorway. He pushed his russet hair out of his eyes and grinned. "The *Marukate* limped into the harbor just after Watch Bells this morning. *Swearing* absolutely that she'd been attacked by a kraken. And everybody knows that there aren't any kraken, but something tore up her hull; Da had to send them over to drydock before they sank in the slip. Come see."

Harrier came to join him, and the two of them began to walk down the dock.

"No kraken?" Tiercel said lightly. "You might as well say there are no unicorns—though I grant neither of us is ever going to see one. But there certainly are kraken—at least there used to be before the Great Flowering, although since they were creatures of the Endarkened, I admit there probably aren't any now."

"Been reading Uncle Alfrin's book have you?" Harrier asked with a relieved grin.

"Ask me anything. Or . . . did you know that there used to be another kind of magic besides the Wild Magic? A kind you don't have to be born with, or Called to by the Gods of the Wild Magic? A kind almost anybody can learn? They called it the High Magick. There are books about it in the Library. They used to call Armethalieh the Mage City."

Harrier regarded him with a combination of exasperation and disbelief. "Is that why you've been spending so much time down at the Great Library these days? I thought you were just studying for your entrance exams for the University."

"Oh, I'm doing that too. But the books I want to read are delicate, and Master Cansel let me borrow some of them, but he won't let me borrow the ones I want to read now. Still, I have to pick a subject to study at school, and I might as well pick ancient history."

"Because it doesn't really matter?" Harrier asked.

Unfortunately, that was a little too close to the truth. "One subject's as good as another," Tiercel answered lightly.

By now they'd reached the area of the docks where the ships that needed more extensive work than could be done on them while they stood at anchor were brought. When a hull needed to be scraped clean of growths—or otherwise repaired—the ship was brought to dry dock, where even the largest hull could be lifted free of the water to be worked on. There were several ships here at the moment, but it was obvious which was the *Marukate*. Her hull was still damp.

And it was obvious why Portmaster Gillain had been in such a hurry to get her into dry dock, even to someone like Tiercel. Her hull looked as if it had been clawed.

There were long white scars in the dark salt-seasoned oak. Deep ones, too, running nearly the length of the ship.

"Could be anything," Harrier said dismissively, startling Tiercel. *He* thought the gouges in the hull were pretty impressive. "Rocks—even whales."

"Then why would the captain say it was a kraken?"

Harrier grinned. "If the bondholders can prove the ship's master was negligent, they won't have to pay off on the damage. And running your ship up on a shoal—or into a pod of whales—counts as negligent seacraft under bond. But a kraken is the same as a storm. The bond would have to pay off then."

"So . . . who's going to win?" Tiercel asked, blinking slowly. "The bondsman or the ship's master?"

Harrier shrugged. "Probably the bondsman." He stepped up onto the timber balks holding the ship upright and pulled out his belt knife. "This ship has been badly maintained. See how soft the timber is?"

He set his knife to the hull beside one of the gashes and, without any great difficulty, carved away a long splinter of wood. "I shouldn't be able to do that," he explained for Tiercel's benefit.

He stepped down onto the dock again and handed the splinter to Tiercel. Tiercel examined it. The wood *was* soft.

"It doesn't look like any rock—or whale—damage I've ever seen," Harrier said reluctantly. "But all the bondsman will care about is that the *Marukate* is a sloppy ship whose master has probably been sailing close to the wind for a long time. So he's not likely to believe in . . . kraken." Harrier shrugged, taking a last look over his shoulder at the ship. "It's strange, though. The captain said he was just beyond the farthest of the Out Islands when it happened. Couldn't have been much further out, or they'd never have made it to port, with their hull racked up the way it was. And there just aren't any reefs out there that could do this to a ship."

⧼⧽

*BUT there aren't any kraken.*

Second Night Bells had just rung, and the entire Rolfort family was safe in their beds.

Except Tiercel.

He was in his bedroom, true, but not in bed.

The scrap of wood Harrier had carved from the hull of the *Marukate* sat on his bedside table, on top of the journal in which Tiercel had taken to using to keep his notes on the High Magick.

Tomorrow the bondsman would meet with the ship's master at the port to look over the damage, and decide what part—if any— of the repairs would be paid for out of the bond. It didn't seem fair that the man should lose his ship. Harrier had said that was probably what would happen if the bond wasn't paid. The ship would be sold up, probably as scrap timber, and the *Marukate's* captain would have to go to work as a hired master on a ship he didn't own. Not the worst fate in the world, but it would be better if there were some way to prove that he was telling the truth about there being *something* out there that had grabbed his ship. Tiercel wondered if there was anything he could do to help. Maybe there was.

There were a lot of spells in the High Magick.

TIERCEL had been stunned to discover, once he'd really started digging through the books in the Closed Collection in the Great Library, that instead of being lost, or even locked up, everything he wanted to know about the High Magick was right there on the shelves, mixed in with the Histories. Spellbooks and manuals, practical information, nearly everything he needed to know.

It hadn't seemed right somehow just to play around with it for fun, though, so even though he'd copied out several of the simplest spells—High Magick seemed to be very elaborate and complicated— he'd never actually tried to do any of it. But this would be for a good cause.

There was a spell called *Knowing.* It didn't seem to be very complicated, and didn't require all of the elaborate tools that some of the other spells did, just some wine and candles and some Light-incense, and a few incantations. There were some other things—about shielding and fasting and ritual hours and proper preparation—but he didn't really understand them, and they looked like things he could afford to skip. Besides, Mama would certainly notice if he tried to skip meals.

The description of *Knowing* said that you would understand an object in its entirety once you had cast the spell upon it. If he cast *Knowing* on the piece of the hull of the *Marukate*, well, then, wouldn't he know how it had come to be damaged? Then he could go and tell Portmaster Gillain what he'd learned.

Assuming the High Magick was actually real, and the spell worked. Even Tiercel had to admit that sounded like a lot of "ifs" and assumptions.

WHEN he was certain that everyone had settled in for the night, Tiercel made his way down to the household Light-shrine and removed a small handful of the Light-incense from its silver box. He also took one of the charcoal cakes to burn it on. Folding both items carefully into a handkerchief, he went from there to the kitchen and took five candles from the candlebox. That should be enough—the spell just said "candles," and he wasn't sure how many to use. Most of the spells he'd seen seemed to do things in multiples of four, though, so he figured that four should be enough. And one for the center.

He went back to his room and made the rest of his preparations.

He rolled away the rug in the center of the floor, and used a piece of blackboard chalk from his study to carefully draw the symbol he had copied out of one of the old books into the middle of the floor. Next, he placed four candles at the corners and one in the middle, and set the piece of wood from the *Marukate* next to the middle candle.

Then he realized that he'd forgotten something to burn the incense in.

A quick scavenger hunt through his study turned up an old pottery bowl. It was thick and heavy; a souvenir from a Flowering Fair a few years back. He used it to hold spare pen-points, and to hold down his papers when the windows were open. It would certainly do. He emptied it out, rubbed it clean with his sleeve, and carried it back into the bedroom, setting it down in the middle of the chalked diagram. There. Everything was ready.

Tiercel admitted he'd never felt sillier in his life. He was much too old for games of "Let's Pretend." And deep in his heart, he was sure that was all that this could possibly be. Certainly he believed that the High Magick had worked once, centuries and centuries ago. But he also believed that if it still worked, people would still be using it. After all, wouldn't everyone want to be a Mage if they had the chance?

Still, he was committed to trying, so he sat down crosslegged beside the diagram, and opened his notebook, and carefully read out the spell for *Knowing*, slowly sounding out the unfamiliar syllables and making the strange gestures that had been depicted in the books. He knew he was supposed to have a wand for that, but doing the spell had been pretty much a spur-of-the-moment idea, so maybe it wouldn't matter.

He finished.

Nothing happened.

*Well, what did you expect?* Tiercel thought, feeling more than a little embarrassed. Even though he hadn't expected anything to happen, he'd hoped, more than he wanted to admit even to himself, that something would. *The Time of Mages is definitely over.*

Just then he started to feel sick.

The room seemed to be getting darker.

THE year before he'd met Harrier, Tiercel had been so sick that the
Healers of Armethalieh—the best in the Nine Cities—had told his
parents that his only hope for survival lay in the Wild Magic.

In those days even Hevnade hadn't been born yet. He'd been
Lord and Lady Rolfort's only child, and to save his life, they'd taken
him immediately to the Temple of the Light in Sentarshadeen,
hoping against hope that a Wildmage could be found to heal him.
Fortunately one was there—waiting for them, in fact—and Tiercel
had quickly been restored to health. He'd remembered nothing at
all of his illness—supposedly you never remembered anything
much about being a child, though Tiercel did—but he'd always remembered the strange dreams he'd had while he'd been ill, even
though it had happened so very long ago. They'd been vividly real,
yet impossible; he'd known that even then. And now, after so many
years, he was having another one without even falling asleep. He
was looking at a Lake of Fire.

Instead of being blue like a proper lake, it was orange. The air
above it shimmered with heat, and its entire surface danced with
flames, as if somebody had taken an ordinary homely hearth-fire
and just made a huge pool of it somehow. It was almost pretty. And
standing at the middle of it was a woman.

That was wrong, because if it was fire, she shouldn't be able to
stand *on* it, but she was. And she was utterly naked, but though
he tried very hard, Tiercel couldn't look away. And he couldn't
wake up.

He'd seen statues of naked women in museums, and he tried to
tell himself that that's all this was, but her long hair moved in the
heat of the flames below her, and the fire gleamed off her skin, so
that he couldn't really tell what color it was. Somehow she saw him
watching her, and when she did, she raised her arms and held them
out to him. Beckoning to him.

He had to go to her, Tiercel knew he did, but as that excited, ashamed, half-formed thought worked its way toward the front of his mind, it was met by another reaction equally strong.

Terror.

No. More than terror. *Revulsion.*

Because there was something horrible about the Fire Woman—something he could sense but couldn't see—and the fact that he didn't quite know what it was made it even more frightening, even though this was only a dream, and the things that frightened you—or didn't—in dreams weren't the same ones that scared you when you were awake.

She was beautiful, but the longer Tiercel looked at her, the stronger his desire to *run away* became. Because he knew—he *knew*—that if he stayed here one moment more, something terrible would happen. Only he didn't know what it was. And he didn't know how to get away.

⤝⤞

*"FIRE!"* Henmon's shout jarred Tiercel out of the dream-not-dream. The footman was pounding desperately on his locked door. He took a deep breath and began to cough wildly. Everything in his room was on fire and the room was rapidly filling with smoke. His bed—the curtains—even the rug that he'd pushed to one side—all were sheets of flame. With a yelp of dismay he snatched up his workbook and ran to unbolt his door. Fortunately, the area between the glyph and the door didn't contain anything that could readily burn.

Henmon took one step over the threshold, stared, and yanked Tiercel out of the room, shouting for servants and water buckets.

⤝⤞

FORTUNATELY, though everything in Tiercel's bedroom that could possibly burn had caught fire, the fire hadn't had time to take a really good hold before it had been discovered. By the time the Fire Watch arrived at the Rolfort townhouse, the flames had already been extinguished.

"Do you have any idea what caused the fire, Lord Rolfort?" the Fire Warden asked.

The family and most of the servants were gathered in the main parlor. It was after Midnight Bells. The room was chill, since the fires had been banked for night two bells ago and now every window in the place was open to air the house of the lingering scent of smoke.

"Candles," Lord Rolfort answered, with a look at Tiercel that was both irritated and disappointed. "My eldest decided to try reading in bed by candlelight, Light knows why. He fell asleep. It won't happen again."

"Beds are for sleeping, chairs are for reading," the Fire Warden said firmly, as if reciting a watchword. "If more people would remember that, there'd be fewer home accidents." He glanced at Tiercel, and frowned. "Your boy doesn't look at all well, if you don't mind my saying so, Lord Rolfort."

In fact, Tiercel didn't *feel* at all well, either. Once the initial terror and excitement of the fire had worn off, he realized that he felt feverish and exhausted. The clothes he'd been wearing when he did the spell were as soaked in sweat as if Henmon had been pouring water on him, not the flames, and despite that, he couldn't keep his teeth from chattering.

In fact, he could barely keep his eyes open.

It was that—and not any lie he'd told—that had led his father to say what he had to the Fire Warden. Henmon had seen the candles in his room as he'd dragged him out, but the old footman had been too rattled to say quite where they'd been. And they were gone now, in any event, consumed by the flames.

Tiercel felt guilty—as much as he felt anything other than

weary—but he thought it would be just as well to let the misunder-standing stand. He really didn't want to explain to his parents that he'd been doing magic up in his room tonight. Especially since the spell hadn't worked.

Only it had. He just hadn't cast the spell he'd been meaning to. *"Fire is the first and simplest spell of the High Magick . . ."* It said that over and over again in all of the books on the High Magick that he'd read. He'd cast Fire. And maybe the woman and the Lake of Fire were just a hallucination and wouldn't happen again.

TO Tiercel's great relief, the rest of the night—what there was of it—was unencumbered by dreams of any kind. But when he finally awoke it was nearly First Afternoon Bells, and he'd slept long past the time the Ship's Bondsman would meet with the Captain of the *Marukate*. He felt far too giddy and light-headed to even get out of bed anyway.

*Not that it would have done me any good if I'd been there,* he thought ruefully. He'd wanted to help, but all he'd done last night was nearly set the entire townhouse on fire. He hadn't learned a single thing that would account—one way or the other—for the in-juries to the *Marukate's* hull, and now it was too late for it to matter. He was truly sorry for that, because it was very likely that the cap-tain *would* lose his ship, and, as Harrier had said, it was pretty un-likely he'd run it onto some rocks if it had been wrecked where he said it had.

Still, there was nothing Tiercel could do.

*But someday there will be. It isn't fair for it to be one man's word against another in a situation like this, with both of them having some-thing to gain from being right. Someone should investigate who has noth-ing to gain. If I am ever a Magistrate, I promise I will make sure that that is always what happens. Someone should care about the truth, and only the truth.*

❧

THAT evening Tiercel received a stern lecture from his father about his carelessness with candles. He apologized sincerely—he truly hadn't meant to set anything on fire, no matter how he'd done it—and promised truthfully never to light another candle in his rooms. He'd certainly learned his lesson. High Magick belonged in books, and in the past. He never intended to try to cast another spell.

He hated to deceive his parents—even by accident and omission—but he simply felt too embarrassed and ashamed to admit what he'd *really* been doing when the room caught on fire. Besides, he *had* been reading. Sort of. Just not in bed. And if he said that the room caught on fire because he'd cast a spell—not *trying* to cast a spell, but *actually* casting a spell—and not because one of the candles fell over and rolled, they wouldn't believe him anyway. *He* didn't quite believe him, and he'd been there. Better to leave matters the way they were.

So he apologized sincerely, and promised to do better, and Mama dosed him with strengthening cordials and kept him home from Preparatory School the next day too, and on the whole, Tiercel was grateful to get off as lightly as he had.

Only he hadn't.

❧

IT was almost a sennight later, and Tiercel had done his best to forget the whole frightening and humiliating incident. It was the first night since the fire that he wasn't sleeping on a trundle bed in his study, because the repairs to his bedroom were finally complete. The fire-damaged room had been scrubbed to within an inch of its life and completely repainted, but even with new curtains, new rug, and new bedding, it still smelled faintly of smoke and scorch. It looked very bare—all the odds and ends that used to clutter it up were gone, lost in the fire, and most of his clothes were still at the fuller's and tailors being cleaned and repaired. And now Harrier would never have to make his report on his Naming Day gift, though he would have to confess to loaning it to a friend (hardly a major transgression, really), because the *Compendium* was one of the many things that had been lost in the blaze. Tiercel promised himself that he'd buy Harrier a "replacement" gift, and something that Harrier would probably like better.

He lay on his back in the center of the bed—it was a new mattress, and felt strange—and was certain he'd never manage to fall asleep in this room turned strange and new.

But he did. And suddenly he was back on the shore of the Lake of Fire again. Only this time it was far more real than it had been in his last vision. This time he could feel the heat of the wind on his skin, could feel the breeze blowing through his hair, smell the scents of burnt rock and sulfur, hear the pop and hiss of the burning lake, feel the itch in his eyes as the hot wind dried them.

And most of all, he wasn't *him*.

"Welcome," he heard. "I had nearly given up hope that you would come. Are you ready at last to accept the gifts I have for you?"

It was as if when she spoke he could suddenly see her, although Tiercel knew she'd been there all along. The Fire Woman from his vision—and now, dream. The one who was horrifying and terrifying, though she only looked beautiful. The one that he wanted to go to, even though the thought revolted him. She was calling to him, just as she had in the vision. But it wasn't him.

And he knew, if whoever she *was* calling went to her, or if she noticed that Tiercel was there too, and could see her, something really terrible was going to happen.

Suddenly her gaze sharpened, and Tiercel realized she *had* noticed he was there—or at least that something was. In another moment she might see him.

⟡

HE awoke with a strangled yell, shaking with utter panic. For a moment he was convinced that the Fire Woman was right here in his room with him, and was half out of the bed before he was able to stop himself. But no. He was alone in his bedroom.

*She might not be here, but she's real.* He had no idea why he was so convinced of that. *A dream. It was only a dream.*

He tried to convince himself of that, but he couldn't. Tiercel had never been very good at lying to himself. This was something unlike anything he'd ever imagined to be possible—at least possible now, in the modern world—but he believed in it, and that frightened him even more. Things like the Fire Woman belonged to the Time of Mages. He knew she wasn't human, but he didn't even know what kind of Otherfolk she might be. All he knew was that if she got what she wanted, something terrible was going to happen. Unfortunately he didn't know what it was. It was like starting a book in the middle.

What he *did* know was that all of a sudden, magic wasn't something safely locked away in the history books—or safely in the hands of the Temples and the Wildmages. It was right here. Stalking him. And he didn't have the faintest idea of what to do about it.

Eventually Tiercel calmed down enough to light his bedside lamp, and then managed to talk himself into getting out of bed and opening his curtains. The cheerful familiar light from the

street calmed him further, pushing the images from the dream farther away. He lit more lamps, then got up and read in his study until dawn.

~≋~

IT was hard to concentrate on his schoolwork that day—both because of having missed most of a night's sleep, and because every
time he closed his eyes, Tiercel saw the face of the Fire Woman.
Even in broad daylight in the middle of his familiar classroom, with
the scents of a cool spring day coming in through the open windows, the images from his dream were still vivid in his mind.

She was as bright as fire. She ought to have been exotic and
beautiful. Even—he shifted uncomfortably—arousing. Instead, she
made him think of all the frightening and ugly things in his life.

There hadn't really been a lot. But once he and Harrier had
snuck down to the Docks to see the fishermen bring in one of their
own who had drowned. The man had been laid out on the wharf beside the boat that had brought him in, bloated and tattered and
white. And as the two of them had stood, gawping, at the edge of the
crowd, the dead man's slack lips had begun to twitch and work, and
several small black sea-crabs had crawled out of his mouth. Tiercel
had thrown up most of the way home. The Fire Woman made him
feel worse.

Part of him wondered if he was going to dream about her every
night for the rest of his life. If he was, what was he going to *do*
about it? He couldn't sleep if he did, and he couldn't go without
sleep.

And there was worse. Last night he'd been convinced that his
dream was real. In daylight, he wasn't quite as sure, but what if it
was? If it was real, and happening now, shouldn't he *do* something
about it? Tell someone?

After his classes were over for the day, he went down to the Port.

He found Harrier there with a sheaf of papers in his hand, going over something with a Ship's Master. This was one of Harrier's jobs, and Harrier was working, so Tiercel waited patiently until he was through. At last Harrier handed over the papers to the Ship's Master, received a scroll in return, and turned to go.

"Tiercel," Harrier said in surprise.

Tiercel got to his feet—he'd been sitting on a large coil of rope waiting for Harrier to finish. "I've got to talk to you."

"Now? I'm here for two more bells, and I have half a dozen ships to check in."

"It's important."

"Then it will have to be quick. Come over here to the storage shed. It's out of the wind."

When they were safely inside the shed, Harrier leaned against the door and folded his arms. "Now. What's so urgent?"

"You know that day you showed me the *Marukate?*"

Harrier frowned, then his brow cleared. "Oh, aye. Da took a skiff to the Out Islands with the captain so he could show him where she'd been hulled. Nothing there—at least not rocks. Bondsman didn't pay the full damage, but he did pay a bit, and Seaman's Assurance will loan the rest. He'll have some lean years while he pays back the loan, but he won't lose his ship. Hit some floating wreckage, more than likely. Was that what you wanted to know?"

At least the captain wouldn't lose his ship. Tiercel felt better for hearing that.

"No. That night, I—Well, I wanted to help. So I did a spell of the High Magick. I'd found it in a book, you see, and it should have told me how the ship was damaged. I thought it would help."

Harrier was staring at him as if he'd completely lost his mind. "*This* is what you came to tell me?"

Tiercel took a deep breath.

"Yes. Because the spell went wrong. It didn't show me that. It showed me a vision of a Lake of Fire, and a—a woman. It was horrible. And I can't stop seeing them. And I don't know what to do about it."

There was a long silence.

"Your mother said you'd been sick after you set your room on fire," Harrier finally said.

"Yes, because, well, you see, I think I cast a Fire Spell, because the books on the High Magick say that—"

"Stop. Tyr. Come on. Good joke, but I'm busy. You didn't cast a spell. You're not a Wildmage."

"You aren't listening. I said I used the High Magick, and—"

"And you also told me that the High Magick was over and done with about a million years ago. So why would it work now? And even if it did, how could *you* use it? No. You fell asleep, you had a bad dream. End of story."

"But I'm still seeing her!"

"So you're still having bad dreams," Harrier said patiently. He shrugged, the gesture saying more clearly than words that while he was sorry about the problem, he was certain it was going to go away and he really didn't see what all the fuss was about.

"Har, you *know* that doesn't make sense. If the High Magick used to work, then it still works. And I did something. I know I did!"

"Damned right you did, you set your house on fire. Tyr, if you were a Wildmage, you'd have the Three Books. Everyone knows that."

"And I keep telling you, it's not the Wild Magic, it's the High Magick. Something anyone can learn if they want to." He knew he was dangerously close to arguing with Harrier, and from the look on Harrier's face, Harrier would be happy to make this into an argument. Harrier didn't want to hear what he was saying. It was just too unbelievable. And when you tried to push Harrier in a direction he didn't want to go, he got angry. That wouldn't solve anything at all.

"Okay," Tiercel said, raising his hands. "I'm sorry I bothered you here. I guess I really was still worried about the *Marukate*. And maybe the dreams will stop."

"Sure they will," Harrier said, relaxing. "You've just spent too much time on Uncle Alfrin's book—and I have to say, I'm not all that sorry to see it go. And everyone comes down with odd fevers when the seasons change. Look, I've got to run. I'll see you soon, though, right?"

"Right," Tiercel said.

But he didn't see Harrier soon.

He knew that if he did, all that would happen would be that they'd just have that argument they'd barely managed to avoid, and the very last thing he wanted to do was argue with Harrier. Harrier couldn't see things his way and he, well, he couldn't manage to see them any other way. He'd have to solve this problem himself.

But by a moonturn later, Tiercel was at his wits' end.

The dream hadn't gone away, and he'd done everything he could think of to make it stop.

First he spoke to his tutor at school about his strange dreams—leaving out the part about casting a spell of the High Magick, of course, but including every other detail. His tutor simply thought he was working too hard preparing to enter University this fall, and assured him confidentially that there was absolutely no doubt at all that he would get in, even if he didn't attend another class from here until the end of term. His marks were excellent and always had been. He had nothing to worry about, and now that he'd chosen Ancient History as his field of study, all he really had to do was show up at University at the beginning of term and start his classes.

No help there. Tiercel knew perfectly well that he wasn't having these dreams because he was worried about University.

Next, he went to his spiritual Preceptor at the Temple of the Light and told him everything, absolutely everything—including that he'd cast a spell of the High Magick and that all of his troubles had started after that. He'd been sure everything would be fixed then, but to his horror, his Preceptor also dismissed his dreams as "the sort of dreams a boy your age often has." No matter how long and how hard Tiercel argued with him, he could not convince the man otherwise. In Preceptor Maver's mind, Tiercel's problems could not have anything to do with the High Magick because . . . the High Magick simply didn't work. Hadn't worked for hundreds of years. And if it hadn't worked for hundreds of years, it couldn't be a problem *now*; could it?

Tiercel would have liked to have lit a candle with magic to prove to Preceptor Maver that it *did* work, but Tiercel actually had no idea how he'd done it the first time. And he had absolutely no intention of fooling around with magic ever again.

By then his lack of sleep—because he slept as little as possible—was visibly taking its toll, and his mother had taken him back to the Healers again. He'd told the Healer, perfectly honestly, that his problem was that he was having nightmares so bad that he was afraid to sleep, and the Healer gave him a strong sweet cordial that—she said—would allow him to sleep without dreams.

She was right. But he could only take it for a sennight, and after that the nightmare was back, more frequent and vivid than ever. It was always the same one, and he took what comfort he could from the fact that while it was undoubtedly *real*—whatever that meant when you were dealing with magic—it was also symbolic. He'd learned a lot more about symbolic dreams in the past few sennights, too, since he spent every free moment he had in the Closed Archives of the Great Library, reading through everything they had on the High Magick. He was hoping to find out what his dreams meant, and how to cure them, but instead all he found out was what an idiot he'd been.

Protective shields, for example. He should have had them up

around any place he was working, if he actually meant to do magic. He should have drawn Glyphs of Protection before he'd cast his spell, too. And *Knowing* was a Student Apprentice spell, not an Apprentice spell, as he'd thought. Far beyond his capability, even if he'd had an actual capability. You needed to study for years to become a High Mage. The Mageborn had begun their training at the age of eight.

Mageborn.

Another thing he'd apparently been wrong about was the High Magick being a magic that everyone could learn. It was true that a lot more people could learn it than could be Wildmages, but apparently you still had to be born with a mysterious something called the *Magegift*. And if you didn't have it, you could study the High Magick forever and not be able to cast a single spell.

Still . . .

Apparently many more people had been High Mages in the old days than were Wildmages now. And certainly the training was long and hard—but so was the training to be a Healer, or a Ship's Pilot, or an Architect, or even a Blacksmith. So why weren't there any High Mages anymore? Had people stopped being born with this Magegift? Or was there some other reason? Unfortunately, Tiercel knew just enough by now to know how much he didn't know, because although there were an enormous number of pre-Flowering books in the Closed Archives, and in the past moonturn he had (with his teachers' approval) cut a lot of his classes to spend most of his time down there reading them, comparatively few of them dealt directly with the High Magick, and a lot of those assumed you already *knew* about the High Magick to begin with. Many of them referred to books that the Archives didn't have, and the more he read, the more it seemed to Tiercel that a lot of the High Magick had been taught directly, Mage to Mage.

And that meant—as far as he could tell—that he was really in trouble now. Because—if he *had* really cast that Fire Spell—he had the Magegift. And not only were there no High Mages left to teach him, but the one thing the surviving books were all very clear on was that an awakening Magegift *had* to be taught.

Or else the new Mageborn died.

# Three

## The Beginning of the Quest

IT WAS THE noon break from his classes, and Tiercel was heading across the Quadrangle. It was already the middle of Windrack—nearly three moonturns since Harrier's Naming Day celebration—and the soft winds of early Summer made the day a pleasure to be out in. In a fortnight the term would be over for the year. Tiercel would graduate with his year-mates, and start the Long Vacation. University would loom in the autumn. Assuming he lived that long.

He didn't *feel* as if he were facing imminent death.

If he had the Magegift, he was. If he didn't, he wasn't. He didn't really feel like experimenting with any more magic spells to find out for sure. He kept dreaming about the Fire Woman almost every night, and despite the fact that it was essentially the same dream over and over, it was still as awful every single time. All he'd been able to find out from reading just about every book on the High Magick that the Great Library held was that he'd done nearly everything wrong to cast his spell—and that the High Mages didn't have dreams and visions. Or if they did, they didn't discuss them in the books available to him.

He was thinking of cutting his afternoon classes—of course it wasn't really cutting when you went to your teachers and asked to be excused, and he really *was* working on a special project of his own—when a voice behind him stopped him.

"Tiercel! Tyr! Wait up!"

HARRIER hadn't seen his friend since that day on the docks when Tyr had come to him with some wild story about suddenly having magic powers. He'd been so mad that day that he'd wanted to shake him. Tiercel was moonturns away from even having to go off to University, but Harrier had to be an adult *now*. His mornings were still spent in Normal School, but every afternoon was spent at the Port, where his Apprenticeship had informally begun. If he played around during work hours, there were plenty of watchers ready to report that fact to his Da, who wouldn't be at all pleased to hear it.

So maybe he'd been a little more abrupt than a friend ought to have been. He'd expected to see Tiercel again that night, or at least next evening, because when Tyr got a hold of an idea—or the other way around—he just didn't give up on it. But Tyr didn't come, and then it was Light-Day and he *still* hadn't come to see Harrier, so Harrier had gone to the Rolfort townhouse when he figured the Rolforts would be back from Temple only to hear that Tiercel had stayed late to talk to his Preceptor. And since Harrier wasn't going to hang around like a lovesick maiden, he'd left.

He'd stopped by a couple of times after that—making time out of his workday, knowing he'd have to work extra late to make up for it—only to be told that Tiercel was down at the Great Library, studying. Harrier had known Tiercel all his life, and while Tyr found the Great Library fascinating, he didn't find it *that* fascinating. He'd figured his friend was avoiding him, ashamed of having been an idiot, and figured Tiercel would come and see him when he was good and ready. But one morning Harrier had been in the middle of his schoolwork and realized it had been an entire moonturn since he'd seen Tiercel. He hadn't gotten so much as a note of explanation. And he'd realized he had to go find out why.

The Preparatory School was in the same district as the Normal School, so his detour wouldn't make him *too* late getting home. The more Harrier turned matters over in his head, the more he decided he was worried. Tiercel was exactly like one of the little ratting-dogs they kept down at the docks to go after vermin. Once he got an idea in his head, he just didn't let go of it. And while he might have gone off on this whole magic thing by himself—there were many interests the two boys didn't share—the thing he *wouldn't* have done was shut Harrier completely out of his life without a single word. Not even if their families were fighting. Which they weren't. There must be something wrong.

When Tiercel turned around in response to his shout of greeting Harrier got the biggest shock of his life. He'd suggested, that day in the shed on the docks, that Tiercel was just having one of the usual early spring fevers. If this was a sample of it, maybe his father should consider closing the Port, because Tiercel looked . . . ill. His eyes were sunken, and had deep shadows under them, as if he hadn't slept well for sennights. If he hadn't been sick before, he was now. Even Harrier could see that.

"What is wrong with you?" he blurted out.

"You didn't believe me the last time I told you," Tiercel said.

Oh. Still thinking about magic, then. If he'd sounded smug, or proud, or anything to indicate that this High Magick he thought he had was a wonderful secret that set him above everyone else, Harrier wouldn't have believed him now, or even listened. But Tiercel just sounded tired and more than a little confused.

"Tell me again."

The two boys sat on a stone bench in the corner of the Quadrangle, and Tiercel told Harrier everything that had happened to him in the past moonturn.

"And everybody—my Tutor, my Preceptor, the Healer—says they're just dreams. And that they'll go away by themselves."

"But you don't think so," Harrier guessed shrewdly.

"Oh, Light, Har, I *hope* they go away! But if you'd had even one of them, you'd know they aren't just dreams. Somehow they're true—a kind of truth, anyway. And what if . . . they were supposed to warn somebody of something, and I got the warning instead? Like a message delivered to the wrong house?"

"It doesn't seem really efficient," Harrier said consideringly. "If there's a problem, wouldn't it make more sense to have something happen in a Light-shrine? Or send a vision to all the Light Priests at once?"

"I don't know," Tiercel said. He sounded very depressed.

"Well, okay. So what are we going to do about it? You can't spend the rest of your life not eating or sleeping. Your parents are going to notice, soon, if they haven't already."

"Oh, they've noticed. Mama has a whole row of bottles from the Healer that she doses me with," Tiercel said dolefully. "Some of them help. Just not very well, or for very long."

"Well, you can't keep taking that stuff. It turns your teeth funny colors. So? We're going to do something, right?"

"You want to help?" Tiercel asked doubtfully.

"Tyr, have I *ever* let you go off on an adventure by yourself since you learned to walk? Doesn't matter what it is this time. I'm in. And it seems to me that if you got yourself into all this trouble with magic, you're going to need a Mage to get you out of it."

"You mean a Wildmage?" Tiercel said doubtfully.

Harrier snorted rudely. "Of *course* a Wildmage! It's not like we're going to turn over a rock and find one of your nonexistent High Mages under it, is it?"

"But . . . where are we going to find one?" Tiercel asked.

Harrier shrugged. "I don't know. I guess we go look until we find one. We could start in Sentarshadeen. There was one there once, wasn't there?"

"I guess," Tiercel said dubiously. "But that was when I was a baby, and for all I know, he made a special trip to the Temple there. I don't know much about Wildmages, but I do know that they don't stay in one place for long."

"Well, we can go and look, can't we?" Harrier said reasonably. "School will be over in a fortnight for both of us. Why don't you see if your family will let you go on a hiking trip with me? Fresh air and exercise; I bet the Healers will say it's just what you need. We'll tell them we're going to Sentarshadeen—and we will be, so you won't even be lying. I'm sure my Da will let me go away. Sort of a farewell trip, you know, because, well, we won't see much of each other after this summer. I'll make all the arrangements. Don't worry, Tyr. Maybe a nice long rest is just what you need to stop having these dreams."

Tiercel stared at him for a long moment, his blue eyes burning feverishly. Harrier had always thought of his friend as being so much younger than he was—in more than the near-year that separated them in age—but just now he looked so much older.

"You don't really believe me, do you?" Tiercel asked sadly. "About the visions?"

Harrier really didn't. It was just too impossible. And he hated to hurt Tiercel's feelings, especially now. Still, he owed his friend the truth.

"I don't know what to believe," Harrier answered with a heavy sigh. "But I know that *you* believe it and that's good enough for me. Besides, you *are* sick, and the Healers aren't helping, and you *were* fooling with magic. So you should see a Wildmage."

Tiercel snorted with laughter despite himself. "You make more sense than anyone else I've talked to! You're a good friend, Harrier Gillain."

"Nobody else would be crazy enough to put up with you," Harrier answered matter-of-factly.

❧

THE next fortnight was a busy one. To Tiercel's surprise, both their sets of parents willingly gave permission for the vacation trip, a moonturn's jaunt up to Sentarshadeen and back. Tiercel was pretty sure that his parents hoped that the country air and change of scene would put an end to his mysterious "problems," but that hardly explained how Harrier got permission to go wandering off for an entire moonturn just when he was supposed to start working at the Port full time.

Harrier wouldn't explain, either. He just looked cheerful and mysterious and stubborn, and said his Da didn't need him underfoot *that* badly. Of course Harrier hadn't told his parents the real reason he was going—to find a Wildmage because Tiercel had been dabbling in magic—and neither had Tiercel. If this didn't work out, though, he supposed he was going to have to.

So Tiercel really hoped it did.

There were a great many preparations to make for a journey of that length. Of course there would be inns all along the way— the Delfier Highway was broad and well-traveled, and they could be sure of finding somewhere to stay at every stop—but they were taking bedrolls and cooking equipment just in case, and they needed proper clothing for the journey, and supplies.

And, apparently, mules.

Harrier took care of most of that. When cargo came into the Port, it had to go somewhere, and as often as not it was on to one of the other Nine Cities by muletrain or cargo wagon. While Harrier wasn't a Cargomaster himself, nor even a Cargomaster's Apprentice, he certainly knew where to go to get advice on planning a journey. All Tiercel had to do was get his own items together and show up on his own doorstep at the designated time.

Early.

Harrier had warned Tiercel the night before that he'd be on his doorstep four chimes after First Dawn Bells. Henmon—who, as far as Tiercel had ever determined, never slept anyway—roused him from his nice warm bed when First Dawn Bells was still ringing, and he stumbled through his morning preparations half-asleep. Fortunately, the previous night had been one without the dream.

To his great surprise, his mother and father were awake to see him off. His mother hugged and kissed him good-bye, and—to his slight embarrassment—his father did the same, though Tiercel felt he was really a bit old for that. Just as he was about to go out the door, his father pressed a pouch into his hand. He could feel the shapes of coins in it: small demi-suns, the larger silver unicorns, and to his shock, even something that must be an actual Golden Sun. An enormous amount of money!

"But—You know—" he stammered. He'd already arranged for the funds for his journey, and the coins were tucked safely away in his belt.

"I know," his father said, smiling. "But things do come up on the road, you know, Tiercel. And it's always best to be prepared for any problem that money can solve. You don't need to spend it, you know. But if you have to . . . it's there."

"Thank you, sir," Tiercel said, tucking the second coin-pouch beside the first. "I'll try not to get into trouble." *Any more trouble than I'm already in.*

He turned away from his parents. Henmon opened the door and handed him his traveling bag. He slung it over his shoulder and walked quickly down the steps.

WHEN he reached the mules—there were two riding mules, and one to hold their gear—Harrier took the bag with Tiercel's clothing and added it to the collection of packs already there. "I don't see why we have to leave in the middle of the night," Tiercel grumbled.

"Middle of the night? First Dawn Bells rang four chimes ago," Harrier answered in mock-outrage.

"And decent people don't get up for another bell and a half."

"Well, then, I guess neither of us is particularly decent," Harrier answered with a grin. "Well," he said, shrugging. "Come on."

They walked off, leading the mules.

THE Delfier Gates that had once permitted—or denied—access to Armethalieh still endured after over two millennia, but of course the walls that they'd once hung from were long since gone. They now stood, a single shining slab of time-worn bronze, in the center of Council Square, with a plaque beneath them that said they'd once marked the boundary of Armethalieh. On the left of the Square, Tiercel could see the Law Courts and the Magistrate's Palace—new buildings, only a few centuries old—and in the distance, off to the right, he could just glimpse the towers of the University.

Just as he passed the Gates, Tiercel felt a sudden strange sensation. As if he were about to be sick, or as if the sun had suddenly gotten much too bright. He staggered, abruptly dizzy, and stared around himself suspiciously.

"Tyr?"

"I'm all right." Had something just happened? He looked back at the band of paler stone in the cobbles. All he'd done was step over the old boundary of the City Walls. That couldn't mean anything, could it? But suddenly, looking back down the long avenue that led through the heart of the City, Tiercel had the sudden horrible feeling that this was the last time he was ever going to see any of these things. That he was leaving Armethalieh, not just for a moonturn, but forever.

"Are you *sure* you're all right?" Harrier asked suspiciously.

"I haven't been getting much sleep lately." He walked on, and after a few more steps he started to feel a little better. Not completely better, though.

❧

EVEN at this hour there was a lot of traffic on the streets of the District—mostly farm carts and delivery vehicles, since the eastern way out of the city led to the Delfier Highway—but the mules were steady and placid, and took no interest in any of the traffic around them. By the time Second Dawn Bells was ringing through the air, they'd reached a small garden park in the New City, and thought it was probably time to try riding for a change.

Though neither of them was an expert rider, Harrier had spent enough time around the dock-mules used for loading and unloading cargo to be well aware of their habits, and Tiercel had gotten the same riding lessons that all the other boys of his age and social class had gotten. And their rented mounts were both steady and gentle. If they weren't exactly the fiery steeds that legendary adventurers setting off on a quest ought to have, then they were at least unlikely to dump their novice riders into the nearest ditch.

A bell of riding brought them to the edge of the City. For the last several chimes they'd seen fewer and fewer houses at all, and those they had seen were surrounded by large gardens, for no one in

Armethalieh had ever ceased to venerate the moment when the world had suddenly turned bright and green again. If they remembered nothing else of their history—they remembered that, and even the poorest home in Armethalieh had its pot of flowers at the family Light-shrine.

Beyond the last of the houses—and the thick white marker stone, which marked the official boundary of the City—Tiercel could see the rolling fields of the vast farmlands that surrounded Armethalieh. Once, centuries ago, this whole area had been forest and small isolated villages. But that was back in the Time of Mages, when Armethalieh had been a walled city considerably smaller than its present size.

They kept to the edge of the road, staying well out of the way of the freight wagons that took up most of the center of the road. Early morning was the time of heaviest traffic, with the carts from the farms heading into the City for the morning markets, and the freight wagons heading off the docks by the North Road, which joined the Delfier Highway just outside the City. Even this late in the day—it was already Midmorning Bells—traffic was still heavy.

"Is it going to be like this all the way to Sentarshadeen?" Tiercel asked Harrier, after they had to ride completely off the road so that two large vehicles—one freight wagon, one farm cart—could pass each other without injury.

Harrier looked contemplative, and Tiercel reminded himself that Harrier didn't have any more experience with the Delfier Highway than he did. "Pretty much, I'd say," Harrier decided, after thinking it over. "But once we get past the farms, there should be less traffic." He pulled out a map and consulted it. "According to this, there's something called the Old War Road that splits off the main road once we ride a bell or so farther on from here. It parallels the Delfier Highway, but it looks like the wagons don't use it. Why don't we take that instead?"

Tiercel grinned in relief. He'd just as soon not spend the entire trip to Sentarshadeen dodging wagons.

"Sounds good."

"And maybe you can tell me what it is—if you don't make the explanation too long."

"Deal."

BY the time they reached the turn-off for the Old War Road, Tiercel had managed to remember what little he'd read about the Old War Road in his recent reading, and since it was about battles, Harrier was willing to listen to it. It was also time to stop for lunch—or at least a snack, since they'd gotten up very early that morning.

Here the road out of Armethalieh became the Delfier Highway, broad and well-marked, heading straight east. The trees were well cut back on both sides of the road, and the mile-markers clearly indicated distance. The Old War Road was not nearly as clearly marked. It was far narrower, and the trees grew right up to its edge. It was obviously a well-traveled road, as its broad surface was free of any sort of vegetation, but it was obviously only meant for horses and foot traffic. And from the map that Harrier had brought, it didn't run nearly as straight as the Delfier Highway, which Tiercel thought was odd in something called a War Road. If you were going to war, wouldn't you want to get there as fast as possible?

At the edge of the forest—it was actually what remained of the ancient Delfier Forest, Tiercel knew from his reading—cattle and foraging deer had reduced the grass to a parklike shortness, and there was a pump-well with a watering trough and some tethering posts. They stopped there and gave the mules a chance to drink before tying them up, and then spread out a blanket from their gear and got out one of the hampers of food.

"Mama says we can ask the landlords at the inns to sell us cold lunches for the road," Harrier explained, setting the provisions out on the colorful Centaur-woven blanket. "That way we won't have to find an inn to stop at for lunch if we don't want to. So. You were saying that this is an old Elven road?"

"According to the books I've been reading, it runs all the way from Ondoladeshiron to Armethalieh. North of Sentarshadeen, the War Road passes by Fort Halacira and Kellen's Bridge. Maybe we can ride up and see them if everything works out. Kellen's supposed to have built that bridge himself, you know. By magic."

"You sound like a guidebook," Harrier said good-naturedly. "And I don't believe anybody ever built a bridge by magic. Kellen Knight-Mage was a Wildmage, and Wildmages don't do that. But I'd like to see Fort Halacira. Say, if it's a fort, do you think there was ever a battle there?"

"I don't know. But since I'm going to study Ancient History at University, maybe I can find out and tell you."

"You're *still* going to study Ancient History?" Harrier asked in disbelief. *After all this?* his expression said plainly.

"Why not?" Tiercel said stubbornly. "It's not as if I'm going to be studying magic. Although . . . that's what they used to teach there," he added teasingly.

"No."

"Yes."

"No."

"Really."

"You can't *teach* magic. When a Wildmage gets his—or her— Three Books, that's it. They just *have* their magic."

"And I keep telling you, that's not how the High Magick worked. It was like Maths, or, or, or training to be a Ship's Pilot. You studied for years. At the Mage College. Which was where Armethalieh University is now. And only Mages went there. To study magic."

"Well, *you* didn't study for years. So how come you were able to cast that spell?" Harrier demanded to know.

"Well, you see—"

But Tiercel's explanation—not that he expected to be allowed to get all the way through it before Harrier interrupted him—was cut short by a sudden commotion in the forest.

A troop of Fauns—Fauns rarely traveled alone—came tumbling out of the forest. It was hard to say how many there were. Five? Eight? They were constantly in motion, their child-sized bodies— human to the waist, though with long caprid ears and small curling horns, and entirely goatlike below—caroming off one another with the exuberance of a tumble of puppies.

Fauns were one of the races of Otherfolk who had elected to remain in the west when most of the Bright Folk had gone off with the Elves. Not that Fauns were particularly bright—in any sense of the word. Cheerful and good-natured, yes. But scatterbrained was the kindest word that could describe them. Those who were feeling less kind called them "thievish" and "destructive"—but having no possessions of their own, so far as anyone had ever discovered, it was hard to expect them to care very much about the possessions of others. In fact, even after having lived in close proximity to the Fauns for so long, no one knew very much about them. No one was even really sure how long—or where—they lived. They just seemed to show up anywhere there was food and drink and music—if anyone had ever seen a Faun village, they'd never mentioned it.

"Saw you—"

"—heading for the forest—"

"—down the old road—"

"—nobody takes the old road—"

"—not for a long time—"

"—some people do—"

"—not many people—"

"—but some—"

"—and you have food—"

"—tasty food—"

"—*lots* of food—"

The Fauns gathered in a group at the edge of the blanket and re-garded the contents of the hamper hopefully. Tiercel looked at Har-rier and shrugged. They'd barely started on their meal, and the Fauns would certainly eat it all, but neither boy would starve for missing a meal. He picked up a loaf of bread and tossed it to the Fauns, who grabbed it and divided it eagerly, stuffing it into their mouths with absolutely no regard for table manners. Now that they were holding fairly still, it was possible to count them. There were six of them.

"Here. You can have some more if you like."

As Tiercel had been pretty sure they would, the Fauns took that as an invitation not only to have *some* food, but *all* of it. They clam-bered onto the blankets—swarming over Tiercel and Harrier as if they were both just part of the landscape—and fell upon the food as if they'd been starving for sennights, though every single one of them looked plump and sleek. Cheese, sausages, bread, fruit, and even an entire pot of jam vanished within less than half a chime.

Other things vanished too, or almost did.

Tiercel only noticed when he saw first his coin-pouch, then his pen-case, appear in the Fauns' hands. With a sigh, he collected both objects—the Fauns didn't look particularly upset—and sat on them this time.

"Hey! That's my map!" Harrier wasn't quite as calm about things. "And my eating knife! Give that back! That's sharp!"

"You can't have those," Tiercel said patiently, plucking the ob-jects from the grasping hands of the Fauns. "They belong to my friend."

"Want to see—"

"Want to touch."

"All gone anyway—"

"—in the forest."

"Scary place."

"Dangerous."

"Dark."

"Dark and dangerous."

"Lose things in the forest."

"Why not here?"

"Easier to find them here."

"Yes?"

"No?"

*"Give me back my knife,"* Harrier growled. Tiercel blinked, and realized that not only had he somehow managed to lose his grip on Harrier's knife, he'd also managed to lose his own pen-case again.

This was going too far. He got to his feet—at least he still had both coin-purses—and went over to the pack mule. Digging through one of the packs, he found a large bag of lump sugar. Harrier had packed it because—so he said—there were times when you just needed to bribe a mule. He hoped one of those times wouldn't come up before they could replace it.

"See what I've got?" he said, holding up the large paper sack invitingly. All the Fauns stopped and looked at him.

"What?" one of them said.

There was a chorus of "What's?" It sounded like a flock of birds.

"I've got candy," Tiercel said temptingly. He hadn't grown up as the eldest child in the Rolfort household without learning a thing or two about diplomacy and outright bribery. "And I'll trade you."

A short time later, he'd traded pieces of lump sugar for Harrier's knife and map, for his pen-case, for the empty jam jar, and for a couple of other things that the Fauns had gotten from their belts and pockets that the two boys hadn't noticed at the time.

"And I'll give you the rest of the candy—look, it's a whole sack—if you promise not to ever touch—or take—any of our things again."

All of the Fauns began chattering at once, but by now Tiercel was getting used to the way they talked, and could figure out what they wanted to know. *For how long?*

"Forever," he said firmly.

He was pretty sure the Fauns wouldn't get the idea if he said anything more equivocal. Or they'd find a way around it somehow.

The deal was made, and Tiercel handed over the rest of the sack of sugar lumps. He was a little surprised that the Fauns didn't fight over them, but they didn't. They carefully shared out the contents of the sack equally. There was enough to go around. He'd counted before he'd offered it to them, taking out the extras and slipping them into his pocket.

With their mouths stuffed full of candy—and obviously seeing no more entertainment to be gained from the strangers—the Fauns ran off over the hill and were quickly gone from sight. At least most of them did. Their leader—for lack of a better term—hung back, gazing at Tiercel and Harrier unreadably. He looked puzzled.

"Other road," he said firmly, pointing. Then he ran on to join the others.

"Well, *that* was interesting," Harrier said, getting up to retrieve his things from the saddlebag in which Tiercel had stashed them for safekeeping.

"I think it was partly our fault," Tiercel said. "If we'd told them not to touch anything before we offered them food, they probably would have behaved themselves. A little better, maybe."

"Huh," Harrier said, unconvinced. "And what about all this danger in the forest?"

"Well, what's going to be dangerous for a Faun probably isn't going to be dangerous for us," Tiercel said, thinking it over. "And it's the Delfier Forest. Not that far from the Delfier Highway, if your map is right. What can possibly go wrong?"

And it couldn't be, Tiercel told himself, as they headed off down the Old War Road, that "nobody" took this road to Sentar-shadeen, as the Fauns had said. Not only was the road itself bare and level—which meant that somebody was keeping it in repair—but it was clear of felltimber. Obviously the road was in use. It just wasn't as heavily traveled as the Delfier Highway. And that suited the two of them just fine.

⋙

"THE map says we'll find a side-trace that should lead us over to the inn we want to stop at tonight," Harrier said.

"That's good," Tiercel said obligingly. He was looking forward to a hot bath and a soft bed—and somebody else to take care of the mules.

It was quiet and peaceful along the Old War Road. If it *was* traveled, there wasn't anyone else in view just at the moment. The only sounds were the birds in the trees and the wind rustling the forest canopy. If he pretended—not very hard—Tiercel could imagine that he was a thousand leagues from anywhere. Not going to Sentarshadeen because he was in real and mysterious trouble, but an ancient hero out of the wondertales with no problems of his own, going off to solve the problems of other people. It was a comfortable fantasy.

They'd ridden for about four chimes—long enough to be well along the trail; not far enough for Harrier to start hinting that this would be a good time to stop and dig further into their supplies for another little snack—when three men stepped out onto the trail ahead of them and stopped. Automatically, Tiercel and Harrier stopped, too.

Tiercel vaguely remembered seeing the men ahead of them on the Delfier Highway, and thinking that they must make the trip often because all three of them had heavy walking boots and equally-heavy walking sticks. The three looked very much alike, and Tiercel had automatically assumed they were a family.

"Can we help you?" Tiercel asked.

"You'll be wanting to get down off those mules, now, boys," the eldest—probably the father of the other two—said.

"I, um, what?" Tiercel said.

"No," Harrier said comprehensively.

The man smiled an ugly smile. "Oh, 'no' is it, young master? And I say, we're three to your two, and my sons are men grown, and you're a long way from Armethalieh. And if you don't want to add a good thrashing to the rest of your misery, you'll get down now."

Harrier opened his mouth again. Tiercel held up his hand. "But the mules aren't ours. We really can't give them to you. It wouldn't be right. If you'll just tell us what you really need, we can certainly help you, though. We have some food we can give you, and I think we have some blankets and some clothing. And if it's money—"

"Spoiled brat! I'm not bargaining with you!" the man growled. He raised his staff threateningly and lunged forward.

HARRIER reached out to grab the headstall of Tiercel's mule, hoping he could turn both beasts and make their escape before the brute reached them. But he'd forgotten about the pack mule behind them, blocking their retreat. It simply wasn't going to happen. They were trapped.

Just then, a flurry of small stones came whizzing out of the forest, striking the three men—hard—with unerring aim. They yelped with pain and shock, recoiling from the rain of missiles, but they couldn't defend themselves from an attacker they couldn't see. One of the flying stones had struck the oldest of the three men on the temple, and he was bleeding freely.

"There's more where that came from!" Harrier shouted furiously, but he was shouting to an empty path. Almost as soon as the stones had begun to fly, the three men had turned tail and run, directly up the trail. The hail of stones followed them until they were out of range, then suddenly the forest was quiet again.

"What do we do now?" Tiercel asked nervously.

"*I* don't know! Light and Darkness, Tyr, *you* were the one who wanted to *talk* to them! Offering them half our things! And money, too!" Harrier said in exasperation.

"Well if they were so badly-off that they had to steal, all I thought was—"

Harrier was prevented from attempting to throttle his friend by the arrival of yet another person at the edge of the path. She was obviously the source of the recent hail of stones, as she still held a sling in her hand. As she stepped further out onto the path, Harrier saw that she was a Centaur.

"Not that it isn't interesting listening to the two of you yell at each other, but I think we ought to move along before they pluck up their courage and come back. My name's Simera, by the way. Who are you?"

Harrier grinned at her. "I'm Harrier Gillain. My idiot friend is Tiercel Rolfort."

"I'm pleased to meet you. I'm a Student Forester—and you're lucky I am, by the way, or I might not have been armed."

"We're glad that you were," Harrier said politely, since Tiercel was still just staring. Now that she'd mentioned being a Student Forester, he could see that her outfit—a forest-green leather tunic and vest, and matching panniers slung over her withers—were a plainer version of the distinctive uniform worn by the Forest Watch. Her flaxen hair and tail—Simera had the chestnut coloring common to many of the Centaurs who lived near Armethalieh—were both bound firmly in webs of matching dark-green leather to keep them from getting tangled in the tree branches and the undergrowth through which she might need to pass. In addition to her sling, she carried the short Centaur bow, and a belt-knife that was larger and heavier than Harrier's.

"Come on, then," she said.

❧

THOUGH they proceeded cautiously—and Simera kept a sling-stone nocked and ready for use—they saw nothing further of the three men who had troubled Tiercel and Harrier. As they traveled, the boys learned that Simera had seen the brigands earlier, but had doubted her ability to pass them safely. She'd also been more than a little worried about the safety of any travelers the thieves might encounter, so, rather than simply going through the forest to avoid them—something she could easily have done—she'd waited at the side of the road, hoping to give them a good scare and to find companions whose numbers would allow her to travel along the road without trouble.

"They're bullies, you see, and will only attack if they're sure of an easy victory. Frightening them off this way should make them think twice about attacking anyone else," she said.

"I still wonder why they were attacking us," Tiercel said musingly. "We aren't even a day from Armethalieh. There's work there. And almshouses, too."

Harrier sighed. Sometimes Tiercel could be unworldly to the point of insanity. "Tyr, some people just don't want to work."

Tiercel darted him a disgusted glance. "Maybe. But it seems to me that attacking people in the forest is a lot harder work than, well, *working*. And more dangerous, too, considering that you can be hanged for it. Wouldn't you do something honest if you had the choice?"

"Tyr, some people just don't—" Harrier began again.

"Maybe so," Simera said. "But they don't want to be hanged, either. And these roads are *very* well patrolled; the Watch comes along here at least twice a sennight, and you can almost always find someone at the larger inns. If they hadn't killed you, you'd have reported them. If they *had* killed you, someone would have found your bodies within a day or two at most. And the Watch wouldn't stop until it brought them in. This has to be the first time they've tried this, because I haven't heard a single report of outlaws. We should stop at the next inn, so I can leave a warning for the Watch there. And I'd better go on to Sentarshadeen and report this in person to the Guildhouse, too, because I saw them myself."

"That's where we're going," Tiercel said. "We could travel together, if you liked. I suppose we'll have to cut back over to the Delfier Highway, though, if you're in a hurry," he added, sounding reluctant.

Simera swished her bound tail in amusement, never breaking her swift, even stride. "The War Road can be just as fast—faster, since we won't have to keep pulling off the road to let the freight wagons have right of way. And if you don't mind taking a few short-cuts through the forest. Don't worry. I won't let you get lost."

"That sounds like fun," Tiercel said eagerly. "Right, Har?"

"More fun than losing our mules to a bunch of bandits," Harrier said.

Tiercel was doing it again.

He'd lost count of the times he'd gotten dragged into some wacky adventure by Tiercel's conviction that everybody he met was his new best friend. Granted, most of them turned out perfectly fine. And—granted again—not only had Simera gotten them out of a bad situation, but the Forest Watch was known to be a force for Good, doing much the same thing outside the Nine Cities as the City Watch did within them, though over a much larger area.

As they made their way toward the Bell and Horn—the nearest inn on their route—they exchanged stories—including the puzzling matter of the warning the Fauns had given Tiercel and Harrier—and soon knew as much about each other as any of them cared to tell.

Simera was about their own age, and like Harrier, in her Apprenticeship year. In Simera's case, since she intended to enter the Forest Watch, this meant she would be spending the next year on her own, traveling through the forests that the Watch traditionally guarded, both in order to get to know them, and in order to learn to survive on her own in every season.

THE Bell and Horn was a large and busy place. Tiercel stayed with the mules at the edge of the inn yard while Harrier went in to buy them cider and cold pies, and Simera went to look for someone to whom she could report their encounter in the forest.

When she came back, Harrier had already returned with food. Simera took her share, saying that she'd only been able to leave a message, and that the Watchman had been through here only yesterday, so it would be almost a sennight before someone from the Forest Watch would receive it. But certainly the landlord would tell the story to everyone who stopped—if for no other reason than it was an exciting one—and word would spread swiftly up and down the Delfier Highway.

"And he hadn't? . . ." Harrier asked, around a mouthful of mutton pie.

Simera made a rude noise. "Heard of any such trouble as this? My great-grandmother hadn't been foaled the last time there were bandits in these woods, Harrier Gillain! Oh, beyond Sentarshadeen, yes, you'll see outlaws in the Avribalzar Forest and parts east now and then, but here in the Delfier? The Delfier is an old tame forest."

"I wonder why now?" Tiercel said.

"Well don't go trying to find out," Harrier said hastily, and Simera looked at both of them curiously.

But by the time they reached the Three Trees, they discovered that the master of the Bell and Horn had been ignorant, or over-cautious, or a combination of both.

The Three Trees was filled to overflowing. It was the second inn they tried, pushing on till much later in the day than they'd intended to stop, as the first one they'd tried, the Happy Faun, was so crowded they simply hadn't bothered to seek beds for the night once they saw the condition of the innyard. Now Harrier wished they had.

Tiercel had seemed fine all day—well, after that little bobble while they were leaving the central City this morning—and in the high spirits of the trip, Harrier had really managed to forget that Tiercel was actually *sick*. But as the day wore on, Tiercel had gotten very quiet. And then, after they passed the Happy Faun, he'd started swaying in his saddle as if he'd been riding for days instead of hours. So, although the Three Trees was even more crowded than the Happy Faun had been, Harrier was determined: they were stopping here if he had to unroll their bedrolls behind the stables.

"No room!" the landlord said, catching sight of them as they crowded into the Common Room. Every table was filled, and so many people were standing in the spaces between that it was hard for the servants to make their way from the kitchens with platters and mugs. "I can give you feed and water for your animals, but I have no beds. A corner of my hayloft, though, at a fair price. I won't turn you away," he said kindly, looking at Tiercel.

"What's going on?" Harrier asked, raising his voice to be heard over the sound of too many people talking all at once.

"Trouble on the road ahead," the landlord said, wiping his hands on his apron. "I see there's just the three of you, and one in Forester Green besides. Watchman, have you not heard the news? The Watch says it isn't safe for parties of less than twenty to travel.

Warning was just set by the Watch this morning for all travelers along the Delfier Highway."

"We came by the War Road," Harrier answered.

The landlord stared at him as if he'd gone mad.

"Well," he finally said, "the War Road's no worse than the Delfier. But *I* wouldn't take it."

"But that's outrageous!" Now Simera had forced her way through the press of people and had come to stand beside Harrier. "When has the forest ever been unsafe?"

"Since Kindling, Forester," the landlord said simply. Though the inn was busy, he obviously relished the chance to rest and impart his tale to those who did not know it.

"Oh, nothing that the Watch could rightly speak to. Just accidents. Trees falling. A woodsman's axe going awry. Just what you'd see in any springtide, but never so many as this year. Then folk started wandering off. At first it was just them getting lost and going astray that never had before. And soon enough found. And if a few more pigs and dogs and deer disappeared than normal and *weren't* found again, nobody noticed that . . . until people started vanishing too; and last night, a whole caravan in a lay-by not half a mile from here—well, they came to me for supplies three days ago and bespoke breakfast, and when I sent my boy out with the breakfast hampers the next morning, there was nothing there at all but their carts. It's worse east of here; there's been travel proscriptions on the road since Kindling, but now they've extended them into the Delfier. Until the Forest Watch finds out what's wrong, well, nobody's going to be going anywhere alone. You'll find every inn along the road as crowded as mine—or more. Folk stop until they find enough others heading for their destination."

Harrier glanced at Tiercel. Tiercel was swaying on his feet, looking as if he'd be on the floor in another moment. "We'll take the hayloft," he said quickly.

THE innkeeper was as good as his word, and fortunately the season was mild, for their animals, along with those of a number of other latecomers to the Three Trees, could not be properly stabled at all, but would spend the night hitched to hastily-constructed hitching-posts at the back of the innyard. So close to the Delfier Highway, there was no danger that the inn would run short on provisions, but the idea that foot travelers, caravans, and even freight wagons must queue together for safety was more than disturbing. It was frightening.

"It started at Kindling," Tiercel said, as Harrier led him out of the Common Room.

"Is that supposed to mean something to me?" Harrier said. His mind was on the problem of getting their gear into the stable, and the pack-mule's gear into the hayloft, for with so many people in the inn, they would have to do most of the work themselves. Fortunately, he was no stranger to hard work.

"Kindling was when I—"

"Shh!" Harrier said, for just then Simera arrived to join them.

"We can't get dinner for at least an hour," Simera said with a sigh. "That's half a bell, Armethaliehan time. That should give you time to get the mules settled. You might as well do a good job of it. Who knows how long you'll be here waiting to make up a traveling party? I wish I'd known. If I'd been on the roads—instead of in the forest—I *would* have known. Then I could have warned you to—"

"I can't wait," Tiercel said with a groan. He staggered over to one of the benches in front of the stable and sat down with an inelegant thud. "I have to get to Sentarshadeen *now*."

Simera stared at him. "What could possibly be that urgent?"

"I'm—"

"Tiercel—"

"I'm looking for a Wildmage to interpret a vision I've had," Tiercel said defiantly, glaring at Harrier miserably.

To Harrier's profound relief, Simera didn't laugh. And to his faint disgust, she seemed to think it was a perfectly reasonable reason for tearing off somewhere as if your tail was on fire. She thought the matter over for a moment, and then nodded.

"Oh. Well. You're going to have to go farther east than that, I guess. I don't think there are any there, though they don't always reveal themselves. The Light Temple will know. And if you really need one—"

"I really need one," Tiercel interrupted.

"—one will probably find you. But if you're seeking one out, you'll probably have to go as far as Ondoladeshiron or Ysterialpoerin to be sure of finding one."

"But—they're moonturns away!" Harrier groaned. "We're only supposed to be gone a few sennights."

Simera shrugged. "Maybe a Wildmage will find you," she repeated.

Harrier sighed. "Well, a Wildmage won't find us tonight. And those mules need to be unsaddled. Tiercel, you stay here."

"I can help."

"You can sit."

"WHAT'S wrong with your friend?" Simera asked, as the two of them made their way to where the ostlers had left the mules.

Harrier shrugged. "Nothing. I don't know."

"If you don't want to tell me, fine."

"I've just told you as much as the best Healers in Armethalieh know," Harrier said defiantly. "Maybe he's just . . . worried."

"He kept a cool head with those brigands. He seems very nice."

"He *is* nice," Harrier said, a little more forcefully than he intended to. "That's why he's always getting into trouble."

"And I suppose you're always around to keep him out of trouble?" Simera asked perceptively.

"Not that it works," Harrier said, grinning in spite of himself. "I don't know what's wrong. Nobody does. But something's . . . wrong."

*And it started at Kindling.*

"Well, in that case, you're *sure* to find a Wildmage, if you just keep looking. They keep the Balance, you know. So when there's wrong, they put it right."

*In that case,* Harrier thought, *why didn't one just come to Armethalieh and save us all the trouble of going to Sentarshadeen?* "Come on, let's get these mules unsaddled," he said firmly. "You have *no* idea how much trouble Tiercel can get into when your back is turned."

But for once Harrier's dire predictions about Tiercel's trouble-finding abilities didn't come true. When they returned to the front of the stables—making the first of what would have to be several trips—all they found was Tiercel at the center of a ring of human and Centaur children. From the sound of things, he was telling them fascinating wondertales of times gone by. And by the time Simera and Harrier had completely unloaded the pack mule and brought the equipment into the stable, Harrier had heard enough of the story to recognize it.

"—but of course Kellen didn't realize that he was a great Knight-Mage, you see, because he was a Poor Orphan Boy, and his only relative, the Blessed Saint Idalia, had been taken away from him as a child and enchanted into the form of a Silver Eagle by the wicked Endarkened. And he was beaten and starved and forced to work on the docks of Armethalieh as a slave. And one day he broke a *whole crate* of Elvenware, and so he was cast out of the City in the depths of winter to *starve.*"

Tiercel's audience "oohed" and "aahed" in sympathy.

"—and as he was lying in the snow about to die, who should come along to save him?"

"Shalkan! Shalkan!" Tiercel's audience cried.

"That's right. The magic unicorn Shalkan. And he dried Kellen's tears and told him of his glorious destiny, and that he was the true son of the Arch-Mage of Armethalieh and the Wildmage Queen of the High Reaches, and that to claim his destiny he must draw the Sword of Light from the Black Cairn in the heart of the Lostlands and use it to turn his sister back into a human girl again, so that she could marry the King of the Elves, Jermayan Dragon-rider. And the two of them would unite the Armies of the Light and slay the Endarkened, so that Spring would return to the world. And now, I think, I have work to do. And your parents are probably missing you."

There were groans of disappointment from his audience as the children reluctantly got up to leave.

"You tell stories well," Simera said.

"I've heard that one every year since I was a child," Tiercel said, getting to his feet and reaching for one of the packs. "I'm not sure, anymore, that any of it's true."

LATER that night he lay awake in the hayloft beside Harrier, sur-rounded by their gear—and the slumbering bodies of the dozen or so other travelers to whom the landlord had sold sleeping space in the stable's second story. It was comfortable, and even warm, and after a long day on the road, Tiercel was exhausted, but he fought sleep with a desperate intensity. He feared his dreams.

The worst part was that there was nothing in the dream *to* fear. A woman made of fire, standing in a lake made of fire. When you described it that way, it sounded pretty. Other than being made of fire, she looked perfectly normal. And she wasn't even looking at him. Not really. He'd been having the dream for long enough that he knew there was someone else in it. Someone he could never see. *That* was the person the Fire Woman was calling to. The one who—if he reached her, and did whatever it was she wanted him to do—would cause all the horrible things to happen.

Whatever they were. Whoever he was. Assuming the dream was real.

But it was real in *some* way, Tiercel knew, because even though the Fire Woman's calling wasn't meant for him, he'd gotten tangled up in it somehow. So that even though she was actually calling to this other person, somehow he was—or could be—visible to her too. He didn't think he was, yet. But the moment when he would be, came closer every time he had the dream, and he had no idea what would happen then. So he really hoped that Simera was right, and that a Wildmage would show up—soon—and tell him what was going on, and how to fix it. Meanwhile, he'd just better stay awake.

But that didn't turn out to be possible. And this time, when he slept, he dreamed a different dream entirely.

# Four

# A Life Between Sand and Stars

IS NAME WAS Bisochim, and he had been born in the Isvai Quarter of the Madiran Desert, far south of the Armen Plains. The Isvai was a sea of sand, harsh and trackless, and one must live by the desert's own law to survive here.

The desert held little of kindness, but there was no cruelty here. Its inhabitants did what they must to survive, but no creature made another's burden heavier. That was the first and most ancient law of the desert, for Bisochim's people, like all the peoples of the world, followed the teachings of the Wild Magic.

Wildmages plotted the routes the nomadic herdsmen took through the great dune sea of the Isvai; Wildmages told them when the Sandwind would blow; Wildmages led their herds to new pastures when old ones failed; and when the deep wells that meant survival in the arid desert ran dry, Wildmages led them to new ones.

Bisochim had never expected to become a Wildmage.

The Three Books had come to him when he was a child. Like all the other boys and girls too young to perform any more useful tasks, his duty was to guard the flocks of the Adanate Isvaieni, for the hardy desert sheep and goats were both their wealth and the life of their tribe. But Bisochim had ambitions to become a hunter someday, and a hunter must have a falcon, both to take small game, and to drive larger prey into the waiting jaws of the hunter's fleet-footed Ikulas. And so he had left the sheep and the goats to the care of the other children one morning and climbed the rocks where he had seen a pair of nesting falcons. If he were careful, and lucky, he could take one of the chicks for his own and raise it himself, taming it to his hand.

But when he reached the nest, it was empty, though he'd been watching it for many days and had been certain that the young falcons were all far too young to fly. The only thing that had been in the nest were three small books bound in brown leather. He'd recognized them at once.

*The Book of Sun.*

*The Book of Moon.*

*The Book of Stars.*

He'd stuffed them into his tunic and scrambled back down the cliff with a lot less care than he'd taken getting up. He hadn't dared look into them, nor had he told any of the other children what he'd found. It wasn't until that evening, when he had returned to the camp, that he had even dared think about what he'd found. The Books of a Wildmage.

He'd taken them from his tunic and wrapped them carefully in his best shirt, and gone off to tell his father.

❧

BISOCHIM'S father was seated at the loom in the main room of the tent, working while there was still light to see. Nedjed's body was small and twisted; what had once been strong muscle was now gaunt sinew, and skin was stretched tight over bone.

Nedjed was a man only in his middle years, but the desert life was hard. He had been one of the tribe's greatest hunters until a battle with a desert lion had left him lamed and crippled. The tribe could support none who could not earn their keep, so Nedjed had learned a new skill, weaving the yarn that his wife spun from the hair and wool of the flocks into the heavy sturdy cloth from which Bisochim's people made so many things. He was neither good nor fast, having come to the trade so late in life, but the work was enough to earn him life, and the respect of the tribe.

"Father," Bisochim said, kneeling beside his father's weaving-stool. "A thing has happened today, and I seek guidance."

"Instruction is the only gift freely given," Nedjed replied. "Tell me what is in your heart, son of my heart."

"Today I found the Three Books of the Wild Magic," Bisochim blurted out after a long agonized pause. "And I do not know what to do."

Nedjed pulled the shuttle to rest and sat back, reaching for his crutch to steady himself. "And is it truth that you did find them, or did you take them from the hands of another?"

"They were in a falcon's nest. I had hoped to take a fledgling. I found the Books instead," Bisochim answered honestly. Theft was not unknown in the Isvai, but the greatest crime possible was to steal from your own people.

"Bring them here," his father said.

When Bisochim had returned with the Three Books, Nedjed regarded his son for a long moment.

"Open one and tell me what you see."

Hands trembling, Bisochim did as he was told, tilting the page toward the sunset light streaming in through the open tentflap.

"It is filled with sayings," he said, after a moment. "Like the ones Socorro the storyteller ends his stories with on feast days." He closed the Book again.

"Then the Gods have made their judgment. These Books have been sent to you. They have chosen you to keep the Balance. You must read them, and learn from them, and hold their wisdom in your heart. Your mother will be pleased."

Bisochim stared down at the Three Books in his hands. He was a Wildmage, now, even though he didn't feel any different than he had when he had gone out with the flocks before dawn. He turned his father's words over in his head.

"Are you, Father? Are you pleased?"

"Son of my heart, it is a great destiny to keep the Balance. Some men yearn to be so chosen, thinking of the glory it may bring them. But the tales tell us it is the hardest life the desert can send. I take great pride that the Gods think you are worthy of it. But for a child of my body, I would wish an easier future between Sand and Stars."

Bisochim bowed his head. His father had never been one to praise lavishly or lightly. "Thank you, Father. I shall always try to be worthy. And I shall never seek glory."

"If you were one to do so, the Books would never have found you. Now go and wash yourself. It is time to eat."

THOUGH he was now a Wildmage, little in Bisochim's life changed immediately. His days were still spent herding goats and sheep. But in the evenings, when once he had played *shamat* and *gan* with his brothers and sisters, now he studied the Three Books. Soon the magic came to him, and the tribe flourished.

He could not Heal Nedjed—though he tried. No spell of Healing could restore what was gone forever, merely encourage that which was damaged to heal quickly and well, and the wound-fever that had settled in his father's leg after the lion's attack had forced the tribe's Healers to cut most of the leg away. But he was able to ease much of his father's pain, just as he eased the hurts of all who came to him, for all the Adanate were eager to lend Power to his spells, and the Mageprices he was called upon to pay were light, and easily discharged. But the more Bisochim delved into the deep mysteries of the Wild Magic over the years, the more he became convinced that there was something . . . out-of-Balance in the world.

The Wild Magic held all things within its grasp. Life and Death. Dark and Light. All in a perfect balance, just like the life of the desert itself. And something wasn't right. He knew he had to find out what it was. The time had come for him to leave.

His people had been expecting the day to come for a long time, for the Wildmages did not belong to any one tribe alone. They went where they were called, across the whole of the Madiran—and even beyond, if that were their fate. Some were called out of the Isvai to live in the cities at the edge of the Madiran. These things went as Sand and Stars willed.

When he went, Bisochim took a proper share of the tribe's wealth, enough to keep him alive in the desert, for that was only proper, and he had earned it by his magic. Waterskins, bedroll, the weapons of a Master Huntsman—for Bisochim had achieved this childhood ambition over the years—he would take all these things away with him when he left the tent of his mother for the last time, but these things had been his for many years, as had been his falcon and his *ikulas* hounds. His share of the tribe's wealth lay in the animal he would ride away upon: a fine riding *shotor*, the hardy, swift, long-necked beast, more enduring than a horse, that could go days without water and traverse the burning sands of the Isvai in speed and comfort.

The second thing he had earned by his magic, Bisochim donned for the first time upon the day he left; the blue robes of a

Wildmage of the Madiran, so that every desert-dweller would see him and know him for what he was at once. Their blue was as bright as the desert sky at morning, before the sun had bleached it to whiteness, and they were woven of the finest, whitest wool of the young kid and dyed with the costly flaxflower blue usually reserved for the weavings sent to the cities as trade goods. The robes ensured that Bisochim would be seen, and known, and welcomed at every oasis and cookfire. To host a Wildmage was never charity. It was service to the Balance.

Gazing down at himself in his mother's tent as he stood there, dressed, for the first time in his life, as a Wildmage, Bisochim felt very odd and uncomfortable. There had never been any need to wear the blue among his own people, for every one of them had known what he was. And though he had not hidden his Wildmage gifts when his tribe had encountered other tribes in their travels, that was a different matter than meeting another tribe as a lone wanderer. In the desert, lone travelers were viewed with suspicion, and the Wild Magic could not protect him from an arrow in the dark. So now he would wear the blue robe. The color of water. Of life.

When Bisochim stepped from his family's tent for the last time, garbed in his new finery, all the tribe was gathered to see him depart. There was cheering when he appeared, but it quickly fell silent. The people he had known all his life, who had known him as a Wildmage for ten cycles of seasons, suddenly saw him as something entirely apart from them now that he wore the blue robes. He had been *set* apart. This, Bisochim realized, was how it would be for the rest of his life.

The people before him cleared a space, and he walked quickly through them to his kneeling *shotor*. Placing a booted foot upon its knee, he swung himself up into its saddle and clucked to it, giving it the command to rise. It lurched to its feet and he gathered the reins, tapping it on the shoulder with his goad to command it to move forward.

Soon Bisochim left the only home he had ever known far behind.

❧

FOR sennights he traveled through the Isvai, seeing no one. The Wild Magic made it a simple matter to arrive at wells and be gone from them before others came, to seek out solitary grazing for Sharab, to call such game as he needed for himself and his *ikulas* to his snare. If he chose, he could live out the rest of his life in this fashion—but if he were the sort who would make such a choice, it was very unlikely that the Three Books would have come to him in the first place.

It was not impossible, of course. The Wild Magic was as mysterious as the desert. Who could say that Bisochim did not serve the Balance by spending the rest of his life wandering as a lonely hermit pondering the intricacies of the Balance? Perhaps the whole purpose of his life was to die in a certain place so that his Books could be found by another? There was truly no way to know, and life in the Isvai did not encourage idle speculation on things one truly could not affect. Bisochim did not spend a great deal of time worrying about it. What he did worry about—alone, between Sand and Star—was his growing belief that there was something flawed in the Balance of the World. For if the Balance was flawed, didn't that mean the *world* was flawed?

It was true that the world had gone out of true before. Many times. But when that happened, so the old tales said, the Wild Magic itself defended the Balance, calling up extraordinary creations out of itself: Knight-Mages and War Mages. They were the essence of Light itself—not of Balance as the Wildmages were— and were just as out-of-tune with true Balance as any creature of Darkness. This was why they appeared only rarely, in moments of great peril, and vanished again once the danger was past, for in their own way, they were just as dangerous to the Keeping of the Balance as the unchecked Darkness. The Balance's tools of Pure Light burned brightly and briefly against the threat to the Balance, giving up their lives so that harmony could be restored; they were not meant to last longer and draw the Balance out of alignment in the opposite direction. Thus the storytellers taught, for had not the War Magic once lingered beyond its time and become a yoke about the neck of its own people, ultimately forged by the Darkness as a blade against their throat?

But none of this was useful *now*. The War Magic had been gone since the Great Flowering, and Bisochim knew that he wasn't a Knight-Mage. All aspects of the Wild Magic flowed strongly through him, and he lacked the Knight-Mage's special gifts—and limitations. So he did not understand why it was he should have received such a warning.

*Perhaps*, he decided at last, *it is so that you can convey it to one who needs it but cannot sense it.*

He could not imagine who such a person could be. The only ones who would need such a warning would be those with the power to act upon it. And any with such power would be other Wildmages, who would certainly be able to sense for themselves that the Balance was out of true. At any rate, with little more than a sense of *wrongness* to go on, there was little he could do. It wasn't even possible to seek out the source of the wrongness, for it was far too subtle. All he could do was watch, and wait. And so, after many moonturns of solitude, Bisochim re-entered the life of the Isvaieni, wandering among the tribes, and doing what he could to serve the Balance and grow stronger in the ways of the Wild Magic. The spells he was called upon to cast were as humble as a Finding Spell that uncovered the location of a wandering goat, and as sophisticated as a Shield spell that protected an entire encampment from the Sandwind's destruction. His Mageprices were always light ones, for his solutions to the problems he faced were always simple and elegant. He became—though it was the last thing he would ever have wished to be—a legend among the tribes. They gave him a veneration he did not want, as if the power was his, and did not come from the Gods of the Wild Magic. Soon they began to speak of him as if he were more important than other Wildmages. As if he were more important than the magic itself. To be set apart in that fashion angered him, and such anger was against all he had been taught of the Balance, and so, less than a score of moonturns after he had left the tents of his own people, Bisochim withdrew once again, this time to the deepest part of the Isvai, a place where the Isvaieni did not go, for there was no grazing to be had there, and no water.

But once, long ago, the land had been otherwise, and there had been cities here, though not cities of Men. The Wild Magic led him to a city carved into the walls of a deep canyon, and there Bisochim coaxed long-dry wells back to life, and with water and labor caused ancient gardens to bloom once more. In silence and solitude he found peace, and only the greatest need called him back out among the Isvaieni. When he went, he no longer wore the blue robes. Like his cousins to the north and east, he worked in secret whenever he could. And then one day something happened which changed his world forever.

Her name was Saravasse.

❧

IT was a fine cool spring morning, and Bisochim was hunting. By now his little canyon held a small herd of goats as well as a few chickens—for the valley had bloomed under his care—and he did not truly need to hunt for meat. But pig and antelope made a nice change from chicken and goat, and stretched the time he could go without looking for a caravan to trade for supplies. Besides, he liked to hunt. He was good at it. A skill unused was wasted, and the desert abhorred waste.

His falcon circled above him in the high sky, wings outspread. His *ikulas* paced along beside him, jaws open and tongues lolling. His *shotor's* pads made soft drumbeats in the sand.

The water he had summoned to the canyon's wells had brought life back to the Deep Isvai, for that was the way of the desert. The plants that had flowered in the brief winter rains did not die, but sunk their taproots deep, so now there was thornbush and dagger-grass to keep game here that once would have migrated elsewhere. Over the years it had grown tall. That the desert creatures came down into the valley as well did not bother him particularly, since Bisochim hunted them for food in turn. That was the Balance.

Suddenly his falcon ceased its lazy hunting circles. For a moment it almost seemed to flounder in the air, then it banked and turned, fleeing as if from an enemy. But falcons fled only from eagles, and there were no eagles here. Bisochim whistled, and swung his lure, but in the end it took magic to bring the falcon to his glove. Only when she was safely hooded and on the block was he willing to investigate what might have frightened her. Whatever it was, it was something in the rocks ahead.

He whistled his *ikulas* to heel and rode cautiously forward. He had only gone a little way into the rocks before the hounds' hackles began to rise and they began to whine uneasily. He silenced them with a gesture. He could smell what they could not. The scent of magic.

At his touch, Sharab knelt, and he swung down from his saddle. She settled herself in the soft dust with a grunt, too lazy to get to her feet since he would obviously be returning soon. He scratched her absently behind one large hairy ear—receiving an echoing groan for his troubles—and walked cautiously forward.

"Man. Come no closer."

The source of the deep soft voice was still hidden by the rocks ahead. All that Bisochim could tell from the sound was that the speaker was female—and not human.

"Are you in trouble?" he asked, stopping where he was. "I am a Wildmage. I can help you."

There was a faint scraping noise from the rocks ahead. "In trouble, yes. But beyond your power to aid," the voice said.

Bisochim scrambled forward through a narrow cleft between two rocks. And saw . . .

A dragon.

Dragons were known in the story-songs of the tribes of the Isvai. They were among the Otherfolk who had been reborn in the War Against the Endarkened, and who had gone into the East when the Elves had withdrawn across the mountains in the aftermath of the Great Flowering, when the Great Desolation had become fertile once again. He had never expected to see one.

She was larger than the largest tent he had ever seen. Her head alone was larger—far larger—than Sharab. She was scaled like an adder, and her scales glinted as brightly as polished metal, in the deep fiery golden red of garnets. Her wings were like the wings of bats—enormous sails of skin and rib—and at the moment they were swept out behind her at an awkward angle, their membrane pierced and shredded by the stand of thornwood trees she'd tumbled into.

"I told you to stay back!" she cried, rearing up. The movement pulled sharply at her wings, causing her to hiss in pain.

"I can help you," Bisochim repeated quietly.

The red-gold dragon chuckled painfully. "You might be the greatest Wildmage born in a thousand years. But the Mageprice to make my wings whole would be more than even you could take upon yourself." She hesitated, as if she would say something more, but she did not.

"It would indeed," Bisochim agreed, once the silence had stretched for a while. "But you must agree, they will heal far better once they have been untangled from these trees."

The dragon blinked in astonishment, as if the idea had never occurred to her. "So they would, Man," she said at last.

"Shall we begin, then?" Bisochim asked.

It was hot, back-breaking work to untangle the dragon's wings from the grove of tall thornbush into which she had been driven by the storm. The Sandwind that had been her undoing had been a violent one, as deep desert winds often were. It had caught her by surprise, she told him, as she flew low to the ground nearly a hundred miles from here, catching her up in its violence, hammering her into near-insensibility before flinging her to the ground in the midst of a stand of thornwood. The tall twisted branches, nearly as hard as metal, had pierced and torn the abraded membrane of her wings, shredding them so thoroughly that she was now incapable of flight, even if she had been able to work herself free.

Bisochim was forced to ride back to his canyon for axe and ropes to cut away branches and—in some cases—cut down entire trees. It was evening by the time he was finished, and at last—for the first time in many days—the dragon was able to fold her wings to her sides once more and straighten herself into a comfortable position.

"I suppose I must thank you for your aid," she said, still with the same odd reluctance with which she had spoken to him at all in their infrequent exchanges. "It is only fitting that you know my name. I am Saravasse."

"And you already know that I am Bisochim. You must be tired and hungry. I know nothing of the ways of dragons, but there is a canyon a little way from here where you can find shelter. There is grass and sweet water—"

Saravasse snorted in amusement.

"—and I can offer you goats."

"I know little of the desert, Bisochim. But I know it does not offer charity. Once I have rested—and I can repay you for your shelter with tales of the lands beyond the mountains—I shall be able to
hunt my own food. Just not on the wing."

"Will your wings heal?" Bisochim asked. Having seen the damage they had sustained, he was greatly worried. He had offered to
sew the torn flaps of skin together—as much as that was possible—
but Saravasse had refused.

"In time," she said quietly. "And I have time. Without a Bond, I
shall live forever. And now, young Wildmage, I suggest that you
look to your *shotor*. Were I to make a sudden appearance, you would
find yourself walking home."

⤬

IN the sennights that followed, Saravasse was as good as her word.
In exchange for her shelter—water was a gift of the desert itself and
was never seen as charity—she told him tales of lands beyond
Bisochim's imagining. Of a world where it was so cold that water
froze at midday, and fell from the sky as snow. Of Elves and unicorns, of forests that stretched as far as the widest desert, of Elven
cities as exquisitely made as the most beautiful lacquerwork box.
She spoke to him, also, of dragons.

Even now, a thousand years after Jermayan and Ancaladar had
brought dragonkind back to life, they were rare, for in a time more
ancient than Bisochim could imagine, the dragons had made a
Great Bargain with the Elves, for the safety of all the peoples of the
Light. Creatures of magic, they had bound their magic first to Elven
Mages and then, when the time of Elven Mages was no more, to human Mages. Since the Great Bargain, only when Bonded to a Mage
could a dragon express its innate magic . . . and produce offspring.

The Mage to whom the Dragon was Bonded became powerful beyond others of his or her kind, for with the Bond, all Prices were paid, and the Mage possessed an endless wellspring of Power from which to draw. But the Bond came at a high price for both of the Bonded, for the death of either meant the death of both. And though an unBonded dragon had an infinite natural lifespan, it was no more invulnerable than any other natural creature, as Bisochim had already seen. A dragon could be killed—by mischance, or by a creature more powerful than itself. And the Bond did not lengthen the human Mage's years at all. Were Saravasse—a young dragon still, as her kind counted time— to Bond, her life would be shortened from eternity to decades.

This was the reason she had been so curt and distant with him. A dragon recognized those with whom a Bond could be forged long before their potential human partners did. And while either—or both—parties could refuse to accept a Bond, refusing what was meant to be came at its own price. One of heartbreak, longing, and eternal regret.

⤙

"I knew the moment I saw you," Saravasse said sadly. "But I did not wish to believe."

It was high summer now, but the desert nights were cool. They sat together in the meadow that had grown up in the depths of Bisochim's canyon home. He had dug the irrigation canals himself last winter, and now the floor of the canyon bloomed lush and green, even in summer, for there was plenty of water.

"You must leave," Bisochim said urgently. "I do not have long to live."

Saravasse chuckled sadly. She was nothing more than a shadow to him, for the moon had not yet risen over the canyon wall, and her eyes were closed so he could not see their light. "You are but a child," she answered softly.

"I am more than a man grown, and the balance of my life will be measured in a few decades, not so very much more. The desert is harsh. The Isvaieni do not make old bones. Nothing to the life that you should have," Bisochim answered.

"Where shall I go? Shall I walk back across the mountains? Even a dragon needs water. It will be long before my wings are healed enough for me to take the wind again."

"Then *I* will leave and never return. I shall give you this place and all it contains. A gift."

"Gifts are only given between lovers, Bisochim. Would you leave me to mourn you?"

"I would leave you to live."

"Once I thought that was important. As did another of my kind. He is a legend, I believe, even among your people."

"You speak of Ancaladar the Star-Crowned."

"Such a fancy name. Ancaladar did not wish to Bond, either. And in those days—I speak now of a time thousands of years ago, of a war that your people have forgotten, the war that Elves and humans once called The Great War—the Bond between Mages and Dragons could not always be counted even in decades, child. Often it was counted in only so many years as you can count on your fingers. For it was wartime, and the Endarkened were powerful. Not even the spells of the Dragon-Bonded could save them. When I was . . . younger than I am now, I heard those stories. They terrified me beyond reason. Child, I have *slept* for longer than the lives of those Bonded. And I vowed—oh, yes—that I would never succumb. Just as, I imagine, Ancaladar vowed, in his time. It is why there are no dragons in human lands now; when the Bond is made, now, it is made among the Elves; their lives are short, but not so short as humankind.

"Those who had Bonded assured me it was a fair bargain—as it must be, since it was set by the Wild Magic itself—and that I should not fear it if it came to me. It does not always. Some seek it, and never find it. Some avoid it, and are sought out. But I was determined to take matters into my own claws, and control my own fate absolutely. I could have retreated into a deep cave and slept away the centuries, but I did not want that. I wanted to explore the world, to cross Great Ocean. They say there are no Mages on the other side. I thought—perhaps—there . . . Instead, the winds blew me to your feet."

"I shall refuse the Bond," Bisochim said, though the words nearly choked him. There was nothing he had ever wanted more in his entire life. Not to be a great hunter. Not to become a Wildmage. Not to Heal his father and see him standing before him once again hale and whole. Nothing. But to accept what he wanted with all his heart would doom the creature he loved most in the entire world to death.

"Will you refuse me, Beloved?" Saravasse asked softly.

"*Yes!*" Bisochim groaned.

"Then you will doom me to an empty and meaningless life," the dragon said implacably. "I shall grieve for the loss of you every hour that I live."

"You will find another!" Bisochim said without thinking.

"And Bond with them? And die with them?" the dragon asked. She laughed bitterly. "Beloved, tell me how *that* is a better bargain!"

"You'll be in the Elven Lands," Bisochim said. "So your Bonded will be an Elf. You'll have thousands of years."

"Hundreds of years," Saravasse corrected. He heard a rustling of scales as she got to her feet. "But you're right. It's possible—if I start looking immediately—that I might find someone else with whom I can Bond in a century or two. I'd better get started." The ground shook with her footsteps as she began to walk away.

"Wait!" Bisochim yelped, scrambling to his feet. "Where are you going?"

"Back to the Elven Lands," Saravasse said over her shoulder. The sound of her voice came from several dozen feet in the air.

"What? Now? You're going to *walk*?"

"I can't fly. And I won't stay here."

Bisochim ran after her, but even though she was walking sedately, she was a dragon and her steps were long. He fell farther behind at every step.

"Come back here!" he shouted. "You can't do this! You'll die in the desert! You'll never get there!"

The ground stopped shaking as Saravasse stopped moving. "I might survive. It's a chance I'm willing to take. You have no claim on me, Bisochim. You want none."

"I want you to live!"

He heard Saravasse sigh in the darkness. "To live is good. I wish to live. But I do not wish to live an empty meaningless life filled with pain. Do you? I am a creature of magic, governed by its laws. You are a Wildmage, keeper of the Balance. Mageprices are harsh things, so I have been told. I do not know; you are the first Wildmage I have ever met. Yet I know that I did not know what happiness was until the moment I saw your face, and I would trade all the long years of a dragon's unBonded lifetime to know that happiness in full. You think only of what I will lose. Think of what we both will gain."

"You would be happy, Saravasse?" Bisochim asked uncertainly.

"I would. For all my days."

"They would be short."

"I could have died a moonturn ago if the rocks had been sharper or I had fallen from a greater height. Nothing in life is certain."

"Are you sure?"

"I am certain of you if you are certain of me," the dragon answered softly.

"I have never wanted anything so much as I want you, Saravasse."

The great red-gold dragon turned around and paced slowly back to where Bisochim stood. For the first time she lowered her head to a level with his own and looked deeply into his eyes. Her eyes were the glowing gold of the rising desert moon.

*Ah, so this is it . . .* Bisochim thought distantly. Power poured into him like a torrent of sweet water, and with it, more than he could ever have imagined. Acceptance. Love. Knowledge.

Later that night he Healed her wings—and then, for the first time, he saw the desert from the air. He was changed utterly.

NO longer did Bisochim need to count Mageprice, or go to the tribes for assistance with the spells he cast for their benefit. Thanks to Saravasse, all Prices were paid forever. He had an endless wellspring of Power to draw upon, limited only by his own strength. Where once he could coax dormant desert wells into life, he could now—did he wish—summon rivers to flow where none had ever been.

But to do that would be to go against the ancient ways of the desert. It would change too many things in the Madiran. Respect for the balance of life in the desert was bred into the bones of all who lived in the Madiran, and so, though Bisochim could easily have turned the sands into a garden with his new power, he did not. He continued to help the Isvaieni, but now he did not have to ask their aid to do so. At last he could remain utterly apart from them if he chose. To trade wild game for needed supplies was a small matter, and thanks to the spells he could cast with his new power, he was always able to convince those he spoke to that he belonged to a trading caravan that was just out of sight. Two things only eroded his peace.

The knowledge that the years of his Bonded were now as short as his. And the conviction that had been born in him the first time he had opened his Three Books that somehow the Balance was out of true.

The spells Bisochim could cast now were beyond the imagining of even dreamers and story-singers. More years passed, and he searched as he had never searched before. Not in written books, for the wandering tribes kept few of those, and it would never have occurred to Bisochim to search for his answers there. But in spells, and dreams, and the riddles Saravasse taught him. And at last he found his answer. He'd had it all along.

Every child in all the world was taught one thing about the Wild Magic if they knew nothing else: that it was the magic of Balance. North and south, east and west, city-dweller and tent-dwelling nomad, hunter and farmer, craftsman and artisan, all knew this one thing about the Wild Magic. Though they might never see a Wildmage in the flesh, never come closer to magic than saying their prayers to the Eternal Light that was the aspect of the Wild Magic given to Men to revere, everyone knew that. The Wild Magic was Balance.

And a millennium ago, the Creatures of the Light had gathered together and smashed that Balance beyond all resurrection, by destroying the Endarkened and all their creations. Half the Balance.

What was Light without Darkness?

The Sandwind that scoured the desert was a terrible thing, feared by all, but without its destruction, the desert would not bloom, for many plants relied upon its scouring winds to carry their seeds to new places. Without the Sandwind, those plants would die, choked by their own growth.

In the Elven Lands, so Saravasse told him, there were moon-turns of darkness and cold every year, a season when the land lay buried beneath drifts of frozen water. Yet without this time of renewal, so she told him, their crops would not grow at all, and the land would suffer. So it was even here in the west, in the lands far to the north. Saravasse and Bisochim had flown north one winter, and he had seen the frozen water that fell from the sky with his own eyes. Only his spells had protected him from freezing to death. He had never imagined such cold. Without Balance—even harsh balance—all things suffered, in the end.

Even when presented with the evidence of his own eyes and senses Bisochim did not wish to believe, for the stories he knew, and the stories he learned from Saravasse, of the battles that had led to the Great Flowering, convinced him that the Endarkened were truly terrible things. Yet he was a child of the Isvai, raised in a harsh land, and knew the pitilessness of Nature's balance. There was no balance if the world was all softness and light. And he was a Wildmage, sworn to serve the Balance. If the Balance had been damaged, he, above all people, must restore it.

Yet he would not act hastily. With Saravasse, he journeyed deeper into the desert, going farther than anyone had ever gone before, to places of which there were not even legends. He was drawn only by a conviction that somewhere there in the Barahileth—the deepest part of the Isvai where even the Isvaieni did not go; the very center of the Madiran—would be the proof he sought, for if Bisochim were truly being called upon to restore a measure of Darkness to the world, he must be very sure it was the right thing to do before he began. He must have utter and absolute proof that he was right to do the things he would be called upon to do. And there, in the Barahileth, he found what he sought.

Thousands of years before, the world had been filled with races destroyed by the Endarkened. They had worshiped at places of Power that had wrapped the land in a jeweled net. Once there had been nine for each of the races that lived beneath the sky. These ancient Shrines had been born with the land itself, wellsprings of eternal power, as indifferent to Good and Evil as Sand and Star. Most of the ancient Shrines had been lost to war, to treachery, and to Time itself. One remained.

Even if humans had remembered its existence, they could have made no use of it. The creatures who had worshiped here so many centuries ago had been the essence of Fire Itself: the Fire-sprites. The marking stones of their shrine were buried beneath the surface of a lake of fire that shimmered and seethed and boiled, just as it had in a time long before even Elves had walked the surface of the land. The moment he first saw it, as he flew high above it on Saravasse's back, Bisochim knew that this was the place he needed to be—a place that had once echoed to the magic of the Endarkened.

The ancient story was told everywhere, the story of the victory of the Blessed Saint Idalia over the Endarkened Queen, and of how the Great Flowering had begun with her dying blood. How that war had been not merely a war of Men and Otherfolk, but of Gods as well, for the ancient Land-Gods of the Elves had roused up from a sleep of ages to fight so that the Black God the Endarkened served could be chained forever. And because the Black God of the Endarkened had come so near to the world at the now-lost Shrine where the Blessed Saint Idalia had died, it was possible for Bisochim to reach out to touch the faint echo of that Darkness here, for what touched one Shrine touched all.

To conjure up the Dark Forces merely to consult them was madness and evil, and Bisochim would not have considered doing such a thing for a moment, no matter how desperate his suspicions that the Balance was currently in grave disarray. But here, in this untouched place of ancient power, older than the Wild Magic itself, the echo of the Darkness was preserved like an insect in amber. Here he could study the Darkness without being touched by it, and determine if that Darkness were truly a part of the Balance.

He would, of course, be very careful.

❦

AT the edge of the Lake of Fire Bisochim created for himself a new home that rivaled in majesty the dwelling-places of the ancient Kings of Men. This task he had set himself would surely be the work of years, and perhaps the rest of his life. It did not matter. There were others who could shepherd the people of the Madiran through the turmoil and crises of their lives. Only he could solve this riddle. And he must have a place to live while doing so. With Saravasse's power to draw upon, he summoned up water from the depths of the desert and used it to create fountains to protect himself from the Lake of Fire's killing heat. Here, at last, he created the garden that his power permitted, a paradise for himself and Saravasse. He withdrew from the world entirely, leaving his garden stronghold rarely, and only to gather those things his magic could not bring to him. He no longer traded with the tribes of the deep desert. When Bisochim required something, he went to one of the cities at the edge of the Madiran and bought it, for gold, like a merchant. Gold was easy to summon from beneath the sand; a pretty yellow metal that the city-dwellers placed great value upon, though it had never yet saved a man's life on the sands of the Isvai.

As time passed, his needs from the outside world grew fewer, for he had gardens to provide his food, and that of his animals, and spell-conjured servants to tend them both. Saravasse ranged wide, hunting her own food and riding the high winds of the desert. Bisochim studied, dreaming and casting spells of augury and prophecy. Ranging, through his dragon-fed magic, deeper into the depths of the ancient Earth Power that fed the Firesprite Shrine than any Mage before him had ever delved. And slowly he became aware that to solve this riddle would do more than redress the ancient Balance gone wrong. If he were to set right the ancient Balance of Dark and Light in a proper fashion, he would be able to adjust the Bond that linked him and Saravasse.

Their years would still be linked, it was true. But her life would not be as short as his. His life would be as long as hers. If he brought

Darkness back into the world, Saravasse would not have to die. It was that which made Bisochim certain at last that restoring the Balance was a good thing, for how could saving his Beloved's life be wrong?

⁓

EVEN though he had at last made up his mind to attempt the restoration of the Balance, it was no quick and easy thing to conjure back into Being what had been so thoroughly destroyed. It was necessary, too, to convince Saravasse that it was right for him to do so, for though the Bond ensured that she would never act against his wishes—and that, in fact, he could use her magic just as he chose—he hated to make her unhappy. He wanted her to see that what he did, he did for her good, and for the good of all who lived between Sand and Stars.

He went to her in her special garden, the largest of them all, the one at the edge of the cliff where she could take off and land easily. It was sunset, and the rocks radiated the heat of the day, but the fountains here had been carefully designed, and a constant veil of fine mist filled the air, making it just cool enough—at sunset—for him to join her here.

"You are happy," she said, lowering her head so that he could stroke the fine soft skin just behind her jaw-hinge. It was the only part of her body that was even remotely soft.

"I have found my answers at last," he said.

"It has taken you many years."

"That does not matter now," he said. "For we shall have all the time in the world, Beloved."

He told her everything, then. How the Balance must be restored—that though he did not entirely know how to do it yet, the pattern for the restoration of the Darkness was locked, in its faint echo, into the very fabric of the Shrine itself, and that all that was needed was to work it free and make it whole once more. How he had been uncertain at first that this was the right thing to do, but that he had always known that the Balance was flawed and that he was the one who must set it right. And that he had known that setting the Darkness free again was the right thing to do when he had realized that in doing so, he would be able to claim immortality for himself, so that Saravasse need not die in a few brief years. He had expected joy at his news.

He had not known a dragon could weep.

It angered him. He'd thought her so wise. Instead, she was as foolish as any of the Isvaieni he'd wasted so many years of his life protecting when he could have been doing this instead. Perhaps linking her years to his had destroyed her ability to see beyond the moment.

It was that realization that made Bisochim understand that he must save her in spite of herself, so that he could return her to the glory of what she once had been. Fierce, proud, independent—not this fearful creature who begged him to come away and forget what he now knew to be his life's work. Could she not see that he was doing this for her, and for the Balance? There was no Light without Darkness.

The voice in the fire told him so.

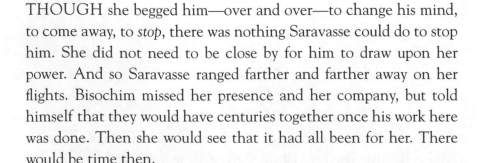

THOUGH she begged him—over and over—to change his mind, to come away, to *stop*, there was nothing Saravasse could do to stop him. She did not need to be close by for him to draw upon her power. And so Saravasse ranged farther and farther away on her flights. Bisochim missed her presence and her company, but told himself that they would have centuries together once his work here was done. Then she would see that it had all been for her. There would be time then.

He threw himself into the work, drawing on Saravasse's power to bring the world back into order and balance once more. The voices in the fire told him what to do, and how to do it. They told him more. They told him that there were those who did not wish him to succeed, who wished the Balance completely destroyed past all repairing.

The enemy was still weak—as weak as the Darkness that Bisochim was coaxing toward life—but Bisochim knew that the enemy's power would grow. That power was tied to the Light, and the Light was out of Balance. His enemy would gain swiftly in power and strength, and destroy all that Bisochim had labored so long to create. Long before another who shared Bisochim's vision could be born, the Great Balance would have been shattered forever.

He did not wish his enemy any personal harm. Whoever it was, Bisochim knew that the enemy acted in ignorance of the damage it was ultimately causing. But Bisochim dared not fail—for his own sake, and for that of Saravasse. A terrible death for his enemy would serve as a warning to any allies that enemy might have—and perhaps do something, in a small way, to redress the Balance Itself. And so, from the shores of the Lake of Fire, Bisochim sent the worst death he could imagine.

*Cold.*

# Five

## A Killing Frost

PAIN WOKE HIM. He'd never been so cold in his life.

The dream he'd been having vanished the moment Tiercel opened his eyes, leaving his head stuffed full of jagged uncomfortable images that slithered away when he tried to think about them. His lips were cracked and bleeding.

He tried to move, and the hay beneath his blankets crackled as if it were shards of glass. Cold-cramped muscles protested, shocking him further awake. The loft was pitch dark. No lanterns here, of course, but there should be lanterns burning in the stable below, and light should be coming up from there through the open trap door.

It was *cold*.

So cold his eyes burned with it, so cold the blood on his mouth froze and flaked. The queasiness he'd felt that morning as he and

Harrier had been leaving the City was back—stronger now—and with it, the same sick terror he felt in his dreams of the Fire Woman and the burning lake. But he was awake now, and this was not fire, but cold. Unnatural cold.

"Harrier." He meant to shout, but his voice came out in a whispery croak. He rolled over to shake Harrier awake. Harrier didn't wake up.

Fear for Harrier did what fear for himself could not. Tiercel's only thought was a need to lash out against the cold before it killed everyone sleeping here. Magic against magic. He knew in his bones what this cold was. Magic. This was summer in the Delfier Forest— not the High Mystrals at Midwinter—and cold like this should not be. There was only one thing that could save them. The first spell, the simplest spell of the High Magick. It spilled into his conscious- ness like water through a gate.

*Fire.*

With a sudden *whoosh* the hayloft was burning.

NO one blamed Tiercel for setting the hayloft afire, but of course, no one knew he had. The moment he cast his spell, the killing cold vanished.

The men sleeping in the hayloft were groggy with cold, but managed to rouse themselves to smother the fire before it spread too far. Fortunately, the cold had not affected those sleeping in the inn as badly. The smell of the smoke roused the kitchen boys, who man- aged to get to the warning-bell and awaken the rest of the inhabi- tants of the inn. They ran to the loft, pitching its burning contents out to the bare ground below, smothering the burning hay with boards, blankets, anything that came to hand. The fire *had* to be smothered. There was no water. The well, the trough, even the wa- ter in the buckets in the stable was frozen solid. When the fire was out, the damage was assessed. The chickens penned behind the sta-ble were dead of cold. The stable cat was dead as well. Their bodies were frozen.

⤜⤛

"WE have to leave," Tiercel said.

He was huddled next to Harrier in the inn's Common Room. Both fireplaces had been built up with roaring fires—despite the season—and everyone who had been in the stable was huddled around one or the other, wrapped in blankets. Those who had slept in the loft were as cold as if they had slept naked in the snow at Midwinter, and their lungs were wracked with smoke, but all would live.

"Now?" Harrier asked shakily. His hands were wrapped around a mug of steaming cider, but he was still shivering so hard he was spilling nearly as much as he drank.

"As soon as it's light," Tiercel said in a low voice. A spasm of coughing shook him, and he huddled closer to the fire. He didn't think he would ever be warm again.

"You think this was you."

Tiercel shot him a look of fond disgust. "I *know* it was me. When are you going to admit it? I had another dream, then I woke up, and we were all freezing to death."

This time Harrier glanced around to see if they were being overheard before speaking. Simera was standing before the other fireplace. Fortunately she'd chosen to sleep outside that night, near the animals, and so had been away from the worst of the cold. It had centered on the hayloft.

"About that woman?" Harrier asked.

"I don't remember this one, actually. But it was the same kind of dream, I think. The cold woke me, and I knew I had to do something."

"And you . . . set the hayloft on fire." For the first time Tiercel heard belief in Harrier's voice. Belief. And fear.

"I had to do something."

"You set the hayloft on fire," Harrier repeated. He sounded as if the fact that Tiercel might have done so were a personal insult.

"Keep your voice down. I'll pay for the damage."

"And explain that how?"

"I'll think of something. But we have to leave. If we stay, and something else happens . . ."

*It will be my fault. And I don't think I can live with that.*

"You're right," Harrier said with a sigh. "I just don't . . . This is crazy, you know. You. Casting spells."

"It was just one spell."

Tiercel looked around the room. The Common Room was full, though it was only a little after Watch Bells, as close as he could guess. Everyone the Three Trees held was here, filling the Common Room and all four of what were usually the private parlors. They were gathered together in small groups, talking in low voices, trying to make sense of something that could not be explained.

"Everybody's really scared," Harrier said.

Tiercel looked at him. "Me, too."

A few moments later Simera came over with a steaming jug, working her way carefully through the knots of standing travelers.

"You should drink more," she said, refilling both their mugs. "There's Allheal in the cider. Smoke hurts the throat."

"I'm so thirsty," Tiercel said hoarsely. He gulped at the fresh mug of cider, wincing only a little at how hot it was.

"It's because of the cold," Simera answered. She frowned faintly. "It was an unnatural thing. If that fire hadn't started when it did, I think we would have all died—in the stable and the stableyard both."

"Lucky thing," Harrier said quickly.

She glanced at him sharply.

"Is this why you're looking for a Wildmage?" she asked Tiercel, taking care to keep her voice low.

"Nothing like this has ever happened before. I swear by the Light," he answered, his voice a low whisper. "I don't . . . Simera, do *you* have any idea what happened?"

"Me?" The Centauress looked surprised. "A whole inn nearly freezes to death at the beginning of summer—you think it's your fault—and you want to know if *I* know why? What I think is that you should go back where you came from and get somebody to help you."

Tiercel shook his head. "They can't. I know they can't. And . . . what if what happened tonight had happened in Armethalieh? What if I hadn't woken up?" He looked at Harrier. His friend's face was grim.

"There are thousands of people in Armethalieh," Harrier said quietly.

"Well, Sentarshadeen isn't that small, and you're planning to go there. What if it happens again in Sentarshadeen?" Simera asked reasonably.

Tiercel shook his head wearily. "I don't know. But I'll have a couple of sennights on the road to figure something out—away from people. Maybe it won't happen again at all. Maybe a Wildmage will be waiting for me in Sentarshadeen. There was one waiting the last time I was there. Maybe . . . I don't know. But I can't stay here. And I can't go back."

Simera studied his face for a moment, then nodded.

"All right. But I'm going with you." At both boys' look of surprise, she made a face, then continued. "I may not be Forest Watch yet, but almost. It's my duty to protect you—*and* the forest. You need to stay away from people and still get to Sentarshadeen. I can help you. You need to survive in the forest, and I bet neither of you has ever done that before. Am I right?"

Tiercel and Harrier both reluctantly nodded.

"You need someone who can hunt for food, because we won't be going near any inns. I can do that too. And if there's something chasing you, well, I'm not afraid of it. You're a good person, Tiercel Rolfort, and whatever this is that's happening to you, I'm sure you don't deserve it." She glared meaningfully at Harrier, as if daring him to argue with her.

Harrier just shrugged.

⁓

WITH the inn in such turmoil, it was easy for them to make their departure unnoticed a few hours later. Before they left, Tiercel managed to slip a large handful of silver unicorns into the inn's cashbox—one of the Golden Suns would have been far too conspicuous—without anyone seeing what he'd done. He hoped it was enough to pay for the damage to the hayloft and the destruction of the fodder that had been stored there. He felt bad about that, but he didn't see anything else he could have done. If he *hadn't* cast the spell—and he still wasn't sure how he'd done it— they'd all be dead now.

Simera had helped them collect their gear. The heavy packs were still in the lower portion of the stable, and their personal packs had been thrown out the window of the loft along with everything moveable that had been burning or might burn, and they'd brought those packs with them when they'd come into the inn's Common Room. Everything smelled of smoke.

"And to think I'd been looking forward to a hot bath last night," Tiercel joked feebly, as they saddled the mules and put their gear once more on the pack mule's saddle.

The horses inside the stable had taken the worst injury from the cold. The sudden sharp drop in temperature had not been good for them, and some of them were now sick. The animals picketed outside had fared better, though all of them—even the usually placid mules—were bad-tempered and skittish this morning.

"At least you'll be able to get a cold one in a few hours," Simera said, holding the pack-mule's head firmly as Tiercel and Harrier worked. "There's a pool a few hours from here. I don't think we should go any farther today. You both need more rest, and it's only by the Herdsman's Grace that you escaped frostburn last night. I know you're in a hurry, but a day of rest now will mean we can travel faster later. And your animals can use the additional rest as well."

"What are we going to feed them?" Harrier asked suddenly. "I mean—"

"They're mules, and it's summer. They aren't going to starve," Simera said briskly. "Now come, before someone thinks to ask us where we're going."

THOUGH the thought of stopping so soon had filled both Harrier and Tiercel with reluctance when Simera had proposed the plan, they were both glad to do so by the time they reached her destination, for last night's unnatural cold had left their muscles stiff and aching. By the time they'd unsaddled the mules and hobbled them so that they could graze without wandering too far, neither of them wanted to do anything but sit where they were. But Simera insisted that they gather wood for a fire, and prepare a camp before they rested. She then announced that she was going off to hunt their dinner, and that if they intended to be finished with their swim before she got back, they'd better hurry.

"That water looks cold," Tiercel said mournfully, when he was sure she was gone.

"Today everything looks cold," Harrier said.

"Still, I'd rather be clean," Tiercel added musingly. "I don't think I've felt this grubby since I was eight, and talked you into exploring the old sewers with me."

Harrier snorted. "One of your lamer ideas."

"Well, I wanted to see where they went. How was I supposed to know they'd still be . . . icky?"

"Everybody in Armethalieh knew after the City Watch rescued us," Harrier reminded him. He pulled off his vest and began to unlace his shirt. "Let's hurry."

Once they got into the water, it wasn't as cold as they feared. The day itself was warm, and their own exertions warmed them further. Still, their swim was brief, and they hurried out of the water and into dry clean clothes.

Standing beside the pool, clean and dressed, eating cold pastries out of their packs—the last of their supplies would be gone by tomorrow's breakfast, but there was no point in trying to save anything, for the bread and pastry would only spoil—it was hard for either of them to quite believe in what had happened only a few hours before. Magic like that belonged in wondertales, not in people's lives. And why should these things be happening to *them?*

It was true that Tiercel had experimented with the High Magick. Once. But he wasn't terribly important, even if he was the son of the Principal Secretary to the Chief Magistrate. He wasn't a prince or the son of a King or even a Wildmage. And it was true that Harrier was the son of the Harbormaster, but there wasn't anything remotely magical about that. And while Harrier was supposed to become the next Harbormaster, he had three elder brothers, and, well, from everything Harrier had said (and hadn't said), Brelt was *much* better suited to the job. If both of them vanished tomorrow, their parents would grieve, certainly, but it wouldn't affect the administration of the City one little bit. And if it didn't affect the running of Armethalieh, it was hard to see how it could affect anything beyond Armethalieh.

And if—it was the only thing Tiercel could think of—he'd somehow managed to intercept a message meant for somebody else, somebody who was *actually* important—he really couldn't figure out why the cold had come last night. Because his dreams had always just been the same vision over and over again. And the cold was something new.

He didn't have enough information to figure this out. He didn't think he could figure it out even if he went back to the Great Library of Armethalieh and read every book there. Twice. He only hoped there were answers in Sentarshadeen. And he hoped they got there alive.

For the first time, it occurred to Tiercel that he might *not* get there alive, and he found the idea profoundly disturbing. Almost as disturbing as the idea that Harrier was in danger because of something he, Tiercel, had or hadn't done. Harrier had almost died last night, along with a lot of other people at the Three Trees. Because of him.

"Look, Har, I've been thinking. We've got a good compass with us, and Sentarshadeen is almost straight east of here. There's no reason you need to go with me. I'm sure I can find it by myself. Why don't you turn around and head back?"

"Uh huh. Think we ought to wash these?" Harrier said, regarding their discarded clothing dubiously.

Tiercel looked at Harrier. Harrier was staring fixedly at the pile of clothing. He obviously had no intention of responding to Tiercel's remark, or even admitting that he'd heard it.

"I'm not sure how," Tiercel finally replied, giving up. "We were supposed to get our laundry done at the inns. I suppose we could just throw it in the pond for a while and then see if it dries."

Harrier shrugged. "Maybe we'll wait and see if Simera has some ideas. I do know something you should do, though," he added.

Tiercel looked at him inquiringly.

"Well, if you really think you can cast spells, maybe you ought to practice them."

" '*Practice?*' " Tiercel echoed in surprise.

"Maybe you'd stop burning things down all the time," Harrier said pragmatically. He shrugged. "Hey, it's a thought."

Tiercel stared at him, his mouth hanging open in shock.

"I still don't believe you can do it, you know," Harrier added.

Without a word, Tiercel turned his back and stalked over to their packs. He'd brought his notebook with him, the one in which he'd written down everything he'd found out about the High Magick. He'd drawn all the glyphs in it, the ones he now knew he'd used so incorrectly the night he'd tried to cast the spell of *Knowing*. He opened the book and paged through it until he found the one he was looking for.

The one for *Fire*.

"If I do this wrong, I'm going to burn down the whole forest," he warned, brandishing the book.

"Well, we've got plenty of water this time to put it out," Harrier said. "What are you supposed to do, anyway?"

"Concentrate on something. See this symbol—in color—over it. Well, draw it with my mind. Then whatever I'm concentrating on is supposed to catch on fire. Why don't you try first?" He handed the book to Harrier.

Harrier studied the symbol. "It looks a little like the Good Luck signs the Selkens paint on their ships. Maybe the Selkens are all High Mages," he suggested. He handed the notebook back to Tiercel, then concentrated on the neat stack of firewood they'd piled at the sandy edge of the pond. He made a good job of it, standing very still for several minutes, brows drawn together as he stared silently. Nothing happened.

"Nope," he said at last. "I think the firewood's pretty scared of me, though."

Tiercel grinned faintly. "My turn," he said.

And there it was. Easy. Quick. The symbol in his mind, a shimmer of movement, not a static thing as it was on the page, but a flash of *coming into being*, and just as it did, he felt an instant where he almost—almost—understood what he was doing. And the pile of wood burst into flames. With a startled gasp, he let the image in his mind dissolve and again he felt that strange moment of weakness, as if, just for a heartbeat, the ground was insubstantial beneath his feet.

"Oh," Harrier whispered, staring from Tiercel to the fire. "Oh. Okay. Oh."

The fire burned brightly. Tiercel walked over to it cautiously. It was a real fire, as normal as if he'd lit it with coals and kindling. He held out his hands to its warmth, reassured by the fact that the flames weren't blue, or green, or black. That it was just like any fire that might burn on his hearth at home. Only he'd lit this one with a spell.

"I'm sorry," he said.

"For being weird?" Harrier said roughly. "You've always been weird." There was a long pause, as if he was trying to work something out in his mind. "But the High Mages and the Wildmages were on the same side, right? In the war?"

Tiercel let out a long breath he hadn't realized he'd been holding. He'd been afraid of . . . what? That Harrier was going to run screaming into the forest? Pick up the nearest rock and bash his brains out? Harrier had been his friend since, well, since before he'd actually been all that good at walking. He couldn't remember a time when Harrier hadn't backed him up, no matter what his moon-addled scheme had been. Even the time he'd tried to make *umbrastone* (which fortunately hadn't worked).

"Right."

"So that's okay. It's not like you're turning into an Endarkened or something, like Kellen's evil stepbrother Anigrel the Black."

"And thanks for bringing that up."

"We'll just find a Wildmage who can get rid of this High Mage thing, and you'll be fine."

Tiercel sighed. Harrier was his best friend, but Harrier liked things to be simple. He was always sure that problems had simple solutions. Tiercel's problems had started because he'd been playing around with the High Magick? Get rid of the High Magick, and everything would be fine.

Tiercel only hoped he was right.

"I see you've gotten the fire going," Simera said when she returned. Three large rabbits—skinned and gutted—hung from her belt, and she looked pleased with herself.

"You'll need to gather more wood, though, to keep it burning through the night. What you have here should do to cook these beauties, though. Take a knife and cut some green sticks from the trees so we can roast them."

She showed them how to secure the carcasses to the sticks so that the rabbits wouldn't fall into the flames as they cooked, and then they settled by the fire to roast their midday meal.

"I've no taste for raw meat myself," she said conversationally, as she insinuated her stick closer to the flame. "Burnt is better, but properly-cooked is best. I'm glad you have a teapot with you. It will be nice to have a good cup of properly-brewed tea. It's just not the same when you make it in a saucepan."

Tiercel laughed, and almost dropped his rabbit.

"I warn you, ashes do *not* improve the flavor," Simera said. "But if you're hungry enough, you'll eat it."

"I'm hungry *now*," Tiercel said, watching grease bubble to the surface of the rabbit's skin. The smell of the cooking meat was wonderful. He didn't think he'd ever been so hungry in his life.

"It isn't done yet," Simera and Harrier said, nearly in chorus.

They looked at each other, and Harrier shrugged and smiled.

"My mother always said a good tale made the cooking go faster," Simera said. "That cold last night . . . you thought it was after you. Or because of you. Why?"

Tiercel shrugged. "I don't know why. I only know—I think I know—that it was. Maybe something like that happens to *all* High Mages when they first start doing High Magick. I don't know."

Simera frowned curiously. "What's a High Mage?"

"Now you've done it," Harrier muttered.

Tiercel explained. In detail. And by the time he was done, so were the rabbits.

"So," Simera said, as they ate, "you say that once there were two kinds of magic and now there aren't except you found out you can do the other kind?"

Tiercel shrugged. "Pretty much."

"Only you don't understand it, and that's why you need to find a Wildmage? But how is a Wildmage going to help you understand it if it isn't the Wild Magic?"

"I have no idea. Harrier thinks a Wildmage can get rid of it for me. The important thing—I think—is that a Wildmage can explain these . . . dreams. Because I think they mean something, too."

"Maybe every High Mage has them," Simera suggested helpfully.

"Oh, I hope not. Because if they did, I can't imagine why there would ever have been any High Mages at all."

ONCE they'd finished their meal—and brewed tea—they spent quite a long time scouring the nearby woods for enough felltimber to keep the fire burning through the night. Simera took the opportunity to show them some of the edible plants that filled the forest—and to warn them away from the dangerous ones. Some of the most enticing-looking berries and mushrooms could be deadly— or at least make the eater very sick.

While it was too early in the season for most of the forest fruits, Simera harvested a fine crop of mushrooms and a few early berries, and by the time they returned to their campsite with the last load of wood, it was late afternoon.

"Now you should rest," she said. "I'll keep watch. At night the fire will keep most creatures away—and I sleep lightly enough—but in daylight, anything might happen."

"Watch?" Harrier asked, slightly startled. He hadn't seen a single living soul on their way here—and every forest creature had fled their (admittedly noisy) approach.

"There's always something to keep watch for in the forest," Simera said firmly.

⚘

THE next morning, while mist still hung over the pool, Simera roused the two of them out of their bedrolls. Though Harrier was used to keeping early hours, apparently the Centauress was an even earlier riser. She showed them, first, how to prepare the fire to brew their morning tea, and then, to break camp.

"There's a game trail that runs fairly straight a few miles from here," Simera said, as she helped them pack. "Once I've set you on it, I'll cut through the forest to the nearest inn. They should be able to sell me a fletch of bacon and a few pounds of meal, and maybe some raisins and some grain for the mules. With that and the game available in the forest, we should reach Sentarshadeen without difficulty. Or any need to tighten our belts overmuch," she added, grinning, for Harrier had complained all through breakfast about their lack of provisions. Except for some tea, salt, and sugar candy, breakfast had finished off their supplies.

"Oh, sure," Tiercel said. Before Harrier could stop him, he'd taken the coin purse from his belt and handed it to her.

"Why didn't you just give her the mules, too, while you were at it?" Harrier demanded later. It was the middle of Morning Bells—or, as they counted time outside the City, the fourth hour of day. Simera, having set them on the game trail, had departed for the inn.

The trail, as she had warned them, was nothing more than a wide spot in the trees; a trail made and used by animals, not people. The wandering bare-earth path was only a few handspans wide; more of a guide than an actual road. But they could follow it if they paid close attention, and Simera had said it was going in the right direction.

"What?" Tiercel asked blankly.

"You gave her all your money. What makes you think she's coming back?"

"Oh, by the Light, Harrier! Are you just looking for things to complain about? Since when does the *Forest Watch* go around robbing people?"

"Apprentice Forest Watch. And we've only her word for that."

"She's wearing the livery. She saved us from those brigands. Although I still think I could have talked my way out of things."

"You always think that. All right. Say she's everything you think she is. What if she's attacked on her way to—or from—the inn? Even *you* have to admit the woods are dangerous—after the brigands, after last night. She *still* has all your money. What if she's hurt, or killed, and the money's lost?"

"Money isn't everything."

Harrier sighed. "It is when you need it to travel on."

"I thought you trusted her," Tiercel said, hurt.

Now it was Harrier's turn to look surprised. "What does that have to do with whether she's hurt or killed? And no, I don't. Why should I?"

"Well, she saved us from the brigands, and she's traveling with us to Sentarshadeen, and—"

"And none of that has cost her much. She needed someone to travel with, as she said. She thinks you're cute. She's going to Sentarshadeen anyway. I don't trust her and I don't *not* trust her . . . not if there are evil things out here that wouldn't find it that hard to *pretend* to be Forest Watch. Tiercel . . . if you want me to believe that you're in some kind of danger, well, one of us ought to act like it."

"I just don't think you should always assume that everybody you meet is out to get you."

"And that's why I'm always the one dragging you out of sewers," Harrier finished triumphantly.

SIMERA did not return until several hours later. By then both boys were hungry and thirsty, and the mules were doing more browsing than moving, despite their best efforts to urge them forward.

She trotted onto the trail a few yards ahead. She was moving carefully, because strapped across her flanks were two large wicker panniers that creaked with every step she took.

"I thought you'd have gotten farther than this," she said, sounding slightly cross.

"I thought you'd be back sooner," Harrier answered equally grumpily.

"Well, she's here now," Tiercel said hastily. He pulled his mule to a halt—not a difficult task—and swung down from the saddle. "It looks like you were successful. Let me help you unpack that. We wanted to look for water—we could hear it—but we didn't want to leave the trail."

Simera smiled. "That was well done of you. There's a little stream not far from here, but it's easy to lose your way in the forest. We'll put the hampers on the pack mule, then go to the stream and eat. I bought buckets and waterskins as well—I'm afraid your purse is much lighter than it was this morning, Tiercel."

"I don't mind," Tiercel said, smiling. "You know what we need better than we do. I'm grateful for your help."

In addition to necessities that would keep over the fortnight they'd need to reach Sentarshadeen, Simera had bought a game pie to eat now, and a dozen berry tarts. Harrier's mood lightened appreciably after he'd devoured all of his share of the food and a good portion of Tiercel's. The remaining supplies were repacked, and the hampers abandoned, a gift to whoever came across them next. They filled the waterskins and went on.

THAT day set the pattern for the ones to follow. That night, at twilight, they made camp. Tiercel and Harrier arranged the camp and took care of the mules while Simera hunted. She brought back whatever she'd managed to catch—that first night, it was squirrels—and they cooked and ate them before rolling up in their bedrolls—at least in the case of Harrier and Tiercel. Simera, like all Centaurs, slept standing.

Tiercel slept without dreams.

"SOMETHING'S coming."

It was the middle of the night. It had been eight days—eight blessedly dreamless days—since they'd left the Three Trees.

Tiercel sat bolt upright in his bedroll, shivering at the shock of the night air on his skin. Above him the summer stars burned brightly.

He'd been dreaming again. One of the *odd* dreams, the ones he didn't remember the moment he awoke, the ones that left his mind feeling jumbled. He looked around. What had it been? He strained to call it back. Nothing. But there was nothing *here*, either. In the last sennight or so, he'd gotten used to the sounds the forest made at night. Simera had told him that the forest kept its own watch. Nothing seemed out of place. And it was certainly no colder than it ought to be, he noticed with relief.

"Coming." Harrier rolled over with a groan. "What?"

"I have no idea."

Harrier sat up, rubbing the sleep out of his eyes. "Tell me you were dreaming."

*The last time I dreamed, a stableful of people almost froze to death.* "I was," Tiercel admitted.

Harrier had always been one to wake up quickly; something Tiercel had found out years ago when attempting to play the usual childhood pranks on his friend—or even to sneak out of a shared room in the middle of the night. Harrier said that if you had older brothers, you learned to sleep lightly. He was fully awake now.

"So?" He sounded irritable. But the irritation didn't come from interrupted sleep, Tiercel knew. It came from the suspicion that Tiercel was about to tell him—once more—something he wasn't going to understand.

This was the part that Tiercel hated most. Not the part where he thought he might be dying. Not even the part where he worried that he might be being stalked by a monster out of a wondertale that might kill his best friend, his new friend, and any strangers they might meet. After all, those things were so unbelievable that he managed to forget them most of the time. The part he hated was that he really believed in the High Magick and Harrier really didn't. No matter how many fires he saw Tiercel light just by look-ing at them. It was as if Tiercel had accidentally stepped around a corner and found himself in a completely different world, one from which he could see his old world, but wasn't a part of it anymore. His world had become . . . different. No matter how much he explained things that seemed logical and ordinary to him now, even reasonable, Harrier just shook his head, like a bull trying to drive away a fly. It was driving the two of them apart.

"So . . . I think my visions are changing. Or else I'm having more of them. And different kinds."

Harrier sighed. "Well, I guess these are better than the other ones, if you can't remember them. But you said 'something's coming.' What?"

"If I knew, I'd tell you."

"That's just great."

Simera walked over to them, her hooded sleeping-robe wrapped tightly around her.

"The forest is quiet," she offered.

"It's the only thing that is," Harrier said in disgust. He reached for his pants and shook them thoroughly, then began to put them on. "How long until dawn?"

Simera glanced at the sky, reading the time by the position of the stars. "A couple of hours. You should go back to sleep."

Harrier simply shook his head, reaching for his tunic.

BISOCHIM was so certain that his spell had worked that he did not look to check its results for many days.

To send the cold into the north had required him to draw greatly upon Saravasse's power, and though she always yielded to his will—as she must—she had begged him not to do it.

Other spells—to turn the Sandwind, to bring water to the wells, to cause the desert plants to bear or bring game to his nets—those she gave her power to gladly. She had even helped him build

this fortress without complaint. But she was unwilling to do the
things that he knew would keep her safe. It was frustrating. For that
reason alone Bisochim had delayed, and delayed again, in seeking
out the proof of the success of his spell. Yet at last prudence had required it, even though Bisochim was certain of his success. The
desert taught its children not to assume.

On the seventh day after he had sent the cold into the north, in
the innermost chamber of his fortress, Bisochim set out to see *what
would be.*

It was not a simple Scrying Spell, such as he had cast all his life,
using date wine and desert lily and a pool of still water. This spell
was far more powerful, calling for blood and powdered bone. Nor did
it show him, as the Scrying Spell did, what he might need to see in
the world as it was. It showed him the shape of the world to come.

THERE were many wellsprings within his fortress, for when he had
first built it, the desert Wildmage had delighted in his newfound
power to summon water from beneath the living rock at will. Fountains filled the courtyards, wasting water into the desert air, for by
his magic Bisochim had procured an inexhaustible supply of the
desert's most precious element. But here, in the deepest room of his
fortress, was a special pool.

The room itself was one he had found, not made. Its walls and
ceiling were a domed bubble of smoky glass, cast up from the Lake
of Fire at some time in the unimaginable past. He had smoothed
the floor, though he had made no other changes, and in the center
of the chamber he had called up a small, perfectly circular, pool of
water from the deep earth. The pool was still and black, and he
used it for no purpose but his magic.

Despite being surrounded by fire, the glass-walled chamber was
cool, for it was deep beneath the surface of the earth. Bisochim en-

tered, crowned in Coldfire, and the pale blue-white light reflected off the myriad cracks and bubbles in the walls, making the whole chamber glitter until it appeared as if he were not beneath the earth, but beneath the stars. He knelt before the pool, arranging what he would need. If he had been successful—as he was certain he had—the vision he would see would change.

But when he sifted the bonemeal across the surface of the unmoving black water, and starred the now-pale surface with drops of his blood, the vision that rose up before him was unchanged. His enemy still lived.

Bisochim paced the chamber in angry confusion.

How could this be?

His enemy, he knew, was weak, while he was powerful.

His spell had been strong.

It should have worked.

But it hadn't, and wondering *why* it hadn't would not save Saravasse or avert the terrible future he saw: fire and pain and marching armies and her death. He closed his eyes. He would waste no more time in wondering why what was, was. That was as useless as weeping over the dead. One could not change the truth. One could only change the future. He had been trying to change the future for years.

For years the vision had been the same.

*He stood upon the ramparts of the Lake of Fire, looking out over the sand. Below him, two vast armies galloped toward each other, their weapons glittering in the sun. One was his. One belonged to the Enemy. He raised his hands, summoning up the Sandwind. It was their only hope: it would destroy the Enemy's army.*

*But it would also destroy his own.*

*He heard Saravasse scream, and knew, in that terrible moment, that an army of merely human warriors was not the Enemy's only weapon. . . .*

No. That day must not come to pass. The Enemy must be destroyed now, while he was still foolish and weak. Before he had gathered his army. Before he had found Bisochim's fortress. Before he attempted to keep Bisochim from restoring the Balance.

*"Do not be either too quick or too slow. Too much thought is as great a flaw as too little."*

Suddenly the words of *The Book of Sun* came to him, making him pause. The future had not changed.

But what if he'd succeeded? What if his spell had worked, and the future *still* had not changed? What if he had more than one Enemy?

Bisochim groaned in exasperation, running his hands through his long black hair. The work to bring the Balance back into alignment once again—without allowing it to slide over toward the Dark, of course—was painstaking, and took all his concentration. He could not spend his time seeking out the Enemies of the Balance and destroying them one by one.

He needed an ally.

⟿

TO create an artificial being that would do his bidding was not beyond the skill and power of a Dragon-bonded Wildmage. But such creatures lacked the imagination that Bisochim suspected would be needed to track down and destroy all the Enemies of the Balance as they presented themselves.

In the Lands Beyond The Mountains there were many Shining-folk. But he was not certain that any of them had the power for this task. Nor was he entirely certain he could trust them. A Balance was a delicate thing. Something long out of true would not, necessarily, seek to be set true again. Rather, it would seek to remain as it was, even if that was in . . . imbalance.

Fortunately, there was another way. Difficult, but barely possible.

In the time before first the Elves, then Men, had taken up the

Keeping of the Balance through the service of the Wild Magic, the land had resounded to the interplay of Elemental Forces far greater than any power that might be wielded by the races that had lived between Sand and Stars. The races that had worshiped at the Shrines had observed them, given them names, and called upon them for aid. The Elves had worshiped the Starry Hunt. Men had worshiped the Stag King and the Mare Queen.

The Firesprites—long vanished—had worshipped the Firecrown. Here, where Bisochim now made his home, had once been the Firesprite Shrine. And something of the Firecrown must remain.

To waken a god, even a dead one, was a delicate task, yet it was one Bisochim preferred to attempting to create an artificial creature to seek out and destroy his Enemy. And best of all, though Saravasse would know what he had done, it could be accomplished without drawing upon her power, for even the shadow of a dead god contained all the power he would need.

⟥⟤

PROPERLY, he should call the Firecrown at noon of the Longest Day, but he dared not wait. Cloaked in stored magic, Bisochim walked across the surface of the Lake of Fire until he stood over the spot where once, thousands upon thousands of years before, a race of beings whose shape he could not even imagine had danced and sang in communion with the being he was about to summon. His offering was a carafe of perfume. As soon as it left the protection of his spells, it exploded in a burst of flame.

The ancient words he had learned in his quest for knowledge left Bisochim's lips in a whisper. Even cloaked in the most powerful spells he knew, the heat was punishing. He could not stay here long.

*One . . . calls . . .*

It was not the Firecrown Itself. It could not be. At best, it was the Shrine's memory of the Firecrown, wakened into life by Bisochim's power. But it was the echo of a Greater Power, and he hoped it would be enough. For Saravasse must live, and so her enemies must die. When he felt the Shrine's power begin to waken, Bisochim poured into that awakening all he knew of the Enemy, and all his will that the Enemy—in all its shifting guises—must be stopped. He felt a flicker of interest from beneath the fire.

*A . . . test? . . .*

"Yes!" he said aloud. "The Enemy is unworthy! Test him and see for yourself!"

*So I shall, Child of Water.*

As Bisochim's shields began to crumble against the punishing onslaught of the searing heat, he felt a sudden sense of *absence*. The Firecrown—or its echo—was gone. But he was content. It would seek out his Enemy. If the Enemy had survived Cold, he would not survive Fire.

Nor would any who followed in his footsteps.

# Six

# The Temple at Sentarshadeen

ND *THIS* IS the River Road into Sentarshadeen.
We're two miles outside the gates." Simera stopped
and indicated the milepost with a flourish.

"No bandits? No tigers? No wolves? No falling
trees? No sudden blizzards? No unusually irritable
rabbits? No—" Harrier seemed willing to go on list-
ing possible dangers for quite some time. Tiercel reached out and
swatted at him.

"Not even bad dreams," he said with a sigh. And no Wildmages,
either. Which was pretty unfair.

The Temple of the Light taught that the Wildmages kept the
Balance and would *always* show up if there was a real need. And
sometimes they showed up anyway, when there wasn't a real need,
to do things that were just nice, but not really vital. Or so he'd always heard. And certainly saving his life—back when he'd been a

baby—had been nice, and certainly his parents had appreciated it and so did he (or he would have if he'd been a little older) but he couldn't really see how it was vital to the Great Balance. Unless it had been vital to the Great Balance for him to live to grow up so that he could get into trouble now. Which didn't really make a lot of sense to Tiercel. He'd been thinking about that a lot, on his way to Sentarshadeen, and he couldn't see how the Great Balance could have any use for an untrained (and untrainable) High Mage.

But even if it did, certainly it would want to stop things like what had happened at the Three Trees from happening again. Just because it hadn't happened again *yet* didn't make Tiercel think those kind of problems were over. Ever since that night he'd awakened in the forest from that dream he couldn't remember, he'd had a sense of being . . . watched.

Neither Simera nor Harrier had noticed anything, of course, so after the first couple of times he'd brought it up, Tiercel had stopped saying anything. He already felt like a freak. And nothing had happened. Yet. Maybe that was why no Wildmage had showed up. Maybe one would be waiting for them in Sentarshadeen.

"So," Simera asked, impatient with the byplay, "do we go on?"

Harrier looked at Tiercel. "Nothing's happened since we left the Three Trees. Maybe that was . . . it."

"Or maybe it's just waiting until I fall asleep around a bunch of people again," Tiercel said.

"Or maybe it was a coincidence," Simera said. "The innkeeper there said they'd been having trouble in the forest long before you arrived. It could have been more of the same. Oh, don't glare at me like that, Tyr Rolfort. You know it could."

"Maybe," Tiercel said reluctantly.

"What about this?" Simera proposed. "The Temple of the Light has a guest house. I know it's horribly expensive, but you told me your father gave you a couple of Golden Suns for emergencies, and

I guess this would count as an emergency. If you aren't safe at the Temple guest house, where *will* you be safe? And they'll certainly know if there's a Wildmage anywhere in Sentarshadeen, or if one is likely to be coming."

"That makes sense," Tiercel said reluctantly.

"Hot baths," Harrier said yearningly. "Soft beds. And we can get everything washed. With *soap*."

"And I'll go to the Guildhouse and report the bandits," Simera said. "And that . . . cold snap."

That was, Tiercel supposed, one way of describing it.

His sense of being watched didn't decrease as they entered Sentarshadeen. In fact, it increased. He knew that hundreds of years ago, this city had belonged to the Elves, but try as he might, he could see no sign of it now. His imagination painted the glittering golden towers of an Elven city, the roaming herds of unicorns, the vast and spectacular tracts of an ever-blooming Flower Forest, but what he saw instead were neat rows of shops and houses that didn't look all that much different from Armethalieh. Just like at home, the city was built around a grand central park with spacious and extensive gardens, edged by the Law Courts and Magistrates' Temple to one side, and the Libraries and the main Light Temple to the other. Tiercel was a little disappointed. He'd hoped for something more exotic.

"The Guildhouse is just up ahead," Simera said, stopping along the edge of Temple Road. "Are you sure you can find your way from here?"

Harrier snorted derisively. "I can *see* the Light Temple from here, Simera. It will be hard to get lost in sight of it, but to please you, I suppose we can manage."

Tiercel grinned to himself, though he was careful not to let either of them see it. Harrier's early distrust of Simera was long-gone now, and he treated her with the same rough friendliness that he granted to Tiercel's sisters.

The Centauress tossed her head. "If you do, I suppose you have wit enough to ask directions. At least Tiercel does. Well, I've gotten you here safely. That counts for something."

"It does. Come to the Temple guest house for dinner tonight, too," Harrier said impulsively. "We certainly owe you a good dinner after all this."

Simera grinned at him, switching her long braided tail back and forth. "If you hadn't offered, I was planning to invite myself. After traveling with you for so long, I certainly want to see how the story ends, you know!"

IF the Light Temple's steward was surprised to find two scruffy boys seeking lodging rather than the rich merchants the guest house usually played host to, he was far too well-trained to betray the fact.

Tiercel paid in advance, even before being prompted, and the sight of the Golden Sun in his palm ended the last of the steward's qualms. A young novice led them to a good plain room with an attached bath. Tiercel had specified that, though he had turned down the lavish suite they had first been shown, and even though Harrier secretly felt it was wastefully extravagant, he was just as happy not to have to trudge down the hall to a public bathing area.

"Let us know when you are ready to depart, young Goodsirs, and what services you require during your stay. You will receive a full accounting, and of course, any balance due you."

"Thank you," Tiercel said. "I'm afraid we have quite a lot of . . . laundry."

"Simply ring for one of the lay servants," the novice said, smiling. "There is also a full schedule of Temple services posted in your rooms—we observe the full ritual here, every day, and you will hear the bells for service. There are also four chapels for private devotions, and Preceptors are available for private counseling."

"Thank you," Tiercel said again.

"What about food?" Harrier asked.

"The Refectory serves at Second Dawn Bells, Noonday, and Evensong Bells, but bread, cheese, and cider are available all day, young Goodsir."

"I'm sure that's everything. Thank you for your time," Tiercel said.

"It is part of my work. The Guesthouse funds the Temple," the novice said, smiling. "If you need something that the servants cannot provide, ask for me. I am Brother Kelamen." He bowed and departed, closing the door behind him.

"First dibs on the bath," Harrier said instantly.

"Are you sure you don't just want to go down to the Refectory?" Tiercel said. "Honestly, Har."

"Well, you never know. They might think there were more important things than food. It's better to be sure," Harrier said, heading into the bathroom.

While Harrier bathed—and Tiercel had to admit he was looking forward to his own turn, because even if he didn't *quite* stink, a fortnight or so of bathing in lakes and streams hadn't left him feeling quite clean either—he sorted through their packs, pulling out the things that needed washing.

It turned out that everything did, pretty much. They'd saved one clean change of clothes each, knowing they'd need it for Sentarshadeen, but everything else was grey and grubby, and some of it was torn, too. He supposed the Guesthouse could do mending as well as washing. When he'd finished making a tidy pile, he went over to the writing desk in the corner and stared down at the pen and paper there. He supposed he should write a letter to his parents, and let them know that he'd gotten to Sentarshadeen safely. If he paid for fast post, it would be there in a few days. But what could he say? He'd never lied to his parents. Not really.

He supposed a letter could wait until he'd talked to the Wildmage. He was sure there'd be one here.

"Your turn," Harrier said, coming out wrapped in a large towel. "There's plenty of hot water."

❧

"OKAY," Harrier said, when they were both clean and dressed. "Now we go over to the Temple and find a Wildmage."

Tiercel hesitated. "Why don't you go on to the Refectory?" he said. "I'll meet you there."

Harrier studied him for a long moment. "Okay," he finally said.

❧

THE Temple of the Light smelled of incense and fresh flowers. It was a comforting smell, one that Tiercel had always liked. He'd come in in the middle of the Litany to the Light and took a seat in the back, letting the familiar words wash over him.

The Light Temple meant safety and comfort. Light-Day services sitting between his parents and his sisters. Light-Day dinners at home. His father never worked on Light-Day, no matter how busy he was during the rest of the sennight. Light-Day was for family, Lord Rolfort always said. For being grateful to the Light and the Flowering, to the Blessed Saint Idalia and Kellen the Poor Orphan Boy who had given them back the world and shown them how important Family was, to the Wildmages who made the whole world their family for the sake of the Great Balance.

They'd always been soothing words when his father said them. But not quite real. Not that it wasn't true that Family was the most important thing, and that the Light taught that you must treat everyone you met as your own family, for the sake of Kellen the Poor Orphan Boy, who had none.

But until all of this happened, Tiercel had never really thought of Kellen and Idalia as real people, although he supposed they must have been. He'd never thought of magic as being something that could barge into your life and take it over, whether you wanted it to or not. Right now, if he wanted to, he could set the Temple of the Light on fire. The thought frightened him.

At the end of the service, he went up to the front of the Temple to speak to the Light Priest. He didn't have to wait long; it was Second Afternoon Bells and the Temple had been fairly empty. He waited until the Golden Bowl had been put away and the incense had been quenched.

"Can I help you?" the Light Priest asked.

"I . . . I don't know," Tiercel said.

Suddenly he felt a terrible urge to just run out of the Temple. He'd been fine for *days*—since they'd left the Three Trees—and fine coming into Sentarshadeen, and into the Guesthouse, and into the Temple, but suddenly he felt his old sick dizziness return.

The Light Priest put an arm around his shoulders. "Come into my robing chamber. We'll talk there."

THE Light Priest's robing chamber was a small room just behind the altar. The walls were hung with robes, but there was a desk and chairs as well. He urged Tiercel into a seat, and quickly poured him a small glass of a bright green cordial. "Sometimes the service is quite long, and I come in here to rest for a bit. The Light does not ask more of a person than he or she is capable of. Drink this. I warn you, it has a vile taste, but it will soon set you right."

Quickly, Tiercel did as he was bidden. The Light Priest had spoken no more than the truth—the liquid tasted like bitter grass—but his sick weakness quickly faded.

"I am Preceptor Maelgwn. It is an Elven name; outlandish, I know; I was much-teased as a child, but here in Sentarshadeen they are still sometimes given. I think you are a visitor to our city, for I have never seen you at service before," Maelgwyn said, taking the decanter and setting it aside. "This is a decoction I brew in my own stillroom to refresh those who have traveled hard and far. But as I say, it does not have a very pleasant taste. Now, how may the Light ease your way?"

Tiercel took a deep breath. After so long, he barely knew how to begin. "My name is Tiercel Rolfort. I've been here before, but it was a long time ago. My parents brought me. I need . . . I was wondering . . . There was a Wildmage here, then, and you see . . ."

Preceptor Maelgwn pursed his lips. "You know that we are taught that the Wildmages seek out those whom the Wild Magic believes need their help."

"Yes, I know. But . . . this is different."

"Is it something that you think you could explain to me, my son?"

"I told them in Armethalieh. I told everyone. My tutors. The doctors. My Preceptor. No one listened." The bitterness in his voice surprised Tiercel. But it was true. He'd asked for help and everyone had said he didn't have a problem at all.

"Armethalieh . . . a lovely city, I took my training there. And 'Rolfort' is an old Armethaliehan name, of course. Did you tell your parents?"

"Not . . . everything," Tiercel admitted, blushing. "But it wouldn't have helped. It's . . . magic, Preceptor. I have a problem with . . . magic. I swear this to you by the Light."

Preceptor Maelgwn sat in silence for a moment.

"Many young people just your age come to me every year, Master Rolfort, convinced they have been Called to be Wildmages, and asking me to provide them with the Three Books," he said quietly. "The Books come as they will. They are not mine—or any Priest's—to provide."

Tiercel shook his head. "It's not that. I can prove it to you, if . . . if you have a candle."

Preceptor Maelgwn's eyebrows rose, but he said nothing. He merely opened a drawer of his desk and removed a fat white candle, silently setting it in the middle of his desk.

Once Tiercel would have been uncertain of his ability to do this, or afraid he would set the entire room on fire. But he had practiced it over and over on the journey here—as much to reassure himself that he wasn't simply losing his mind as because, well, it was so *convenient* to be able to make a fire quickly whenever you wished. Though it took more effort than it usually did—he was tired, he supposed, just as Maelgwyn had said—he set the candle alight with nothing more than a thought.

Maelgwn took a deep breath. "So you are already a Wildmage."

"No," Tiercel said. "I'm something else. There used to be—a long time ago—another kind of magic. A good magic called the High Magick. I don't know much about it, but I can do, well, this. I don't really want to try anything else, because all I can find out says that it's dangerous if you aren't trained by another High Mage, and they're all dead. But I need . . . I was hoping . . . I have to find a Wildmage. I need to understand why this has happened to me. I just . . . I'm afraid that something bad will happen. Or maybe it already has."

Haltingly at first, and then with increasing fluency, Tiercel told his story once again, leaving nothing out. The first spell he had cast. The Lake of Fire. The Fire Woman. The terrible cold at the Three Trees. The sense of being watched. "I don't know what to do," he finished.

"You are doing, I believe, all that you can," Preceptor Maelgwn said quietly. "And it grieves me deeply not to be able to offer you help. But so far as we of the Temple know, no Wildmage has come to Sentarshadeen in many years. You will have to continue north, and hope one comes to you."

"But—" Tiercel said. He'd been so sure that there'd be a Wildmage in Sentarshadeen!

"You may stay here in Sentarshadeen as long as you wish, of course. But from all you have said, I think it would be best if you slept in the Temple itself. I shall have a bed prepared here in this room. We will hope that the sanctity of the Eternal Light will protect you."

Tiercel nodded reluctantly. "Thank you. I won't keep you any longer."

He found Harrier in the Refectory at one of the long tables. Harrier was eating as if his last meal had been days before and his next one was likely to be days away, but he stopped as soon as he saw Tiercel's face.

"No Wildmages," he said, guessing.

"No," Tiercel said levelly. "I talked to Preceptor Maelgwn. He thinks I should ride north and hope one of them finds me."

"North?" Harrier said blankly. "That would be . . ."

"North," Tiercel finished. "And that means not going home."

"Have some cheese," Harrier said.

⟜

"SO what do you want to do?" Harrier asked.

The two of them had left the Temple grounds and were walking through the streets of Sentarshadeen. Neither of them had any particular destination in mind, but it was a warm late afternoon in an unfamiliar city, and with nothing else to do, Harrier had suggested they might as well see the sights.

"I guess I'll go north," Tiercel said, after a long pause. "At least there aren't any people there."

"Well, I *did* want to see Fort Halacira and Kellen's Bridge," Harrier said. "And then . . . what? Ondoladeshiron? Ysterialpoerin? How far are you going to go?"

"Until I find a Wildmage who can explain all of this to me," Tiercel said evenly. "Or I die."

"*Die?*" Harrier said blankly. He stared at Tiercel for a moment,

then grabbed his friend's arm and dragged him back against a building, out of the flow of traffic along the busy street. "You're not going
to die. You've been lots better since we left Armethalieh, and—"

"And all the books I read about High Mages were from the time
of the High Mages, and just *assumed* I knew the whole story. They
left a lot out. But there's one thing they all hint at. The Magegift
starts like a fever; that's how it was recognized in the old days. After that, it either had to be trained, or destroyed. Or—" He stopped.

"Or?"

"Or whoever had it died."

Harrier stared at him for a long moment, his hazel eyes wide.
Then he blew out a deep breath. "Okay. We find a Wildmage. And
maybe you can train yourself. I mean, there had to be a first High
Mage, didn't there? Who trained him?"

"Train myself *how?*"

"Well, you've got all those notes . . ." Harrier's voice trailed
off to a stop. "You're not going to die," he said firmly. "I won't
let you."

Tiercel smiled, just a little. If sheer stubbornness could solve the
problem, Harrier would solve it.

"So what are we going to tell our parents?" Harrier added. "Because we obviously aren't going to be home at the end of the moonturn. And don't tell me *I* can go back. I'm not going back without
you to explain things to your mother. Or mine."

Tiercel sighed. "I'll think of something before we leave."

IT was nearly Evensong by the time they'd reached the horse-
market. They'd come to an agreement that even though they were
going on, they would return the mules to Armethalieh just as they'd
planned; their journey would go faster on horseback, anyway.

Tiercel wasn't sure how much horses cost, but even if he didn't have enough money left in his purse to cover the cost, there was a bank here, and he was sure he could get an advance on his allowance there. And maybe Simera would know what they'd need to buy for an extended trip to . . . nowhere.

It was summer, so the horse-market would not close until First Night Bells: the Second Hour of Night, as it was otherwise reckoned, though in summer it would be only an hour or so after sunset, and the sky would still be light. They had a little time to look around before going to meet Simera for the evening meal at the Temple Guesthouse.

As they walked, Tiercel asked the prices of riding horses, and realized that a Golden Sun—he had two left—would be more than enough to buy two of most of the animals here.

"These look good," Harrier said uncertainly.

They were stopped before a line of horses whose coats all gleamed. Knots of ribbon were braided into their manes and tails, and they wore halters of brightly-dyed leather. As Harrier stepped forward, the nearest animal tossed his head and stepped back.

"The finest animals in all Sentarshadeen, young sir," the horse-seller said, coming forward and placing a hand on the skittish animal's neck. He was a burly Centaur of middle years, with a full russet beard as elaborately-braided as any of his charges' tails.

"In fact, I venture to say, you could find no faster nor more spirited beast were you to venture to Vardirvoshanon itself! You seek a fine riding horse?"

"Two horses, actually," Tiercel said.

"And not these horses, Garan," a familiar voice said behind them.

"Simera," Garan said. He sounded disappointed.

"'Simera,' you old horse-leech," she agreed, stepping forward. "Still glossying up wind-broken nags and attempting to pass them off as prime stock, I see?"

"Now, Simera," Garan said coaxingly, "you know I would never—"

"Oh, certainly not," she agreed. She glanced at the horse Harrier had first approached, the one who was still sidling and tossing his head. "Sometimes you offer up half-wild beasts with no manners at all. Of course, their new owners don't realize that until whatever potion you've given the poor beast has worn off. But that's hardly your fault, is it? Come on, boys. There are other dealers in the market to buy from."

"But isn't that *dishonest?*" Tiercel asked, when they were walking back the other way.

Simera shrugged. "Only a fool goes to the horse-market to buy without knowing anything about horses. And Garan's reputation is well-known." She glanced sideways at Tiercel, raising her eyebrows in a silent question.

"The Preceptor at the Temple said I'd need to go farther north to find a Wildmage," he said. "Since we need to send the mules back to Armethalieh, I thought we could buy some horses here."

"I know someone who will have what you need. I'll take you to her tomorrow," Simera said. "Halyon's beasts aren't cheap, but they're gentle, steady, and reliable. We'll need that, if we're traveling north."

"Ah . . . 'we'?" Harrier asked, raising his eyebrows.

"I said I wanted to be there for the end of your story, and it doesn't look as if it's over yet," Simera replied. "Properly, you should hire a Forest Guide here; one of the Forest Watch's duties is to protect people in the Wilderness, and I know *exactly* how much experience you two have. So I'm offering my services."

"But what about your Year? And being alone?" Tiercel asked.

"Oh, this will count toward that," Simera said. "I'll have to spend a little more time finishing my Circuit at the end, but I really don't want to miss this. Besides, I'd like to see a Wildmage myself, and if Tyr is going to set anything else on fire, at least I'll be there to put it out. So tomorrow we'll buy horses, and then we'll buy the rest of what you need. Those boots you have wouldn't do for a walk in the city park, and your cloaks are already in rags."

Tiercel shook his head. It was one thing to drag Harrier along on this crazy journey—especially since he couldn't see any way of making him go home—but he had no intention of involving anyone else.

"Thank you, Simera," Harrier said. "We'll need your help, and we accept."

"Good," Simera said, with a smile. "Now, let's go back to the Temple Guesthouse where you can treat me to an exceptionally fine dinner and we'll make our plans. And tomorrow morning I'll meet you and bring you back to the market and introduce you to my friend Halyon."

FOR the next three nights, Tiercel slept in Preceptor Maelgwn's Robing Room. He drank a dose of the terrible-tasting cordial every evening before he went to bed, for Preceptor Maelgwn assured him it would do him no harm, and might do him much good. Sleeping there was a little embarrassing, but nothing terrible happened, so he supposed that embarrassment was a small price to pay for safety. In addition, he had heard the Litany of the Light so many times over the last three nights that not only could he recite it by now without thought, he probably wouldn't need to enter a Light Temple again until his thirtieth Naming Day. Of course, he *liked* Light Temples.

With Simera's help, he and Harrier purchased two gentle geldings; neither the youngest nor the prettiest animals in the Sentarshadeen horse-market, but—according to Simera's friend Halyon—they were steady well-trained animals, good for inexperienced riders, who were also what Halyon called 'easy keepers.' Simera explained that this meant they would be happy with forage and a little grain, and not require the quarts of rich food each day that some animals needed to stay in condition.

Halyon had also advised them on the purchase of a pack-pony to carry their supplies, for while their horses would carry small packs, they would not be able to carry everything that Tiercel and Harrier would require. And so, in addition to Cloud and Lightning (who was named for the blaze on his forehead, and not for any turn of speed) they now possessed a small black pony named Thunder, who had apparently been named for his disposition. Thunder tended to kick, and had snapped at Harrier more than once, but once he was harnessed, he would follow Cloud and Lightning docilely wherever the two horses went. And since Halyon had assured them that the pony was strong, sound, and a willing worker, Tiercel and Harrier could only hope he would eventually grow fonder of them.

Making the rest of their purchases took every last coin the two boys had, since Tiercel had no idea of how long they'd have to travel, and Simera said it was always better to prepare for a long journey than a short one and end up with more than you needed. Tiercel was able to get the advance on his allowance that he'd hoped for at the counting house, so they wouldn't be traveling on without coins in their pocket, but the amount of money he had to spend in Sentarshadeen worried him. His parents had never stinted him, but they'd always made sure he knew what things cost, too. What he and Harrier had spent to equip their expedition . . . well, it would keep a working-class family in food for a year, back home, or pay his first-year's tuition to the University.

The hardest part of everything he had to do was write his letter explaining why he wasn't coming home. He really didn't know what to say. He hadn't told his parents about the High Magick back in Armethalieh, and he didn't think the explanation would sound any better on paper. But *not* telling them—now, when he knew he was a High Mage, or something like it—and when he was certain that things were becoming worse than they had been in Armethalieh, seemed so dishonest that he couldn't bear it. Finally he settled on a compromise.

*Dear Mama and Papa: I am writing to tell you that I am not coming home for a while, but that I am safe and well, because Harrier is with me, and he will be writing to his parents to tell them that he will be staying with me until I can come home again.*

*I know you have been worried about me since Kindling, and hoped that this trip to Sentarshadeen would make me feel better. Believe me when I say that I hoped for the same. I came to believe that I needed to find a Wildmage to help me, and when I reached Sentarshadeen, I consulted with Preceptor Maelgwn at the Main Temple of the Light here. He said that no Wildmages have come to Sentarshadeen for many years, but suggested I look farther north. I am being very careful, and Harrier and I are traveling with a member of the Forest Watch to guide us (this was not precisely a lie, as Simera was an Apprentice) so we will have no trouble on the roads. She has helped us buy a pair of good horses, so we are returning the mules.*

He chewed on his pen for a moment, considering, but he really couldn't think of anything else to say.

*My love to you all. I shall write again when I can, but it may not be for a long time. With Harrier to look after me, you can be sure I shall be perfectly safe. All my love.*

There was really nothing to add to that.

IT was Second Dawn Bells when Tiercel came to their room. Harrier—of course—was already up and packed, and they did not need to meet Simera at her Guildhouse until two chimes past Morning Bells.

"I guess sleeping in the Temple agrees with you?" Harrier said with a grin.

"If I'd known I was going to be doing that, we could have gotten a smaller room," Tiercel grumbled.

After breakfast, they went looking for the Guesthouse steward to settle their accounting. After that, they would head for the stables, where their new animals and most of their equipment was, and from there they would go to collect Simera. After three days in Sentarshadeen, both boys knew their way around the central city well enough to avoid getting lost. A few questions of a passing acolyte got them directions to the steward's office.

"Ah, young Lord Tiercel, Master Harrier. You are leaving us so soon?"

Tiercel kept himself from making a face with an effort. It was true that since his father was Lord Rolfort, he was actually "Lord Tiercel," but no one ever used his title much and it sounded very odd to hear it.

"Yes, Steward Fairgan. It's a very nice place, but . . ."

"But your business in Sentarshadeen is completed. I understand. And you will wish to receive an accounting for your records." Steward Fairgan opened a drawer of his desk and pulled out a heavy bronze cashbox, opening the lid.

"Here you are, Lord Tiercel," he said.

He placed the Golden Sun—the entire amount Tiercel had given him to begin with—atop the desk.

"At the request of Chief Priest Maelgwn, there will be no fees for your visit with us."

Tiercel blinked. Harrier cleared his throat.

"I. Ah. That's very kind." *But it isn't fair.*

He thought about what Brother Kelarnen had told him; how the money to run the Temple came from the Guesthouse. And then he thought for a moment more. "Can you tell me how much our stay *would* have cost?"

When they left the steward's office, they passed by a tall jar. Such jars were commonplace around the Temple grounds—and, in fact, all over the city. They were used to collect money for the Temple. The money was used to feed the poor and to care for the sick, and to perform other works of compassion in the name of the Light.

Tiercel stopped beside the jar and dug in his coin-pouch. He pulled out a handful of silver unicorns—a few more than would have covered the cost of their stay—and tipped them into the jar. It was a heavy handful; the coins clattered to the bottom of the jar.

"Ah . . . What are you doing, Tyr?" Harrier asked.

"We don't need the Temple's charity," Tiercel answered. "And there are others who can use it. Come on. Simera's probably already waiting for us."

FROM an alcove near the doorway where he could see but not be seen, Preceptor Maelgwn watched the two boys walk out of the Guesthouse in the direction of the stables. As they left, he felt a sense of release. His Price was paid.

He had paid harder ones, over the years, and lighter ones. Serving the people of Sentarshadeen as both Light-Priest and Wild-mage was sometimes a difficult task, and often called for him to tell far less than he knew.

To lie to that troubled, terrified child, however—to drug him with the cordial that kept the magic in his blood from resonating to the presence of the Wild Magic . . .

It had been Maelgwyn's Price. And he had Paid it. He dipped a hand into the pocket of his robe and ran a hand lovingly over the worn leather of the Three Books there.

Yet it had troubled him enough that he had done something he had rarely done before. He had asked the Wild Magic why such a Price should be set. He had received no clear answer—nor had he expected any—just the suggestion of a test he might set for young Tiercel, if he chose to.

If Tiercel Rolfort had not passed that small test, would he have found some way to call him back? To keep him in Sentarshadeen? Even . . . convince him to return home?

No.

Danger was coming, such as the world had not faced in a thousand years. He must trust the Light and the Wild Magic to deal with it in Their own way. This small test had been only for the peace of mind of an old man whose part in Tiercel's story was over. And, perhaps, to strengthen Tiercel, just a little, for the greater tests to come. There would be many others.

Maelgwn could Sense it.

⚬❧⚬

AT half-past Morning Bells, the three of them rode out along the Old War Road. Simera was leading Thunder, as the pony seemed to like her better than it did either of the others.

"Lunch?" Harrier suggested cheerfully.

"It isn't even Midmorning Bells yet," Tiercel said with a groan.

"And we're not stopping until we reach Fort Halacira," Simera said firmly. "We'll have lunch there, see Kellen's Bridge, ask about the condition of the road east, and go on."

"And ask after Wildmages," Tiercel said with a sigh. He didn't think they'd find any just waiting around at Fort Halacira, though.

"Might as well ask after unicorns," Harrier said.

"If you want to," Simera said.

⚬❧⚬

FORT Halacira had once been a storehouse or a barracks—nobody was quite sure which—centered around extensive mines that were no longer worked. These days, Fort Halacira was a mill town. The River Angarussa gave power to the machines that ground grain and milled lumber for half the villages around, and they heard it long before they saw it.

"It's louder than the Docks," Harrier said, wincing.

"Just be glad we're on the War Road and not the Delfier Road, or we'd have been run down by freight wagons half a dozen times already," Simera pointed out. The road between Fort Halacira and Sentarshadeen was even more heavily-traveled than the road between Armethalieh and Sentarshadeen. "There will be less traffic north and east of here."

"And fewer inns," Harrier pointed out.

"The War Road goes as far as Ondoladeshiron, if you want to follow it," Simera said. She looked at Tiercel.

He shrugged. "I have no idea." *But I think I know how I can find out.*

Fort Halacira was used to travelers—both those who came on business and those who came to view the remains of the ancient monuments at the center of the town. The three of them stopped for a meal, then, at Tiercel's insistence, went to see the old mine.

"It was built by Elves thousands of years ago," Tiercel said.

"It's a *mine*," Harrier said.

Mine it might be, but it had been one of the Ancient Wonders of the Elven World, and the *Compendium* had mentioned the Jeweled Caverns in the chapter about Elves.

But when they got to it, there wasn't much to see. Only a very large stone building that identified itself as the Fort Halacira Granary Stores and Office of the Magistrate. In front of the building's imposing façade was a tall stone monument, crowned with the shape of the Eternal Light, which stated that upon this site had once stood Fort Halacira, an ancient stronghold of the Elves, where the Knight-Mage Kellen had fought a great battle against the Endarkened.

"So much for ancient history," Harrier said with a rude snort.

"It was a very long time ago," Simera said gently, looking at Tiercel's face. Tiercel just shook his head. He knew he was stupid to be disappointed. It was ridiculous to think it would all still be *here*. He just needed it to be.

"Can I help you?" a young man asked, walking down the steps.

He was dressed in clerk's robes, not a laborer's tunic. Obviously he worked in the Magistrate's office here, and was leaving the building on his way to his midday meal.

"Oh," Tiercel said, blushing faintly. "I was just wondering. My friends and I . . . we've come from Armethalieh and we were wondering . . . is any of the old Fort left inside? The part that was built by the Elves?"

The young man smiled at them. It was obviously a question he was used to hearing. "Oh, no," he said. "All that was cleared away a long time ago."

KELLEN'S Bridge was less of a disappointment.

It was less than an hour's ride north along the river, but the town had not grown in that direction, and though the Avribalzar Forest had long since vanished into the sawmills of Fort Halacira, the meadow that played along the Angarussa's banks was sunlit and peaceful. Even the Light-shrine that stood beside the bridge was deserted at the moment.

"Made by magic," Simera said. Even she sounded impressed.

"Huh," Harrier said. He dismounted from Lightning and walked forward to take a closer look. "It looks like one piece of stone. Think you could do that, Tyr?"

"No." Tiercel didn't even have to think before he answered. Everyone knew the story of Kellen's Bridge, where ice had turned to stone when Kellen had led his troops across the river to fight against the Endarkened. He wasn't exactly sure, anymore, that it was true. It was a pretty story, though.

"Well, the War Road is on the other side," Simera said firmly. "Let's go."

Unlike the War Road farther south, which was little-used and had few travelers, the War Road between Sentarshadeen and Ondoladeshiron was the road that took most of the light traffic. The Avribalzar Road—wider and with a good stone foundation—had been constructed for heavy freight wagons and for driving the herds down from the northern pastures. This meant that while the road wasn't exactly clogged with travelers, they met—and were sometimes passed—several times that day, and both Tiercel and Harrier had plenty of cause to be grateful that they had quiet gentle mounts. Horses who took exception to every cart—or other horse—on the road would have made things difficult.

"WELL?" Simera said. "Sun's westering. And there's an inn up ahead. Do we stop there and burn it down or freeze it out? Or do we turn off the road and look for some place to sleep under the stars?"

They had long since passed the last of the farms beyond Fort Halacira. The open country they rode through now, Simera told them, was devoted to the needs of cattle and sheep, and the few villages that tended to the needs of the drovers lay far from the road, built close by wells and open water. They would not return to true forest until they passed beyond Ondoladeshiron, assuming they continued heading eastward.

Both of them looked at him, and Tiercel realized that both of them were waiting for him to make a decision about what they should do next. He thought about it. It wasn't as if they were actually going anywhere in particular. "Ride north until you find a Wildmage" wasn't much of a destination. If they rode north for long enough, they'd bump up against the border of the Elven Lands—and then, he supposed, they'd have to turn back. It would take them a good long time to get there, though. He wasn't really sure where it was. Nobody was. He supposed the Elves liked things that way. He wondered why.

But right now Harrier and Simera were waiting for him to make up his mind. Not that they paid any attention to him most of the time. Simera was sure that neither of them could take care of themselves outside the bounds of a city, and while they were learning fast, she was more right than not, so half the time she ignored anything either of them suggested. And Harrier, well, ever since the day Harrier had fished him out of the Harbor when he'd been two and Harrier had been three, Harrier had gotten it fixed in his head that most of Tiercel's ideas involved killing himself somehow, and once Harrier made up his mind about something, it was impossible to change it. Tiercel wondered if his friend might be right. His ideas hadn't been turning out too well lately.

But now—*now*—the two of them wanted *him* to decide where they were going? Well, why not? Because if they weren't actually going anywhere, one direction was almost as good as another, wasn't it? And he didn't want to get any more people in trouble than he had to.

"I don't think we should sleep at any more inns," he said slowly. The feeling he'd had of being watched was back. It had been gone in Sentarshadeen—while he'd stayed in The Temple of the Light—but it was back now. "And I'd like to head north. *Straight* north. Can we do that?"

Simera glanced up at the sun, taking her bearings. "I don't see why not. Nobody will mind if we cross open land, and if the cattle can find water, so can we. Come on. See those trees in the distance? We'll stop there for the night. From the look of the land, there's a stream not too far beyond."

❧

NOT surprisingly, Simera had been right. By the time they reached the copse of old oaks, they could hear the sound of a stream a few yards beyond it. As they led the horses and the pony down to it for an evening drink, Simera explained to Harrier what signs she had seen in the landscape to let her know the water was there.

"Your horse can lead you to water, of course," she added. "But only if he's thirsty enough. Silly beasts," she added affectionately, stroking Cloud's shoulder.

There was still a little light in the sky by the time they had the animals settled and their camp set up. By now, after a fortnight of practice, both Tiercel and Harrier were getting good at it, and the new equipment they'd bought in Sentarshadeen helped. Lanterns to light the camp at night. A cooking-brazier, so they would not always have to gather wood. With it they could heat soup or tea, make griddle-cakes and fry bacon.

Simera had also insisted on the purchase of a number of basic medical supplies, since while they didn't really expect to ever be more than a day's travel from an inn or a village, it was a good idea to be prepared. She'd also taken advantage of the stop to expand her collection of hunting gear, and as Harrier and Tiercel laid out the cold meats they'd bought in Fort Halacira, Simera set several snares in the tall grass. In the morning she'd collect them, hoping to have snared a rabbit or two for tomorrow's supper.

After the meal, they took the remains far from their campsite to dispose of, and then hung the packs with their food carefully from a tree, where nothing with an appetite for a quick and easy meal could get at them. Harrier settled down in his blankets then—or on them, since the night was warm—but Tiercel pulled the last lantern they'd left burning over to him and took his workbook out of his pack. He wished he'd written down more about the High Magick when he'd had the chance. He wished he'd brought the Spellbooks he'd read at the Great Library with him, come to that.

"What are you doing?" Harrier asked, sounding faintly grumpy and entirely disbelieving.

"Thinking," Tiercel answered shortly.

He knew he could cast a Fire Spell. That meant there must be other spells he could cast, and one of them would *have* to be useful now. The ancient High Mages had built Armethalieh with magic, after all.

Unfortunately, while everybody talked a lot about magic in the books he'd read—and there were a lot of spells written down— nobody said anything very specific about the *why* of the High Magic, and—as he kept discovering—there were so many important details left out. Take MageShield, for example. All the books said that was a vital spell to learn. But he suspected that he didn't have all the details of how to cast it. And what—exactly—did he have to defend himself from? And even if he *could* cast it, he didn't need a defense right now, he needed information.

There was Knowing. Knowing provided information, and he was pretty sure he'd be able to cast it correctly now. But you had to have an item to cast it on, and he didn't have anything. There was Mage- Light. That one seemed to be the same as Coldfire, at least the description was: *to create a ball or nimbus of spectral light which answers to the will of the Mage, or to imbue objects with such radiance.* Wild- mages could do that. That one was another spell involving glyphs, and a Wand. He didn't have a wand—though from the description they seemed fairly simple to make. After the last time he'd thought a spell of the High Magick was "simple," though, he thought he'd wait a while before trying to make a wand. And anyway, making things light up didn't seem to be immediately helpful either.

There was Lightning. He had no idea of how to cast that one, and was just as glad; apparently High Mages had been able to summon lightning bolts down out of the clear blue sky and that just sounded dangerous.

But then there was Conjuration. That seemed as if it might be helpful.

One of the books he'd read had been called *Ars Perfidorum: the Book of Forbidden Things.* One of the chapters had discussed the

Conjuration of Illusory Creatures. That had been interesting, because it had raised more questions than it had answered. Why—not
to mention *how*—conjure up something that didn't exist? It hadn't
gone into details—the *Ars Perfidorum* had seemed to be mostly interested in explaining why a bunch of fascinating things were a really bad idea, and as far as Tiercel could tell, most of the
information it contained was incorrect, though he'd read it
anyway—but another of the books had given more information on
Conjuration. What the *Ars Perfidorum* called Illusory Creatures
were actually Otherfolk; the ones who had gone east with the
Elves; not the ones like Fauns and Brownies and Centaurs, but the
ones people—usually—couldn't see. So what Conjuration really
was, was a spell to summon up one of the Otherfolk, and if you left
out a lot of the preparation, the actual Conjuration looked fairly
simple.

He knew this was exactly the way he'd gotten into trouble in
the first place—leaving out all of the preparation. But maybe the
preparation was necessary because High Mages had all lived in the
middle of a city. Maybe it had all been to protect everyone else.
Wildmages were Mages, and they stayed out of cities for the most
part. Maybe that was why there were still Wildmages, and there
weren't any more High Mages.

Tiercel knew he was guessing, and guessing wildly, but he was
running out of ideas. He had to try *something*, and while he knew
that Wildmages could Scry the future—at least, such powers had
figured prominently in the Flowering Fair plays—such spells had
never even been mentioned in anything he'd read about the High
Magick. He needed to ask someone for help, that was all there was
to it. And if a Wildmage wasn't going to show up, and if the little
he knew about the High Magick couldn't provide him with a convenient spell that could either solve all his problems or tell him
what to do, then all he could do was try to use the spells he *could*
figure out how to cast (hoping they weren't too dangerous) to call

someone and hope they could help. Conjuration looked like his best choice.

His decision made, Tiercel tucked his book away, blew out the lantern, and settled himself for sleep.

# Seven

# The Apparition in the Grove

E'D BARELY BEEN asleep for a few minutes—at
least so it seemed—when the agitation of the horses
woke him. Harrier and Simera were already awake.

"There's something out there," Simera said in a
low voice. "Something big."

"A cow?" Harrier asked hopefully.

"No."

Tiercel got to his feet at the same time Harrier did. The campsite was in darkness; the moon had set, and it was dark under the
trees. They hadn't bothered with a fire, and of course they'd doused
the brazier and the lanterns when they'd gone to bed.

"Should I light the lanterns?" Tiercel whispered nervously. Inside his mind he could feel the glyphs of the High Magick crowd-
ing just below the surface of his consciousness: fifty-two symbols
that, used alone or in combination by someone with the Magegift,

could do amazing things. He had less than a quarter of them memorized.

"Shh!" Simera hissed.

She was frightened, and that scared him. He could hear it now: something big, moving around through the grass. He could hear a wet snuffling, and felt a sense of *size,* even though he could see nothing.

The horses and Thunder were really upset now. Only their hobbles kept them from bolting, but they were jerking at them, trying to run, and the straps would break in a moment.

Under the sound of the horses' panic, he heard rustling as Simera reached her weapons. He realized that she was afraid that whatever it was might try to attack, and was preparing to shoot it if it did.

"Bear," Simera said in a low voice. "Find a tree. And light the lanterns."

Tiercel understood everything she didn't say, because Simera had spent the last fortnight warning them about bears. Bears liked forest, not open country. Bears didn't generally wander around in the middle of the night. Bears were very very rare south of Ondoladeshiron. You could never be sure what a bear would do.

And he knew one thing more. While he and Harrier could probably climb a tree and be reasonably safe from the bear, Simera couldn't.

The grunting noises were coming closer, and now Tiercel could make out a faint shadowy shape in the grass beyond the trees. If it was a bear, it was bigger than the horses. *Much* bigger than the little black bears Simera had warned them they might possibly encounter in the Delfier Forest. She was an excellent shot, but she'd told him over and over that a wounded animal was very dangerous, and he didn't think she could either kill it or drive it off—considering how big it was— with her arrows.

He could use the High Magick to set it on fire. But even as he considered the idea, Tiercel felt a pang of revulsion. Burn an innocent animal to death just for being in the wrong place? There had to be another way!

Maybe there was.

He took a cautious step forward, feeling his way in the dark, and struggled to remember the shape of the glyphs he'd been studying before he went to sleep. He could almost feel the shape of a wand between his fingers. . . .

"*Tiercel!*" Harrier's agonized whisper had all the force of a shout.

Tiercel could smell the bear now. It smelled like burning and old leaves. The dark shape in the grass stopped its slow prowl when it saw him. It raised its head, grunting, and Tiercel saw its eyes flash, coin-bright, in the darkness. Then it began to trot forward purposefully, as fast as a trotting horse. Tiercel raised his hands above his head.

He should have been terrified instead of embarrassed, but all he could think of was that he wasn't wearing pants and he must look exactly like the Mock Mage in the Midwinter Plays, the one who wasn't really a Wildmage at all, only thought he was. Then the glyph he needed rushed to the front of his mind and uncoiled itself and he wasn't thinking at all.

Coldfire. MageLight. He didn't really need a wand at all. . . .

A ball of bright blue light, brighter than the full moon, bloomed between his outstretched hands. *A ball or nimbus of spectral light which answers to the will of the Mage* . . . Larger. Brighter. He flung it toward the onrushing bear. *Follow.*

When the ball of MageLight had first appeared, the bear had stopped its headlong rush and reared up, making a startled "whuffing" noise, but Tiercel hadn't really been paying attention. Now he did, and if he hadn't already done what he'd needed to do to cast the spell, he would have been doomed, for all he could do was stare. The bear was only a few yards away. He could see it clearly in the light from the globe of MageLight, and wished he couldn't.

*That was what I figured I could scare off?*

Tiercel stood transfixed in terror.

It was easily twice his height. Its fur was a bright coppery red-gold, and its claws were as long as his fingers. It roared out a challenge as the globe of light scudded toward it, and at the sound, the animals in the oak grove snapped their hobbles and bolted. The bear slashed at the hovering globe of MageLight, as if it were a swarm of bees, but the blow passed right through the shimmering azure substance. Tiercel was certain he'd miscalculated disastrously. Instead of frightening the animal away, the MageLight would only enrage it to the point of attacking.

It stared into his eyes.

Then it dropped to all fours, turned, and ran. The globe of MageLight followed.

Tiercel stared after the retreating animal, feeling waves of nausea and terror and relief wash over him. Suddenly a blow to the back of the head knocked him sprawling.

"Don't you *ever* do that again!" Harrier stood over him, fists clenched. "You could have been *killed!*"

One bare foot kicked out at Tiercel's thigh, flipping him over onto his back. "Ow," Tiercel said weakly.

"Stop that!" Simera demanded, trotting over, a lantern in one hand. "You're both idiots." She reached down and helped Tiercel to his feet.

Tiercel looked at Harrier. Harrier's fists were clenched, and he was breathing hard. Tiercel did not need to be able to see his eyes to know that they'd gone quite green.

"Hit him again and I'll kick you until you can't walk," Simera said firmly. "What he did was stupid. There's an end to it."

"I scared it away, and no one was hurt," Tiercel said placatingly.

Though his heart was still racing, he was sure he'd done the right thing. Simera could not possibly have killed that bear with her arrows. And come to that, neither he nor Harrier could have climbed high enough to escape from something that size.

"You," Harrier said with great emphasis. "Could have been killed."

"But I wasn't," Tiercel said coaxingly. Now that they were safe from the bear, they really didn't need to fight with each other. "And I don't think climbing a tree would really have helped. And Simera couldn't climb a tree anyway. Simera, you saw that. What . . . *was* it?"

"A bear," Simera said, but her voice was troubled. "Like no bear I've ever seen. I've heard there are bears like that in the Girizethiels, but that's far to the north and east of here. And even in summer coat, they're brown, not red."

"Well," Tiercel said, "we're going north. Maybe we'll see more."

"I don't *want* to see more," Harrier said feelingly.

"Neither do I," Simera said. She shook her head. "Come back to the camp. I don't think any of us will get any more sleep tonight, but it's useless to try to look for the horses before morning."

As they walked back under the trees, Tiercel looked over his shoulder. In the distance he could see a faint spark of blue.

They spent the rest of the night huddled together around the brazier, drinking tea and trying to make sense of what had happened. While it was true (Simera said) that the Great Bears of the north sometimes wandered south to attack livestock, normally only those who were old or ill chose that path, and the one they had seen looked both young and healthy.

"It's a good thing you figured out another spell," Harrier said doubtfully.

"I've got notes for a lot of spells I could do," Tiercel pointed out grumpily. "It's just that most of them need . . . things."

Harrier made a pained face, and Tiercel kindly spared him the rest of the explanation.

He did, however, make up his mind to start looking for a suitable piece of wood to make a wand with. He wasn't sure he'd ever have the nerve to use it, but at least he'd have it.

⤳

WHEN dawn came, they began the difficult process of locating their horses and pack-pony. It took until noon to track them down, but they found them at last, grazing contentedly in the midst of a herd of cattle. Upon seeing Tiercel and Harrier, Cloud and Lightning trotted up to them as if nothing had happened, allowing their halters to be slipped into place. When he saw that the two horses were being led away, Thunder followed.

Simera had told them that she wanted to track the bear and see where it had gone. Tiercel didn't know how long the globe of MageLight he'd cast would last—he knew it would dissipate, from what Master Cansel back at the Great Library had told him, but he wasn't sure when. And it wouldn't be all that visible in strong sunlight, anyway. But tracking a rogue bear was certainly a part of the Forest Watch's duties. And if it had come after them once, there was a chance it might circle around and come after them again. At least the bear was nowhere nearby now—at least, he hadn't seen his globe of MageLight anywhere, though he'd kept a wary eye out for it, and he was fairly certain it would last at least a day.

The bear's first tracks were easy to follow. The large clawed paws had dug deep gouges into the earth as it ran from the luminous globe of blue fire that inexorably followed it wherever it went. It ran in a straight line, and Simera had no trouble tracking it.

Then the tracks . . . stopped.

At the place where the tracks stopped, they were about five miles away from the oak grove where Tiercel had cast his spell, at the far side of a low hill. And though Simera circled the area for almost an hour before giving up, she found no further trace of tracks.

And Tiercel's MageLight was nowhere to be seen.

"That's good, right?" Harrier asked, as they turned their horses's heads north once more.

It was midafternoon by now. Between finding and catching the horses, and tracing the bear, they'd lost most of the day. But it was hard to see that it mattered; Tiercel was the only one who felt as if they were running out of time. And even he couldn't say exactly how. Or why. He had to stop someone he'd never met from doing something he wasn't quite sure of. And he wasn't actually certain whether that event lay in the past or the future, and he *really* didn't know why he knew about it at all.

"The bear just vanished?" Simera answered irritably. "Bears don't just *vanish*, Harrier. They wander off. If it had stopped running, it would still have left tracks. And if you *dare* suggest that it *did* leave tracks, and I just couldn't find them—"

"Nobody's suggesting that, Simera," Tiercel said quickly, although he suspected that those would have been the next words out of Harrier's mouth. "But . . . maybe the bear *did* just vanish."

Simera rounded on him, looking very much as if she'd like to hit him.

"Think about it," he said quickly. "I mean . . . you said it didn't look like a normal bear. And . . . wasn't there only one set of tracks?" He hadn't realized what he was going to say until he said it, but it seemed so *right*.

"The ones leading *away*," Simera said, looking stunned as the meaning of his words sank in. "Herdsman's Path—how could I have been such a fool! Not a single print leading down to the trees. Only the ones leading away."

"Another thing like the inn," Harrier said. His voice was flat.

"I guess," Tiercel said. But he wasn't quite sure. Somehow, this attack hadn't seemed quite the same.

"Magic ice-storms, vanishing bears . . . I hope we find this Wildmage of yours soon, Tiercel," Simera said. "I'm not sure I can take any more *strangeness*."

"Oh, well, about that. I sort of have an idea," Tiercel said.

⤜⤏

"DO you really think that would be such a good idea. . . ?" Simera said doubtfully, once Tiercel had explained his plan.

"No," Harrier said flatly. "It wouldn't. He almost burned down his family's house in Armethalieh the last time he tried anything like that," he explained.

"That was completely different," Tiercel said.

"You started a *fire*!" Harrier said. "Will you look around? We're in the middle of grazing lands. Do you want to start a fire *here*? We'd never put it out. Not to mention that a grass fire would cause a stampede that would probably kill us all," Harrier added. His expansive gesture took in the herd of cattle on the horizon.

"I wouldn't start a fire," Tiercel protested.

"You think. You hope. You have no real idea what would actually happen if you did another . . . spell," Harrier said forcefully. His voice was loud enough to make Lightning flick his ears nervously.

"Okay. You're right about that. But I don't see any Wildmages around here. Do you? So we go north, cross the Mystrals, reach Ysterialpoerin—in another couple of moonturns—*don't* find a Wildmage there, either—keep going—cross the Bazrahil Range, go through the Gatekeeper Pass—if we're lucky enough to manage to get there before winter sets in—cross the mountains of Pelashia's Veil, and reach the Elven Lands. Then what? It will certainly be winter by then, and you know that we won't be able to make it back through the Bazrahils in winter. And the Elves won't want us in the Elven Lands, and do you know what? I bet we still won't have found a single Wildmage!"

The other two were staring at him in astonishment. Harrier, because Tiercel simply never lost his temper. And Simera, well, she was just staring.

"What else am I supposed to do?" Tiercel finished quietly.

Harrier just shook his head.

"Do you always set things on fire when you cast your spells?" Simera asked, after a long pause.

Tiercel just shrugged. Not counting MageLight and Fire— simple "baby spells" according to all the books—he'd cast exactly one spell deliberately in his entire life, and wasn't really looking forward to trying it again.

"You did back in Armethalieh. And at the inn," Harrier said, although Tiercel wasn't really sure that was true—and anyway, if you were actually casting Fire, you shouldn't be surprised if things caught on fire, should you? Harrier sighed. "Nobody's gone as far north as the Bazrahils in . . . I don't know."

"Hundreds of years," Simera said, sounding troubled. "Maybe . . ."

"Maybe a Wildmage will *just show up?*" Harrier's voice was thick with frustration and anger. "It's been three moonturns since Kindling, and that's when Tyr set fire to his bedroom and all this really started." He glanced at Tiercel, and Tiercel could see exactly what Harrier was thinking. He had always been able to read his friend's thoughts as easily as he could read a page of print. Harrier hated to have to think, and was slow to make up his mind, but—possibly for that very reason—when he did come to a decision, his decisions were sound ones. Which was a good thing, because it was nearly impossible to get him to *change* his mind.

"I know they're supposed to come when we need them," Harrier said slowly, reasoning it out. "That's what the Light teaches. And I guess the Herdsman, too."

Simera nodded.

"But if Tyr doesn't need one after practically burning down his house, and getting so sick, and having all those dreams, and then *something* happening at the inn, and now the bear coming, who does? But we haven't seen one. Maybe . . ." he took a deep breath. "Maybe one isn't coming."

Harrier looked sick at the very thought, and Simera simply looked disbelieving. But it had been almost five days now since the three of them had arrived in Sentarshadeen to find that there was no Wild-mage waiting for Tiercel there, and Tiercel had had time to get used to the idea. The Light taught that everyone must do their best to keep Balance in the world, not rely upon the Wildmages to do it alone.

The Light gave no gifts without reason.

Maybe he'd discovered his High Mage gifts so that he could *use* them.

It was a frightening thought to think of using the High Magick again—deliberately—but if he *did* have to use it, well, better here—out in the middle of nowhere—than in the middle of a city.

"Maybe a Wildmage isn't going to come along and solve my problems," Tiercel said carefully. "Maybe I have everything I need to help myself already. If I do, then this spell will work. If not . . ." He shrugged.

Simera looked around. She was obviously still trying to come to terms with the idea that a Wildmage *wouldn't* arrive to offer aid when aid was so obviously needed, but the practical side of her nature won out.

"What about the fire that comes when you use your magic?" she asked.

"I don't know what will happen. I think it was an accident the other times."

Simera made a rude noise. "Best be sure. Before you try this stunt of yours, we'll find a place where you can't set anything on fire."

Harrier shrugged. "I'd rather be safe than dead."

⸫

AS they traveled north, looking for a location that Simera would deem suitable for Tiercel to make his first attempt at Conjuration, Tiercel looked for something to make into a wand. There was no detailed information about wands in the books he'd found, so he assumed that any wood would do. He found a willow tree growing by one of the rivers they passed, and, with Harrier's help, he cut a nice straight length of wood, one that was not too thick. Simera helped him trim and smooth it. They all agreed now that he should practice, though none of the three of them was really certain what it was he was practicing. But the books Tiercel remembered reading back in Armethalieh seemed to imply that the wand was used to draw the sigils in the air as a component of the spellcasting (so were the sword and the staff, but he wasn't likely to be able to get his hands on either of those any time soon), so he'd thought he'd give it a try. The sigils weren't actually spells, so practicing them should be fairly harmless.

The first time he tried using his new wand to draw the sigils in the air, Tiercel dropped it with a shriek.

⸫

"WHAT! What happened?"

It was evening. Simera and Harrier were gathering firewood a little distance away. Tiercel had balanced his notebook on a convenient flat rock, open to the pages where he'd written down the sigils, and started to draw the first of the sigils.

"Aleph—"

And there it was, hanging in the air in pale-colored fire. He'd shrieked in surprise, and his friends had come running. By the time they'd gotten there, it was gone.

"I—I—I—*Look!*"

With shaking hands, Tiercel retrieved his dropped stick—wand—and did it again.

"Aleph" appeared again, hanging in the air.

"Well, that's impressive," Harrier said in a deceptively-calm voice, watching as the glyph slowly faded away again. "What does it do?"

"It makes Fire, if I tell it to," Tiercel said. He drew a shaky breath. "But I didn't know it would actually *appear*. Maybe it's because of the wand."

Harrier took the wand from Tiercel's hand and stared at it suspiciously, then waved it around experimentally before handing it back. "No," he said, in the tones of one thinking the matter over. "I think it's you."

❧

TIERCEL shooed the two of them back to their wood-gathering and resumed his practice, drawing as many of the sigils in the air as he could: some of them were too complicated for him to manage without more practice. Each one appeared as a different color. They all faded quickly.

He would have practiced longer, but after a short time he started to feel dizzy and weak again, the same way he had when he'd cast MageLight on the bear. Just as he had back at the inn, and back in his room in Armethalieh.

In fact—Tiercel was coming to realize—every single time he used the High Magick in any big important way, he got sick. And that didn't seem right. Magic was supposed to be normal and natural, wasn't it? He wouldn't have the Magegift if he wasn't supposed to use it.

Unless he really *was* dying.

He shook his head. He'd better not let Harrier find out, or the one thing he'd be hoping for was to die *sooner*. He grinned in spite of himself. And when Old Mother Death showed up, Harrier would be certain to want to fight with her, too.

Then he sobered. He didn't want to be sick, and he didn't want to die, and more than he wanted both of those things, he wanted to know the meaning—and the purpose—of his visions. He hoped they'd find a suitable place to try the Summoning soon.

That night he dreamed again.

~⁓~

IN his dream, once more Tiercel was back on the shore of the Lake of Fire. The Fire Woman was there, and as always she seemed familiar and desirable and terrible all at once. The other presence was there as well—the one he could never see—the one who was the true subject of her attention.

She wanted something from him—the other one. Tiercel only wished he knew what it was. But he didn't even know what *she* was. And in the middle of the dream, he never wondered. He only watched in terror as she coaxed the other unseen watcher to come to her, over and over.

But this time, when he woke up, he realized, for the first time, that he had sensed something of the unseen watcher's thoughts as well as of the Fire Woman.

And that he had reason to fear the unseen watcher's plans as well.

~⁓~

A sennight's journey due north brought them onto the Great Plains. The Mystrals were visible in the distance, their highest peaks still covered with snow. Simera would be able to take them through the mountains; it would take them a moonturn, two at most, to reach them.

Assuming they had to go that far.

By now their letters would have reached Armethalieh, and their parents knew that they weren't coming home. Tiercel tried very hard not to think about that. His constant practice with his wand helped distract his thoughts, though he was careful to practice out of sight of the others at all times. The bouts of weakness that came from using his Magegift didn't fade, and he didn't want the others to worry. He didn't know what the problem was, but it didn't get better, and it didn't go away. It was as if—each time he used the High Magick—he hit some sort of invisible wall, and afterward, he couldn't even see the shapes of the glyphs inside his mind. As if whatever fuelled his power to do magic had vanished for a while.

It was always back by the next evening, though.

EVER since they'd met up with the bear-that-wasn't-a-bear, Harrier had done his best to keep his thoughts and feelings to himself. Letting the others know what he thought wouldn't do anybody any good anyway.

This was crazy. But he didn't have any better ideas.

Had there been a Wildmage in Sentarshadeen, that would have solved all their problems. They could have done . . . whatever . . . turned around, gone home, and gone on with their lives.

They wouldn't have had to do this. Or maybe gotten to do this. Sometimes Harrier wasn't sure, even in his own mind, which way he thought of it anymore. If everything hadn't been so just plain weird, this journey would have actually been fun. He'd spent all his life in a big city next to the ocean, growing up around ships, with the sound of the waves in his ears and the smell of the sea in his nostrils.

This was nothing like that.

From Armethalieh to Sentarshadeen they'd traveled through woodlands—nice enough, but just as closed-in as a city, really, when you stopped to think about it. And north of Fort Halacira, the land was cut up by little hills and groves of trees and herds of cattle, so you never really got a sense of how *big* it was, though he'd never lost his sense of strangeness at not being able to smell or hear the ocean.

He'd liked it.

This was what he wanted to do with his life, Harrier realized. Go new places and see new things. Not just hear about them from the captains of the ships that docked in Armathalieh Harbor, but go and see them himself. And not see them from the deck of a ship, either, but on his own two feet—or at least from horseback. It almost felt like treason, to want to give up the sea so completely, but he guessed he was more like Uncle Alfrin than anybody in the family had ever suspected.

But when they reached the Great Plains, that was when Harrier truly fell in love with the land.

AS the gentle rise and fall of the Avribalzar grasslands disappeared behind them, the horizon dropped away, receding to infinity. Here the landscape was as flat as a dish, with nothing between them and the distant Mystrals but the wind.

It was like riding across the ocean itself. Just as empty. Just as trackless. Ondoladeshiron lay somewhere far to the west, but it was nowhere to be seen. Except for the hawks wheeling through the sky—and a distant glimpse, once, of what Simera said was a Silver Eagle—there was nothing to be seen but summer-yellow grass.

Of course the Plains were not as empty as they looked. They were home to deer, and wild bulls, herds of free-roaming horses, and hundreds of other animals. Simera's snares were always full.

But they never saw any of them. It was strangely peaceful. And everything would have been perfect, if Tiercel weren't waving a wand and making things glow in the dark and behaving like something out of a Flowering Fair play, because Harrier just didn't know what to think about that at all. Especially if a Wildmage really *wasn't* going to appear to set things right.

All his life Harrier had been used to pulling Tiercel out of scrapes. And now this was the biggest scrape ever, and all he could really do was watch as things kept getting worse in new and exciting ways. He didn't like the idea that the only thing Tiercel could think of to do was cast another spell, because Tiercel was compulsively honest, and if they hadn't known everything that could go wrong with this Summoning thing a sennight ago, they certainly did now.

But Harrier also knew that the only alternative was to keep going north the way they were until they either ran into the peaks of Pelashia's Veil or met up with a Wildmage who might not be coming at all.

One of the things he really hated to admit (and wouldn't admit unless there was a really good reason for it, which there rarely was) was that Tiercel was often right about things. Well, more than often. Usually. Even most of the time. He didn't brag about it, or even make a point of it, and he certainly didn't draw attention to it. And that didn't mean that his *ideas* weren't pretty half-baked most of the time. But when Tiercel said something like "I think it's going to rain" or "that dog won't bite" or "Javiard Kalborn is going to try to pick a fight with you during lunch," Harrier had learned to pay close attention, because Tiercel was almost always right.

So when Tiercel had said that a Wildmage might not be coming—because he might already have the power to solve his own problems—Harrier had hated the thought. But he'd listened.

And he'd hated the idea of Tiercel trying another spell. But he had to admit that he couldn't think of anything better to try. Magic had caused the problem. Magic had to be the solution.

～

"SOMEONE'S coming," Tiercel said.

He only saw it first because on horseback he was taller than Simera, and because he happened to be looking ahead while Harrier was looking off to the side, marveling once again at the sheer amount of *space* all around them.

At Tiercel's words, Harrier looked to where Tiercel was looking. There was a faint speck on the horizon. Someone on horseback.

～

THE lone rider reached them by midday. Because the Plains were so very flat, they had, literally, been watching his approach for hours, seeing him grow from a speck on the horizon to a rider on a roan horse leading a pack mule, with two large red dogs loping lazily along beside the horse's legs. When the rider got even closer, they could see that the long hair curling from beneath his broad-brimmed hat was as red as the coats of his dogs.

"Greetings," he said, reining in and tipping his hat to Tiercel. "It's been a long time since I've encountered a traveler."

"Hello," Tiercel answered. "I'm Tiercel and this is Harrier and Simera. We're heading north—"

"To Ysterialpoerin," Harrier added, since it would seem odd if they didn't have a destination, and *very* odd if Tiercel told him the truth.

But: "Where to?" the stranger asked, just as if Harrier hadn't spoken.

The easy pleasant expression on his face didn't change, and it was plain to Harrier—and, he hoped, to Tiercel—that the stranger wasn't ignoring the two of them.

He simply didn't see them.

"I thought I'd go to Ysterialpoerin. Have you heard of it?" Tiercel said.

"Of course. The city has been there for a very long time," the stranger said. "It might not be the best place for you to go, though."

"Really," Tiercel said noncommittally.

"Sickness tends to strike there in the summers."

"Um, Tyr?" Harrier said.

Tiercel and the stranger both ignored him.

Harrier looked at Simera.

"Does it strike anybody but me as a little odd that this guy doesn't seem to know that anybody but Tiercel is here?" Harrier said, very loudly.

"Do you think he's like the bear?" Simera asked, taking a nervous step backward and switching her tail.

Tiercel gave them both a determined glare of warning, but Harrier was tired of just sitting there and watching. He kneed Lightning forward, determined to make the stranger notice him, or ride off, or . . . *something*.

TIERCEL did his best to block out the sound of Harrier's voice. There were times when he really admired Harrier's determination and courage, and there were other times—like now—when all Tiercel wanted to do was dig a really deep pit and drop Harrier at the bottom of it.

He kept his eyes fixed on the stranger's face.

He was pretty sure the stranger was *exactly* like the bear, which meant they were all in deep trouble. But for some reason, this time their trouble hadn't shown up trying to kill them or rip them to pieces, but trying to trick them in a way that was so pathetically obvious a child could see through it. At least, he was pretty sure that was what was going on.

"I'll be careful," he said to the stranger.

"You can never be too careful," the stranger said. "I have some medicines in my pack. They've been very useful to me in the past. I'd be happy to share them with you."

"That isn't necessary," Tiercel said firmly. "You might need them yourself later. I'll be fine." He was careful not to mention his friends again.

The stranger was persistent—far more persistent than a chance-met stranger making a casual offer of aid ought to be. He even opened his pack and brought out the medicine that he was offering to Tiercel. The vials glittered in the sunlight like the rarest of jewels. They were so beautiful that Tiercel was tempted to take them for the sake of their beauty alone; their contents glowed in all the colors of the rainbow, and the bottles themselves were tiny works of art. He was actually reaching for them when a thread of suspicion stopped him.

Why would someone keep medicine in bottles like these?

For that matter, why would medicine look like this? Tiercel had been taking medicines all his life for various ailments. It was usually some shade of brown. Not green and blue and purple and red. He withdrew his hand and refused again.

"YOU'RE quite certain?" the stranger asked at last. "You don't want the medicines? You might get sick in Ysterialpoerin. And the bottles are very pretty."

"I'm sure," Tiercel said evenly.

He'd never been so afraid in his life. It was the way the stranger talked. He spoke so reasonably, but the things he said bordered on nonsense. He couldn't really expect to trick someone, talking that way. It was as if the stranger were crazy, or didn't care whether he fooled Tiercel or not. Or—despite what he looked like—as if he were something farther from being human than Cloud was, or even the hawk circling lazily above them in the sky, and though he was doing his best to impersonate one of Tiercel's kind, it wasn't much of a best.

"All right then," the stranger said.

And just like that it was over. The stranger dug his heels into his horse's sides. It trotted past Tiercel, with the mule following along behind, lugging at the end of its tether. The dogs loped eagerly afterward, making wide circles around horse and mule.

When they had passed, Tiercel felt as if he'd been sitting on Cloud's back without moving for hours. He stretched and sighed.

"I'm glad we—" he began, turning to the others.

He stopped.

His friends were gone.

⨎

HE barely had time to begin to panic when he located them. Simera was only a few yards away, slightly behind and to the right of him, standing as if she'd fallen asleep. She'd dropped Thunder's lead-rope, and the sturdy black pony had drifted away from her and was grazing as if he didn't have a care in the world.

It took him a little longer to find Harrier, but he finally managed. Harrier was several miles ahead, still mounted, but slumped forward in Lightning's saddle in a way that suggested that he, too, might be asleep. Tiercel swallowed hard and rode toward Simera. She woke as soon as he approached, straightening with a grunt of surprise and staring at him with wide blue eyes.

"Harrier tried to attack the red-haired man," she said, looking around in confusion.

"I don't think he was a man," Tiercel said. "But I managed to get him to go away." He pointed into the distance, where Harrier sat on his unmoving mount. "Let's go get Harrier."

⤙⤚

HARRIER was much harder to wake than Simera had been. Tiercel thought it might be because he'd actually *touched* the stranger (Simera said she thought he had, though Tiercel hadn't even seen him ride forward), but for whatever reason, it took dumping him from Lightning's back to return him to consciousness.

⤙⤚

HARRIER stared up at both of them indignantly. Lightning nosed at him optimistically, obviously hoping for food.

The last thing he remembered was riding toward the redheaded stranger who could see neither him nor Simera. And now he was staring up at the sky, lying flat on his back in the grass, and from the position of the sun it was a couple of hours later than it had been the last time he'd looked, and he had no idea how he'd gotten here.

He didn't like the explanation at all when he got it. No one who worked around ships—and Harrier had done that, in one way or another, ever since he'd been old enough to be of use down at the Port—was a stranger to the tales ships crews told themselves and each other. Some were lighthearted, some were heartbreakingly grim, all filled with inexplicable events and all sworn—by their tellers—to be absolutely true. He'd never expected something out of a True Sea Story to happen to him. And on dry land, besides.

"So he's the bear—or he's like the bear—and he wanted to show up and offer you a lot of medicine in fancy bottles because he wanted to kill you. And he couldn't see me or Simera because he's magic?"

He glared at Tiercel.

"If I actually knew the answer to that, Har, or what I was doing, or why we're here, I'd tell you," Tiercel said with irritated patience.

What Harrier knew was that he was getting very tired of running into things that made no sense at all but were apparently dangerous that he couldn't hit.

Of course the stranger was gone when they looked for him, though he couldn't have ridden out of sight in the short time they'd been distracted.

"THIS looks like the best place we're likely to find for what Tiercel wants to do," Simera said a few hours later.

Harrier looked around.

They'd come to a break in the endless sea of grass. It was a wide flat expanse of gravel and bare earth. Down the center of it trickled a narrow stream. At its edges, the grass was cropped short, heavily grazed, though of course there were no animals in sight. After what she'd told them about the possible consequences, neither of the boys wanted to set a grassfire, and Tiercel couldn't be sure that he wouldn't, when he cast his spell.

By now, with the benefit of Simera's constant patient teaching, Harrier could recognize the tracks of the animals that had visited the water's edge. Hares and deer, and even birds. As they approached the stream, the horses pulled forward, eager to get to the water.

"A streambed," Tiercel said.

"It runs full during the Spring Melt, and during the autumn rains, but at this time of year it dries down to a trickle," Simera confirmed. "There's nothing to burn in the riverbed, and at this time of year you won't need to worry about being flooded out, either."

"But there's water if we need it," Harrier said, swinging down from Lightning's saddle and leading the horse forward. The bay gelding plunged his nose into the water, blowing and slobbering as he drank. The stream was shallow, but it ran strongly.

Cloud and Thunder quickly joined him.

"Here, then," Tiercel said, nodding.

"WHAT do you want us to do?" Harrier asked.

By now it was late afternoon; they would have been stopping to make camp for the evening in a few hours anyway. They'd set up camp with the ease of long practice: the horses unsaddled and hobbled and set to graze, their gear set out where they could get at it easily, and the fire started for tea and soup. On the Plains, there was no firewood to be had, and Simera had advised saving their charcoal for occasions when there was nothing else to burn. Dried dung made an adequate—if far too fragrant—fuel, and they'd been gathering it whenever they came across it.

"Well, nothing, pretty much," Tiercel answered, shrugging. He looked down at the wand in his hands—just a stick, really, though by now it had been worn smooth by constant handling. "I'm going to walk up the streambed a little ways so the horses don't spook. I figure . . . there was a spell in the Library called MageShield. I think I can cast it. It's supposed to protect the High Mage, though I'm not really sure from what, but after what happened earlier, I think it would be a good idea to use it. So I'll cast that first, then do the rest. I'll need the lanterns. It's supposed to be candles, but the lanterns will have to do." He shrugged again.

Harrier nodded.

He didn't like this at all—especially after what had happened earlier. But their encounter with the traveler—whatever he'd

been—only underscored the fact that there were *things* coming after them—or at least after Tiercel—and if they didn't figure out
some way to deal with those things soon, well, Tyr might as well
have stayed home in Armethalieh and kept getting sicker.

He and Simera watched as Tiercel put the six lanterns into one
of their bags, picked up the bag, and began to walk along the
creekbed away from them.

It all seemed very quiet and ordinary.

"I guess we wait," Harrier said unhappily.

THEY could still see Tiercel clearly when he stopped. There was
no reason not to watch. He set the lanterns down in a circle, looked
up at the sun—gauging direction, Harrier realized—and then there
was a flicker as all the lanterns came alight at once. Even in the
bright sunlight of midafternoon, Harrier could see the pale spark of
flame inside the lanterns' glass cases.

"I wonder why he needs the lanterns?" he said quietly.

Simera shook her head. "He keeps saying that his High Magick
has rules. Maybe the lanterns are a part of that. It sounds very
complicated."

"I suppose that's why nobody does it any more," Harrier answered. Why use magic to light a lantern when flint and steel were
so much easier? And anybody could use those, not just somebody
who was born with this Magegift of Tiercel's.

He wondered if he should stop staring, and at least pretend that
he thought everything was going to be fine, but he couldn't. And
neither, he saw, could Simera.

He saw Tiercel look around again. Tiercel was holding his workbook in his other hand. He tucked his wand under his arm and
paged through the book for a moment, then closed it and set it at

his feet. Then he took his wand into his hand and began to draw in the air.

Since that first night, Tiercel had never let the two of them watch him practice when he drew the magic letters, so Harrier and Simera had no idea what to expect. They saw the air fill with colored lines, layer after layer of them, color building on color, simply hanging in the air. Simera gave a soft gasp of wonder at the sight.

Suddenly a pale purple globe began to appear around Tiercel. At first it was so faint they weren't certain they saw it at all, but in a matter of heartbeats it had grown so bright that Tiercel was invisible.

Then it vanished like a popped soap bubble, and Tiercel was lying on the ground, not moving.

"That wasn't supposed to happen!" Harrier said with frightened certainty.

He began to run.

# Eight

# Gifts and New Beginnings

IMERA GOT THERE first, of course—four legs were faster than two—and was kneeling awkwardly beside Tiercel by the time Harrier reached him.

"He's fainted," she said tersely. "Get some water."

Harrier did as he was told, bringing water from the stream in his cupped hands and dashing it into Tiercel's face. But though that caused Tiercel to groan and stir, it didn't really revive him.

Harrier desperately wanted to ask what had happened, but the only one of the three of them who might possibly know the answer to that was lying unconscious on the ground.

"When he fell out of a tree, he was just like this," Harrier said, taking a deep breath. Panic wouldn't help anything. "He'd hit his head. He was okay after a few minutes."

Tiercel didn't look as if he were dying, Harrier told himself firmly. On the docks, you couldn't avoid seeing death. Accidents happened. He'd seen a man crushed to death when a crane slipped, once, as well as seeing plenty of broken bones and hard knocks—and getting a few himself. Tiercel's color was good. The two of them had both started to tan pretty dark, but beneath it, his skin hadn't gone grayish or flushed or turned any other peculiar color. He wasn't sweating hard. If not for the magic—and the fact that Harrier had seen him standing out in the middle of nothing a moment before, he'd just have figured Tiercel had been hit with something.

Or fell out of a tree that wasn't there.

A few minutes later Tiercel opened his eyes and blinked at them. "Tired," he said, closing them again.

"Dammit, Tyr!" Harrier snarled. He kept himself from shaking his friend with an effort.

"I don't know what's happened, but we'd better get him back to the camp," Simera said.

AT Simera's urging, Harrier lifted Tiercel onto her back. She assured him that she was much stronger than she might look, and perfectly capable of carrying Tiercel the short distance to the camp.

When they reached it, there was someone there.

The old woman looked up from the brazier as they approached. She was squatting beside it, poking at the contents of a saucepan—not one of theirs—with a wooden spoon.

"Youth," she said calmly, "is far too impatient. Another moon-turn—two at the most—and I would have reached Armethalieh. You could have waited there in perfect comfort and safety for me. Or even Sentarshadeen, if you insisted on a bit of an adventure. But Armethalieh, I think, would have been safer. Yes, indeed. But youth never listens. Always in such a hurry. Hmph!"

Simera made a choking noise.

"Don't do anything," Harrier said warningly. Though what

he could do to stop her—if she had the same sort of powers as the last traveler they'd encountered on the Plains—he had no idea at all.

The old woman made a rude noise and rose from her squatting position. Though she stood tall and straight, she was a tiny thing. The top of her head barely came to Harrier's shoulder.

She wore the wide-brimmed hat, long vest, and full split-skirts of the Mountainfolk, and the durable homespun was faded to shades of dun and grey by hard use and long wear. Her hair was white with age, pulled back and braided firmly into a coil at the nape of her neck. The only spot of color about her was a bright red scarf knotted about her throat.

"Do nothing? When you have been doing nothing but searching for me for sennights? Shall I take Mouse and go home, then?" she demanded mockingly, gesturing toward the small grey donkey that browsed contentedly beside the horses and Thunder.

"You're a Wildmage?" Simera asked hopefully.

"I am. And it's entirely your own fault that you've run into enough misfortune to doubt that fact. As I said, Harrier Gillain, if you and Tiercel had simply waited for me in Armethalieh, you wouldn't be in this situation now."

"But . . . We didn't know you were coming," Harrier protested weakly. "And who *are* you?"

"Such courtly manners from a son of the Portmaster!" the woman scoffed. "I am Wildmage Roneida. And you might as well put your friend down on the blankets, Simera. I'm sure your back is beginning to ache."

⁂

HARRIER helped Simera lay Tiercel out on his bedroll. They couldn't run, and they couldn't fight, and despite his suspicions, he was beginning to believe that Roneida really *was* a Wildmage. She didn't behave at all like the traveler, and she seemed to know a lot about all three of them. Besides, she could see him and Simera, and the traveler hadn't been able to.

"When this tea is ready, we'll wake your friend up and give him some. That will help him a great deal," Roneida said.

"But aren't you going to Heal him?" Simera asked.

"Why waste the spell?" Roneida snapped. "You youngsters! Magic this and magic that! As if the Good Gods hadn't given you a brain to think your way out of your troubles with. Now, a little less talk and a lot more action—especially out of you, young Centauress! Mouse needs to be untacked and brushed down, and frankly, I've seen better camps organized by a troup of Fauns. You'll never make Forest Watch if this is how you go about things."

By the time the camp was rearranged to Roneida's satisfaction, the tea was ready. She poured out a generous serving into a large earthenware cup that she removed from one of the packs that Simera had taken from Mouse's back, and Harrier sat Tiercel up and shook him awake.

"The Wildmage is here," Harrier said.

"Oh. All right," Tiercel said groggily. He took the cup without complaint, but after the first taste he choked and tried to spit it out.

"Now, now," Roneida said reprovingly. "What's good isn't always pleasant. Drink it all."

Whatever was in the tea did a great deal to restore Tiercel's strength, for as soon as he'd finished the entire cup, he was sitting up and regarding their new guest with interest.

"What happened to you?" Harrier demanded.

"I'm not sure. As soon as I started casting MageShield, I started to feel weak and dizzy. It always happens, but . . . never that bad."

"And you keep doing it?" Harrier demanded indignantly.

"I thought it would go away," Tiercel said. "Do you know what the problem is?" he asked Roneida.

"How in the name of the Gods of the Wild Magic should *I* know?" Roneida snorted. "Do *I* look old enough to have ever seen a High Mage in the flesh? Oh, I know that's what you are—born with both the Magegift and the will to use it—and if that doesn't worry you, it should, because the Gods don't send us gifts we don't need. I'd stop trying to cast spells though, if I were you. But that's just me."

Harrier sighed with exasperation, seeing Tiercel's shoulders slump in disappointment. Somehow he'd thought a Wildmage would be more, well, *useful.*

Roneida shot him a sharp look.

"Can you at least tell me what's going on?" Tiercel asked plaintively. "I think I'm in a lot of trouble. Well, actually, I, um, I'm not really sure," Tiercel stammered.

"If I knew what was going on—in the sense that you mean—I'd be a great deal wiser than I am. I'm a servant of the Wild Magic, not a princess in a wondertale. All I know is that I was minding my own business in Vardirvoshanon, looking after my garden, when all of a sudden nothing would do but I should come south at once to find the Fire-Crowned boy—meaning *you,* young man. Not a light Price, to undertake a journey that long before the snows had melted, but one I'd been expecting to pay for years—which is a story that is nothing to do with you, nor do I intend to tell it to you. And having gotten here, and found you wandering halfway to Ysterialpoerin doing your best to break your neck or set yourself aflame—Fire-Crowned boy indeed!—pray, tell me what the Gods of the Wild Magic would have me do for you, young High Mage?"

The three of them looked at each other. They'd been spending so long looking for a Wildmage—at least Tiercel and Harrier had—that now that one had finally found them, they weren't quite sure what to say.

Roneida sighed.

"This has all the earmarks of a long story, and will undoubtedly go better with food. I've a rabbit in my pack that will thicken your stew nicely, and I'll make the griddle-cakes while you tell me all you know."

BY the time the stew was cooking—thick with pieces of bacon and rabbit, and the second brazier had been set up to fry griddle-cakes—Tiercel had stumbled through his entire tale, having gone all the way back to Harrier's Naming Day celebration, with the help of Roneida's none-too-gentle prodding.

There were parts of the story that neither Harrier nor Simera had heard before. Until now, Harrier hadn't known that untrained High Mages died—or that Tiercel's periods of sickness had been getting worse since he'd left Armethalieh.

He'd thought Tiercel was getting better.

"Most of the time I'm fine," Tiercel said. "But whenever I do magic—unless it's something simple and quick, like lighting a fire—I'm weak afterward. Like I've held my breath too long. But it takes hours to go away."

Roneida smacked him—very hard—with the wooden spoon she was holding. "I told you: stop doing magic."

"But what if—"

She hit him again.

"That, or get used to falling down a lot. I told you: I know *nothing* about the High Magick."

"But what about the visions?" Tiercel asked. "I was hoping you could make them go away."

"Well, that's a new one," Roneida said, but this time her tone was more gentle. "Usually, people come to me asking to *have* visions. They want to know who they're going to marry, or they want to see the face of their first child before it's conceived—or find a lost horse, when they should have kept the gate locked in the first place. Ah well. You don't want to hear about my problems, and you aren't going to like my answers. So we might as well eat first."

There was no shifting her from her decision, and Harrier was already afraid she wasn't going to tell them anything they wanted to hear, so he helped distribute the food without arguing at all.

Roneida's pack contained many luxuries their own did not—jam for the griddle cakes, extra spices and dried vegetables for the stew, and even a bottle of fruit cordial to round out the meal. When they were all comfortably full—and had washed their dishes in the stream and packed them away, something she insisted on—she settled back on her bedroll and sighed.

By now it was twilight. Tea-water was brewing on the brazier, and the pot was set ready for filling. The lanterns ringed the campsite—Harrier had gone back and fetched them earlier, along with Tiercel's workbook and wand—but no one had lit them yet. He supposed—based on what Tiercel had said earlier—that if they wanted them lit tonight, they'd have to do it the old-fashioned way. In fact, he wasn't sure if he ever wanted to see Tiercel doing any magic ever again.

"Now," Roneida said. "You obviously have little experience with Wildmages, and that, children, is much as it should be, for the world would be in a sad mess if people were always running to us to solve every little problem instead of relying on their own limbs and wits. And, as with everything one sees little of, people develop a lot of silly notions—oh, we see the plays and stories, and get a good laugh out of them, too! As the Blessed Idalia certainly would, if she were here. But I will tell you this: all Wildmages are not alike. Some are great in power, some are less so. All do the work of the Gods of the Wild Magic in the world, keeping the Great Balance, paying their Prices. We're born as the world needs us, each to fulfill our destiny. Some are great Healers, others know weather best, others have a great gift for caring for animals, or knowing what is best for the crops. Some have every talent in moderation. Some simply see the best way that things should go, and try to persuade others to live simply and kindly together. It takes no magic to do that; just a clever tongue and a great store of patience, and I tell you no secret when I tell you that this is *not* the aspect of the Wild Magic that the Gods have seen fit to favor me with."

Harrier laughed out loud, and even Tiercel smiled. Roneida favored them both with an approving look. Now that she had settled in to tell her tale—for a tale it was, in some ways—her demeanor had changed. Harrier suspected that whatever she said about her store of patience—or lack of it—back in her own home, her own gifts lay in teaching.

"But to each of us, the Three Books come at some point in our lives, and we all do our best to live by the wisdom set out in them.

"What I mean to say to you, young Tiercel, is that I have no magic cure to offer you, though your problem and your danger is very real. Certainly you have been touched by magic, but I cannot see or sense it—it is High Magick, to which the Wild Magic is blind. And I am not fool enough to meddle with that which I cannot see. You sense danger, and I will not blind you to it, even though you ask me to. What it is, and where it lies, I do not know. Perhaps the High Magick can tell you, if you can master it."

Harrier opened his mouth. Roneida held up a warning finger. "I told you I knew nothing of the High Magick, and that was the truth. But I know this: the Elves have memories longer than ours, and the dragons, longer still. If you need to know about High Magick and High Mages, ask them."

"Ask the Elves?" Simera said, sounding dismayed and startled.

"Ask *dragons?*" Harrier echoed.

"Should I have stayed in Vardirvoshanon? Yes, witling children, the Elves—and the dragons!" Roneida sniped. "I have told you I know nothing of the High Magick—and that is true—but I know that the Elves remember it, and I *do* know the Elves. They'll tell you what they know if they think there's need. Go east through the Mystrals, find the Gatekeeper Pass, and keep heading east through the Bazrahils. If you're lucky, you'll reach the Elven Lands before you freeze."

"Oh, there's a comforting thought," Harrier muttered under his breath.

"I'll give you what help I can against what's following you—but you shall have to make your way by your wits. And you shall certainly need your wits, if what I suspect is true."

"It would be really helpful if you'd just tell us what that is, instead of dropping all these hints," Harrier said, louder this time.

He'd been pretty sure the wooden spoon had been washed and put away with the rest of the cooking supplies, but suddenly he felt a stinging crack to the back of his head, and instead of the spoon, there was a long slender stick in Roneida's hands, very similar to Tiercel's wand, but of a darker wood. Apparently she just liked hitting people, and came prepared to do it.

"Oh, and then you would be convinced you knew exactly what dangers you faced, and precisely how to deal with them, wouldn't you? Never mind *my* opinion, that it is far better to send you on your way afraid of everything, so that you won't trust something you shouldn't by mistake! Idiot child: you believe in only what you can touch, and what touches you. Just as before, many of the dangers you will face will be of that sort. Many will not. Many will be both, or will seem to be one and be another. There? Is that plainspeaking enough for you?"

"No," Harrier said simply.

He'd pretty much changed his mind about ever wanting to meet a Wildmage. Apparently all they ever did was hit you and talk incomprehensibly. And thanks to Tiercel, he was already *very* tired of magic.

"But now you have had the bitter and the sour, so I will give you the sweet. Since I knew before I left Vardirvoshanon that I would be meeting you, I brought some objects you will find useful on your journey." Once more she rummaged in the packs spread around her.

The first items she came out with were three white quartz stones the size of pigeons' eggs. They were threaded on leather cords. The stones were slightly flattened, and the natural action of water had worn a hole through the center of each, through which the waxed leather cords were looped and knotted.

"Wear these," she said, handing one to each of them, "and never take them off. I believe they will confuse the enemy which pursues you—and who knows, young man? It may allow you to get some sleep at night," she added, with a nod to Tiercel.

When Harrier put his on, slipping the knotted cord over his head, he wasn't sure what he expected to feel, but he felt nothing at all. The stone was just a stone, heavy and smooth, like any stone he might pick up out of a riverbed. He turned his attention back to Roneida, not quite sure she wasn't going to hit him again. She was removing another object from her pack; a bundle of arrows tightly wrapped in a case of oiled cloth.

"If you'd been sensible enough to go north by way of Ondoladeshiron, you could have replenished your supplies there. As it is, you're likely to run out of arrows long before you reach Ysterialpoerin, young Centauress, and you'll never find a decent fletcher at any of the small towns you pass," Roneida said, passing the bundle to Simera. "I'd suggest you stop for supplies at Windy Meadows, by the way. You'll need to head a bit east of True North to run across it, but that pony of yours could pull a cart without trouble, and then you won't have to live like savages. But I suppose you'll do just as you please." She sniffed disapprovingly—reminding Harrier forcibly of a nanny he'd had long ago—and continued removing items from her pack.

The next item was three large knives in their sheaths. All three were larger and heavier than their own knives—even Simera's sturdy practical hunting knife—and obviously weapons rather than tools.

"And if there is something that my Talismans cannot turn aside, nor Simera's arrows discourage, then you shall be forced to fight, and a strong edge is a compelling argument."

They regarded the blades in their hands doubtfully. Of the three of them, Simera had the most experience with keeping the peace, and even she looked as if she'd rather be somewhere else. No matter how many times they told themselves—or Tiercel told them—that there was danger involved in all of this, no matter how many bandits, bears, ice-storms, and bizarre vanishing travelers they encountered, none of that was the same thing as holding a knife in your hands that had been forged for one purpose: to draw someone's blood.

And thinking you might have to use it.

"But if these will not serve . . ."

Last of all she pulled the largest of her packs toward her and pulled out a long bundle wrapped in coarse cloth.

"Then Harrier shall at last have what he so ardently desires. The chance to hit something." She placed the bundle in Harrier's lap.

It was a sword. He felt its shape through the cloth, and unwrapped it quickly, swallowing hard. The sword was sheathed, and there was a swordbelt. He pulled the blade partway from its sheath and stared at it.

The silvery blade was slick with grease and gleamed like bright glass in the deep twilight. He knew better than to touch the blade itself—if he knew nothing of swords, at least he knew something of knives, and the grease was there to protect the metal of the blade. Besides, it looked sharp.

Very sharp.

There was no particular ornamentation to either sword or sheath, just good plain leather for the one, and plain metal for the other. The hilt was wrapped in plaited horsehair; the rough wiry surface would give him a good strong grip, no matter how much his hands sweated as he held it. He ran a finger over the hilt experimentally, feeling the roughness.

"I don't know how to use a sword," he said aloud.

"You'll learn," Roneida said unsympathetically. "And until you do, simply think of it as a long sharp club."

Tiercel snickered nervously. Harrier turned and glared at him. *Tiercel* was the High Mage! *Tiercel* was the one talking about needing a sword for his stupid magic spells! Why hadn't Roneida given *Tiercel* the sword?

"I, ah, um. Thank you," he said awkwardly. It was a present, after all. And you thanked people for presents, even when they gave you things you'd rather not have.

It occurred to him that this had all started when he'd been given a present he hadn't wanted—The *Compendium of Ancient Myth and Legend*. He hoped that this present didn't mean the start of even more trouble. And he *really* hoped he wasn't going to have to hit anything.

"And now we'll have a nice cup of tea, and go to bed," Roneida said briskly. "We all have a long way to go in the morning, and you've all had a very busy day."

❧

BUT even after the evening tea—something from Roneida's pack; spicy, fragrant, and unfamiliar—Harrier couldn't sleep, though Tiercel dozed off immediately and even Simera seemed perfectly able to sleep just as if this were any other night. He couldn't stop thinking about what Roneida had told them.

Go find the Elves.

It would take them two moonturns at least to cross the Mystrals and reach Ysterialpoerin, and he had no idea how far beyond that the Bazrahil Range was. A long way, he thought. The edge of the world. And Pelashia's Veil was farther still.

Their parents were going to think they were dead.

They might actually *be* dead before they got that far, it occurred to him. Roneida hadn't said her rocks could protect them—he fingered the white stone around his neck—she just said they might help. Whatever was chasing Tiercel would keep coming. None of them really knew much about fighting. Simera could defend herself against bandits—if there weren't too many of them—but what if something worse came along? Since they all seemed to be falling into a Kindling Day play, why not expect icedrakes and dwerro and bearwards and minotaurs to come charging over the next hill? And unicorns and Frost Giants too? If they were going to visit the Elves, and see dragons, maybe they'd get to see *all* the creatures of ancient legend, wonderful and monstrous.

He really hoped not. It was one thing to imagine them safely in a wondertale—that was fine—and quite another to imagine actually meeting any of them. The bad ones would kill them outright, and Harrier couldn't really imagine that even the good ones would have much interest in them.

And why wouldn't Roneida just *do* something about Tiercel's visions, if they were so dangerous, instead of sending them off to the Elves? What were the Elves going to do? Train Tyr as a High Mage? From everything Tiercel had said, that took years. If what he was seeing was an actual problem, wouldn't it be over by then, one way or the other?

Harrier was definitely going to ask Roneida about all that in the morning. From a safe distance. Although actually he wouldn't even mind getting hit, so long as he got answers as well. She really hadn't told them all that much, though she'd made Tiercel feel better. And the stew had been good.

Eventually he exhausted himself with unanswered questions, and slept.

TIERCEL awoke feeling better than he had in a very long time. The nagging almost-a-headache he'd had for moonturns was gone and he felt alert and wide-awake, even before his first cup of morning tea. He even felt cheerful, which was pretty weird, considering that they'd finally met the Wildmage he'd been looking for ever since he and Harrier had left Armethalieh, and she'd basically told him that she couldn't help.

But at least she *had* told him who could, and that was more than he'd known before. And since she'd done so much for them already, maybe he could persuade her to tell them something more today. Like how she'd known where to find them. And why she'd brought them the things she had. She must have brought those particular things for a reason, after all.

He sat up in his blankets, yawning and stretching, and looked around. Harrier was still an unconscious lump in his blankets, and Tiercel smiled. It was nice to be awake first for a change. Even Simera was asleep. He wondered—not for the first time—if it was uncomfortable to sleep standing up. He supposed it was natural, if you were a Centaur. After all, they had four legs, and wouldn't fall over. He looked further.

Roneida and her donkey were gone.

"Hey!" he yelped, throwing his bedclothes back. His good mood of a moment before had vanished utterly. He felt betrayed. He'd expected Roneida to be here in the morning. He'd expected her to stay with them.

Simera jerked upright with a huff and a gurgle, and Harrier came thrashing out of his blankets as if an entire army of Endark-ened were about to come rushing across the Plains.

"What? What is it?" he demanded, grabbing for the sword Roneida had left them. And that was the single scariest thing Tier-cel had seen in the last moonturn. Harrier with a sword. Harrier was the *Portmaster's son*, for the Light's sake!

"Roneida's gone. She's left us," Tiercel said tightly.

"She did *what?*" At least Harrier's eyes were all the way open now, and he'd put the sword down. He hadn't even managed to get it all the way out of its sheath.

"She isn't here," Tiercel repeated. He stood up and looked around, half-hoping she might be hiding somewhere, but he already knew what he'd find. She wasn't here, and he couldn't see her anywhere on the horizon.

"She *left?*" Harrier sputtered.

She had. And—obviously—she was not only using Wildmage magic to conceal herself—because otherwise they should still be able to see her in the distance—but, as they soon found, had appar-ently used Wildmage magic to conceal her tracks as well, because Simera could find no trace of either her or the donkey.

VOICES carried a great distance over the High Plains. It took no great enchantment—though Roneida carried many with her—to hear the sounds of dismay at the awakening camp less than half a mile behind her.

She stopped for a moment, savoring the cool of the morning. Even through the thin fabric of the *tarnkappa* that concealed her, she could feel the morning breeze.

This was definitely the best part of the day.

Behind her, Mouse waited patiently. She could not see him—he

was veiled, just as she was, in an all-concealing shroud of magic—
but he was well-trained, and would follow the pull of the lead-rope
even though he could not see his mistress.

A hard Price, and a complicated one, but as soon as she had
gotten safely away from the children, it would be paid in full. She
thought she would go to Sentarshadeen. She hadn't seen Maelgwn
in years. He would certainly want to know that the Fire-Crowned
had reached her safely.

With as much safety as there was left in the world.

Praise the Gods of the Wild Magic that the Fire-Crowned was
as ignorant as he was! It had been hard indeed not to tell him all
she knew—little as that was—but she could not help him gain his
Mastery, and without it, ignorance of his peril—true innocence—
was his only shield.

Tiercel and his friends were worried, and that was good. But
they obviously had no inkling of precisely how serious a matter it
was when the Wild Magic called back into the world the ancient
War Magic that had been created in the Light's hour of darkest
peril to save all that lived from the Endarkened.

Should they realize it—truly and properly understand it—they
would do what any sensible well-brought-up youngsters would do.

They would go to their elders for help.

They would spend time trying to convince others of the danger
they were all in.

They would stay somewhere they thought was *safe*.

And—since there was nowhere safe, and, even if they could
convince someone in Armethalieh that Tiercel had the powers of a
High Mage, nobody there would have the least idea of what to do
about that—it was far better for him to be doing precisely what he
was doing now.

A slim hope was better than no hope at all.

Roneida tugged on Mouse's lead-rope and continued walking in
the direction of Sentarshadeen.

≈

"BREAKFAST?" Tiercel said with a sigh.

Simera was angry at not having found a single trace of Roneida's tracks. She'd said the Wildmage had just *appeared* the day before, and apparently she'd vanished the same way today.

Harrier was just as irritated, but Harrier didn't particularly like surprises, good or bad.

"I suppose," he agreed, sitting down beside Tiercel with a sigh. "I thought she was going to go with us to the Elves."

"I guess she had something else to do," Tiercel offered.

"What?" Simera demanded. "What could have been more important?"

"Than nursemaiding us?" Tiercel asked with a wry grin. "Well, think of it this way. We can't be in very much danger if she just went off and left us, can we?"

"That's not what she said last night," Harrier grumbled, reaching for the teapot.

"She said we might run into trouble," Tiercel said, thinking back. "I guess she thinks we can handle it. And at least she won't keep hitting you."

Harrier rubbed the back of his head reflexively. "I bet she teaches school back in Vardirvoshanon," he said.

"So what do we do now?" Simera asked.

Tiercel shrugged. "Find the Elves. And I guess we stop at that town she suggested and buy a cart for Thunder, first."

≈

WINDY Meadows was—so Simera told them—a typical plains town: little more than a long street and some holding pens for cattle. There were a few settlements nearby—"near" being a relative term—for Windy Meadows was one of the towns along the road that led through the Northern Pass through the Mystrals. Though most of the traffic went by way of the more southerly route that led close to Ondoladeshiron, the traffic along the northern road kept towns like Windy Meadows well-supplied, and this early in the year, the mountain passes would be clear.

The sun was setting as they reached the town, and despite Tiercel's uneasy protests, Simera and Harrier were both looking forward to spending the night at whatever local accommodation the town might provide.

"I'm sure Roneida's magic will protect us," Simera said hopefully.

"And . . . have you noticed that the whatever-they-are's have been getting, well, less harmful?" Harrier said, frowning. "That cold-snap *killed* a lot of things. And the bear could have killed us. But that guy only tried to talk you to death."

"He was . . ." Tiercel stopped, sighing. There was no way to explain to the other two—especially Harrier—that the stranger had been as dangerous—and maybe more dangerous—than the cold-snap. Not because of what he'd done. But because of what Tiercel had sensed that he *could* do.

He shrugged. "I guess one night won't hurt."

⇜

"ARE you sure it's supposed to be *this* deserted?" Tiercel asked, a short time later.

He was standing in the center of the High Street of Windy Meadows. It was also the only street, so far as any of them could tell: a wide dirt track with a line of stone-and-brick buildings on either side. At the far end of the High Street were barns, cattle pens, and a wind-driven pump. The pump's sails spun strongly in the brisk wind of evening, making a faint steady clacking sound. It was the only sound there was, other than the wind and the sound of their own voices.

"No," Harrier said.

"Roneida said she'd been here," Simelda began uncertainly.

"Did she?" Harrier said. "Or did she just say *we* should come here? I've been thinking about what she said, and it wasn't much."

"But . . . she *was* a Wildmage," Simera said. "She knew so much. About all of us."

Harrier just looked at her.

"Whatever—I mean *whoever* she was, I don't think she was one of the Bad Things," Tiercel said.

" 'Bad Things'?" Harrier said mockingly. "Tyr, *how* old are you?"

Tiercel flushed. "Well, what would *you* call them?"

Harrier's smile faded. "You're right. Bad Things it is. So. She was a Wildmage. And she sent us here, and, if she'd come from Vardirvoshanon, she must have stopped here on the way, right?"

"So it must have been perfectly safe then," Simera said. She didn't sound completely certain. "But . . . there don't seem to be any people here," she added.

"Hello?" Tiercel shouted. His voice echoed through the dusk.

"Don't *do* that!" Harrier said, sounding as if he'd very much like to swear. He was good at it, Tiercel knew, though he didn't do it often. Either the situation wasn't bad enough for bad language, he said—quoting his father, who was mild-spoken for all his loudness—or it was much too bad for it. Tiercel suspected they were heading for the second category. Fast.

"Didn't you say the stranger kept warning you about plague?" Simera asked.

"In Ysterialpoerin," Tiercel said, sliding down off of Cloud's back. The big bay gelding stood placidly. Whatever had happened here apparently wasn't upsetting to horses, though that wasn't really reassuring. He walked Cloud over to the nearest hitching post and looped his reins through one of the rings.

"What are you doing?" Harrier asked.

"I'm going to take a look around."

"So—in case it *is* plague—you can catch it and die. Great idea," Harrier grumbled.

"I'll take my wand," Tiercel said mildly.

"Even better. You can dazzle the plague with colored lights and then pass out. In that case, I'm coming with you. And I'm taking my sword."

"So you can hit the plague over the head. Great."

"Whatever's wrong here," Simera said firmly, "I'm bound by law to find out what it is and help if I can. So you might as well stop arguing and start looking around."

IT took Harrier a moment to get the sword and belt down from the back of Lightning's saddle and buckle them into place. The unfamiliar weight dragged at his hip, but Roneida had been right; if nothing else, he could use it as a club. And this place worried him.

He was *almost certain* Roneida wouldn't have knowingly sent them into danger. But it had taken them all of today to reach here, and they'd met her in the middle of yesterday, and she'd been on foot, not on horseback. She would have been traveling more slowly. So even if she *had* stopped here, it would have been three or four days ago, at least, since she'd been here, and possibly more. A lot could happen in that time.

He tied Lightning beside Cloud and followed Tiercel.

THEY started with the inn. It was the largest building, and the doors stood open.

"We should have brought the lanterns," Harrier said dubiously. The common room was dark. And empty.

"I think I can—" Tiercel said.

Before either of them could stop him, he sketched a shape in the air with the wand. A ball of blue light appeared, about the size of a loaf of bread, and floated up over his head. He sighed with relief.

"I'm all right." He looked at them. "I could make one for each of you, I think."

"Oh, no," Harrier said hastily. "Why don't we just stay together?"

They went inside.

"Hello?" Tiercel called again.

The inn stood empty, and this should have been its busiest time.

The light over Tiercel's head—Harrier tried not to think about that, with some success—was brighter indoors. The inn's common room was completely dark; there were windows, but they had shutters, not glass, and the shutters were closed and latched. Simera crossed to them—moving carefully; this place had not been designed for Centaurs—opening them.

Tables, benches. No people.

The benches were pushed back, as if people had gotten to their feet suddenly. There were mugs and plates on the tables and all of them contained half-eaten meals. Harrier dipped his finger into a bowl of stew. Cold and congealed, but not dried up. Not like something that had been sitting here, say, four days or more. So it hadn't happened before Roneida had been here. And the Wild Magic hadn't warned her not to send them here.

He didn't like this.

The floor—wooden planks laid on a frame above the bare earth—was wet.

Harrier squatted down and touched his fingers to the wetness and sniffed them.

"Cider," he said, frowning. They would have smelled it when they'd walked in if the door hadn't been open. Most of the cider had trickled between the gaps in the planks, but from the marks on the floor, a lot had spilled.

He followed the traces back across the floor, past the serving board, to the row of wooden kegs racked along the back wall. The names of the contents were chalked on the sides of the barrels: several kinds of beer and ale, several kinds of cider, even water.

There was a pewter mug lying on the floor, and the tap to one of the kegs was open and dripping. Harrier rapped the side of the keg. It was empty.

The landlord had been filling a mug when . . . something . . . happened.

"Guys?" he said.

The room had suddenly gone dark.

"There's nobody in the storeroom, either," Tiercel said, walking back into the main room again, bringing the light back with him.

"This isn't right," Simera said, frowning as she gazed around the room.

She wasn't frightened. Harrier had noticed that about her; Simera didn't get afraid of things when something went wrong, she simply got angry that everything wasn't going the way it was supposed to go. She sounded irritated now.

"If there *were* a plague, this is where the people would gather," she said, working it out. "They'd come in from the steadings to the town, because it's nearest the road. And they'd turn the inn into a hospital—or if there were too many sick, and they used the barn instead, they'd be using the inn to cook for them. They'd be here."

"Whatever happened, they left so fast the landlord let one of his kegs run dry instead of shutting down the tap. Let's get out of here," Harrier said. *And whatever happened, it happened so recently that the floor's still wet.*

# Nine

# A Town Filled with Shadows

**T**HEY'D ONLY BEEN inside the inn for a few minutes, but by the time they came out into the street again, it was already enough darker that Tiercel's MageLight crown was bright enough to cast shadows. Both of the horses raised their heads and looked at it inquiringly. Thunder paid no attention.

"Everybody just vanished," Tiercel said. He sounded as if he were saying it to see if he liked the sound of the words any better aloud. From his expression, he didn't.

"In the middle of eating their stew and pulling a pint of cider," Harrier agreed.

"We should check the other buildings," Tiercel said next.

"For *what?*" Harrier demanded in exasperation.

"To see if—"

"I saw something," Simera said abruptly.

Both of the boys turned to look at her.

"I don't know," she said, having no trouble at all interpreting their looks. She pointed up the street. "Maybe an animal."

"We should look," Harrier said reluctantly. "But let's take the horses with us."

Tiercel had just settled into Cloud's saddle, and Harrier had one foot in his own mount's stirrup, when Simera let out a sharp yelp of surprise. There was a creature in the middle of the street where none had been before. It was about the size of a two-year-old child, but it was obviously not human, or a member of any race that Harrier recognized. It was completely naked and its body was as featureless as a child's doll. Its purple-grey skin was slick and hairless—reminding Harrier of a frog—and it looked a little more like an ape than it looked like anything else. Its head was round and nearly featureless; it had a lipless mouth so wide it seemed to be smiling; no nose that he could see; and large round silver eyes that it kept squinting and blinking, as if even the dusk was too bright for it. Harrier swung up into his saddle, trying to do it silently.

As he did, two more of the things appeared. They didn't come from behind the buildings, or up the street. They came up out of the street itself, sliding through the hard-packed surface as if the street were water.

"Get rid of that light," Harrier said quietly.

Tiercel gestured, and the globe of MageLight went to hover over the roof of the inn. The creatures turned their heads to watch it move. Their mouths hung open, and now Harrier could see that their mouths were filled with long, needle-sharp fangs.

Simera was stringing her bow. She knew even better than Harrier did that no creature had teeth like that if it weren't a predator. From the expression on her face, the creatures were as strange to her as they were to Harrier, but she recognized them as dangerous none the less.

And the fact that they appeared in a town where all the inhabitants had vanished was too gruesome a coincidence to *be* a coincidence.

"Let's go," Simera said. "Slowly. Maybe they won't follow."

They moved their horses down the center of the Main Street at a slow walk.

Harrier looked back.

There were five of the creatures now.

FOR a few moments Harrier dared to hope that they'd actually be able to just walk away. Simera had told them both various stories of her encounters with wild animals, everything from unexpected meetings with bears—the small black kind—to facing down lynxes and rutting bucks and even angry foxes. Sometimes you could avoid a disastrous—or violent—encounter simply by walking slowly away, as they were doing now. Both Harrier and Simera were watching over their shoulders. Tiercel was leading Thunder, and looking in the direction of the road. They would have to follow the road now; it was getting much too dark to strike off over the Plains.

The pony was restless, shaking his head and pulling at the lead rope, obviously unhappy to be where he was. They made it as far as the end of the street, and the road was in sight, when suddenly the creatures began moving down the street after them, swinging themselves slowly along on their elongated forearms. They weren't simply going to let them leave.

Simera stopped, turned, and shot.

Her arrow flew true, straight into the eye-socket of the lead creature. It fell back among its fellows with a shriek of pain, and in an instant the other four fell on it like a pack of starving dogs, devouring its body before it had stopped twitching—possibly even before it died.

That was the final straw for the horses. Whether it was the smell of blood, or the sounds, or some combination of both, they laid their ears flat back and bolted.

Thunder's lead-rope was jerked from Tiercel's hand immediately when Cloud stretched his neck out and began to run. The pony had been built for endurance, not for speed, and Thunder was left behind as soon as Cloud jumped the ditch at the edge of the main road and began running through the long yellow grass of the Plains.

Tiercel flailed as he tried to get both hands on the reins without either dropping his wand or simply falling from the saddle. He tried to remember everything Halyon had told him back in Sentarshadeen about what to do if Cloud ever ran away with him, but he couldn't think of any of it. He finally got both hands on the reins and was pulling back as hard as he could, but it was useless. All he could do was try to stay in the saddle as Cloud galloped, in a line as straight as the flight of an arrow, away from the town of Windy Meadows. He didn't even know where Harrier or Simera were.

Behind him, he suddenly heard an unearthly shrieking.

"TIERCEL!" Harrier shouted.

"The road!" Simera shouted back.

Harrier had been slightly more fortunate than Tiercel had. When Lightning gathered himself to bolt, Harrier had given the reins a savage jerk and kept the gelding from getting the bit between his teeth. He couldn't stop his mount from running—and considering what was after them, he didn't want to try—but he could control the direction the two of them went.

He couldn't see Tiercel anywhere.

He and Simera galloped up the road. Thunder followed them, running free, but the pony was dropping farther behind with every passing moment.

And the *things* were following.

He hoped they could outrun them.

Then Harrier heard a scream behind him, and realized he was alone on the road. He sawed frantically at the reins, forcing Lightning around in a tight circle. The gelding danced and bucked, but at the end of a long day's travel even so short a run had tired him, and Harrier was able to force him back the way they'd come.

The scream he'd heard was Thunder.

The pony lay in the middle of the road in a spreading pool of blood. The creatures—more than five, now, many more—swarmed over his corpse, devouring every scrap of flesh and bone. Simera stood in the road a few yards distant, loosing arrows into the seething swarm of creatures, but it was almost fully dark now, and often her arrows didn't find their mark. The creatures seemed willing to turn on dead and wounded alike, however, devouring them just as they had the one Simera had killed in the town. But no matter how many of their own kind they devoured, their appetite seemed endless.

"Go!" Simera shouted when she saw Harrier. Her voice was ragged as she gasped for air after her long run, and her flanks were foamy with sweat. "Find Tiercel!"

"Come on!" he said urgently. "Why did you stop?"

Despite the animal's exhaustion, it was taking everything he had to hold Lightning in place. The poor beast was tossing its head and stepping backward and sideways, desperate to be away from this place.

"I can't outrun them," she said, never stopping her careful mechanical aiming and loosing into the feeding mass of creatures. Despite the additional fodder she was providing them, they would have finished consuming the pony's carcass in only a few minutes more. "Maybe you can."

"No."

He slipped from Lightning's back quickly, before the gelding could shy again and trip him. The moment it realized it was free, the horse turned and galloped away.

Harrier drew his sword.

"Damn you, stupid city boy," Simera panted.

"Yeah," Harrier said.

"There's a lantern in my pack."

Harrier found the lantern and lit it, setting it behind them on the side of the trail.

The creatures were starting to advance again. Less than half a dozen remained, but from all that Harrier had seen, half a dozen would be more than enough to kill the two of them. He clutched the sword tightly and tried to imagine what he was doing here. He would have been afraid, except for the fact that this all seemed completely unreal.

Then Simera was loosing more arrows again, and for a moment he thought—with a pang of relief so sharp it almost made him dizzy—that everything was going to be fine, and they were going to get out of this okay, because the creatures kept stopping to eat their dead, and that made them easy targets. She'd kill the rest of them, and the two of them would go find Lightning. They'd *escape*. . . .

Then Simera threw down her bow with a sob and Harrier knew she was out of arrows. She drew her knife. Four left.

There weren't even bones where Thunder's body had been, just a few chewed pieces of the packs' contents and the saddle.

"Get away from them!" he heard Tiercel shout.

But they couldn't. The creatures sprang forward, moving fast now, and one of them jumped at him and Harrier hit it, the sword twisting in his hands, and there was a sudden sharp terrible smell in the air as the creature came apart with the force of the blow—not blood, but it still made him want to gag—and Simera screamed, because one of them had jumped at her; she'd turned and kicked it but it was holding on, fangs buried deep in her rump.

There was a rush of heat and light.

Screaming.

Harrier pulled the knife Roneida had given him. He rushed toward Simera and stabbed at the one that was biting her, pulling it free and throwing its body down into the road. It wasn't quite dead, but it was dying.

Simera staggered away, and that one burst into flames, too.

Tiercel leaned over the side of his horse and threw up.

Harrier dropped his sword in the road and ran over to Cloud. He grabbed the horse's reins; the animal was foam-flecked and exhausted; obviously too exhausted to stir a step, but Harrier still didn't want the horse bolting again.

"Simera!" he called over his shoulder. "Are you all—"

"No," Tiercel said, his tone one of quiet protest.

Harrier looked back over his shoulder. Simera was down on her knees. Harrier dropped the reins and ran back to her.

She'd rolled to her side. Her long legs were twitching, as if she were running, and her flank was dark with blood from the gaping bite-wound.

"Simera?"

He knelt on the road beside her and attempted to drag her torso into his lap. Her skin was ice cold. The fires from the creatures Tiercel had set alight had gone out, leaving small stinking splotches on the road, and the only light came from the one lantern they'd lit earlier.

"Poison," she whispered, gasping for air. "If you— Don't let them *bite* you."

Tiercel skidded to his knees in front of her, a small bottle in his hands. "Simera? I have the brandy. Drink it."

He tried to pour it into her mouth, but she couldn't swallow. She choked and coughed, and then she gasped for air.

And then she died.

"Why didn't you get here sooner?" Harrier said, getting to his feet.

Tiercel stared up at him, his face blank with shock and the growing horrified realization that Simera was dead.

"I got here as soon as I could," he said after a long silence. "I couldn't find you. Then I saw the lantern. And heard . . . the sounds."

He pushed himself slowly to his feet and walked back to Cloud, his back to Harrier.

⇜

THE gelding was standing where Tiercel had left him. Cloud had run himself nearly to exhaustion when he'd bolted, which was the only reason Tiercel had been able to bring him around. If Harrier and Simera hadn't lit that lantern, he never would have found them as quickly as he had. Sound carried weirdly on the Plains at night, and by the time he'd gotten Cloud to stop running, he hadn't really been certain of where he was.

Harrier was right.

He should have managed to get there sooner.

He should have set those things on fire when they'd first seen them back in the town.

But he still recoiled from the horror of what he'd done. They were alive, and he'd burned them to death.

But if he'd done it sooner, Simera would be alive now.

He led Cloud back to the road. The gelding's nostrils flared as it approached the road, and even Tiercel could smell the stench— burning, and something worse—but the animal was too tired to make much of a fuss.

Harrier was still standing over Simera's body. He rubbed at his face with the back of his hand when Tiercel approached.

"Come on," Tiercel said quietly. "We can't stay here."

"We have to—" Harrier said thickly. "We can't just—"

He gestured to Simera's body.

"Centaurs don't," Tiercel said. "They just . . . out in the fields. They say it's the Herdsman's Way."

"Can't just leave her in the road," Harrier said thickly, drawing a shaking breath.

"No."

&

IT wasn't a pretty business. They needed Cloud to move her. They tied a rope from the gelding's pack around Simera's body and used it to drag her out into the tall grass. They wrapped as much of her as they could in a blanket from her pack first, but it still seemed a terrible way to treat the body of their friend. Both of them were crying openly by the time the brutal work was done.

"I don't know any words for Centaurs," Tiercel said, staring down at her body.

"I guess it doesn't matter now," Harrier said harshly. "My Da says prayers are for the living." He picked up the lantern and began to walk back to the road. Tiercel took Cloud's reins and followed.

&

THEY walked up the road in silence with Tiercel leading Cloud. Both of them were too grief-stricken and exhausted to talk. While they'd been setting Simera to rest, the moon had risen; it was full, and gave plenty of light to see by.

Harrier was stunned, still aching with the suddenness of the loss of Simera, but despite his cruel words earlier, he didn't blame Tiercel for her death. Cloud had bolted. Tiercel had regained control of his horse and ridden back to them as fast as he could.

As for the rest . . .

He still wasn't sure how he felt about Tiercel being able to cast spells, even though Tiercel didn't really seem to be that good at it.

And the idea of having Tiercel use magic against the monsters disturbed him almost more than the idea of being killed by them.

He wished Simera were alive; there was no question of that. If it had been a clear-cut choice, if *he* were the one with the magic, he would have used it unhesitatingly. But it wasn't the first thing that you thought of doing. It wasn't like having a sword in your hand.

And in the end, magic or not, it was still burning something alive to death. Thinking of it that way made it harder to decide what was the right thing to do.

At first they were both nervous and on-edge as they walked, wondering if every flickering shadow held more of those monsters, but at last they'd given up worrying. There was nothing they could do about them if they *did* come. Not really. Tiercel might be able to force himself to burn some of them, but if there were a lot of them, and if they surrounded them . . .

Harrier didn't know how much control Tiercel had over his magic-called fire. Maybe he could set fire to all of them if a whole pack of the creatures surrounded them—without setting fire to himself and Harrier in the process. Maybe not.

Harrier preferred to hope that all of the creatures were dead.

"What's that?"

Harrier stopped and raised his sword. He'd brought it with him, of course—it was still covered with the monsters' blood—and hadn't put it back into its scabbard.

There was a large dark shape ahead in the road.

At the sound of his voice, it raised its head and started forward. The metal on its bridle jingled.

"Lightning!" Harrier said, his voice ragged with relief. "I really ought to beat you senseless."

"According to Halyon, that wouldn't take much," Tiercel said. "Did he throw you?"

"Ran off," Harrier said shortly. "But not far enough."

He approached the gelding cautiously, but Lightning seemed

delighted to see him, butting and nuzzling at his chest in obvious hope of reward. Harrier didn't have anything to give him, but as soon as the reins were safely in his hands, he gave the gelding a good scratch behind the ears before leading it back to Tiercel.

"We might as well ride," he said. "I'm tired of walking, anyway."

＊

THEY rode at the slowest possible walking pace through the rest of the night, only stopping at dawn when they came to one of the Light-shrines that were set near the road at regular intervals. It was easily seen from a distance by the wind-pump that marked it, an indication that it would also have a well.

They were truly grateful for that. By now the horses were thirsty, and so were they; nearly all of their provisions had been in Thunder's packs. They each carried a water bottle, but those had been empty when they'd reached Windy Meadows.

Fortunately they knew enough about thirsty horses not to let the animals drink their fill at once. Harrier held the animals back while Tiercel pumped the trough full of water, then Harrier let them have a short drink—less than they wanted—before tying them to the tether-rings at the front of the temple. In a few minutes, he'd let them drink more.

"We might as well stop here for a few hours," Tiercel said. "The horses could use the rest, and so could we."

He pulled Cloud's saddlebags off and began unbuckling the saddle girths.

＊

ONCE the horses had been watered and turned out to graze (their hobbles, fortunately, were one of the things packed in their saddlebags), the boys went into the shrine.

It was a typical roadside Light-shrine, of the sort they'd seen many of along the way; a three-sided structure, barely large enough for two or three people to enter at once. The back wall was carved in a relief of the Eternal Light, painted in gold, and below it was an altar-shelf set with a heavy stone bowl where offerings could be burned. There were flowers beside the bowl on the altar, but they were withered and brown. Nobody had been here in a while.

Tiercel scooped them up and set them into the bowl. They blazed into sudden life and burned brightly for a moment before crumbling away into ash.

"Are you sure you ought to be doing that?" Harrier asked.

"It all comes from the same place," Tiercel answered. He set his hands flat against the back wall of the shrine and closed his eyes. Blue light began to spread from his hands, out across the stone, until in moments the entire interior of the shrine—walls, ceiling, floor, the altar itself—was glowing a bright radiant azure. There was so much light that it was like standing in sunlight, except that it came from below as well.

"For Simera," Tiercel said.

"The next person who shows up here isn't going to want to come in," Harrier said, stepping back and shaking his head.

"I think it fades eventually," Tiercel answered. But he didn't sound as if he really cared.

They went back outside.

THEY rinsed and filled their water bottles, and did their best to wash away some of the dust and grime of the long night in the water trough. Then they went to see what supplies they had left.

Not much.

They had their heavy traveling cloaks. Some food—enough for a couple of days, though of course no grain for the horses. Tea, but no way to brew it. Money—but no place to buy anything. Tiercel's books. An extra shirt of Harrier's. Medicines for themselves and the horses. A coil of rope. A lantern. Tiercel's guidebook with its maps.

That was about it.

Harrier squinted out at the rising sun, munching on a bar of trail rations as he leaned against the side of the shrine. Most of the ones they had were compressed bars of seeds, nuts, and dried fruit, held together with honey; useful for bribing the horses as well as making a meal on when they didn't want to stop to cook. There was a little jerky as well; you could make soup out of it if you were patient. And if you had a pot and some water, of course.

"So what do we do?" he asked Tiercel.

Not that he hadn't made up his own mind already. It was pretty obvious. Mostly he wanted to be sure that Tiercel agreed with him.

Tiercel was down on his hands and knees, squinting at the folded-out map in his guidebook. He'd bought the guidebook in Sentarshadeen, and while he constantly complained that it wasn't as detailed as he wanted, it *did* cover all of the Nine Cities and the principal roads between them.

"There should be another town near the road a day or two north of here; a place called Thunder Grass. It's hard to tell. The trouble is, we don't have any way to carry enough water for the horses. And I'm not sure where the next well is. Or which of the rivers are still running in summer."

Harrier sighed. Simera would have known. "That's a problem."

"Or—" Tiercel continued doggedly, "whether there's going to be anybody alive in Thunder Grass when we get there."

"That's a real problem." Harrier watched the sun rise for a while. "We could stay here," he said. "Somebody's going to come down this road eventually." He was sure they could figure out some way to explain why the shrine was glowing.

"I think it *was* a kraken," Tiercel said.

Since Harrier had known his friend practically from the time Tiercel had learned to walk, he didn't find anything particularly unusual in the abrupt change of subject. That didn't mean, however, that he knew what Tiercel was talking about.

"Krakens live in the ocean," Harrier reminded him.

"The captain of the *Marukate*," Tiercel explained patiently, "said his ship had been attacked by a kraken."

"Oh, yes," Harrier said, nodding. "That makes perfect sense."

"And krakens are creatures of Dark Magic. They were in your uncle's book."

"And haven't been seen in . . . how many hundred years?"

"A lot. And neither have Goblins. I think those things last night were Goblins. I'm not sure. If they were, we're safe during the day. They only come out at night."

"The Blessed Saint Idalia destroyed all the creatures of the Dark," Harrier said uneasily.

Tiercel glanced up at him, folding the map back into the guidebook. "I know. She made the Great Sacrifice at Kindling and broke the power of the Endarkened, and they and their creatures were all destroyed, which is why the land flowered again. Everyone says so. And the Priests and the Wildmages said it was forever, but . . . But I think they're coming back."

*I don't want to hear this,* was Harrier's first, automatic thought. *But I'm only seventeen!* was his second.

He looked around. Empty sky, empty earth.

And the blue light flooding out from the door of the Lightshrine. Light that Tiercel had put there.

*"The Gods don't send us gifts we don't need."*

Roneida had said that.

Was that why Tiercel had the powers of a High Mage? Because the Darkness was coming back? But Tyr had no idea of what to do with them!

And there was only one of him.

Even Kellen the Poor Orphan Boy had had an army.

"Because you did one little Dark-damned spell?" Harrier demanded angrily.

"I don't think so," Tiercel answered slowly. "I just think everything's all unraveling at the same time. I think the fact that it's unraveling is why there are krakens and Goblins and probably other things out there that we haven't run into. And why I'm having visions."

"Although you don't know what they're visions of," Harrier pointed out.

"Maybe I do. Har, what do the Endarkened look like?"

Harrier sighed deeply. "You went to all the same Flowering Festival plays that I did. They're giant black monsters with wings and tails that live—well, lived—under Shadow Mountain."

"That's just what we think they look like. Nobody really knows. The only thing we know for sure is that they could look like anything."

"I really hate to break this to you, but Knight-Mage Kellen and the Armies of the Light killed all the Endarkened a thousand years ago. They're gone."

Tiercel just kept looking at him, in the way that he did when he wasn't going to argue about something any more. And Harrier didn't want to argue either. This was too important for that. Tiercel was right: the Endarkened could look like anything. That was how they'd snuck into Armethalieh to steal Saint Idalia from her cradle, and how they'd managed to place the Demon Queen's own son, Anigrel the Black, in a nobleman's house to be raised as a Prince of the City.

"We have to tell somebody," Harrier said. But tell them what?

That the ancient evil that had been destroyed forever was—somehow—coming back? Who was going to believe them?

Tiercel laughed bitterly. "I've told everybody I can think of, Harrier: my tutor, *three* Healers in Armethalieh, my Preceptor, the Chief Preceptor in Sentarshadeen. I've even told a Wildmage."

"You didn't tell them this," Harrier pointed out. Not that the Creatures of the Dark were coming back. It was almost proof. It would be proof—providing anyone saw them besides him and Tiercel.

And lived to tell. He took a deep breath, trying not to think of Simera.

"I don't think it's going to make any difference. I can't prove any of it, any more than the captain of the *Marukate* could prove he'd been attacked by a kraken. The only thing I *can* prove is that I have the ability to do High Mage magic, and while that might prove something to somebody eventually, I don't know if we have, well, *time*. I think it's just going to keep . . . getting worse. Roneida said we should—I should—go find the Elves. That's what I'm going to do," Tiercel said stubbornly.

"This is crazy," Harrier said desperately. "Things like this don't happen to people like us. Things like this don't happen to *anybody*."

"They happened to people once."

"About a thousand years ago."

"One thousand and eight years ago this last Kindling."

"Pedant."

"Dock-rat."

"Book-nose."

"At least I can read."

Harrier stuffed the last of the trail-bar into his mouth and chewed noisily, spraying crumbs. "So," he said, after he'd swallowed. "Elves?"

Tiercel sighed. "We'll stop in Thunder Grass first and see what we can pick up in the way of supplies, I guess. Then go on over the Southern Pass."

Harrier nodded. It was pretty much what he'd decided as well. He just hoped Thunder Grass was . . . there. "We might as well catch a few hours sleep first."

❧

THEY headed up the road around midday. Their luck turned, and they spent that evening in the camp of a wagon train heading west toward Sentarshadeen.

The wagonmaster thought it was odd to find two boys in the middle of nowhere, traveling with little more than the clothes on their backs, and Harrier wasn't at all sure what to say to him by way of explanation.

Tiercel, of course, told him nearly everything.

He left out the part about being a High Mage, about having visions, and about intending to go visit the Elves—for which Harrier was profoundly grateful—but he told him about meeting Simera on the road to Sentarshadeen, and traveling north with her, and meeting Roneida, and stopping in Windy Meadows and finding it completely deserted. About encountering the strange creatures there, and being followed by them. About Simera's death.

"And why were you and your young friend heading all this way north?" Wagonmaster Matteus asked.

"I'd wanted to see the Great Library at Ysterialpoerin," Tiercel said simply. "I'm going to be entering University in Armethalieh to study Ancient History, and Master Cansel—he's the Chief Librarian at the Great Library in Armethalieh—said that the Library there had an excellent collection of ancient texts."

Harrier attempted to keep his face completely blank. Had Tiercel actually just *lied?*

Matteus shook his head in disbelief at the foolishness of boys, but there was no doubt that he accepted Tiercel's explanation. "I am very sorry for your misfortune. You're welcome to travel back with us to Sentarshadeen, if you wish. Your horses look as if they can stand the pace."

But Tiercel shook his head in turn. "No, I'd rather keep going. We've come so far already. Isn't there a town near here where we can buy a pack-horse and supplies to take us through the Mystrals?"

Matteus pursed his lips, thinking. "Thunder Grass should be able to sell you what you need. It's about three days up the road, and half a day off it, but the turn-off is well marked. There's a post-inn and a Light-shrine between here and the turn-off. Both have wells, so you won't lack for water, and you'll be able to buy food and drink at the inn, though there's no place to sleep. And we could let you have a bit of food as well."

"We'd be happy to pay for anything you can spare," Harrier said quickly.

⤳

THAT night, curled up in a new set of bedrolls—Matteus had insisted on making them a gift, saying the information they'd given him about what they'd encountered in Windy Meadows was well worth the reward—Harrier took the opportunity to quiz his friend.

"Tyr, did you actually *lie* to the Wagonmaster?" he asked, keeping his voice low.

Tiercel chuckled in the darkness.

"Well, I *am* going to study Ancient History. And I *do* want to see what the library has at Ysterialpoerin. But no, Master Cansel didn't actually suggest I go there. I guess I'm picking up bad habits from you."

"Good thing."

"Go to sleep."

In the morning they continued north.

⌘

THE Posting Inn was a simple one-room structure, designed mainly to serve the needs of the dispatch riders who took the northern route. There were not so many riders as on the other road, for most of the traffic went by way of Ondoladeshiron, and took the southern pass across the Mystrals before swinging north to Ysterialpoerin. But the northern pass was the most direct route between Sentarshadeen and Ysterialpoerin, and the needs of those who rode this way must be served as well. If Harrier and Tiercel had followed the road instead of riding directly over the Plains, they would have seen Posting Inns set all along their way. Anywhere there was not a town set close to the road—such as Windy Meadows—there would be a Posting Inn, each one set a day's ride apart.

The inns could provide food and drink for travelers and their horses, but were really only intended as brief stopping places for the post-riders who carried the Magistrates' most urgent messages—and those letters that private individuals were willing to pay the premium to get to their destination in sennights instead of moonturns. Tiercel checked with the innkeeper, and discovered that a westward post-rider was expected to come through the day after next. They would be able to send a letter with him, if they wished.

It had been far too long since their parents had gotten word from them. Their last letters had been sent from Sentarshadeen; it was possible that there might be a response waiting in Ysterialpoerin, though it would only be an exceedingly lucky guess on the part of either of their families that would lead them to address a letter there. And what might it say? "Come home"?

Tiercel couldn't do that, even though he wanted to. But certainly both of them owed their families fresh word, even if it couldn't be the words he knew his and Harrier's parents wanted to hear. And so, after a brief consultation, he and Harrier bought paper and ink, and borrowed pens, and sat at one of the tables in the small common room with mugs of watered ale to compose the letters they needed to send. The cost of sending anything by a Dispatch Rider was high, but Tiercel didn't want to wait and hope a caravan that was willing to take their letters stopped here. This method, at least, was certain.

They also wrote a letter to Simera's Guildhouse in Sentarshadeen, giving an account of how and where she had died, and signing both their names to it. They weren't certain what else to do—she'd never spoken much of her family—but the Forest Watch would be able to get word to any family she had. They might even be able to find the Wildmage Roneida and get her account of matters; in a part of his mind, Tiercel was thinking that no matter how carefully he phrased his account of what had happened at Windy Meadows, it would sound very suspicious. At least the Wildmage could vouch for their honesty and innocence.

What both boys were certain of was that Simera shouldn't simply vanish without a trace. And it was just as important that the Forest Watch should be told about the creatures that had killed Simera, and that might well attack others. A letter taken from the Posting Inn by the post-rider would be in Sentarshadeen within a fortnight, and certainly Tiercel had told the story of what had happened at Windy Meadows to the Inn's proprietor as well. They were both determined to spread the warning as far as possible.

By mutual consent, they did not mention Simera's death, or the Goblin attack, in the letters they wrote to their families, but when Tiercel sat down to write, he found himself telling his parents nearly everything else. Unlike some of his age-mates, who'd bragged about how little they told their parents, Tiercel had always been honest with his. He had always been rewarded: with their understanding, with their advice (sometimes it had been useful, sometimes not), and with the perspective of two people who had simply been alive much longer than he had. He'd been very guarded in what he had put into the letter he had written from Sentarshadeen, but now he told his parents everything about the reason for his journey, including that he'd met a Wildmage who felt he should seek out the Elves.

He didn't want to imagine their reaction when his letter finally reached them—it would go by regular post after it reached Sentarshadeen—but he felt a great sense of both guilt and relief at having finally told them the truth.

He had no idea what Harrier had written—beyond not telling his parents that they'd been attacked—and Harrier didn't say.

TO their great relief, Thunder Grass was just what Windy Meadows ought to have been: a small town of herders and farmers, untouched by any taint of disaster. There, they were able to buy a pack mule and replace most of their supplies.

After they left Thunder Grass, they entered the foothills that would lead them to the pass through the Mystrals. This far to the north and east the land was changing again; they were back in lush settled farming country. After the isolation of the Plains, it was almost a shock to see evidence of civilization on every side, but now the road that they followed led them through orchards and fields, and the only cattle they saw were fat and lazy and safely penned behind fences.

They saw no sign of Goblins, but in a town called Pinehold, where they stopped because Lightning had thrown a shoe, they heard news nearly as disturbing as the sight of Goblins would have been.

"GOING over Breakheart Pass, are you?" the smith asked. Harrier grinned at him good-naturedly.

"Not much else to do here, unless we want to turn around and go home," he answered. Beyond Pinehold there was only one more village close to the road, and after that, they were on their own. All they would encounter from here to the other side of the Mystrals would be other travelers like themselves, and the roadside inns that served them. For the last sennight, he and Tiercel had been arguing about whether it would be safe to use the inns, or whether they would need to try to camp out under the stars. Harrier argued that Roneida's talismans would protect them from anything that might still be following them, but after Windy Meadows, Tiercel wasn't willing to take the risk. Whether the Goblins had been drawn to his magic, or were simply a sign of the coming disaster, just as his own Magegift was, Tiercel wasn't willing to take the risk.

The smith nodded. "There's that. I'm just saying. You might want to be careful."

Tiercel—who'd been examining every item in the forge, the way he always did in a new place, as if every unfamiliar item might hold the key to the mysteries of the universe—turned around and regarded the smith curiously.

"It's late in the year for snow-slide, isn't it?" he asked. Which also meant that sleeping out as they went through the passes would be cold, Harrier knew. Not that Tiercel cared.

The smith interrupted his careful tapping at the shoe on the anvil. "Oh, Breakheart's been dry for moonturns. T'isn't snow you've got to worry about. It's wolves."

Both boys looked at him.

"Best you take me serious, now," the smith said, watching their faces. "You can go down to Eldon's house when you're done here and see the skins. No trouble all winter, when you'd think there'd be—not that we've had trouble with wolves here since my great-grandsire's time—but come the springtide, the beasts come down out of the hills like there was something chasing them. Haven't been able to send the sheep out to the far pastures at all."

"Springtide?" Harrier asked, when it became clear that Tiercel wasn't going to say anything.

"Oh, ah. Nigh about Kindling. Before Breakheart thawed, come to it. Oh, we've passed word to the Mountain Patrol and the Forest Watch, but they can't be everywhere. So best you keep a watchful eye, and be sure you're safe within doors before night falls."

"We will," Tiercel said quietly. Not that Harrier believed him.

# Ten

## Into the Mountains

**P**AST PINEHOLD, THE road began to ascend sharply, and even in deep summer the air was crisp and cool. Lasthold was the final town close to the road before they ascended to the mountains themselves, and the villagers there corroborated the Pinehold smith's story. Though wolves had not been seen in this area in over a century—and this wasn't the season for raiding wolfpacks, besides—they had come swarming down from the mountains in early spring.

In Lasthold the villagers also mentioned that bears had been seen in greater numbers this spring than usual, and said that westbound travelers had said they'd seen ice-tiger tracks in the higher reaches of the Mystrals, though nobody really believed that. Ice-tigers were fearsome predators, but shy and reclusive creatures, unlikely to come anywhere near humans.

"We'll be lucky to get across the pass alive," Harrier muttered as they left Lasthold.

When they'd arrived, he'd hoped to talk Tiercel into spending the night there, but once the villagers had started talking about tigers and bears and enormous wolfpacks, his heart really hadn't been in it. He'd settled for adding a couple of heavy wolfskin robes to their supplies before they left. Since they were apparently going to be sleeping in the snows of the mountain passes, Harrier had a feeling they were going to need them.

He only hoped that Tiercel would be able to get more money in Ysterialpoerin. He'd drawn the last of his own allowance in Sentarshadeen, and traveling was more expensive than he'd ever imagined. Growing up, he'd never given a thought to the fact that Tiercel was noble-born while he was "merely" a member of the Merchant Class—since in reality, the Harbormaster's Son would be more important in the City, someday, than the son of a Magistrate's Clerk, unless Tiercel became a Magistrate himself—which seemed very unlikely now.

But if Harrier's family was important, well, then he'd always known that Tiercel's was wealthy, though they'd always had the good manners not to flaunt their wealth. And that was a very good thing, since the two of them were certainly going to need more money soon. Their journey wasn't even half over.

It had been Meadowbloom when they left Armethalieh. They'd traveled through Sunkindle and most of Fruits, and would be lucky to reach Ysterialpoerin before the end of Harvest. And even then their trip wouldn't be over. Far from it. He wondered when the Gatekeeper was closed by weather. Vintage? Or earlier? Were they running out of time to reach their final destination?

And even when they'd gotten where they were going, and did whatever they had to do there, they still had to get back again.

*Not this year*, he thought resignedly. He hoped the Elves wanted houseguests, because he wasn't sure what else they were going to do once they got where they were going except wait for Windrack or even Sunkindle to unfreeze the southwestern passes again. *If they even got there in the first place.*

"I'm sure the pass is well-patroled," Tiercel said absently. "Why do you suppose the wolves came down into the farms this year?"

Harrier sighed. It was obvious, but he did wish Tiercel hadn't brought it up.

"Because something's chasing them, Tyr. And whatever it is, I really don't want to meet it."

CENTURIES ago, travel through the Mystrals had been difficult and dangerous, but now—at least in summer—the journey was quick and easy, and they accomplished in days what had taken ancient travelers sennights and more. But in the end, Harrier won his argument. They ended up staying in inns through the Mystrals without Harrier having to argue Tiercel into it, because the Mountain Patrol absolutely forbade them to camp, requiring them to check in each night at one of the Traveler's Inns. When Tiercel asked why, he was told that there had already been several deaths earlier in the year from wild animal attacks. Travelers were being strongly encouraged to organize themselves into large parties for their own safety, and night travel was strictly forbidden. There was even talk of closing the Pass entirely to pleasure travel.

("Not that this is a pleasure," Harrier had muttered.)

Tiercel had been miserable at the thought of being forced to sleep among people. He didn't mention whether he still had the dreams since he'd started wearing Roneida's talisman, but Harrier suspected that he did. There were mornings when Tiercel woke up looking as if he hadn't slept at all, and Harrier had to take care of all of the work of saddling the horses and the packmule, since anything that Tiercel did would simply have had to be re-done anyway.

Despite Tiercel's misery at their accommodations, Harrier was just as glad to be indoors. Even in the inns, they could hear the wolves howling in the night.

BECAUSE of the Mountain Patrol's new regulations, the mountain inns they stopped at were (so they were told) fuller than usual. Harrier got the opportunity to catch up on all the gossip they'd missed crossing the Plains—and to hear the first news from the East.

"It's going to be the ruin of my master, I assure you." The speaker sounded cheerful, for all that he was prophesying immanent doom. Harrier recognized him, from what others had said, as the Wagonmaster of a westbound train. He eavesdropped shamelessly.

"Ah, Kerreld, you say that every year."

"But Baald, this year it happens to be true! In all my years bringing the early harvest down over the mountain, I have *never* seen the crops in the Dragon's Tail fail so spectacularly! With the drought, no one expected the rice to do well, but then frosts killed most of the *naranjes* and my master hoped that the wheat and the apples would make up for it, though he wouldn't be able to compete in the first markets there, of course. But half the fields of summerwheat didn't even come up, and as for the apples . . . I would be ashamed to feed them to my horses!"

"Your horses are unlikely to be in the markets. People will buy them. If they can afford them."

Harrier heard both men sigh.

"With what I've had to pay for extra guards on my wagons—" Baald said, sighing. "Guards! On the Delfier Road! The price of a bolt of Selken velvet will be triple in Ysterialpoerin what it was last year."

"Triple?" Kerreld said, sounding surprised. "You're gouging them, my friend."

Baald snorted rudely. "Not I, but those Light-blasted Selkens! My factor in Sentarshadeen says the cost at dockside Armethalieh has doubled for Selken wares since the spring. Fewer ships from across the sea are coming into Port. No one knows why, only that the list of Missing Ships is longer than it's ever been. But if the goods aren't there to buy, costs must be passed along."

Kerreld chuckled sourly. "Not that anyone will believe that, when a bushel of apples costs four times what it did last year. My master will be lucky not to spend all his time in Magistrates' Court. Before, of course, he must declare bankruptcy."

Baald clapped Kerreld on the shoulder. "There will still be work for the likes of us. And before you must seek new employment, I believe it is your turn to buy the next round."

The two men moved off, leaving Harrier thinking hard.

Once he would have dismissed the talk of drought and blight out of hand as nothing to do with him. But the talk of the late frost reminded him of the cold back at the Inn of the Three Trees that had nearly killed all of them.

Could this, too, have something to do with magic?

The talk of the missing ships worried him far more, for it touched on something he knew well. Travel across the Deep Ocean was never completely safe, of course, and a ship or two was lost each year or so to storms. But to lose so many that it was actually affecting the price of foreign goods at dockside?

That wasn't natural.

If it was no longer safe to sail to Armethalieh, the Selkens would stop coming. Perhaps they already had. The gossip he'd just heard was at least a couple of moonturns old—the Harbormaster's son certainly knew how long it took a wagonload of freight to go from Armathalieh to Ysterialpoerin as well as he knew his sums and letters.

Harrier sighed, draining his tankard of cider. Should he tell Tiercel about this? Probably not. He'd find out on his own soon enough. And it wasn't as if there were anything either of them could do about it.

ON the far side of the Mystrals, the land was still thickly-forested, and it was easy for Tiercel to imagine the great battles that had taken place here against the forces of the Endarkened. Unlike the west, the east was only lightly-settled; outside of the irregular triangle of land called the Dragon's Tail defined by the eastern three of the Nine Cities, with Ysterialpoerin at its base, Windalorianan to the north, and Deskethomaynel to the south, the land beyond the Mystrals was much as it had been a thousand years ago.

Fortunately for them, their path took them directly through the heart of the settled lands: up the Dragon's Gate Road to Ysterialpoerin.

After that, they would take the Triad Road from Ysterialpoerin toward Windalorianan. In Windalorianan, if the weather held, they could take the Bazrahil Road through the Gatekeeper Pass and head through the mountains toward Pelashia's Veil.

There weren't any maps after that.

TIERCEL hoped that even if he couldn't get more money at the Banking House here, that the remains of their funds would stretch to at least a sennight in Ysterialpoerin. After so many sennights on the road, both they and their animals were tired, and the hardest part of the journey lay ahead. He and Harrier had learned the names and locations of some cheap safe inns that catered to travelers, and he still had a few silver unicorns in his pouch.

But to travel farther would require more than a few silver unicorns. Pack horses, warm clothes, a *lot* of supplies . . . things that would require him not only to draw against his quarterly allowance, but against a portion of his inheritance as well. That had been available to him since his last Naming Day, since Lord Rolfort had felt that Tiercel should be aware of what his position in the City would someday be, and begin to learn to manage his own wealth responsibly. He'd always known that his father could revoke the privilege if he abused it, and he certainly never had. He only hoped that the money was there now.

And that Lord Rolfort simply hadn't sent orders to take anyone into custody who called for it.

There was no way to know in advance.

And as much as he hated the idea of stopping in a city—where any sort of disaster could happen at any moment—Tiercel actually *did* want to consult the Great Library in Ysterialpoerin. Before the Elves had given the city to Men, it had been—so the ancient legends said—the capital of their empire, where all their ancient learning was stored. For a century after the Great Flowering, Elves and Men had lived together, as Elves had taught Mankind the secrets of their ancient learning before withdrawing over the mountains to the east. If there were books from before the Flowering in Armethalieh, there might be more in Ysterialpoerin. Elven books.

Maybe there was some shortcut to the Elven Lands.

He hadn't said anything to Harrier, but whatever the talismans Roneida gave them were for, it didn't seem to have had any real effect on the dream-visions he was having. And now that he suspected the Fire Woman was one of the Endarkened, the dreams were much worse.

It wasn't so much that their content had changed—because it hadn't—but the way he felt about it had.

All his life the Endarkened had been the monsters that the Blessed Saint Idalia and Knight-Mage Kellen, the Poor Orphan Boy, had destroyed to bring about the Great Flowering a millennium ago; nothing scarier than sugar decorations on Festival cakes, or the paper demons in Festival plays. Harmless and kind of exciting. When he'd been a child, Tiercel had played at Knights and Endarkened with his sisters, and of course he'd always made them be the Endarkened.

But now the Endarkened weren't wondertale monsters any more. They were in his dreams. They were *possible*. They might be coming back. If he was guessing right.

He didn't want everything to depend on whether or not he was guessing right. Having the Magegift didn't count. It only made sense that hundreds of people might be born with it every year and just never notice. *He* wouldn't have noticed if he hadn't started messing around with the High Magick, would he? And the Goblins, and the kraken, and the wolves being chased down out of the mountains by *something* . . . that didn't *have* to mean that the Endarkened were somehow being reborn, did it?

*You might be able to fool Harrier with that argument, but you can't fool yourself. If it's not the Endarkened, it's something Dark. And if it's not coming this year, or even this century, it's still coming. And the Fire Woman is definitely part of it.* Who was she summoning? And what was she going to do with him when she got her hands on him? Tiercel had absolutely no idea, except that it was something bad.

What was worse—because the danger was more personal—was that he still had the sense of being *watched*. Whatever was stalking him—for whatever reason—was still out there. It was only a matter of time before it came after him—after both of them—again.

⇜

MIGHT *as well get it over with,* he thought nervously.

The Great Armethalieh Counting House had offices everywhere in the Nine Cities. It held all the wealth of the Nine, and bound them together in a web of commerce and trade.

They'd stopped first to find a lodging for the next few days, and a place to stable their horses. Harrier had paid close attention to the gossip in the inns through the pass, and was able to direct them to one that was both cheap and clean. It was far from quiet, and there was certainly no attached bath, but they were able to wash the worst of their journey-grime from them, and ask directions to the Counting House.

"Are you sure this is the brightest thing you've ever done?" Harrier asked. Tiercel had insisted on going in alone, warning Harrier that he might not be coming out. Though what Harrier could do in that case, other than throw himself on the mercy of the nearest Magistrate, Tiercel wasn't entirely certain.

"We'll be starving in the streets in another sennight if I don't. In a moonturn if we sell the horses, maybe," Tiercel said grimly. "Besides. That's only the worst that could happen."

"My Da would do it," Harrier said, with feeling.

"He'd be afraid you'd buy a ship and turn pirate if you could get your hands on that much money," Tiercel gibed.

"Independent trader," Harrier corrected, with a faint smile. "And you know, I *still* don't see why he took against the idea so."

"You were twelve." Tiercel sighed. "I'm going now."

"Light be with you," Harrier said automatically. "Ah, not that you're going to need it, of course."

Tiercel raised a hand in salute and walked into the building.

ALL of the Counting Houses were built in much the same style. He went first to the desk of the Junior Clerk and identified himself—presenting his signet ring as proof—and signed the book.

From there he was passed to a Senior Clerk—to whom he confided his business—and from there to a Director of the Bank, who took him into an inner office.

"Quite a large withdrawal for a young man such as yourself," Director Bernun said idly. "You are making inroads upon your principal."

It was a master merchant banker's talk, and Tiercel was familiar with it. "I expect to recover from it soon. Meanwhile, I am traveling, and my expenses are heavy."

There was a knock at the door, but it was only a clerk carrying a tray. On it were several bags of coin—the funds Tiercel had requested, and he had specified that most of it should come in small denominations—stars and unicorns—as few folk could make change when confronted with a Golden Sun. But there was a bag of Golden Suns as well.

There were also two thick bundles of wax-sealed parchment. With a thrill of shock, Tiercel recognized his father's seal.

"Letters," Director Bernun said. "For you and a Master Harrier— your traveling companion, I presume. They arrived a moonturn past—by post-rider, so the news from home will be fresh."

"Thank you," Tiercel said. He picked up the two letters and tucked them into his tunic. They were heavy, and thick, and he could not imagine what it must have cost to send them by post-rider all the way from Armethalieh. If they had come a moonturn ago, they must have been written soon after his and Harrier's letters reached Armethalieh. Though the letter was proof of the fact that his father accepted what he was doing, they didn't really make him feel much better.

He tucked the money away into his belt-pouches—it made a heavy load—and thanked Director Bernun once again for his help. He could tell that the man was puzzled by the mystery that he represented but—in the tactful fashion of all good men of business everywhere—Bernun asked no further questions. Still, Tiercel didn't really breathe easier until he was outside once more.

⌘

"LETTERS from home," he said, handing Harrier his as he walked down the steps.

Harrier took it, looking as if he'd rather have been handed a live snake. "My Da wrote me a letter?" he asked.

"Someone using the Harbormaster's Seal did. My father wrote me, too. So we know they got our letters."

Harrier swallowed nervously and made no move to open his letter. "So. Where shall we go now? The Great Library?"

"No."

⌘

"I need to report a death," Tiercel said to the clerk on duty.

"This is the Guildhouse of the Forest Watch, not the City Watch. I can have someone conduct you—" The clerk was about their own age. Like Simera had, he wore the unadorned green leathers of a Student Forester. He regarded Tiercel sympathetically, obviously thinking him some lost visitor to the city.

"She was a Forester. Her name was Simera."

The boy got to his feet. "Please come with me."

He led them further into the building, to another room where a graying bearded Centaur stood behind a high table. He, too, wore the green tunic and tabard of the Forest Watch, but there was an elaborate silver brooch on the shoulder of the tabard.

"These men have come to report the death of a Watchman, Watch Commander Nevus," the boy said.

"Very well," Nevus said, nodding. "I'll take care of it."

The boy bowed and retreated, closing the door to the room behind him.

"It's a hard thing to lose one of our Watchmen. When we do, so often we never hear anything at all. I shall be grateful for all that you can tell me. Were you able to recover his badge?" He tapped the gleaming oval of silver metal on the left breast of his tunic.

Harrier and Tiercel looked at each other.

"I don't think she had one yet," Tiercel said quietly. "She was still an Apprentice. Her name was Simera."

Under Nevus's careful questioning, the story was quickly told. They left out Tiercel's spells, saying only that Simera and Harrier had managed to kill all of the attackers with sword and arrows. It was almost true.

"At Windy Meadows?" Nevus asked.

"A little outside it, I think," Harrier answered. "We might have made it a mile up the road before they took down our pack-pony. But everyone in the town was gone when we arrived there."

"And you say they were . . . Goblins?"

There was a faint note of incredulity in Nevus's voice, though not outright disbelief.

"I'm not completely sure." This time it was Tiercel who spoke. "But we—all—saw them move through the earth as if it were water, and their bite was poisonous. I'd read about Goblins in some old books. The description is pretty close."

Nevus shook his head. "We'll send people to look for her body—and for your Goblins. I'm glad you sent word to Sentarshadeen. We'd had word of what happened in Windy Meadows already. It's not the first isolated hamlet from which everyone has vanished without a trace recently. But this is the first time we've ever had anything approaching witnesses. You were very lucky to have survived."

"We would have been luckier if we'd all survived," Harrier said bleakly.

Nevus sighed. "We cannot choose the hour of our death, only, by the Herdsman's Grace, the manner of it. Simera died in the service and the honor of our Guild, and so she will be remembered. When Passing Court convenes a sennight from now, to honor the names of all those of the Forest Watch who have gone to walk the Herdsman's Path in the last Quarter, Simera's name will be read out. We would be honored if you would attend."

⊰⊱

"I don't like the sound of all this," Harrier said, when they reached the street. "Whole villages vanishing? And—I didn't tell you about this before—Selken ships vanishing, too. I heard a couple of carters gossiping about it in one of the inns we stayed at."

Tiercel simply sighed and shook his head. "Even if we could get a hearing before the Chief Magistrate of the Nine Cities—and she believed us—what could she do? Roneida knows everything I know. She won't just do nothing."

Harrier didn't say anything. Neither of them believed that Roneida had sent them into the Goblins' path at Windy Meadows, but it hadn't seemed very much to Harrier as if Roneida was in any hurry to ring warning alarms about the danger Tiercel had told her about. The more he thought about what she'd said and done during their brief time together, the more he was left with the impression that she thought things were going along just fine. Or if not fine, then at least in the way that they had to go.

And even if he was wrong about that, the last they'd seen of her, she was traveling alone across the Great Plains where they'd seen the Goblins. And if whole villages could just vanish, if he and Tiercel had barely escaped from the Goblins with their lives, even a Wildmage might not be safe. Roneida might not do anything because she might not be alive to do it.

"Where to now?" he said aloud.

"New clothes," Tiercel said decisively. "If I'm going to go to the

Library tomorrow, I'd better not go looking as if I've been on the road for the last several moonturns. And then . . . I suppose we should see what our families have to say."

~≋~

THEY'D put it off for as long as possible. They'd bought clothes—and new boots—and a good hot dinner, and even a jug of cider to take back to their lodgings. But now they couldn't put it off any longer without admitting that they were delaying. By the light of several large and expensive candles (one of Tiercel's purchases) in their rented room, the boys settled on their beds and opened their letters from home.

Harrier puzzled over his father's cramped script—Antarans Gillain had a clerk for when he wanted his documents to be legible, but had obviously written this letter himself. Harrier had expected . . . well, he didn't know *what* he'd expected, but what he got was a dry recitation of news, as matter-of-fact as a report to the City Council.

Brelt was continuing to do well as the Harbormaster-Apprentice (Harrier winced). Brelt's wife, Meroine, was expecting their second child, likely to be a Kindling child, and lucky. Divigana was well, and looking forward to becoming a grandmother yet again. Eugens's wife had been delivered of yet another set of twins, and a new Apprentice had been Bonded to assist him in the Customs House, since he would not have his brother's assistance as he had expected there. Port traffic had been light through the Summer—fewer Selken ships than usual had called, and ships from Serjokka, Averi, and the Jaspan Islands had not called at all, and the rumor was that Armethalieh was being named across the sea as an unsafe destination, so that fewer lands were willing to risk sailing across the ocean to the Great Harbor. The roster of Missing and Overdue Ships was longer than Antarans had ever seen it—longer, indeed, than it had ever been in his father's time, or his grandsire's time, and several Coastal Patrol ships had gone missing. . . .

Reading on through the dry recitation of events and family news, Harrier realized that if he was expecting his father to write directly about what he had said in his letter: that he was following Tiercel to the end of the world, and he had no idea when—or even if—he'd be back, he would probably wait in vain. They'd never spoken outright about the important things in life. His father had simply expected Harrier to do his duty, just as every generation of the Gillains back to the Founding of the City had.

And Harrier realized, with a lump in his throat, that this was his father's way of telling him that his choice was all right. Letters cost money. His father hadn't had to write at all, much less to go on for page after page about just the same things that he would have if Harrier had been standing right beside him on the docks at home. He didn't know what place there would be for him at the Port if—when—he returned, or even if he wanted one, but he was sure—now—that there would always be a place for him at his family's table.

At the bottom of the last page there were a few lines in his mother's flowing ornate hand: *We love you. We miss you. Stay safe, and come home as soon as you can. All my love, and all your father's love as well.*

Harrier never doubted it for an instant.

⋙

*"MY dear son Tiercel,"* (he read) *"Your mother and sisters and I are grateful to hear that you are alive and well, as it has been some time since the letter with your rather surprising news came from Sentarshadeen. You will understand that the information which you have chosen to impart to us comes as something of a shock, especially considering that the genesis*

*of these events lies so many moonturns in the past, at a time when you
still possessed the full resources of your family to draw upon—"*

Tiercel sighed, looking away from the letter. He knew that the
full disclosure of, well, *everything*, had to have hurt his parents
deeply. Both the thought that he'd kept secrets from them, and the
thought that he hadn't turned to them for help. He sighed again.
He only wished they *could* have helped.

*"I appreciate your deep confusion at that time, and from your own
account you acted with great level-headedness, seeking counsel from
Healers and Preceptors both, in addition to doing extensive historical research. While I certainly do not endorse your decision to pursue your ob-
jective in secrecy, still less to involve Harrier Gillain in a course of action
that involved lying to his parents—though I quite understand that your
original intention was to have gone to Sentarshadeen and returned with
no one being the wiser about any of this—it is entirely possible that, faced
with the choices and decisions that you were faced with, my own re-
sponses would have been similar to your own. It is a very grave quandary
which you face: not only what to do, but how to do it, and the knowledge
that, if you succeed, you will inevitably take your place upon the wider
stage of History, for good or ill. This, alone, is hardly a small matter to
consider, and considering the nature of the danger that you face, I know
you must be very frightened right now."*

Tiercel blinked hard. He *wouldn't* cry—not with Harrier right
across the room from him. But he'd never felt more like doing so in
longer than he could remember. He *was* frightened—and he'd been
so scared for so long he almost didn't notice it any more. He was
gladder than ever that he hadn't told his parents about the Goblins.
And he was more grateful than he could have imagined for his father's understanding—even if it *did* come wrapped in a gentle scold.
It was one he deserved, anyway. If he'd known back at the very beginning what was going to happen later, while he still might have
concealed the truth from his parents, he wouldn't have told it to

Harrier either. He would have gone to Sentarshadeen—and beyond—alone.

And died on the road half-a-dozen times, he realized somberly. If not for Harrier and Simera, he'd never have gotten even this far.

*"I can only hope that this letter reaches you. You are somewhere where I cannot protect you, in a place where I cannot even help you. I know I've rarely discussed my work with you, but should it become useful or necessary to you, you should be aware that I have performed a number of significant services for Chief Magistrate Vaunnel in times past, which she will be more than willing to return, and her word is not without weight in any of the Nine Cities. While you are entirely aware that I detest the far-too-pervasive custom of trading upon favors and influence instead of permitting Law and Justice to have their way, I believe that your cause is one that merits extraordinary measures, and I know that you will not use her name, nor such influence as I possess with her, lightly, nor except at sufficient need. I believe that over the years you have given me sufficient cause to trust your judgment, my son, and though I could wish that I did not have such great need to place such faith in it now, you have all my confidence, and all my love."*

Now the tears *did* well up, and Tiercel scrubbed angrily at his eyes with the sleeve of his tunic. But they weren't unmixed with shock. Chief Magistrate Vaunnel was not only the Chief Magistrate of Armethalieh, she was first among the nine Chief Magistrates who ruled over the Nine Cities. He'd always known that his father had an important place in the running of the City, but the idea that he, Tiercel, could expect favors from Chief Magistrate Vaunnel was almost as stunning as discovering he had the Magegift. He only hoped he was never in a situation where he needed to call upon them.

*"Your mother, naturally, is greatly distressed at both your departure and your absence, and fears for your health. I have reassured her that you have never come to any fatal harm while in young Harrier's company,*

*and though I would hardly say anything of the sort to his parents, I am greatly reassured that he is with you. Your sisters are also well. I have told them that you have gone upon an extended journey at the advice of a Wildmage—as you may certainly imagine, Brodana and Doreses are heartbroken that they did not get to go with you, and Hevnade and Katona hope that you will have the opportunity to do some shopping along the way—though Hevnade hopes for interesting examples of what she calls 'tribal weavings' and Katona, as always, hopes for new books."*

Tiercel had to smile at that, imagining his little sisters—though Hevnade, at fourteen, was not so very little—all thinking of this as nothing more than a lengthy pleasure-trip. He thought of what it must have cost his parents, through all the long moonturns of worrying about him, to give the impression that all was more-or-less well, and sighed heavily. He loved his family so much! And while he wasn't really sure if he'd even see them again, the very least he owed them was to do his best to solve this . . . problem.

There was very little more of the letter.

*"We shall all miss you this Wintertide, and offer daily prayers to the Light for the safe return of you and Harrier. Your loving father, Barover, Lord Rolfort."*

He took a deep breath. "I miss them," he said.

"Yeah," Harrier said raggedly. "My Da . . . well, he *would* send his best if he'd mentioned you at all. But you know."

"Yeah," Tiercel said. "Hevnade wants me to go shopping."

Harrier snorted rudely. "Oh, like *that's* going to happen. Unless she wants a new stormcloak and new boots—or maybe a pack mule. Pass me the cider jug."

"Get it yourself, it's on your side of the room," Tiercel said heartlessly.

"By less than a handspan. And I carried it here."

"So you've got plenty of practice at lifting it."

Seeing he wasn't going to get his way, Harrier got to his feet, grumbling, and picked up the cider jug. They'd rented a ewer and cups along with the room, and he poured both cups full, handing one to Tiercel.

"So. What shall we do tomorrow?" he said. The subject of home and families was too painful to talk about, and Harrier was good at avoiding subjects he didn't want to talk about. For once, Tiercel was grateful.

"The Library," he said decisively.

〜

BUT to Tiercel's frustration and dismay, he was unable to do what he had hoped to do at the Great Library at Ysterialpoerin.

Certainly the Great Library had an extensive collection of pre-Flowering books. Scholars traveled from all the Nine Cities to consult them. The librarians he spoke to were happy to tell him this much, and even show him the room in which some of the books were kept, row upon row of books in tall glass-fronted cabinets.

But he'd been allowed into the closed stacks in Armethalieh because of his long friendship with the Chief Librarian, and he had no such friendships to ease his way here. Master Librarian Numus kindly explained to Tiercel that such ancient and valuable books could only be made available to trained scholars. He did *not* say that they could not be pawed by scruffy young students on holiday, because he was a kind and patient man, but Tiercel knew perfectly well what he looked like, even in newly-bought travel clothes. Even if he had been wearing his Light-day finest, it would have been difficult to persuade a stranger that a youngster without any formal credentials should be allowed to handle books dozens of centuries old, especially when he could give no good reason for wishing to do so.

He thought about what his father had said in his letter, and he hesitated. He really wanted to see those books. But deep in his heart, he didn't think that something like this was what his father had meant. His life wasn't in danger, and neither was Harrier's. The books would be helpful, but they weren't vital.

So he said nothing, and left.

"IT was a good try," Harrier said consolingly, as they walked down the Library steps. They'd spent the first part of the day on more errands—with money in hand, they'd moved their mounts to better stabling, in a place where they could be turned out to graze for most of the day, as well as treating themselves to a long session at one of the city's many bathhouses. Tiercel had only arrived at the Great Library of Ysterialpoerin in the afternoon, and even without succeeding in his errand, had spent several hours there. By now it was evening, and their minds were turning toward dinner. The hostel they were staying at did not have a kitchen, but there were many cheap eating places in Ysterialpoerin, and a list of those nearest to their accommodations was posted in the hostel's common room. After so long on the road, every meal they didn't have to cook themselves was a luxury.

"I should have known it wouldn't work," Tiercel grumbled.

"You never know until you try. And . . . couldn't you have put a spell on him to make him do what you want, or something?"

"Maybe. If I knew what I was doing. But if I knew how to do something like that already, we wouldn't have to go find the Elves, now, would we, Har?"

"That's a point."

"And I'm not sure it would be right."

"What?"

"To use magic to get what I want. It doesn't seem as if it would be fair."

"But you don't just want it. You need it. And it's important."

Tiercel frowned. "I'll have to think about that."

"It's not like you won't have time. Because you *can't* cast a spell that would get you in there, so you can think about whether you *would* have done it all you like."

Because it was true, Tiercel shoved him. Harrier shoved him back, and a short scuffle broke out. It continued as they moved up the street—neither looking where he was going—as they worked off some of the tension of the unpleasant events of the past days.

"Hey! Watch where you're going, street rats!"

Harrier's last enthusiastic shove had propelled Tiercel directly into the path of a very large stranger.

He was obviously a person of consequence—his clothing alone told Tiercel that—as well as the fact that he was on the street with half a dozen servants in household livery. On second glance, seeing that he wore a household badge on his own cloak, Tiercel decided that he must be the Chief Steward of some noble household in the city. Such men could often be more arrogant than the nobles they served.

"I'm very sorry, goodsir," Tiercel said, stepping back. But the stranger had grabbed his arm and was shaking it violently.

"Don't you know to give way to your betters? I should give you a sound thrashing!"

"Get your hands off him!" Harrier jumped forward and yanked Tiercel out of the stranger's bruising grasp, but when he did, the stranger's servants stepped forward, obviously eager for trouble.

Tiercel shrugged Harrier off quickly. He faced the stranger and bowed. "Once again, my deepest apologies, goodsir. We are strangers to your city, and were not watching our steps. We very much regret all the trouble and inconvenience we have caused you with our hasty and ill-considered brawling."

"As well you should," the stranger growled, though it was obvious he was somewhat mollified by Tiercel's humble words. "Strangers here?"

"We come from Armethalieh, goodsir," Tiercel said, bowing again.

"You've come a long way to make trouble. Family cast you out, I don't doubt. Well, I'll let it go this time. But cross my path again and I'll give you a hiding you'll remember for the rest of your days."

"Yes, goodsir. Thank you, goodsir," Tiercel said, bowing again and stepping back toward the wall.

⤙⤚

"YOU didn't even tell him who you were!" Harrier said, outraged.

"The point was to avoid a fight, not start one," Tiercel said patiently.

"He wanted to hit you!" Harrier sputtered.

"But he wouldn't. Then he'd have to explain to Lord Whoever why it was that *he* was fighting in the Library Plaza. He just wanted me to bow to him. So I did. Problem solved."

"I will never understand you."

"Just as long as you find us something to eat. I'm starving."

The two boys set off once again in the direction of a cookshop they remembered from the morning, where the food was both cheap and plentiful.

⤙⤚

"ARE you sure it's this way, Har?"

"I thought it was."

The sun had set while they'd been walking back in the direction of their lodgings, and the lamps made all the streets look different than they had when they'd set out for the Library in the early afternoon. The two of them realized that they were not only completely lost, but completely lost in a part of Ysterialpoerin where—

from the look of things—it would not be a good idea to stop and ask for directions.

Garbage clogged the drainage gutter running down the center of the narrow street, and rats scuttled through the piles of refuse that lay heaped in drifts along the walls. All of the windows that they saw were barred and shuttered, and the shutters themselves were chipped and battered.

Neither boy was entirely certain of how they'd ended up in this narrow maze of twisting alleyways when they'd been walking down a pleasant—though shabby—merchant street a moment or two before. They'd been on a street that sold books. . . .

"I'd better look at the map," Tiercel said, reaching into the pocket in his cloak.

Harrier looked around. It was already so dark that they could barely make out each other's faces, let alone the fine print and finer lines on the street map Tiercel had bought that morning. The walls of the alley hadn't been whitewashed in living memory, and there weren't any lanterns—even at the intersections—rendering their surroundings even gloomier. And of course, *they* didn't have a lantern. They'd been sure they'd be back at their lodgings before it got dark.

Abruptly Harrier realized what Tiercel was about to do.

"Tyr, I'm really not sure it'd be a good idea to do that glowy thing right now," Harrier said. Tiercel still hadn't figured out how to make the globes of MageLight he could create go away.

"Well, without it we aren't going to be able to see," Tiercel answered, lowering his hand. He sounded irritated. "Find me something to cast it on, then, and I'll use that. We can at least hide it, or stuff it under our cloaks, or something."

Harrier *really* didn't want to go poking around in the trash-heaps at the edges of the alley, but fortunately somebody had dumped the broken remains of an old chair among the debris. He pulled it cautiously free of its pile of garbage and was starting to pull it apart in order to get a handy length of wood when he heard the sound of many pairs of feet coming toward them. Torches flickered on the walls of the intersection at the end of the alley.

"Come out, street rats! It's time to take your thrashing!" an oddly familiar voice bellowed. After a moment, Harrier recognized it as the stranger they'd bumped into in front of the library. He stared at the advancing torchlight, more in disbelief than in any recognition of possible personal danger. How had the stranger found them? And why had he bothered? As he was still staring at the light, Tiercel ran forward, grabbed his arm, and dragged him back up the alley in the other direction.

"I will find you!" the voice bellowed from behind them.

THEY no longer concerned themselves with trying to find their way out of whatever part of Ysterialpoerin they were lost in. All Tiercel cared about now was staying away from the creature that pursued them. He was sure it was the same creature that he'd met before, on the High Plains; whether it had also been the steward he'd bumped into outside the library, he wasn't sure.

It didn't matter.

Whether due to the stranger's magic, or simply because the people who lived in this district, being no strangers to violence, knew enough to avoid it whenever possible, the alleys and backstreets down which they fled were completely deserted, despite the early hour. Tiercel and Harrier knew they were probably running in circles—they had to be; if they'd been running in a straight line they'd undoubtedly have reached one of the main streets by now. Even the few tiny shops that they passed were barred and shuttered, their windows dark.

❧

"WE should stand and fight," Harrier growled.

Both boys were sweaty and out of breath. It didn't matter how fast they ran, or how far—and by now they were feeling their way through total darkness, as the last light had faded from the evening sky—every time they stopped to catch their breath, they heard the taunting voice of their pursuer half a street behind them, and the chase was on once more.

"And get killed?" Tiercel panted. "We don't know how many people he has with him."

"Okay. *I* should stand and fight. You should keep running," Harrier amended.

"That's not any better," Tiercel said.

"Those seem to be our only choices."

They saw the glare of torches behind them and staggered off down the alley once more.

❧

"WE should have turned back there," Tiercel said with resignation.

"It's a dead end," Harrier snarled, kicking the wall.

Tiercel spread his hands, and the air between them began to glow.

"Don't *do* that!" Harrier said, automatically.

"If I'm going to die, I want to see who's responsible," Tiercel said. The small ball of MageLight hovered for a moment, then rose up to hover several feet above his head.

The alley was narrow, barely ten feet wide. Decaying garbage heaped the three walls of the dead end, its scent sickeningly sweet even in the cool night air. Buildings rose up five stories high on all three sides, but there were no windows within their reach. The ancient brick was crumbling and irregular, but not uneven enough to give enough purchase for climbing.

There was nothing anywhere within reach that could possibly

be used as a weapon. Neither boy was carrying anything more threatening than their eating knives.

They waited in silence, panting, hearts hammering.

Nothing happened.

Their pursuer didn't arrive.

"YOU know," Harrier said after several minutes, "none of this makes any sense. Why chase us around this Dark-damned rabbit warren for an entire bell and then—when he's got us cornered—*not* come finish us off?"

"Yes," Tiercel said.

"'Yes' is the answer?"

"It's a riddle. It's not a 'he,' Harrier, it's an 'it.' Something that isn't human. It doesn't think like a human being. When it came after us—me—on the Plains, it didn't act human at all. I think it's learning about . . . us."

"About you, you mean," Harrier said with sudden insight. "It wanted to see what you'd do when you thought it was going to kill you. I don't see why it bothered. It already sent the Goblins after us."

"No," Tiercel said slowly. "I think that's something else doing that. And I think this—whatever it is—is testing me."

"Well . . . did you pass?" Harrier asked, still looking up the alleyway.

"I have no idea," Tiercel answered. "Maybe I was supposed to confront it instead of running away from it. Try to set it on fire or something. But I can't see how that could possibly have been a good idea."

"Probably not," Harrier said with a sigh. "We're still lost, though," he said after a moment.

"Not if this map is at all accurate," Tiercel said with a faint grin, reaching into his cloak pocket once again.

◈

ONCE they were no longer being hunted, and with Tiercel's map to guide them, it took them only a few minutes to work their way out of the twisting maze of alleys they'd been lost in and back out onto one of the main streets. As soon as they could see the glow of street lamps in the distance, Tiercel sent the globe of MageLight to go sailing up into the sky. He had no idea what would happen to it, or if it would just keep rising forever, but until he could figure out how to unmake the things he could so easily make, it was a simpler solution than just having the blue balls of light follow him around eternally.

They came out very near to the place where they'd gone in, back on the street of the booksellers. Though it was fully dark—and had been for some time—the street was well-lit by hanging lanterns, and filled with pedestrians, mainly students from the university. After their recent narrow escape, even Tiercel wasn't tempted to linger, and with the aid of their streetmap they made their way to the main thoroughfare that had been their original destination.

After a late—and on Harrier's part, much-appreciated—dinner at a cookshop, they returned to their lodgings to plan what to do next.

◈

"WE can't stay here," Tiercel said, pacing the small room. "Now that it's found us, who knows what it'll do next?"

"We can't just pack up and leave in the middle of the night. For that matter, the horses could use a good sennight's rest before we set out again. And we haven't even started buying supplies yet. There are towns between here and Windalorianan, sure, but if we want to get a good price—"

"No. I've been thinking. The Dragon's Tail is pretty heavily settled. There will be inns all the way up the road, and no real place to get away from people anyway even if we *do* camp in someone's field. Let's sell the mule here, and buy supplies for over the Bazrahils in Windalorianan when we get there. It will be faster."

"You're sure?"

Tiercel nodded.

"All right. We can sell the mule tomorrow down at the horse market. But it's not going to get us out of here any faster, because the horses still need to rest and fatten up before we head out again."

"I want to leave tomorrow."

"Without me, then. I'm not walking to Windalorianan when Lightning goes lame. They both need to be re-shod, too, and that means finding a farrier, and—"

"What if something happens because we stay here?" Tiercel demanded edgily. "Ysterialpoerin is almost the size of Armethalieh!"

"And has Magistrates, the City Watch, the Fire Watch, a detachment of the Militia—maybe there are even Wildmages here. You can't be responsible for everything that happens in the world, Tyr." Harrier watched Tiercel pace their tiny room, knowing it would take force to make him stop.

"I can when it's my fault."

"You said it wasn't your fault that the Dark was coming back."

Tiercel made a sound of frustrated exasperation and flung himself face-down on his bed.

Harrier leaned against the door, as much to keep Tiercel from rushing out through it as to keep out of Tiercel's way. His sword lay on top of his bed. He could have brought it with him when they'd gone out earlier, but he hadn't thought of it. Why go armed in a civilized place like Ysterialpoerin?

From now on, he didn't care *how* civilized a place seemed—or whether or not he really knew how to use a sword. He was taking it with him everywhere.

The trouble was, Tiercel had a point. Harrier fingered the Wild-mage talisman around his neck, thinking it hadn't been much help this evening. Something was still after Tiercel, and he had no more de-sire than Tiercel did to see innocent people harmed simply because they were in the way when whatever was chasing Tiercel came after him again. But at the same time, the two of them had been traveling fast and hard for sennights, and they needed to stop and rest as much as the horses did. Maybe they were safer in a big city than a small village.

And maybe not.

There was no way of knowing.

AFTER he had dispatched the echo of the Firecrown to its work, moonturns passed as Bisochim devoted himself entirely to his work. In its way, it was a task as subtle as wakening the desert to life in his old stronghold had been: water was life, but too much water, too soon, would have destroyed the life he sought to nurture there. And what he sought, above all, was Balance, not destruction. Above all things, he wished to avoid that which he saw in his vision: the clashing of armies, and war.

But the Light was powerful, and relentless. And the closer he came to success, the more possible it was that one of the Enemy might seek him out.

The voices in the fire were stronger now, urging him to take every care—not only for himself, but for the people he had sworn his oaths upon the Three Books to protect. It was the voices' care for the Isvaieni that convinced Bisochim, once again, that what he was doing was right, for if they were truly no part of the Balance, they would hardly have urged him to a course of action that went so much against his solitary nature. But he knew they were right. The people of the Isvai must be protected, if there were any chance they were in danger.

He must know.

Once again he went down into the deep rock, to his scrying chamber, to the still black pool, and cast bonemeal and blood upon the water.

Once again the vision had not changed, though the Firecrown had walked the world for almost a season now. His enemies had grown beyond its powers, or there were too many. Perhaps it could destroy them all with time, but the compassion the Fire had taught him urged him not to gamble with the lives under his care.

He must defend the Isvaieni against the Light.

Light . . . such a positive word. Light was always good, was it not? But a child of the desert knew that Light was not always good. Light killed. Light sterilized. Light blinded.

And the Light was doing all those things now. Eventually, there would be nothing left but Light. The Light surely recognized what he was doing by now, and would be working to destroy him, destroy Saravasse. Eventually an army would come here, led by the champions of the Light.

In ancient times, armies had been mustered against peril, danger had been recognized, only at the eleventh hour, and so countless lives had been lost that could have been saved. He saw the danger now, long in advance. He would go out among the tribes and bring them to him, deep in the Barahileth, where they would be safe. He would create a paradise for them with his magic, here at the edge of the Lake of Fire. He would turn the desert into a garden. There would be peace and plenty for all.

But he must get them here first.

They would not come merely for his word, not if he told them he was bringing them here to keep them safe. The desert honed its people, burned away all that was not hard and lean and sharp. Desert people were steel forged in the fires of extremity. They did not flee from battle. If he told them that an army marched upon the Isvai, they would unite as he wished, true. But only as a prelude to war. The people of the Isvai lacked only a purpose to become the greatest army the world had ever known.

Very well. He would go among them speaking of war and battle, of fire and the sword. He would promise them death and enemies, and if only he knew that his greater purpose was to save them from both of these things, a small deception did not matter. All would become clear to them in time. Let them gird for battle. If the only way to unify them and lead them to where he needed them to be was for such a purpose, he could give them that purpose.

He *would* give them that purpose.

It was his destiny.

SHAIARA, Darak's only living child, might have inherited her father's staff of leadership at his death, but she would not have kept it if she had not been worthy of it. Though she had become their leader when she was barely a woman grown, she had led the Nalzandar Isvaieni for the past two years as ably as ever he had, and theirs was a way hard even by the hard standards of the desert, for her tribe lived by hunting. *Only* by hunting. They kept no herds, and only the few *shotors* needed to pack the tribe's tents and supplies. They tended no gardens. They settled in no place for longer than a hand of days, because to do so would deplete the game and upset the Balance. They traded what they had in abundance—hides, green-cured in the sun—for what they did not make for themselves. Their diet was meat, a little grain, the few greens and bitter fruits that could be found growing wild. They drank only water; a child could grow to old age without so much as tasting anything sweet. They were hard, lean, bronze. A silent people by nature, more attuned to listening than to speaking, they were set apart by their silence at the yearly Gathering of the Tribes. For that reason, they tended to avoid the other tribes. Shaiara was their emissary. She did the trading, the negotiations for spouses, the needful interaction with those not of the Nalzandar who, to her peoples' eyes, were as soft and alien as the city-dwellers of whom Shaiara had heard but never seen. And though it was that a lone traveler in the Madiran was always viewed with suspicion, all knew the ways of the Nalzandar, and it was a saying oft-repeated in the Isvai: "if one rides alone, that one is Nalzandar."

So it was that Shaiara rode out alone one morning in the cold, grey light of desert dawn, toward an oasis a few hours away. The *shotor* beneath her was swift and strong, for her tribe bred the hardiest beasts in the desert, and she led a pack-*shotor* burdened with a tall stack of stiff, clattering hides. If there was not a tribe at Sapthiruk Oasis when she came, she would wait, for she was patient, as a hunter must be, and she meant to find a buyer willing to trade for the hides she carried with woven robes and desert cloaks. Such things were expensive . . . but these were no ordinary hides. The stacks bound to the back and sides of the *shotor* bore soft fur of russet and honey, the colors of the desert sunset. This was the fruit of three seasons of hunting, the hides of the elusive *feneric*, a carnivore the size of an *ikulas*-hound, whose fur was much prized by tribesmen and city-dwellers alike for its softness and colors.

But as she neared Sapthiruk, she immediately knew that something was . . . off.

It was signaled at first by the unwonted growth of vegetation, long before the oasis itself was in view. There was grass here. Grass! Oh not, perhaps, the sort of thing that a city-dweller would have thought of as grass . . . not a lush meadow, nor rolling turf. This was desert grass, gray-green and growing in tufts. But it should not have been here at all.

And there were herds grazing here. Not just a few, but . . . many. As many as if it were a Gathering of the Tribes, though this was neither the time nor the place for that.

Shaiara's eyes narrowed, and she tucked the scarf that covered her mouth and nose against the blowing sand a little tighter into her headband. Suddenly, she did not want to be recognized as anything but one of the Nalzandar. Not as herself. Not as Shaiara. She did not know why in the front of her mind, but in the back of her mind, the instinct of the hunter was warning her.

The nearer she drew to the oasis, the less she liked what she saw. Too much grass, and the trees were in bloom, all out of season.

Then—long before she was ready to see it—she saw the verdancy of the oasis itself. A garden, a haven from the sun. Young trees. Moisture softening the air. And it was all too soon, she was nowhere near to the wellhead, and even if she had been, that well could not possibly be producing the amount of water it took to tend growth like this.

That was bad enough. Worse was the sheer number of people; all of them were Isvaieni, of course, but—this was not the day of the gathering of the Clans. . . .

She dismounted, and continued on foot, leading the two *shotors*. Listening. Observing.

There was roast goat over every fire—and sheep, too—as if this were a great feast-day. Jars of date-wine uncorked at midday, and strong *kaffeyeh* brewing in open pans. Her eyes widened in shock as she saw a great pool of open water in the distance, surrounded by tall trees and greenery. She stopped and drew a deep breath. The very air was wet.

Unnatural.

People spoke to her as she passed, but there were things that were notably absent from the brief exchanges. Though they recognized that she was Nalzandar by her robes, they were not, and they could see from the pack-*shotor* that she led that she had come here to trade. Yet no one tried to draw her into any casual conversations, there were no friendly interchanges. It was as if all the world had suddenly become Nalzandar, and that was not right.

Instead, and she was glad she had left her scarf over her face when she first heard this, there was much talk, with gleaming eyes and absolute sincerity, of how the Balance was out of true and all the world was rushing headlong to destruction and war.

Now if there was ever a people in the world that understood the Balance, it was the Nalzandar. They more than lived by the Balance, they *kept* the Balance, and it was only by careful observation of the Balance that they were able to survive in the harsh depths of the Isvai. These people, these folk who *looked* like her own, were speaking utter madness.

Worse still, it was clear, the further into the center of the oasis that Shaiara came, that they were preparing for war. That alone would have shocked her senseless, had she not already been beyond shock. War? There had been no war in the world since the time of the Great Flowering. With whom would they make war? The Peoples of the North kept to their places in the Great Cold, beyond the Armen Plains; the city-dwellers kept to their cities at the edge of the Madiran; and the peoples of the Isvai had no energy to spend on anything but survival.

She tethered her *shotors* in the picket lines, and, taking one of the hides as a sample, went to find a trading-partner for what she had brought. Her mouth was set in a hard, grim line beneath her scarf as she walked through the sprawling camp, hearing nothing but talk of the glory of the battle to come. It took her far longer than it ordinarily would have to find anyone interested in trading at all—though trade was as necessary as water in the deep desert—and when she did, Shaiara made the most perfunctory of bargains, letting the *feneric*-skins go with only the bare minimum of haggling. And it was another indication of how very out-of-true things were that the one with whom she bargained did not think it odd that she cut the bargaining short, and did not stay to accept either the customary meal that closed a trade or even a cup of *kaffeyeh*.

Her buyer came and collected his purchase, and she loaded her *shotor* with the robes and cloaks for which she had traded, lashing the pack down tightly. Her business at Sapthiruk Oasis was concluded, but even though her skin crawled and her heart demanded urgently that she leave this place, Shaiara dared not. Not until she had found out everything there was to learn. Not until she knew what was the cause of this madness.

She was a hunter, a Hunter's Hunter, one of the most skilled of her tribe. The Master-hunters of other tribes were as babes to the hunters of her people. Those other hunters read tracks on the sand. Her people read tracks on the wind. And she could read the fading memory of tracks.

Those other hunters forgot to use their skills once back among the tents. Shaiara never forgot and she used them now.

She kept the skin around her eyes relaxed, so as not to reveal her tension or her inner thoughts. She changed the folds of her robes, so she did not look—now—as if she were Nalzandar. She walked with purpose, as if she had a place to be and knew exactly where it was, even though she had no idea of what she was looking for. And she never walked alone. Always she moved with a small group; not so near as to make them pause to look at her and recognize her as a stranger, but near enough to seem a part of them.

She examined everything while seeming to look at nothing; listened to everything while appearing to be paying heed only to the conversation of those she was "with."

Finally she came to the shores of the strange unnatural pool of water at the heart of Sapthiruk Oasis, and there, sitting beneath a tent-awning and surrounded by a large crowd of spellbound listeners, she found the source of the madness, wrapped in robes of morning blue. And in a way, she had almost expected to find this man here, yet it was a shock, a mental blow that left her with the sense of having the ground drop out from under her.

Because she knew this man, both by reputation and by sight. This was one of the most respected and honored Wildmages to be found among the tribes.

This was Bisochim.

But the words coming from his mouth were a blasphemy against everything that the Wildmages stood for.

She worked her way through to the front of the crowd—carefully—and stood and listened, knowing she would have no second chance at this. She must learn everything she could. She could not have come at a more opportune time for this; Bisochim sat among the tribal leaders of half-a-dozen tribes—strong, wise, prudent men; men who had led their tribes safely through all the dangers the Isvai could offer since before Shaiara had first seen the light of day. He smiled upon them as she had never seen him smile before—though he had come, twice, to the tents of the Nalzandar Isvaieni—bending all the power of his mind on them, laying out the impossible before them in such sweet and reasoned words that they were nodding in agreement like children. But Shaiara, who was under no such pressure of regard, could see it as impossible even as the others were seduced.

"The Balance of the world is out of true," said Bisochim. "It has been since the Great Flowering, and has been tipping more and more ever since, and now the Wild Magic is attempting to restore that Balance—here, in the Isvai, where the Balance has always been kept purely. But there are always those who would seek to be enemies of the True Balance, the proper Balance as it was in ancient times, and even now those forces are gathering a great army in a place of darkness and cold, to invade our homeland and destroy our one hope of success, and freedom. They would place all the free people of the desert into chains more heinous than those we had escaped a thousand years ago. But together we can withstand them. I have prepared a place for you, where we all may go, to await the day when we may scour them from the desert sands as the Sandwind scours, and the True Balance will triumph once more!"

The trouble was, without Bisochim's attention on her, Shaiara knew very well that all of this was specious, if not deceptive. The Balance was not out of true. The Great Flowering had restored it, not destroyed it. Bisochim spoke of the world as if it were all now one thing or the other, and Shaiara knew that it was not. There was illness, injury, men still oppressed and persecuted their fellows—yet there was joy, and love, and the freedom of life between Sand and Star to balance those things.

How could a Wildmage—of all people—speak so?

Then Bisochim flattered his visitors. He told them how they were the only creatures in the world who could possibly hear the truth in his words—not the city-dwellers, and still less the Peoples of the North. And it was for that reason that they, and only they, were in danger and must defend themselves when the time came. They must set aside the small differences between tribe and tribe. They must all gather together, in the name of the True Balance, though the road would be as long and as hard for them as it had once been for Kellen the Poor Orphan Boy and the Blessed Saint Idalia. They had but to trust in him, for he knew the way of the True Balance, and he would lead them to victory.

And even as Shaiara listened, and knew that what he was saying was utter madness, his words began to sound . . . reasonable.

And that was when she knew that she had heard enough.

She eased out of the respectful crowd around Bisochim and made her way back to the picket line. There she took her *shotors* and rode, as hard and as fast as she had ever pushed a *shotor*, back to the tents of her people.

Kamar was waiting before her tent, to take her *shotor's* lead-rope and to welcome her home. He was her father's brother, and he had been the first to say that she must follow Darak as the leader of the Nalzandar. He knew instantly that all was not well with her, and his smile of greeting turned to a frown of astonishment, even as the rest of the Nalzandar began to come forth from their tents.

As her *shotor* knelt, she flung herself from its back into the silent welcome of her tribe. But what she had to tell them turned welcome into astonishment.

"Strike the tents," she said abruptly. "We are leaving."

"Why?" Kamar demanded, speaking for them all.

"There is an infection of madness, and it is being spread by Bisochim. He is a Wildmage no more. I think—" She hesitated, and then simply told the truth. "I think he has been Shadow-touched. He is taking the tribes to war." She gritted her teeth. "But it is a war we will have no part of. Pack the tents. I am taking us to where not even our own people will find us. Unless we want to be found, or unless the Wild Magic grants them a miracle."

*And I do not think it will, for I think the Wild Magic has no part in this.*

⁓

HE was dreaming.

Normally Harrier didn't remember his dreams at all after he'd had them, much less *while* he was having them. But right now he knew, just as clearly as if he were back in school hearing his lessons, that he was asleep and dreaming, and that none of this was really happening.

Yet in another way, he knew that it was.

He was faintly indignant that the first dream he'd ever actually managed to notice was so, well, *boring.* All he was doing was standing in a cave. And while he'd never actually been in a cave before, he'd seen a lot of pictures of caves during his school years. When Tiercel had been twelve, he'd spent three entire moonturns completely obsessed with caves. Harrier had learned more about caves than he ever wanted to know then. This was definitely a cave.

It was certainly the largest cave that Harrier could imagine seeing. The cavern he was standing in was as large as the Great Temple of the Light back home. Pale stone icicles hung from the ceiling and rose up from the floor, and the curved walls were banded in all the colors of the sunset. In the distance, he could hear water rushing.

Caves were supposed to be dark, though this one wasn't. Maybe Tiercel was lighting it, Harrier thought vaguely. Harrier was somehow certain that Tiercel was here with him, even though he couldn't see him anywhere.

There was something important about this particular cave, too, although he couldn't imagine what it could be. Elves didn't live in caves, he didn't think, and the only important thing right now was getting to the Land of the Elves. Besides, none of this could be something important for *him*. He was only along on this journey because he was keeping Tiercel out of trouble. That was why he'd come with Tiercel in the first place. Even after everything they'd found out, well, it wasn't as if he were a High Mage or having visions or anything. He was the son of the Harbormaster of Armethalieh. He was supposed to be at home right now starting his Apprenticeship, not off on the other side of the world trying to understand something that even Wildmages couldn't explain.

But here he was, in this cave. Well, not actually *in* the cave. *Dreaming* about being in a cave, for some reason.

And somebody was calling him. . . .

# Eleven

# The Caves of Imrathalion

ARRIER WAS AWAKENED early the next morning by a loud argument in the room next door, and by the time he was fully awake, he'd forgotten entirely about his dream.

THE horse-market in Ysterialpoerin was larger than the one in Sentarshadeen, bustling and filled with color and smells. They'd been to the edge of it yesterday, when they'd found long-term stabling for the mule and their horses, but the market itself was enormous and they hadn't spent much time here. Now they were back to seek out a farrier and a place to sell the mule—and to decide what, if anything, they would want to buy in the way of new saddles and packs.

The horse-market was filled with the smell of horses, of course, but also with the smell of grain, hay, and other feeds, of liniments and medicines, of leather and leather-dressings. Every possible item that could be used on, with, or around a horse was sold in the Ysterialpoerin horse-market, from saddles to plows to every kind of cart and carriage imaginable. Tiercel told him that farming was centralized here in the Dragon's Tail and that was why this horse-market was larger than the last one they'd seen; Harrier told Tiercel that he didn't care.

It seemed to Harrier that the horses came in nearly as many shapes and sizes as the carriages did. He'd seen only a small part of the Sentarshadeen horse-market, since he and Tiercel had only been looking for riding horses there, and besides, they had come too early to see the big farm-horses offered for sale.

Here, though, they were offered year-round, and they didn't come in just one size. There were as many different size and shapes of draft-horse as there were carriages: some simply looked like giant saddle-horses, while others were as heavy-boned and ponderous as oxen.

But the variety of the draft-horses paled in comparison to that of the ponies. Ponies seemed to come in as many different varieties, bred for as many different purposes, as, well, dogs. The pack and cart and riding ponies were easy enough to recognize. Harrier had to stop and ask, though, about another breed, and was told that they were pump and winch ponies, bred to provide the power for farm machinery. They were smaller than Thunder had been, and so massively muscled they were as wide as they were tall.

"This could all be done by magic," Tiercel said, looking at the line of stolid, patient little creatures. "Then you wouldn't have to breed animals to do it."

"Or by wishing," Harrier said, grabbing his arm and pulling him away. "Then *nobody* would have to do it."

⮜⮞

IT took them most of the morning to find out where in the market mules were bought and sold, then to go back to the stabling where their animals were kept and bring their animal into the market. When they located someone who was willing to buy a mule from two students from nowhere in particular, it was already after noon.

The bargaining didn't go well. Harrier was sure they were cheated on the price they got for the mule, especially since they ended up selling the beast for a lot less than they'd had to pay to get it back in Thunder Grass, but Harrier told himself that if they'd managed to rent a mule they would have been out the same amount of money—or more—and still not had a mule to show for it afterward, and he tried to be content with that.

Tiercel—of course—didn't care. Harrier suspected he would have been glad to *give* the mule away just to be rid of it. Harrier had almost managed to forget how single-minded Tiercel could be once he'd settled on a course of action. Even if it was a really stupid one.

Of course Tiercel wanted to get through Pelashia's Veil before winter set in. But a few more days in Ysterialpoerin wouldn't matter one way or the other. And frankly, Harrier was starting to have doubts about the wisdom of Tiercel's plan. Large doubts.

Yes, Roneida had told Tiercel to seek out the Elves because they could tell him how to control his High Mage powers (and possibly keep him from, oh, *dying*) and also because they might be able to tell them—in plain language—what Tiercel's visions meant and what to do about them. And it was pretty clear that nobody else either would or could do that. But they'd come more than a few hundred leagues to get this far, and that had been the soft and easy part of the journey, through settled and civilized lands. Windalorianan was the edge of the world. Beyond its outskirts was nothing but wilderness—*mountain* wilderness at that, and the two of them would be heading into it right at the beginning of winter. With monsters chasing them. It really didn't matter if Tiercel said that these monsters didn't want to kill him; Harrier wasn't convinced. Tiercel always thought the best of everyone.

And even if Tiercel was right about the monsters (at least the ones like the one in the alleyway last night, and the bear, and the Red Rider), there were still the Creatures of the Dark to worry about. What if they ran into more Goblins? Or something else from before the Flowering? Or for that matter, nothing more unworldly than a starving pack of wolves?

The two of them would be dead.

Yes, going to Windalorianan—and beyond Windalorianan— was going to end up, one way or the other, with both of them dead. Harrier was pretty sure of that. And he had no idea how far past Windalorianan the Elven Lands were. No one did.

The annoying thing was that he was also pretty sure that even if he told Tiercel all of these things, Tiercel would nod, and look thoughtful, and agree that he was right. And say that he ought to turn back for Armethalieh, and Tiercel would go on without him.

And Harrier just couldn't imagine himself doing that.

AS they were leaving the farrier's shop—just as Harrier had suspected, the farrier could not fit their horses into his schedule any sooner than three days from now—Tiercel still jittered with nervous energy to the point that Harrier was tempted to simply knock him senseless.

"Look," he said in desperation, "we're here in Ysterialpoerin, there must be *something* to do—because I am *not* taking the horses and heading for Windalorianan today—so why don't we look around and maybe visit some . . . caves?"

Abruptly he remembered his dream of the night before.

Tiercel was looking at him oddly.

"Harrier," Tiercel said slowly, "did you dream about a cave last night?"

"No," Harrier said promptly. "Yes," he admitted, because Tiercel was still looking at him.

"I did too."

TO Harrier's great reluctance, they compared notes as they walked back toward their lodgings. Tiercel told him every detail of his dream and badgered Harrier for every detail of his that he could remember, undistracted by Harrier's constant interruptions to buy food from various street vendors. To Harrier's surprise and secret dismay, now that Tiercel had reminded him of it, he could remember what he'd dreamed as clearly as if it were something that had actually happened. He didn't remember the part of his dream about coming to the cave or leaving it, but he remembered being inside it as clearly and as vividly as he could remember standing on the docks at Armethalieh on a warm spring day.

Both dreams were eerily similar.

"What do you think?" Tiercel said.

"I don't like it," Harrier said, around a mouthful of meat-roll. Their errands at the horse-market had eaten up so much of the day that he'd missed his midday meal, and he was determined to repair that lack.

"You always say that."

"Then why did you ask me? It's weird, and if it's weird, it has to be something to do with that thing that was chasing us around the alleys last night and keeps trying to kill you."

"I'm not sure it's trying to kill me," Tiercel responded instantly and predictably.

"That makes me feel *so* much better."

"And I don't think this has something to do with . . . that."

"So, what? Now there are *three* weird things following us around?" Harrier demanded.

"I guess so. Because the thing that's chasing me can't really see you. When it was the bear and the Red Rider, it only saw me. And I don't think it was after you in the alley at all, only me. But you had the same dream I did." Except for the fact—as Harrier now knew—that Tiercel remembered walking up to the mouth of the cave, and walking down inside, and going beyond the cavern that Harrier remembered, to another cavern beside the underground river that Harrier had heard.

Harrier simply grunted, unimpressed at Tiercel's attempts at logic.

"I think we ought to see if there are any caves around here and see what's there. I think I remember reading about some. Wasn't there a big battle in a cave near Ysterialpoerin during the War? We should go there," Tiercel said earnestly.

"Right."

"I'm going with you or without you, Har."

"Well, you're going without me, because I'm not going," Harrier said firmly, trying to forget that going to explore caves had been his idea in the first place.

IN the end, of course, Harrier went with him, since the only alternative was staying behind and composing a letter to his family, and while he knew that was a task he'd have to perform before he left Ysterialpoerin—and really, he ought to write to Tiercel's family as well—he'd really like to put it off for as long as he could manage. There wasn't really anything he could think of to say. He could tell them he was fine—which was mostly true—and he could *not* tell them a lot of things that he'd seen with his own eyes and barely believed himself.

At least if he wrote to them tomorrow, he could tell them about this.

The Caves of Imrathalion lay a few miles outside the city limits of Ysterialpoerin. According to the history book Tiercel had promptly purchased in the street of the booksellers once they decided to go, several important battles against the Endarkened had been fought there by Kellen Knight-Mage himself, and the caves and much of the forest around them were now a Protected Park.

To spare their own animals, they rented a pair of job-horses for the ride out to the caves from the same stables where their own horses were being kept. Though he felt just a little silly doing so, Harrier wore his sword. He'd been wearing it in the horse-market this morning, too, and he was sure people had been looking at him, but after last night, he'd promised himself that he was never going out without it again, and that was a promise he intended to keep. He wasn't really surprised to see that Tiercel brought his wand and his workbook with him either, although Tiercel hadn't brought them this morning. He supposed it was pretty much the same idea.

"This is a stupid idea," Harrier grumbled, once they were on their way.

"It's a Protected Park. There are tours of the caves. There's a Light-shrine there. What can possibly happen?" Tiercel answered equitably.

"If you didn't think something could possibly happen, you wouldn't be going," Harrier said inarguably. *And you wouldn't have brought your Mage-stuff.*

"I just want to know why I had that dream."

"It was probably the fish-rolls you had for dinner last night," Harrier answered, just to be difficult.

"Well, you had mutton pie, and you had the same dream."

⚬≈⚬

THE Imrathalion Protected Park was faintly disappointing to Tiercel, though even he wasn't certain what he was expecting. Certainly not to see Elven armies massed for battle, with Star-Crowned Ancaladar soaring overhead.

A thousand years ago, according to the histories, the whole area around Ysterialpoerin had been untouched mountain wilderness, for the Elves had built much smaller cities than humans now did. But modern Ysterialpoerin was a sprawling modern city and the largest city east of the Mystrals, so fields and orchards ran right up to the edge of the trees that marked the boundary of the park. They weren't the same trees that had been here a thousand years ago, of course: greenneedle trees had short life-spans, and lived only a few decades—a century at most—before succumbing to age or storm. But the forest that bounded the park was impressive, none the less.

Despite the fact that they were visiting the park late in the afternoon on a work day, they were far from the only guests. The Caves of Imrathalion were famous throughout the Nine Cities, and any visitor to Ysterialpoerin was almost certain to visit the caves as well. They shared the road to the park not only with humans but with Centaurs, Brownies (to Tiercel's surprise), and even Fauns. Both he and Harrier regarded the Fauns warily, but the little creatures made no trouble for anyone on the road—aside from getting constantly underfoot.

THE gates to the park stood open, though even closed they could not have barred entrance, for they were purely ornamental. They were anchored by two stone pillars carved in the shape of gigantic Elven Knights, and the tall wooden gates themselves were carved with a fanciful scene of battle, in which unicorn-mounted knights slew hordes of winged Endarkened. Tiercel regarded the panorama and swallowed hard, his throat suddenly dry. Scenes like this were just decoration to everyone else—even, he suspected, to Harrier—but to him they represented something that was out there *right now*.

Inside the gates they left their horses at the stables, paying two copper demi-suns to have them rubbed down and given fodder. At Harrier's insistence, they also stopped at a vendor selling meat-pies and cider, while Tiercel, naturally, bought a guidebook.

"It's the same one you bought in Ysterialpoerin," Harrier said, around a mouthful of pastry.

"No," Tiercel said patiently. "This one's different. It's about the park. Come on. I want to see the Light Temple here."

A few minutes' walk brought them to the Imrathalion Temple of the Light.

"Just don't make anything glow," Harrier muttered, wiping his hands on his trousers and tossing his empty cup into a nearby barrel.

Tiercel snorted. He had no intention of doing anything that stupid. But Light Temples were often dedicated to specific saints or great events, and according to the park guidebook, the Imrathalion Temple was the oldest Temple of the Light in what had once been Elven Lands. It had been built soon after the Flowering, to honor not only the humans who had died here—so legend said—but to memorialize those who had not merely died, but surrendered near-immortality in the battle. Tiercel wanted to see if it was any different from every other Temple of the Light he'd ever seen.

Besides, he had a plan.

The guidebook he'd purchased said that there were guided tours given of the Caves of Imrathalion. It also said when the last one started. The tally-board they'd passed on the way to the Temple said they'd just have time to take a quick look at the Temple before joining the last tour of the caves.

And then what?

He didn't know.

⤞

THE Eternal Light was without form, its only symbol the flame on the High Altar, and for that reason, Light Temples did not contain depictions of objects from the natural world. But the Imrathalion Temple was unique, dedicated to the victory of the Light over the Darkness.

There was an hour yet before Evening Litany, so the Temple was quiet and nearly-deserted. A few of the long plain wooden benches were occupied by those who had come to offer private prayers to the Light. There were a handful of others who, like Tiercel and Harrier, had simply come to see the place.

"It looks different," Harrier said simply, standing in the doorway.

The entire back wall of the temple, framing the High Altar and the Eternal Flame, was made of thousands of tiny pieces of colored glass, all making up a picture of a flower-filled forest. The sunlight coming through from outside flickered over the intricately-set pieces, making the leaves of the vitreous forest seem to shift and move.

On the paneled walls of the temple, carved unicorns danced and played among graceful robed figures that Harrier realized, after a moment, must be Elves. Harrier wondered if the unicorns had been depicted life-sized; he'd always assumed that unicorns were as large as horses, but the ones carved on the wall seemed to be no larger than deer when contrasted with the Elven figures.

"Look up," Tiercel said, and Harrier did.

The domed ceiling had been painted in the likeness of a summer sky. At its apex, the likeness of a glittering black dragon wheeled in joyous flight, wreathed in a cloud of glittering butterflies. Involuntarily, Harrier took a step back. The painted image almost seemed to move. . . .

"Wow," he said. "It must be really hard to pay attention to the Litany here."

"I suppose the priests get used to it," Tiercel said.

"That wasn't exactly . . ." Harrier began, and shrugged. He walked over to the nearest wall to get a better look at it. There was a sign asking visitors not to touch the carvings, but it was obvious that hundreds of generations of visitors had been unable to resist, for the wood was worn so smooth in places that it glowed like amber. Even so, it was still possible to make out details of the once-intricate carving. The petals of a flower. A bird in its nest, tucked carefully into the branches of a flowering tree.

"Hey . . . Elves wore earrings!" Harrier exclaimed.

Several people turned and glared at him.

"They probably still do," Tiercel said. "They aren't all dead, you know. Come on. We'll be late for the tour of the caves."

THERE were about a dozen people, including Tiercel and Harrier, gathered for the tour, which was led by two of the park's caretakers. There was a cheerful family of Centaurs—the younger of the two Centaur colts still stilt-legged and awkward—a docent from Ysterialpoerin University with a cluster of his students—all of whom looked very solemn and earnest—and three stout white-haired sisters who spoke with the broad flat accents of the High Reaches. They'd sold the family farm last year and were traveling now on pleasure, they said, finally seeing all the sights of the wide world.

"And you?" the eldest of the three sisters—her name was Mereel—asked. "Are you here on business—like Old Prune Face there—" she indicated the docent with a jerk of her chin "—or do you visit the park for pleasure?"

"Well—" Harrier began, but was saved from answering as their guide summoned them all to order.

She introduced herself as Mistress Amalgar, and began with a short lecture on the historic importance of the Imrathalion Caves. Her words were not exactly interrupted, but underlaid, with a constant steady muttering from the Ysterialpoerine docent, who seemed to disagree with almost everything she said. Harrier found himself moving away from the man and his little cluster of students—not because he was particularly interested in Mistress Amalgar's lecture—because he wasn't—but simply because he found the sound of the man's voice so annoying. If the man's lectures were anything like this, Harrier sincerely pitied his students.

After the history lecture, Mistress Amalgar's partner, Guide Eredor, gave a shorter speech on safe conduct within the caves. Harrier paid more attention this time. They were told to stay close together and always keep either Mistress Amalgar or Guide Eredor in sight at all times.

Then they walked up the short path that led to the entrance.

TIERCEL was surprised at how much colder it was inside the cave than out, though the lanterns set at frequent intervals along their path kept it from being dark. Once they were all inside, their guides explained the cave system in detail, and how it had been infested by Creatures of the Dark for thousands of years before Kellen and Idalia had found and destroyed them.

Everything looked vaguely familiar. He'd thought it might.

These were the caves he and Harrier had dreamed about last night. Obviously someone was sending them a message, and one Tiercel was determined to answer, no matter what Harrier might have to say about it. He was sure it hadn't come from the same creature who'd chased them around the alleys, and from what he knew about the Creatures of the Dark, they wouldn't waste their time laying elaborate traps. They'd just eat someone.

He was pretty sure of that.

HE'D hoped to be able to take Harrier and sneak away from the rest of the party in order to find the place he'd dreamed about the night before, but Amalgar and Eredor apparently had years of experience in keeping visitors from wandering off and getting lost, and there was no chance to slip away. Despite his disappointment and frustration, Tiercel found himself being drawn in by the tour. They walked along ancient trails and pathways cut into the living rock. Some were obviously man-made—or made by *something*, anyway—while others were obviously newer, simply marked out by the guides across the floor of larger caverns. Amalgar said that once there had been cities and villages of Darkspawn here, though they had all been destroyed in the ancient battles against the Dark, and Tiercel could certainly believe it. Though they were only shown a small portion of the caves, the cave system honeycombed the mountains in which Ysterialpoerin was nestled.

He gazed down a particularly interesting passageway, one he was pretty sure he remembered from his dream. It was roped off, and marked with a "Do Not Enter" sign.

"What's down there?" he asked Eredor.

"More caverns," Eredor said, smiling, "and some particularly nasty drop-offs, which is why that section is closed. Kellen Knight-Mage might have been able to dance on the blade of a sword, but we don't expect our visitors to." He put a hand on Tiercel's arm, urging him to rejoin the others.

⟨≈⟩

"SO that was a cave," Harrier said, blinking and shivering as he followed Tiercel back out into the evening sunlight.

"Did it seem . . . familiar to you?" Tiercel asked, taking care to keep his voice low. A guilty silence from Harrier was his only reply.

"I'm going to go back in there," Tiercel said. "I think I can find the part I dreamed about now."

"And get killed? Eaten? Die the way Simera did?" Harrier demanded brutally.

"I don't think so," Tiercel said.

"You never think."

They'd reached the bottom of the cave trail by now. They'd been at the back of the group of visitors, and were hanging even further back now. Tiercel glanced back up at the cave entrance. There was no door, of course, but a wooden panel had been dragged into place in front of the cave opening, indicating that it was closed to visitors for the day.

"I've done nothing *but* think since Kindling, Harrier. I *think* this is the right thing to do now."

Harrier sighed and rubbed the back of his neck. "Even if it were—and I'm not saying that it is—how could we do it? There are no more tours today. And you didn't have much luck getting away from the one we were on. I saw you trying."

Tiercel grinned. "The tours may be over, but the park isn't closed. You should have read the guidebook. The park doesn't close until Second Night Bells—the Second Hour of Night. We can sneak back up here when it's dark."

Harrier snorted. "I don't think we'd be the first people to think of doing something like that."

Tiercel poked him in the ribs. "But we've got years of experience. Like the time we snuck into that old foundry, remember? That was your idea."

Harrier sighed. "It was *your* idea. I can't even remember why we did it. I *do* remember the dogs, though. Why in the name of the Light would anybody guard an *abandoned* foundry? It isn't like there'd be something there that anybody would want to steal. . . ."

"The point is, we did that and we can do this. I just want to look around and see if the inside of the cave really does look like what we dreamed. Then we can go back to the city," he said reassuringly.

"Okay. Right. Fine. Let's go get something to eat while we're waiting."

"Again?"

Harrier grinned at him. "It may be my last meal."

❦

DESPITE Harrier's misgivings, it wasn't actually all that difficult to get back into the cave.

They waited a bell and a half—the Temple rang out the bells, just as if they were back in Armethalieh—and just as First Night Bells was ringing, they made their way back toward the cavern mouth. It had already been fully dark for quite some time, and the air was filled with the scent of flowers from the ornamental gardens; the night-blooming varieties had the heaviest perfume.

They had rented a lantern from one of the lantern-booths, but they'd blown it out as soon as they could do so inconspicuously. A number of the park's patrons had left at sunset, and those that remained had gravitated either to the extensive gardens—which were brilliantly lit for evening—or to attend the Evening Litany of the Light in Imrathalion Temple. The building was almost as beautiful from the outside at night as it was on the inside during the day.

At night, the light streamed outward through the many windows of colored glass set into its walls, turning the entire building into a giant ornamental lantern of a sort.

Harrier paused for just a moment to admire it, one part of his mind thinking that with the Temple so brightly lit, anybody in or around it wouldn't be able to see anything outside it—such as the two of them. Then he turned away, following his friend—his idiot friend—into the dark. Tiercel always made his plans seem so logical. That was always the trouble.

They reached the wooden barrier, groping their way over its surface as if they were blind, because by now they were very far away from the lights and any light of their own would attract far too much attention. The barrier was pressed right across the cave mouth, and they had to move it in order to get around behind it. It made a grating sound as they shifted it, and Harrier's heart hammered guiltily in his chest. He didn't think even Tiercel could talk his way out of the situation if they were caught.

But no one caught them, and they slipped behind the wooden panel, shifting it back into place behind them.

"DO you mind lighting that thing now, o great and powerful High Mage?" Harrier asked, when they'd spent a few minutes groping their way along the path by touch. The lanterns that had been lit for the daytime visitors had all been doused for night, and the cave was absolutely lightless. Even though—as far as Harrier remembered— the corridor was straight and the path beneath his feet was smooth, he still found himself staggering and stumbling, bumping into Tiercel and the walls. It was blacker than the back of his closet in here, and he had the spooky feeling that there wasn't any air, though he'd been fine when they'd been down here before.

"Oh. Yeah. Sure." Tiercel sounded a little embarrassed. He stepped away from Harrier, and a moment later the lantern glowed to life.

With the light from the lantern it seemed a little easier to breathe, though it didn't really show them much more of the cave. If Tiercel showed any sign at all of casting one of his MageLight spells, though, Harrier vowed, he was going to smack him so hard he'd forget all about being a High Mage.

They quickly returned to the main cavern they'd been in before. It had taken the tour about an hour to reach it the last time, with all the stops and starts; the two of them, alone, got there in half that time.

According to Amalgar and Eredor, there'd been either a big battle or a village of Endarkened creatures here once; no one remembered which. Though Tiercel's lantern cast only a few feet of light in their immediate vicinity, Harrier remembered that the floor here was as smooth and even as if it had been built by human hands, and the sloping walls of the cave were covered with a thick glittery something that looked like frost. They'd all been told not to touch it, but he had, and it had crumbled under his fingers like salt. Standing in the middle of the cavern now, neither of them could see the walls at all by the light of their single lantern.

"I think we want to go this way," Tiercel said. His voice had a creepy flat sound in the cave, as if it ought to echo and didn't. Harrier had noticed that the last time they were down here. In some places in the cave, sounds had echoed so much it was deafening. In others—like this cavern—sounds were weirdly flat.

"You mean, past the rope that blocks off that section of the cave from people going into it?" Harrier said resignedly.

"That's right," Tiercel answered matter-of-factly.

Harrier didn't ask how he knew. It looked familiar to him, too.

The lantern flame flickered and danced as they ducked under the rope, and Harrier's sword rang loudly against the stone wall as he twisted to follow Tiercel. He hissed in dismay—*that* echoed, as loud as all the Thousand Bells of Armethalieh rung at once—but there obviously wasn't anybody down here at night.

Tiercel held the lantern high as he walked. It occurred to Harrier that they might get lost down here. Back in the other section of the cave there'd been signs, and a marked trail, and lanterns at regular intervals. Here there was nothing but empty places where lanterns could go, and cryptic marks that he couldn't read chalked onto the walls.

They were moving down one of the long narrow corridors, the kind that Amalgar had said had been carved by the Endarkened out of the rock when they couldn't find a passageway going where they wanted it to go. Harrier trailed his hand along the rock as he walked. It was smooth under his fingers, as smooth as any wall built at home. After a few minutes they reached a cross-passage.

"Which way?" he asked.

Tiercel hesitated.

"Well," Harrier said, pointing, "that one leads up, and that one leads down, so we should probably go down, don't you think? Because if whatever you're looking for was waiting for us on the surface, you'd have found it already."

Tiercel looked at him curiously. "How do you know? Where the corridors go, I mean. I thought you'd told me everything you dreamed. And it's all level."

"I did. And I didn't dream this. I just know."

Tiercel grinned at him. " 'Just know?' Now you know how I feel most of the time."

They followed Harrier's lead.

⤙⤚

THAT corridor opened out into one of the drop-offs Eredor had told them about; a narrow ledge surrounding . . . something. Tiercel wanted to light it with MageLight, and Harrier wouldn't let him; there'd be no place to get rid of the glowing ball of light later.

But there was a wind rushing up from below, cold and soft and steady, and if the lantern hadn't been well-shielded it would definitely have gone out. They were obviously standing at the edge of a very deep drop.

The ledge was narrow enough so they had to walk single file and be very careful, and neither of them liked it much. They had no idea how far the ledge extended, or if it would just stop and they'd have to turn back and try to find another way, but soon they came to a set of wide shallow steps. By silent agreement, they followed them down into the dark. Neither of them wanted to stay on the ledge one moment longer than they had to.

It was a long walk.

At the bottom there was a sense of . . . space. Without the stone wall to reflect its light back at them, their lantern was only a dim spark in a great darkness, and they'd never been in this part of the caves before.

"I'm going to make a light," Tiercel said.

"No!" Harrier said instantly.

"I have to." Tiercel sounded slightly panicked. "I thought the lantern would be enough, but it isn't. I can't see where we're going. What if we fall into something? I have to!" Before Harrier could stop him—or hit him, the way he'd vowed to—Tiercel had set the lantern down on the ground and flung his arms wide. The familiar ball of MageLight began to grow between his hands.

But before it quite took shape, the radiance streamed upward from his hands like smoke from a bonfire. It reached the ceiling of the chamber, and swirled through the stone like ink dropped into water, spreading until the entire ceiling of the cavern began to glow a bright unnatural blue.

Now it was as bright as midsummer noon in the cavern, and Harrier blinked, squinting. "I didn't do that," Tiercel said hastily.

"Sure," Harrier said, unconvinced. He looked around.

The cavern revealed by the MageLight was huge—bigger than anything else they'd seen inside the mountain. Without the glowing ceiling, they'd never have seen it all; if Harrier had decided to take a walk across it—he didn't think he would, actually—it would probably take him an hour to get to the other side.

In the center of the floor of the chamber there was a huge lake of black glass. It was perfectly round, and gleamed like a mirror in the brightness of the ceiling. Because of the brilliance of the light, he could see the countless crack-lines that formed a green and gold tracery in its surface.

"*Really*" Tiercel said. "I was just going to make a small one. One I could move around. I wasn't going to do something like this. I just— It just— Harrier, I think somebody did this *before*."

He sounded excited, as if he'd discovered a new fact, and that, more than anything else, convinced Harrier that Tiercel was telling the truth. Not that Tiercel would lie to him in the first place—Tiercel wouldn't lie to *anyone*, that was what was always getting him in so much trouble—but there were actually some rare occasions upon which Tiercel Rolfort was wrong about something.

"Yeah. Okay. Some other High Mage made the ceiling glow," Harrier said.

"Maybe." Tiercel didn't sound as sure this time.

"Can you make it stop?"

"No."

"Great."

"At least we can see now."

Harrier concentrated on the cavern. Tiercel was always at his most irritating when he was looking at the bright side of disasters.

At the edges of the cavern were more of the stone icicles Harrier had seen elsewhere, and along the far wall there were a series of round holes going halfway up the cave wall. They looked like nests for birds or bats—really big ones—and Harrier wondered what they'd been for. Probably, he decided, he didn't really want to know.

Unfortunately for Harrier's temper, it turned out to be a good thing that they could see every detail of this cavern so clearly, because without the cavern's brilliant illumination, they never would have found the exit they were looking for. Even with the help of so much light, it was nearly Watch Bells, as closely as Harrier could guess the time, by the time they found the way out they needed.

THE corridor leading off from the huge cavern was narrow, and their bodies blocked the light coming from the space behind, leaving them with only the illumination from the lantern they carried, but even so, Tiercel didn't suggest using MageLight again.

He could hear water running, and knew that it was the underground river that he'd heard in his dream. He had a crawly unsettled feeling in the pit of his stomach, the same sort that he associated with drawing the glyphs, but much stronger. He hadn't had it around Roneida—but then, his magic had been completely exhausted then, so he probably wouldn't have been able to sense anything at all, now that he came to think about it.

He had no intention of letting Harrier know about it, though. Because Harrier would either want to turn around and head back the way they'd come—and by now they were probably in a certain amount of trouble, because somebody would have noticed that their horses hadn't been claimed when the park closed—or want to find whatever it was and hit it with his sword, and Tier-

cel didn't think either of those things was really the right thing
to do.

Was there another High Mage here somewhere? Could High
Mages sense each others' presence? Only the other times he'd felt
like this—the various points along their journey, and in Sentarshadeen, just at first—there hadn't been a High Mage anywhere.
He was pretty sure of that. If High Mages were all that common,
the Wildmages would know about them. He was absolutely certain
of *that*.

They reached the end of the corridor. It was a relief in one
way, because the passageway was so narrow that it was barely
wider than they were. Harrier's shoulders had scraped along the
sides as they'd walked, and if Tiercel wobbled at all, either left or
right, he'd banged into the sides. He'd been okay before, when
they'd been down here with the tour and the caves were brightly
lit—and they hadn't gone into such narrow spaces—but in the
corridor, even though he knew better, the sense of being trapped,
buried alive, was almost too strong to ignore. He was at the edge
of panic, down here in the dark, and he didn't want Harrier to
know about that, either.

On the other hand, the place they came to was obviously another huge cavern. All they could see was a lot of darkness, and the
puddle of light around their feet from the lantern. The trouble was,
the lantern had been getting dimmer and dimmer for the last several minutes. It was almost out of oil, and when it went out, he was
going to have to cast MageLight again, and Tiercel hadn't liked the
feeling he'd gotten inside when the ceiling had lit up—as if things
were spiraling out of his control in a way that was so far beyond
"dangerous" that he wished he'd agreed with everything that Harrier had ever said.

Suddenly Harrier let out a stifled quacking noise, as if he were
trying to shout, but very quietly, and grabbed Tiercel's shoulder.

When Tiercel looked where he was looking, he saw two globes of orange fire rising up from the floor of the cave. And the crawly unsettled feeling was so strong he felt as if he wanted to run—only he couldn't quite decide on a direction.

"Welcome," a deep voice said. "I have been waiting for you."

# Twelve

## Into the Elven Lands

**D**O IT," HARRIER said in a strangled voice, and Tiercel needed no more encouragement. He dropped the lantern—not even stopping to set it down this time—and spun MageLight from his fingers. At his feet the broken lantern flared into a last brief moment of life as the puddle of spilled oil ignited and burned away with a huff. Tiercel hardly noticed. He was forcing all of his will into the glyph that summoned MageLight, calling his power until the effort left him dizzy and a shimmering foglike ball of blue larger than a haywagon rolled slowly into the air. It showed him a space even larger than the cavern with the glass lake, a cavern filled with stone rivers and icicles and fantastic frozen shapes in a rainbow of colors.

And in the middle of it, something was alive.

It was big, and black, and shiny, and for some reason, even though it was at the bottom of a cave, it had wings. The glowing lights he and Harrier had seen a moment ago were its eyes; its head was the size of a fishing boat and it looked as if it could swallow a horse without choking.

"That's better, isn't it?" the voice said again. The enormous head nodded at the ball of MageLight, and the golden eyes blinked slowly. "I can see very well in the dark, but humans can't, you know."

It was talking.

"You're a dragon," Tiercel said, suddenly recognizing what the creature must be.

"Yes," the dragon said, sounding pleased. "I am."

The dragon was what was making him feel this way, he realized. It was like standing next to a hot stove, but instead of heat, the dragon radiated *crawliness*. Knowing that didn't make the feeling go away, but somehow recognizing the source of it made it much easier to deal with.

"Well," Tiercel said, after a long pause during which nobody said anything, "what are you doing here?"

"Oh. That. I've been waiting for you."

"Waiting for us?" Harrier demanded, sounding outraged. "You couldn't have known we'd be coming."

The dragon sighed. "Harrier Gillain, we've known Tiercel would be coming since before he was born. Oh, I haven't been here that long. Dragons are creatures of magic, but we need to eat, and there's not much to hunt around here these days. Besides, I was promised, well, a very long time ago, that I'd never have to hunt for myself again. And I prefer not to. But I *have* been waiting long enough to get hungry. So we should go."

"Go?" Tiercel asked, hearing his voice slide upward. "Where are we going?"

The dragon sighed again. "We're going to the Elven Lands, which is where you wanted to go in the first place. It's not that I don't think that travel isn't broadening for young minds, but Jermayan doesn't think you'd reach your destination on foot—leaving aside the matter that it would take you another year to get there. So we'll take a faster route."

"I, er, ah, um. Jermayan?" Tiercel asked.

"My Bonded. You know, you really can ask all these questions after I've had dinner."

"We're going to see the King of the Elves?" Tiercel couldn't quite believe what he was hearing. Maybe "Jermayan" was a common Elven name. He hoped so.

"Certainly not. We're going to Karahelanderialigor."

"Kara-Kara-hara-ha—" Harrier stuttered.

"You can learn how to pronounce it later," the dragon said crisply. "Do come along."

It raised itself to its feet—apparently it had been lying down before—and now it simply *loomed*. Tiercel had always known that dragons were big—"as large as the sky," the old nursery-rhyme went—but stories couldn't compare with seeing a dragon in the flesh. It was as big as one of Harrier's full-rigged deep-water cargo ships.

"Please," he said, a little breathlessly. "We can't just call you 'dragon.' And you know both our names."

"My name is Ancaladar," the dragon said kindly.

"No it isn't," Harrier said instantly, and Tiercel groaned. But he felt a sinking feeling as well. *Jermayan-and-Ancaladar; Jermayan-and-Ancaladar*, his mind chanted.

This wasn't just *any* black dragon. This was Star-Crowned Ancaladar, who had fought against the Endarkened, whose Bonded was Jermayan Dragon-rider, King of the Elves.

"Oh?" the dragon responded in offended tones. "Perhaps you know best, young Master Gillain." Without another word, he turned himself gracefully around and began to walk off. There was a loud rasping sound as his scales slithered over the stone.

Tiercel aimed a kick at Harrier's ankle. "*Do you know who that is?*" he hissed.

"He *can't* be Ancaladar!" Harrier snarled back in a loud whisper. "He'd be a thousand years old!"

"*You* argue with him," Tiercel snapped back, and stomped off after Ancaladar. This was impossible to believe—part of him was sure this was all still part of the cave-dream, and he'd never really woken up—but the one thing he was sure of was that when the Star-Crowned Ancaladar told you to do something, you did it.

The ball of MageLight he had created followed.

THEY walked for most of another hour deeper into the caves, into places that Tiercel suspected had never been explored even by the park guides. He'd been cold before, but he wasn't now: Ancaladar's body gave off heat as if it were a giant sun-warmed rock. He walked beside the dragon when he could, and behind him when the passage narrowed—but since the paths they took all had to be wide enough for Ancaladar, there were never any really narrow ones. He wasn't really thinking. He was still too stunned. It would have been more reasonable—in his imagination—for the bronze statue of High Magistrate Cilarnen, who had founded the Law Courts that now ruled the Nine Cities, to get down from its pedestal in front of the Magistrate's Palace and give him advice about his future than . . .

Than to meet someone who had known High Magistrate Cilarnen in the flesh.

Harrier trudged along several yards behind, radiating deep disapproval of the entire proceedings. At least he hadn't opened his mouth again to say anything else irritating or stupid, because Tiercel could tell that Harrier was still refusing to believe that Ancaladar was who he said he was, and Tiercel didn't think that Ancaladar would take kindly to being doubted. Tiercel was pretty sure that Ancaladar wouldn't simply whip his head around and swallow Harrier up in one gulp, but he wasn't *completely* sure. And Harrier could be really annoying when he wanted to prove a point, especially when he wasn't quite sure what the point was.

Finally they stopped.

"We're here," Ancaladar said.

The cavern looked very much like the others they'd passed through, except for the fact that there was a pool in the middle of it. Tiercel stared at it, then blinked. He'd thought it was reflecting the light of the ball of MageLight that was traveling with them, but no—it was glowing all by itself. And he couldn't actually see the surface of the water, just a thin fuzzy layer of mist laying over the surface of where water probably was. It sparkled faintly, and he wasn't really sure whether that was the mist, or the water that might lay beneath. What he *was* sure of was that the faint queasy feeling he'd felt when he'd gotten near Ancaladar—it hadn't gone away, but he'd gotten used to it—had gotten even stronger.

Harrier caught up to them and cleared his throat meaningfully. Ancaladar sighed.

"This is magic," the dragon said, nodding toward the glowing pool. "A doorway that leads from the Caves of Imrathalion to a place near Karahelanderialigor. You need to step through."

"Jump in, you mean," Harrier said resentfully. "It looks wet."

Tiercel bet that it wasn't wet, and even if it was, there were probably dry clothes on the other side. In order to avoid listening to any more of Harrier's grumbling, he stepped quickly to the edge of the pool and jumped in.

❧

HE didn't know what he'd expected when he jumped into the cave-pool, but what Tiercel got was a terrifying sense of *falling*. He felt as if every experience of light and warmth that he'd ever had

had been suddenly stolen from him: this was more than cold, more than darkness, and he had the terrifying certainty that it was going to last, not just for the rest of his life, but forever.

Then it was over.

He staggered forward a step or two, tripped, and fell flat on his face, because though he'd jumped feet-first into a pool, he exited from a standing archway. He was given no time at all to register his surroundings, because the first sound he heard was Harrier's stunned roar of shock as he exited the same portal, and the first thing he was sure he felt wherever he was, was Harrier landing right on top of him.

Harrier rolled away, growling and panting—and muttering something about "bloodsucking spawn of the Endarkened"—and Tiercel opened his eyes just in time to see Ancaladar step, daintily and sinuously, through the doorway and over both of them. Tiercel sat up. He wasn't wet—not jumping-into-a-pool-of-water wet—but the grass was very damp and he was lying on it. It was early morning here, and his mind spun dizzily at the thought. Had they been underground that long? Or had they simply traveled that far East?

There was too much to look at all at once, though he tried to look at all of it. There was Ancaladar himself. Now Tiercel could see the dragon clearly for the first time. He didn't look quite like the drawings and paintings of dragons that Tiercel had seen, and certainly nothing like the creatures in the Flowering Day plays. His neck was much longer, and his forelegs were much shorter—though still quite long enough that Tiercel was certain that Ancaladar could canter like a horse if he had to, but why run if you could fly? Both front and hind feet had long hooked claws—like a bear's— that gleamed as black as the glittering black iridescent scales that covered most of the rest of his body.

He had the huge ribbed wings that were in all the drawings, but none of the drawings had ever shown the way that they caught the light and gleamed like rainbows. Or that his head wasn't covered with scales like the rest of him, but with huge flat smooth plates of—maybe—bone. Or that the long whiplike tail that ended in a flat arrow-shaped barb was easily as long as head and neck and body put together.

Ancaladar blinked his enormous golden eyes, amused by Tiercel's scrutiny, and Tiercel looked back the way he'd come.

There was an archway standing upright in the grass behind him—large enough for Ancaladar to pass through comfortably; thinking back, Tiercel realized that the cave-pool must have been a very tight fit for him. The archway was made of something white and faintly glistening, and was as ornate as one of his sister Hevnade's carved hairclips, and the interior of the semicircle enclosed by the elaborately-carved material was filled with sparkling, shifting blue-green fire. He stared at it, half-hypnotized.

"Don't walk back through that, unless you want to go back to Imrathalion again," Ancaladar said. "You could come back here again, of course—the doorway is always open—but apparently humans find the trip distressing."

There was a heartfelt groan from the ground beside Tiercel, where Harrier lay.

"Is the pool a spell of the High Magick?" Tiercel asked.

Ancaladar snorted in amusement. "That, Master Rolfort, would be most unlikely, since you are the first High Mage to cast a spell of the High Magick in nearly a thousand years. No, this is Elven Magery, merely the product of the labors of several centuries of spells of a dozen Elven Mages. An improvement over the last Doorway Spell I saw cast, which was the Master Spell of a dying Elven Mage, and which didn't last very long at that."

"Oh," Tiercel said.

Harrier sat up with a last fervent groan.

"You did that on purpose!" he said to Ancaladar accusingly.

It was just like Harrier, Tiercel thought, to try to pick a fight with a dragon.

"I don't think Ancaladar knows what going through the doorway feels like to humans," Tiercel said conciliatingly.

"Of course I know," Ancaladar said reprovingly. "Humans described the sensation quite vividly the last time they experienced it, and none of you care for it. But it's unpleasant, nothing more."

"And now we're in the Elven Lands, and our troubles are over," Harrier said sarcastically. He drew breath to add a further comment, then fell silent as he took a first good look at where he was.

Since it seemed as if Tiercel would be spared from having to referee a fight between Harrier and Ancaladar, he looked around too—beyond Ancaladar and the Doorway—and abruptly understood why Harrier had fallen so unexpectedly silent.

The portal stood in the middle of a lush green meadow filled with wildflowers he couldn't name. The broad flat expanse of wild-grass was ringed with trees; a forest in full summer leaf. At its very edge, Tiercel could see a herd of red deer, their morning's feeding over, making their leisurely way back into the forest for a day's sleep. At the back of the party of does, a young buck stopped and gazed at him, head raised; not frightened by these interlopers in his domain, merely curious.

Between Armethalieh and Ysterialpoerin Tiercel and Harrier had seen plenty of trees, forests, meadows, and flowers, but nothing like this. Everything here, as far as the eye could see, was perfect. The grass still glistened with early-morning dew, and there were no withered blades of grass, no misshapen flowers—there weren't even any flowers in clashing colors growing next to each other. And while it was a wild meadow, and not one that had been trimmed or landscaped in any way, seeing it, Tiercel could not escape the idea that someone had come along and *arranged* each blade of grass and every flower, removing every imperfection.

Because it was perfect. Tiercel thought he could sit there on the ground forever, just staring at it. Harrier smacked him on the shoulder. Hard.

"Ow," Tiercel said. "What was that for?"

"I'm wet and I'm hungry, and we're in the middle of nowhere, and—in case you haven't noticed—everything we own is back in Ysterialpoerin, including our dry clothes."

Slowly Tiercel got to his feet and began ineffectually brushing at his own damp trousers, though that would do nothing to dry them.

"And I am very late for last night's dinner," Ancaladar said, spreading his wings with a crisp snap. Open, the black membrane between the ribs of the great wings was translucent, like oiled silk, and shimmered with rainbow colors. "Go that way," the dragon added, swinging his head toward the western edge of the meadow, "and you will find a trail. Follow it, and you will certainly know what to do when the time comes."

"Wait!" Tiercel cried. "Will we see you again?"

"Inevitably," Ancaladar answered.

Tiercel opened his mouth to ask another question, but Ancaladar had already turned to go. As the two boys watched, the dragon bounded away, breaking first into a trot, then a run, then a gallop, his wings half-spread. It seemed to his observers that Ancaladar was simply going to run head-first into the trees and crash, but at the last possible moment, he spread his wings fully and gave a leap upward. To Tiercel and Harrier's amazement, Ancaladar spun almost completely around, like a kite in an updraft, and began to angle upward into the sky in long, seemingly-lazy zig-zags. Long seconds passed before the first time the great black dragon stroked his wings downward against the morning air, and seconds after that he'd vanished against the sky.

"Okay," Harrier said for no reason in particular, finally getting up off the grass. He regarded Tiercel with disgust, as if the fact that he was damp and thousands of miles from home with nothing but the clothes on his back was entirely Tiercel's fault. "Now what?"

"What he said," Tiercel said, sighing. "We're bound to run into some Elves sooner or later." Without waiting to hear what Harrier had to say—about Elves, Dragons, jumping into glowing pools of water, or the extreme likelihood that he was going to miss breakfast—Tiercel turned and began to trudge off in the direction Ancaladar had indicated.

≈

ACTUAL forests—Tiercel couldn't keep from thinking of this one as something different—were messy. Trees fell in all directions and rotted where they lay; new trees grew up haphazardly. Not here.

They'd found the trail that Ancaladar had told them about as soon as they reached the edge of the meadow, though it was hardly worth the name; a narrow deer-track through the moss and low-growing plants of the forest floor, less than a handspan wide. It was obviously the trail they sought; the trace went in the right direction, and the earth was pounded down to claylike hardness with the passage of many feet, both animal and human.

By the time they'd reached the forest, their trouser legs and the hems of their cloaks were both thoroughly saturated with morning dew. But it was hard to be preoccupied with simple physical discomfort—even their own growing hunger and thirst—when their surroundings were so unimaginably strange.

"It looks like . . . Remember the time we visited your cousin?" Harrier said half an hour later.

"My mother's uncle, Lord Morlade?"

"Breeds pigeons, and has a big estate in the Delfier Valley," Harrier agreed. "You know; he had this big fake ruin out in the back, and a bunch of trees planted around it to look like an overgrown forest, only the whole thing was fussed over by his gardeners day and night."

"You mean all this looks artificial, as if someone's taking care of it," Tiercel said.

"I guess," Harrier said doubtfully.

In fact, the forest *did* look like a garden of a sort, and the air was as filled with scent as if this were a perfumer's shop, from the green scent of mosses and leaves, to the intense fruit scent of the berries and the exotic fruit-bearing trees, to the host of sweet scents coming from the flowers that seemed to bloom everywhere. Everything was tidy and organized, polished and tended. Though under Simera's tutelage—remembering her still brought pangs of dull angry grief—he'd started to become at least a little familiar with the forest, and the way it had changed as they'd moved north and east, Tiercel didn't recognize a single one of the trees around him now. There was something like an oak, but it had fruits like apples; something almost like a maple, but it had large pale-orange flowers. Clustered at the bases of the trees were low-growing bushes heavy with bright-colored summer berries. Since there were deer in the forest, the bushes should have been chewed over and stripped of berries, but as far as he could see, that was not the case.

The berries looked delicious, but they also didn't look like anything he'd ever seen before, and poor Simera might not have had time to teach him everything about the edible plants of the forest, but he'd been eating breakfast, lunch, and dinner in the capital of the Nine Cities for the past sixteen years, and Tiercel was pretty sure that if it grew anywhere from the Dragon's Tail to the Western Ocean, it had appeared on the Rolfort table at some point. If he didn't recognize it, eating it was probably not a good idea, whether he was hungry or not. Everything Tiercel saw reminded him that he was far from home.

He wondered if all the caretaking of the forest was done by

magic spells, because it was hard to imagine the amount of labor that would have had to go into tending even the part of the forest they saw—and this forest could be only a small part of the whole Elven Lands.

The birds in the trees were not feathered in the familiar blues and greys of the sea and forest birds of Armethalieh, but in green and yellow and even purple. And birds weren't the only winged things roosting in the trees. Tiercel looked up, his eye drawn to a by-now-familiar flash of color, and found himself staring at what he thought at first was a giant butterfly. He'd thought it was more than a little strange, not only because it was more than a foot across, but because it glowed as if it were made of MageLight.

He supposed butterflies might do that in the Elven Lands, but then the butterfly had reached out a hand to pluck a cluster of berries growing from a vine coiled around the tree branch the butterfly was perched on, and Tiercel realized that it wasn't a butterfly of any kind, but a tiny glowing humanshape with something like butterfly wings. Then another movement caught his eye and he glanced away from it, toward the oak-with-apples, sure that he'd seen a female figure standing there against its trunk, but when he looked at the tree directly, he saw nothing. He looked back toward the tree branch. The winged creature had been joined by several more of its kind. They were all sitting on the branch, eating berries. Tiercel thought they were staring at him.

"You're awfully jumpy," Harrier said idly.

Tiercel stared at him, wondering if Harrier had decided to be particularly irritating, or if it was possible he actually wasn't seeing what Tiercel was seeing.

"The forest is alive."

Harrier regarded him condescendingly. "Ye-e-s-s-s . . . Trees, grass . . ."

Tiercel pointed silently toward the glowing butterfly-creatures and watched Harrier's jaw drop in shock. He felt reassured that Harrier could at least see the little butterfly creatures, but he had the odd feeling that Harrier wouldn't be able to see the tree-women, or the half-invisible shapes in the air that Tiercel thought he might have seen earlier. "I'm pretty sure those are pixies. And I think I saw some women in the trees over there, too. If I did, they're probably dryads. I don't know."

Harrier sighed and hunched his shoulders. "Not Elves?" he asked hopefully.

"Not yet."

There was a pause.

"That couldn't have been Ancaladar," Harrier said, as if he were trying out the idea to see if he could convince himself. "Not the—"

"Why not?" Tiercel demanded. "Dragons live forever."

"So," Harrier said. "The *actual* Ancaladar."

Tiercel nodded. A year ago, if someone had offered him the chance to meet Ancaladar in the flesh—or even see him—he would have been so thrilled he would hardly have been able to breathe.

"Why you?" Harrier asked, in an uncanny echo of his thoughts. "I mean, not that it isn't a great honor and all."

Tiercel shook his head. "To bring me here," he said.

"To meet Jermayan," Harrier said.

Tiercel nodded.

"Not *the*—"

"I don't know!"

They continued along the trail. Unlike the other trails they'd followed in human lands, this trail really didn't seem to be going anywhere in particular, and a couple of times Tiercel was certain they turned around and headed back the way they'd come. To make things worse, he continued to glimpse shapes out of the corner of his eye; moving shimmers that were never quite *there* when he turned to gaze at them full-on. He got the strong feeling that the forest was even more thoroughly inhabited than he could see, with kinds of Otherfolk that were either invisible to the human eye or that were just very *very* good at hiding. He listed the possibilities in his mind: Pixies, Dryads, Fairies, Fauns, Selkies, Salamanders, Undines, Gnomes, Sylphs, Air-Sprites, Water-Sprites, Flower-Sprites, Forest-Fae, Unicorns, of course . . .

"I see you," a voice out of nowhere said formally.

Tiercel stopped with a hiccup of surprise. He'd been staring off to the side of the path at a particularly strange looking tree; its bark was silvery-white—though it looked nothing like the birch trees he'd seen—and its long slender leaves were nearly black. The thing was, when you glanced at the whole forest together, it looked like a perfectly normal forest. It was only when you started looking carefully at the trees that you realized you'd never seen anything like any of them before.

"Hello?" he responded cautiously. He wondered if the stranger had been invisible until he'd chosen to reveal himself. After the events of the past day, Tiercel thought anything was possible.

Besides, he was an Elf.

He was about Tiercel's height—which made him an inch or two shorter than Harrier—and his skin was nearly as pale as whatever material the portal that had carried Tiercel and Harrier here had been made of. He was wearing a hooded tunic and close-fitting leggings in a dull green that blended in with the leaves of the forest— and both tunic and leggings were embroidered with an elaborate pattern of spirals and lines in a thousand shades of brown and grey and gold. The long hood of the tunic was pushed back to expose his waist-length hair, which was elaborately-braided with strips of cloth in greens and browns that matched his clothing. High soft boots in dull fawn suede, stitched with a pattern of green leaves, completed his outfit. A delicate hand-held crossbow was balanced at his hip, and he held a quarterstaff in his other hand. His black eyes gazed at Tiercel and Harrier without expression.

"Perhaps it would be good to be gentle with the human for

whom Father has been waiting, and not simply kill him outright for his presumption in speaking to you," a new voice said.

This time Tiercel was staring right at the first Elf as the second one appeared right beside him, and he still wasn't sure what happened. One moment there was one Elf standing in front of him. A moment later, there were two.

Like the first one, she—he was pretty sure it was a "she"—was dressed in a soft heavily-embroidered green tunic. She, too, had long black hair in a beribboned braid. The only difference between the two of them that Tiercel could see was that her crossbow was slung over her shoulder, and not pointed at him.

"We do not know that this is he," the first Elf said.

"It would make good hearing did you share with me your knowledge of the many other humans whom Ancaladar has brought through the Doorway to Karahelanderialigor in recent years," the second Elf said, and though she did not raise her voice in the slightest, and though her tone was completely courteous, Tiercel had the impression that if this were back home in Armethalieh and they were human, the two of them would already be yelling at each other at the top of their lungs—and not politely.

"Uh, hey? Excuse me? I'm Harrier Gillain and this is Tiercel Rolfort, and this Ancaladar sent us this way, but I think we might be lost," Harrier said, stepping forward.

"It would be difficult for you to lose yourself, did you properly follow Ancaladar's direction," the woman said, preparing to turn back to her argument.

"Well, you see," Harrier plowed on stubbornly, "that's the thing. He said we were supposed to end up at Kara-Hela-Dragon-Lore, or some place like that, and all we've seen is this forest, where we've been wandering around for about a bell and a half. Now it's a great forest, but do you think that maybe—"

"*Harrier!*"

Harrier regarded Tiercel with stubborn irritation. "Tyr, it's either too late or too early to watch a couple of Elves stand around and argue about whether or not you're who you are. I mean, *Elves*. They're supposed to be wise and all-knowing, right? So either they can be useful, or I figure they aren't really Elves."

Both of the Elves were now staring at Harrier with identical expressionless faces. It gave their features an eerie correspondence; that, combined with their identical mode of dress, made them look more alike than twins.

The male of the pair bowed, very slightly. "I greet you, travelers, in the name of Leaf and Star, and welcome you to the lands beyond the Veil. I am Rilphanifel and this is Elunyerin. We see you."

"That's good," Harrier said cautiously.

Elunyerin seemed to stifle a sigh. "Greatfather will know what to do," she said to Rilphanifel. "He has known many humans." She turned and walked off.

"It would be fortunate did you choose to follow us," Rilphanifel observed, as if speaking to the empty air. He turned and followed Elunyerin up the trail.

Tiercel looked at Harrier. "Um, I guess they *are* Elves," he said, and hurried after the pair.

NEITHER of the two Elves gave any further indication that they noticed Tiercel or Harrier's presence, though Tiercel noticed that for all their pretend-obliviousness, they were careful to remain in sight. Dressed as they were, it would have been easy for them to vanish among the trees, so obviously remaining visible was a deliberate choice.

Unfortunately, as Tiercel realized, he didn't know as much about Elves as he'd thought he did. After the Great Flowering, Elves and Men had lived closely-connected for a century or two, as Elves had taught Men their ways and Men—so Tiercel realized now—had slowly given up the High Magick. Then the Elves had withdrawn Eastward in the wake of the Great Flowering's spread across what had once been the Scoured Lands, and after their departure, Men had claimed the ancient Elven cities for their own. All that remained in the West was the memory of the Elves as being kind, powerful, mysterious, warlike, obsessed with perfection and beauty, and a very ancient race. One that, apparently, didn't want to talk to them.

Another hour's walk—at a brisk pace, this time—brought them to the far edge of the forest. Imperceptibly, as they had walked through the forest, the path they had been on had become broader and more well-established, until by the time they left the forest it was edged with large round white stones and wide enough for Tiercel and Harrier to walk upon it side-by-side. At the edge of the forest, the trailhead was marked with two smooth posts of the same white stone that edged the path. Beyond that lay, not a meadow, but a park: the grass was short-trimmed and velvet smooth, and not intermixed with wildflowers as the meadow with the Doorway had been.

Tiercel hadn't realized how dark it was under the forest canopy until they stepped out from its shelter. While they'd been beneath the trees it had gone from dawn to mid-morning, and shapes and colors were bright and sharp in the afternoon sunlight. He blinked in the sudden vividness.

"Do you think we're supposed to walk on it?" Harrier asked uneasily, staring at the grass.

"*They* are," Tiercel replied, shrugging. The two of them followed the Elves.

❧

"HERE we are, brother, in the midst of Karahelanderialigor, about to arrive at our Greatfather's house," Elunyerin observed.

"Indeed, sister, that is so. And we shall arrive soon upon our doorstep. And were there anyone accompanying us—but alas, there is not, for no one has seen us—we would offer them the hospitality of our father's home and hearth. It is indeed sad that no one accompanies us," Rilphanifel answered, gazing off into space.

"Most sad," Elunyerin agreed. "I see you, and you see me, and that is as it should be. For the rest . . ."

"I see you, Rilphanifel. I see you, Elunyerin," Tiercel said, finally getting the idea. "Ah . . . do you see me?"

Both Elves stopped and turned around. They regarded each other for a moment, then looked back at him. "That is very bold speech on such short acquaintance," Rilphanifel said to his sister. "It is possible that there might be cause for reflection on the advisability of leaving foundlings in the forest."

"Equally, one might contemplate the notion that there are more races in the land than Elves, and they are not all alike. Indeed, we do see you," Elunyerin said, answering Tiercel at last.

They waited expectantly.

"My name is Tiercel Rolfort. This is Harrier Gillain."

To Tiercel's surprise, Harrier bowed—well, anyone who spent half their life on the Armethaliehan docks would be used to dealing with foreign ways and customs—at least, once he got over sulking about them. "I see you," Harrier said.

Both Elves seemed relieved.

"We greet you once again and this time in full measure, Tiercel and Harrier, in the name of Leaf and Star, and welcome you to the lands beyond the Veil. Stay as long as you will, and when you go, go with joy. I am Rilphanifel and this is Elunyerin. We have come to escort you to the House of Malkirinath, jewel of the city of Kara-helanderialigor, where Tiercel has long been awaited, and where his friend is welcome."

"Okay," Tiercel said slowly. He really wasn't sure how he felt about having been "long awaited," especially by Elves, but now that he was here there really didn't seem to be a lot of point in making a fuss.

"Nice to know I'm welcome," Harrier muttered.

"Come," Elunyerin said, beckoning them onward.

A few minutes later Tiercel realized not only that he was looking at a house, but that he'd been looking at a house for quite some time.

Elunyerin and Rilphanifel had said they were taking the two of them to a city, but he'd seen no signs of one. The first thing he'd seen that looked man-made—or Elvenmade—was what he was staring at now, and for the longest time, his mind had insisted on telling him that it was not a house at all, but a copse of trees. Then suddenly everything had somehow shifted right before his eyes: trees had become pillars, random boulders had become foundation stones, and between one heartbeat and the next he was staring at a house, and could not imagine how he had ever seen anything else. The house was built on a low rise of ground, and rose up out of the earth as if it were an extension of the forms of the earth. The wood of its walls was silvered with time, and the low sloping planes of its roof was thick with moss. While the houses of the Nine Cities were straightforward and up-and-down, this house seemed to . . . swirl, as if it were somehow in motion, like a drift of leaves caught by the wind.

For all its size—and the house was not small—it had an airiness to it. The walls were pierced by long windows that echoed the shapes of the trunks of trees. They sparkled with light—and had added to the original illusion, Tiercel imagined, that this had been a grove of trees and not a house, but no matter how hard he tried, now, he could not un-see the house and see the trees again. The whole illusion—however it had been created—was disturbing in a way he couldn't quite articulate to himself. Things should be able to appear and disappear this way in twilight and fog, his mind told him, not on a clear summer morning. But the house had appeared before his eyes where a grove of trees had been only moments before, and now he could not decide whether the trees had ever been there at all.

"Harrier, do you see that house?" he asked, pointing.

"Sure," Harrier said after a moment, sounding puzzled.

"Did you see it before?"

"Before when?" Harrier asked, and Tiercel gave up. It was a house. It had always been a house.

⟤

"BE welcome in the House of Malkirinath, in our home and at our hearth," Elunyerin said, stopping and encouraging them to step in front of her.

The house had a deep portico—it was hard to see it until you got right up close to the house itself—and the actual door of the house stood in a pleasant shade. The door was made of a single slab of wood as pale as bone, delicately and elaborately carved with a swirling pattern of dragons in flight, and Tiercel would have liked a chance to look at it longer, but it was opened almost immediately.

The Elf who opened it looked enough like Elunyerin and Rilphanifel to be yet another twin, though she was dressed far more formally, in a gown, underskirt, and long sleeveless embroidered overvest in three harmonizing shades of blue. Her hair, as long as theirs, was coiled neatly at the nape of her neck by a number of small enameled pins, and long sapphire drops swung from her ears.

Harrier cleared his throat nervously.

"I see you, Elunyerin. I see you, Rilphanifel," the woman said.

"We see you, Farabiael," Rilphanifel answered. "Here are Tiercel and Harrier, travelers from beyond the Veil, guests of this house."

"I see you, Tiercel. I see you, Harrier."

"I see you, Farabiael. I thank you for permitting me to enter here," Harrier said, bowing. *On his best manners*, Tiercel thought in relief.

"I see you, Farabiael," Tiercel echoed.

"Come, then, and be welcome in the name of Leaf and Star," Farabiael said, stepping aside to allow them to enter, "Be welcome at our hearth and in our home. I do wonder that you have made it here alive, having been hurried through the Doorwood without thought for food or rest by these foolish children."

Both boys stopped just inside the door of the house staring at each other. They'd thought they were used to the ways of Elves, but apparently they were not.

"It is quite true," Farabiael continued, "that though I raised them myself, there are many who believe they were left in the Flower Forest to be raised by Fauns, though no one would be so uncivilized as to mention the fact. Nor do I feel that either Ancaladar or their Greatmother has formed their characters in the fashion that would have been seen when the Nine Cities lay in the West."

Though none of the three Elves had what Tiercel would actually consider an expression on their faces, he really had the impression that Farabiael was scolding Elunyerin and Rilphanifel and that they were more than a little embarrassed about it. He didn't think their behavior had been out of line, though. Humans and Elves had lived apart for centuries. He and Harrier must be as strange to them as they were to him.

"Despite this, I am certain that now they will wish to conduct you to a place where you may bathe and rest and eat and garb yourselves in more suitable clothing before you are asked to consider matters further. You will rejoice to know that the teas of summer are exceptionally fine this year."

"Thank you," Tiercel said.

"Come," Elunyerin said.

THE house was large, and ought to have reminded him of his uncle's country place—which both Tiercel and Harrier had always found to be very formal and somewhat intimidating—but it actually reminded Tiercel most, of all the places he'd ever been, of Harrier's house, though on the surface it had nothing in common with it. No matter how exotic, and, well, *Elven*, House Malkirinath was, it still seemed like the sort of place where people raised children and children ran through the halls.

"Here are the rooms that have been prepared for you," Rilphanifel said, stopping before a closed door. "I believe you will find all within that you may require—and, as Farabiael most properly reminds me, you will wish to recover from your journey. I shall return later so that you may come and drink tea with our Greatfather, for perhaps you will find that he is the goal of your long travels."

"Ah, perhaps," Tiercel agreed, not really knowing what else to say. Behind him the door began to open, though neither of the Elves had moved. He turned toward it, distracted, and when he turned back again—he had more questions, like *"when are you coming back"* and *"what if we need something"*—both Elves where gone.

"Did you? . . ." he asked.

Harrier shrugged in answer, a sour look on his face. Obviously he hadn't seen them leave either.

However it had opened, the door shut in the ordinary way.

"I'm taking my boots off," Harrier announced immediately, sitting down on the bench just inside the door. "These carpets may be ordinary to the Elves, but I know what they'd cost back home, and I just can't walk on them in muddy boots."

Tiercel looked down at his own feet. He'd scraped off most of the muck from the forest trudge walking across the lawn and the portico—the surface of the terrace might almost have been designed for cleaning muddy boots—but looking at the lush patterned carpet, he didn't want to go tromping across it in dirty boots either. He shoved Harrier sideways and began pulling off his own boots and socks.

"That feels better," Harrier said with a sigh. He wiggled his toes. "Hey, food."

Tiercel sighed. The treasures of the Elven Lands—things that Men hadn't seen for centuries—were spread out before them, and Harrier wanted breakfast. Tiercel's stomach rumbled. Well, maybe Harrier was right.

The room they were in was obviously a sort of sitting room. Low deep benches lined two of the walls, and in the center of the room were several comfortable chairs set around a large octagonal table inlaid with the green and white squares of a *shamat* board, the pieces already set up for a game. In the far corner was a large standing harp with a stool beside it, and hung upon the wall behind it were several other instruments; Tiercel recognized a gittern and a flute. There was a small glass-fronted case of books as well, on the wall opposite the windows, but though he longed to explore it—what sort of books did Elves read?—his immediate attention was claimed by the table beneath the windows, where Harrier was already lifting the covers off of dishes and exploring the contents of baskets.

"Everything's cold," Harrier announced through a mouth full of cheese, "but there's a lot of it. Come and eat."

Tiercel did as he was bid.

THERE was indeed a lot of it; either the Elves had known Harrier was coming, or they were simply excellent hosts. Some of it Tiercel recognized—bread and cheese and jam were pretty much the same everywhere—and a lot of it he didn't. None of the fruits were familiar, though they were certainly fruit, and all delicious. He wasn't quite sure what sort of smoked cold bird he was eating, or what it was stuffed with, or, considering the size, how the cook had managed to get all the bones out, but he ate three of them. And he had no idea what the little pastries were stuffed with (fruit? vegetables? meat?), or what the other meat on the platters was at all. Fish? Pork? But it was pink and tender and he grabbed two slices of it before Harrier ate all of it, because the one thing he was certain of was that nothing here would poison him.

After they'd both eaten as much as they could hold—and tidied up afterward as well as they could—Harrier began to investigate the items on the table that weren't immediately edible.

"There's a brazier here—pretty fancy one—and sugar and honey—so this must be the tea," he said, gingerly picking up an Elvenware canister and opening it. He sniffed, and shook his head. "No. Smells like some kind of leaves. Maybe we were supposed to put it on the food?" He offered it to Tiercel.

Tiercel took the narrow gleaming cylinder carefully. The secret of the manufacture of Elvenware was one secret the Elves had not shared, and the only Elvenware still in Armethalieh was centuries old; in museums or in private collections. While he was sure it was as common as glass in the Elvenlands, he couldn't get over the idea that he was handling something rare and precious.

He sniffed its contents as Harrier had done, but he didn't smell tea, only a faintly peppery grasslike scent. "I don't know," he said slowly. "Well, we don't need tea. There were two kinds of cider."

"And three kinds of leaves," Harrier said, investigating the other cylinders. "Okay. What do we do now?"

"Well, Farabiael said we were to 'bathe and rest and eat.' And we've eaten."

The other doors off the sitting room led to identical bed-rooms. In addition to a bed, each held a small writing-desk and a clothes-press, and the bed was turned down invitingly. After peek-ing into one room, they walked into the other to investigate it more thoroughly.

The clothes-press proved to contain a few items of clothing: a house-robe and chamber-boots, and a tunic, leggings, and boots similar to what they had seen Elunyerin and Rilphanifel wearing.

"Well," Harrier said, holding the pale fawn-colored tunic up against himself, "I guess that settles whose room is which."

"What?" Tiercel said. He was looking out the window. All he could see was more lawn, though the first-floor rooms were obvi-ously at the back of the house, since there was a large garden out-side the window. He didn't see anything that looked like a city. He heard Harrier sigh in exasperation.

"These won't fit me. But they'll fit you. So this is obviously your room. Hope mine has a bath, too."

"If it doesn't, you'll just have to stand outside and hope it rains."

THERE was, naturally, a bath in Harrier's room as well, and the clothing provided for him was all in shades of pale russet. He waved cheerfully to Tiercel and went off to investigate the mysteries of El-ven plumbing, and soon Tiercel heard water running.

The bath in Tiercel's bedroom was very much like what Tiercel was used to back home in Armethalieh, except for the fact that us-ing it was like bathing in a piece of jewelry, which made him just a little nervous. The entire bathroom, just to begin with, seemed to be made out of Elvenware, and Elves seemed to use a *lot* more per-fume than he was used to. But the flowery scents weren't as strong as they seemed at first, and to his relief, they seemed to dissipate quickly—or at least, he couldn't smell them after a while.

When he came out, wrapped in the houserobe, he looked around for Harrier, but didn't see him anywhere. He ate an apple-ish fruit and went to inspect the *shamat* board—only to discover that the game set up wasn't *shamat* after all; there were too many playing pieces and he didn't recognize any of them. And Harrier still hadn't appeared.

He went to investigate Harrier's room, only to discover Harrier sprawled out across his bed, damp from his bath and fast asleep.

*Figures*, Tiercel thought with amusement. They might not have the freedom of the whole house to explore, but there was enough in these few rooms to keep anybody occupied for hours. And all Harrier wanted to do was sleep.

Well, *he* didn't want to sleep. He went back into the other room and turned to investigate the bookshelf.

Several of the books were in an alphabet he couldn't read—fascinating, but frustrating. The next book he selected he *could* read, but it was a book of poems—nice, but not as informative as he was hoping for. The one after that was on gardening, and he spent a few minutes leafing through it, admiring the pictures. The next seemed to be the same book but in the other alphabet, so if he had enough time, he could probably learn the language. The book after that was about fans: how to make them, how to decorate them, how to use them. He'd just about given up hope of finding anything really useful when, at the bottom of the last shelf, he found six thick volumes bound in matching blue leather. The title on the spines was *A Brief Essay on Recent Events*.

This looked promising. He pulled the books out of the shelves and took them over to the chair, moving the not-*shamat* pieces aside so he could pile the books on the game-table. He opened Volume One and began to read.

A few minutes later he looked up, making an amused face.

Brief? Recent? He wondered when this had been written. The un-known author—there was no name anywhere on the books—began with events from two thousand years ago—Tiercel knew that, be-cause the author said at the beginning of his "brief essay" that he would begin his narrative with the founding of Armethalieh. Per-sonally, Tiercel would like to meet someone for whom the founding of Armethalieh was a "recent event."

Still, he liked history, and anything that went back that far was sure to have plenty about the High Magick in it. He kept reading.

# Thirteen

## In the House of Malkirinath

TIERCEL DIDN'T KNOW how long he read, though he got up once to get a cup of cider from the pitcher, and then a couple of times more to refill it, but eventually Harrier came wandering out into the main room again.

"Trust you to find a book," Harrier said, heading over to the table. "See any Elves?"

"No," Tiercel said. He looked around.

From the position of the sun, it was now several hours past midday, and Tiercel was abruptly aware that he was lounging around in a loose robe when their hosts might reappear at any moment; Harrier, of course, was already dressed in the clothing their hosts had provided. He got to his feet.

"I'll be right back."

THE unfamiliar Elven clothing reminded him very much of something he might wear to a Festival masquerade back in Armethalieh, and he was a little surprised that Harrier hadn't insisted on putting his own clothes back on, but Harrier wasn't an idiot, and both of them had heard Farabiael's remarks about "suitable" clothing. Obviously the Elves didn't consider their own clothes suitable. But certainly nobody had dressed like this in Armethalieh for hundreds of years.

The belt gave him the most trouble. It was a long piece of fabric, obviously meant to go around the waist several times, but there was no way to fasten it. He settled for wrapping it around his waist, tying the ends into a knot, and then tucking the free ends into the wrapped fabric. That would have to do.

When he walked back out into the other room again, Harrier was staring at Rilphanifel, who was standing in the open doorway. Rilphanifel had changed his plain green outfit—hunting clothes, Tiercel now realized—for a far more elaborate costume in grey, silver, and blue, with an ankle-length vest and trailing sleeves. It should have made him look ridiculous—he was even wearing earrings—but it didn't.

"It would make good hearing to know that all here was to your liking, and that I arrive to find you rested and refreshed," Rilphanifel said, regarding them.

"Well, I don't think Tiercel slept," Harrier said cautiously. "But we're fine. Would you like to come in?"

Tiercel wasn't sure, but he thought Rilphanifel winced slightly at Harrier's question.

"If it should please you to do so at this time, it would be my pleasure to conduct you to my Greatfather's solar, where you and he could drink tea together," the Elf answered at last.

Harrier looked baffled, and darted a hopeful look at Tiercel. "Sure," Tiercel said. "We can do that. We'd, ah, *like* to do that. Maybe we could ask him some questions."

Now Rilphanifel really did look upset. Tiercel was sure of it, though he didn't actually change expression. "It is our custom to drink tea at this time," he finally said, as if he simply couldn't think of anything else to say.

"Then we'll come and drink tea," Tiercel said, wondering what he'd just done wrong.

The two of them followed Rilphanifel through the house again, this time ascending a broad curving flight of stairs that led to the second floor. By now Tiercel had seen enough of House Malkiri-nath to be able to start thinking about the ways in which Elven houses differed from human ones. Where, back in Armethalieh, the walls would be hung with paintings, here, the walls them-selves were ornamented, either painted, or carved, or simply in-laid. Though the floors were often covered with beautifully-woven patterned carpets—Tiercel hadn't seen an all-of-a-color one yet—the floor beneath was almost always patterned as well, whether it was parquet, or mosaic, or tile. He got the chance to glance into a few rooms as they were led past, and each room, like the bed-rooms and sitting room they had just vacated, was decorated as a harmonious whole. Each item seemed to belong in that room and nowhere else.

At last they reached what Rilphanifel had called the "solar," and as Tiercel had expected, the walls were made of glass. He just hadn't expected *all* the walls to be made of glass.

He didn't know how they could have come up another flight of stairs without his noticing it, but this room was obviously on the roof of the house. Aside from the door they'd come in through, every wall was transparent.

"Wuh," Harrier said, coming in behind him and stopping dead.

The chamber was large, and could have been glaringly bright—though the roof was not glass, but wood—save for the fact that the walls were edged with ornamental jars of varying sizes containing live plants in which the light filtered pleasantly. The floor was tiled, and covered with several small rugs whose purpose seemed to be more to decorate the floor than to cover it. In one corner of the room, a fountain splashed and bubbled, and at the opposite corner stood a large stove, unused at this season, obviously designed to mimic the shape of the fountain.

There were four Elves already in the room: Elunyerin, Farabiael, and two others the boys had not met yet. They were all sitting—or lying, in the case of the man—on the chairs and divans grouped facing the door in a loose semi-circle.

"Enter and be welcome," the man said, raising his hand. "We shall drink tea together—and then, perhaps, Tiercel, you shall tell me how you have at last come to this place."

The speaker was truly ancient, and Tiercel—who had heard all his life that Elves lived for centuries—hardly dared to imagine how old he must be. His hair no longer retained even the faintest trace of black; it was as white as new milk, and lay coiled over his chest in a thin braid. His skin had the soft pallidness of age, and there were deep lines around his eyes, as if he had spent much of his long life staring into the sun.

The woman who sat beside him was nearly as old as he, though her hair had a faint bluish tinge, as if a few strands of black still remained mixed among the white. Despite her age, her back was straight and she carried herself with as much grace as Elunyerin did. She smiled at the ancient Elf's words, and then glanced up at Tiercel, and when she met his eyes he blinked in surprise, for the ancient Elven woman's eyes were a deep vivid violet.

"Come," she said, patting the empty space on the divan beside her. "Jermayan has been eagerly awaiting your arrival for nearly twenty turns of the seasons, Tiercel, but I told him you could not be rushed, for first you must be born, and then you must grow. For myself, I am surprised that we see you so soon. I think you are very young yet."

"He is—if I have my years at all correct—only so young as

Kellen was when he arrived in the Wildwood, Idalia," the ancient Elf said, a faint note of chiding in his voice.

"No. Wait," Harrier said. "Excuse me, I don't want to be rude, and I know that Tiercel's the one you've been waiting for and not me, but, er, you, we don't really know who you are, and, you're talking like you're the Blessed Saint Idalia and Jermayan Dragon-rider. And you can't be. Right?"

The woman with the violet eyes blinked, and the ancient Elf actually laughed.

"Sit before you never have to worry about such matters again," Tiercel heard Rilphanifel whisper in Harrier's ear. Tiercel took Harrier's arm and led him forward to the seats that the woman—it couldn't be the *real* Idalia—had indicated.

"It has been a very long time since I have dealt with humans, and I had forgotten what they were like. I beg your indulgence for ways that must seem strange to you, and let questions be asked and answered here, as on the battlefield. I am Jermayan, son of Malkiri-nath, once, long ago by your reckoning, an Elven Knight, and still Ancaladar's Bondmate, though never have I heard myself named 'Jermayan Dragon-rider.' This is my wife, Idalia, whose spirit was once clothed in the flesh of Men, reborn among the Elves by the grace of Leaf and Star."

Tiercel blinked owlishly at the two ancient Elves, trying to make the words make sense. The man couldn't be saying what Tiercel thought he was. Could he?

Yes, he could. But . . . wasn't Jermayan Dragon-rider the King of the Elves?

Tiercel was determined not to ask that question, and he vowed he'd kill Harrier—on the spot—if *he* did.

"Well, now that you have bound up their tongues, my love, to explain matters to them would make good hearing, I do believe, for neither Rilphanifel nor Elunyerin know the whole of this tale, and it has been two score generations and more beyond the Veil since you last drew sword against the Shadow, and nearly as long as that since the last High Mage chanted out his spells in the Council House at Armethalieh. Human memory is a fragile thing. Though we have long suspected this day must come, they have not, and they are children still. But first, there shall be tea."

At Idalia's words, Farabiael got to her feet and went to the corner of the room, returning with a large footed tray which she set before Idalia. It contained a large teapot with a deep iridescent brown-green glaze, seven matching handleless teacups, and a large plate of little iced cakes as bright as flowers.

"They are not so very much younger than you were when I saw you for the first time," Jermayan said fondly. "And far older than you were when I beheld you for the first time in the flesh you now wear."

Idalia—despite what Jermayan had said, Tiercel could still hardly believe it was her—poured the tea and passed the cups around. He raised his cup and inhaled cautiously. It didn't smell like tea, and he lowered it again without drinking. When she offered him the plate of cakes, he shook his head. How could she be the Blessed Saint Idalia? She was an Elf, just to begin with. And the Blessed Saint Idalia was someone to whom he had prayed every time he'd recited the Litany of the Light for as long as he could remember. . . .

"Um?" Harrier said, balancing his teacup and a cake awkwardly. "Could we . . . Could we, um . . . ?"

"I'm not sure we're supposed to ask any questions," Tiercel said quickly, remembering how upset Rilphanifel had seemed to be at the thought.

"Indeed, questions are permitted here today, though normally, as Tiercel has guessed, they are not customary among us," Idalia said. "But I am certain you have as many as Kellen once did, so if you will permit, I will begin with a story that may answer some of them, and afterward, ask what you will."

"I read a book back in our rooms," Tiercel offered. "I mean, I started to, but—"

Harrier kicked him.

"I do not think that you will find all that I have to say set down in any book," Idalia said kindly. "Though some of the tale is told there, even in the lands of Men, much has been forgotten there, and much was never known. Even here, in a land where even a short tale is long, this is the longest tale of all. The first time the Light faced the Darkness, the battle was fought before there were any Men at all, in a time when the Elves were a savage warlike race and neither the High Magick nor the Wild Magic as they later came to be existed. Great Queen Vieliessar Farcarinon united the Elven tribes and learned the secret of bonding with the Dragons, but to win that war, Elvenkind had to surrender its immortality and much of its magic to the Gods of the Wild Magic, for that was the price of victory. The payment of that price won the races of the Light ten thousand years of peace.

"When the Endarkened struck again, Men walked the land, wielders of the Wild Magic and beloved of dragons. In that age, all the forces of the Light rallied together to fight in a war they nearly lost, for the Endarkened had been cunning and patient, and it took Men far too long to believe in the existence of an Enemy they had never seen. Most of the races of the Light perished in that conflict, and most of the land itself was reduced to barren desert. The Second Endarkened War lasted over a century, and from its battles came the War Magic, which humans later called High Magick. Used in concert with the Wild Magic, it could slay the Endarkened, and its spells were impervious to Their influence, for they were wholly mechanical in origin and design.

"But if the magick itself was untouchable, its wielders were human men and women, and as fallible and corruptible as any other. That war, too, was won by the Light, though at great cost, and everyone thought the Endarkened had been destroyed, this time forever. But in the course of that war, many wielders of the Wild Magic had been perverted to serve the Endarkened, and so the War Mages chose to withdraw from all who accepted the Wild Magic as good—other Men, and all the other races of the Light— and to found a city where they could be safe from all threats, even those that existed only in their own minds."

"Armethalieh," Tiercel said. He felt a thrill of excitement. She was telling him the same story—in a different way—that he'd read in the *Compendium of Ancient Myth and Legend.* Of the Time of Mages, and just before it, and of how—and why—the City had come to be.

"But why would they bother, if they thought the Endarkened were all dead?" Harrier asked.

Elunyerin made an exasperated noise at the question, and Jermayan smiled.

"People who have been badly hurt are not always logical," Idalia answered kindly. "The Second War was won at only the greatest of costs, and went on for the lives of many generations of Men. The Elves and those possessed of the Wild Magic were certain of their victory—and, as it happens, wrong to think so—but others only looked to their losses and betrayals. And if Armethalieh had not been built, certainly those who were needed in the dark times to come would not have been born at all. The Wild Magic goes as it wills, and it is not always easy for us to understand. Despite the pain the High Magick caused to so many, if Armethalieh had not done precisely as it had, all would have been lost.

"Armethalieh endured for a thousand years, becoming *very* set in its ways. And when the Endarkened struck again, They chose stealth, and not great armies. It took a very long time for anyone to realize that Light and Shadow were at war once more, and without my brother Kellen, we would not have known until it was too late. But we *did* have Kellen, and once again the Endarkened were defeated—and this time, all the land which They had blighted and destroyed was made green and fertile once more."

"Which means they were gone forever this time," Harrier said insistently. "The Great Flowering proves it."

"No," Tiercel said slowly, his voice troubled. "They're coming back, aren't they? Somehow."

"The Wild Magic is a magic of balance," Jermayan said reluctantly. "It transforms, but it does not destroy. To destroy something outright would be anathema to everything that the Wild Magic does and is."

"So Idalia didn't kill the Queen of the Endarkened?" Harrier asked. "I mean—" He stopped in confusion, realizing who he was talking to.

Idalia laughed. "The Demon Queen is certainly dead, Harrier, though it was Jermayan who killed her, not I. No. It is that there can be no Light without Darkness . . . or at least, the freedom to choose Darkness. Or create it."

"And the Wild Magic does not give gifts without need," Jermayan added.

There was a long silence. Tiercel realized that the liquid in his cup had grown cold, but he drank it anyway. It tasted a lot like grass. He swallowed it anyway.

Much of what Idalia had said—the later parts, anyway— matched up with what he'd read in the book back in his rooms. After the Second, or Great War—the one that had left so much of the land as a desert—the High Mages had built Armethalieh and sealed it off from everything and everyone, ruling it by magic, until the Great Flowering. His power—the High Magick—had evolved from the War Magick, which had been designed to be something the Endarkened couldn't touch.

"Greatfather says that you're the first High Mage born in almost a thousand years," Elunyerin said. From the tone of her voice, she was trying to be helpful.

"Wait-wait-wait," Harrier said. "You think that because Tiercel's a High Mage the Endarkened are back? But . . . you couldn't have known he was going to be a High Mage."

"We could indeed," Jermayan answered. "For when he was an infant, Wildmage Maelgwn not only Healed him of a sickness, but, recognizing what he was to be, set spells upon him so that when his Magegift began to wake, it would not do so in the disastrous fashion that such gifts had done in centuries past."

It took a moment for the name to sink in.

"*Maelgwn?*" Tiercel said. "The Preceptor in Sentarshadeen? But he was Priest of the Light, not a Wildmage."

"There's no rule—now—that says you can't be both," Idalia answered.

"So if we can ask you all these questions, I've got some," Harrier said belligerently. "If Maelgwn was a Wildmage, why did we have to come all the way here, and why did Simera have to die, and why do we *still* not know what's going on, since Tyr could have just gotten help back in Sentarshadeen?"

"As the Wildmage who *did* eventually find you helped you?" Idalia asked tartly. "It would not have mattered whether it was Roneida or Maelgwyn who said it. The words would have been the same."

"Roneida told us to come here because you'd tell me about High Magick," Tiercel said slowly. "If Maelgwn had told me the same thing, well, maybe I wouldn't have come. But she didn't say you'd tell me what was going on. Will you? Do you know about my visions? Can you make them stop? Or . . . tell me about them? If the Dark is coming back, and you know it, why won't you do something to stop it?"

There was silence. Several times Harrier opened his mouth to say something, and just as many times, Tiercel stopped him, because everyone in the room—even Idalia—was waiting. Finally Jermayan spoke.

"There is . . . difficulty," Jermayan said at last. "Certainly I never expected you to undertake this journey. In a year, or two, when you were older, I meant to send a message to you and ask you to come to the Elven Lands. I would have sent Ancaladar to you to make your journey easy and quick. I had forgotten how impetuous humans could be. For that, I beg your forgiveness. When I discovered you had already set your feet upon your road, I took counsel of others who had also suspected that this day must come, and all agreed that it was now best to let you find your own way as much as possible. Once before, you see, Kellen saw danger to the races of the Light when no one else did because he was untainted by our ancient preconceptions. If there is, indeed, great danger abroad in the world now, we feel it is best for the Chosen Champion of the Light to discover it himself, rather than to be guided—and perhaps misled—by others."

Tiercel stared at Jermayan in stunned disbelief. Harrier gave a yelp of disbelieving laughter, stifled an instant later when he realized, just as Tiercel had, that Jermayan was utterly serious. With a dawning sense of horror Tiercel realized that they'd come all this way, lost a dear friend, and now the Elves were telling him that he was *just going to have to figure things out for himself?*

"So you're not going to help?" Tiercel said. "You brought me all this way not to help? There are *Goblins* out there. And worse things. I've seen them."

"We will give you all the help we dare," Jermayan answered quietly. "I have faced the armies of the Endarkened in battle and I truly wish, Tiercel, that I saw another way."

Blindly, Tiercel reached out and set his cup on the table. He rubbed his face with his hands. "This doesn't make any sense. You knew—you say you knew—that there was trouble coming. You say you knew that the Endarkened were coming back. And you just *sat* here?"

"We did not know that, Tiercel," Idalia said quietly. "We knew that the power of the Endarkened had been broken when the Great

Flowering came to pass, never doubt that. But it is the first law of the Wild Magic that all that lives is free to choose to live its life for good or evil. The Wild Magic is a magic of balance, and there is both dark and light in every balance. When you were born, we suspected the balance had shifted, but—"

"But you still weren't going to do anything," Harrier said roughly.

Tiercel looked at him in surprise. Harrier had been sitting fairly quietly—for Harrier—all through Idalia's long history and even through the stunning declaration that the Elves had known perfectly well for decades that the Endarkened—or something very much like them—were returning and didn't intend to do anything about it.

"The lessons of the last war were hard ones," Jermayan answered softly. "What we knew was what Idalia has told you: that the ancient evil might return. Perhaps not in my lifetime, or even within my greatson's lifetime. That creatures of Shadow again walk the land—and I promise you, Goblins are the least of these—that Tiercel has been born with his gifts, and granted his visions, are signs, nothing more. The greater Darkness could sleep for centuries more. It could already be poised to strike. We have seen too much to be certain of anything but our own fears. Only one who looks without expectation can see what must be seen."

"So you want Tiercel because he's an idiot," Harrier said after a moment.

"I would not, myself, choose to express it in precisely those words," Idalia answered calmly.

"You want to get him killed," Harrier said stubbornly, and Tiercel recognized all the signs of Harrier working himself into a temper.

"Harrier, come on. I'm sure they didn't bring me all the way here just to get me killed. And it's really rude to say so, don't you think?" Tiercel said.

"I have seen too much death," Jermayan said quietly, and Idalia put a comforting hand over his.

"I'm sorry," Harrier said quickly, "but I really don't understand—"

Elunyerin shook her head slightly and Rilphanifel got to his feet. "Come," he said. "We will walk in the gardens."

It was more of an order than a suggestion, and the two boys got to their feet and allowed themselves to be ushered out.

THEY followed Rilphanifel out of the house in silence, this time out through a set of sliding glass doors that led, first to a sunny stone veranda, and then down a broad flight of steps to the gardens Tiercel had seen from his windows.

The plantings in the garden were wide and low rather than tall, beds of flowers and herbs interspersed with broad pathways of small smooth stones laid down in patterns that mimicked the carpets indoors. Stone benches carved to match indoor furniture, exact down to tasseled stone pillows set at the corners, were set at angles along the pathways to provide places to rest. The sharp scent of herbs mingled pleasantly with the sweeter scent of flowers, and for a few minutes there was no sound but that of their footsteps on the path as the three of them walked away from the house.

"Greatfather tires quickly these days. But he and Idalia Greatmother wished to see you immediately. In a day or two, he will see you again, but know that he has already told you nearly as much as it is possible to tell. What he has said is as new to me as to you, and I am no Elven Mage, to understand the necessities of the Wild Magic, but every child of the Veiled Lands learns the story of Kellen's War, and how we nearly lost it through our own blindness."

"I'm sorry I lost my temper. But still . . . it's not much of an explanation," Harrier grumbled.

"Indeed," Rilphanifel answered, "one must suppose it is not. One must also suppose that all round-ears are as incredibly rude as you two are."

"I guess so," Harrier said, stopping. "Are all Elves as vague as you are?"

"I would say rather that we have proper manners, as you obviously do not. It will be well for you to learn polite and appropriate speech in your time in Karahelanderialigor, as War Manners are all very well—in time of war. Greatfather is a forgiving man who has seen much in his life, but if you must go out into the city and meet others, it will be desirable for you not to give offense the moment you open your mouths."

"Is he your Grandfather?" Tiercel asked, staring off into the distance, because wondering about Rilphanifel's family was easier than thinking about all the things he'd just learned.

Rilphanifel sighed. "Just for today, round-ear, I will answer questions as if we were both in the House of Sword and Shield, so you may ask all the questions you can think of—just don't ask anyone but Elunyerin or me. And not where anyone else can hear you, if it pleases you. It would be well for you to be able to pretend to be civilized later. Tomorrow you will begin to learn proper manners, or you shall never be able to leave your rooms. And there is much to see in Karahelanderialigor. Look."

Rilphanifel pointed upward, and both boys looked.

High above in the summer sky, three dragons wheeled, one around the other. None of them was Ancaladar—two were green, and the third was a gold so bright that it blinded them to look at it.

"Karahelanderialigor is the city of dragons, where the Elven Mages live. I am certain you will wish to meet them—the dragons, if not the Mages. And now, to answer your question, Jermayan Greatfather is not my father, nor my grandfather, nor my grandfather's father. Five generations of House Malkirinath lie between us, of which my sister and I are the youngest."

"Why wouldn't we want to meet the Mages?" Harrier asked, still watching the dragons.

"Perhaps you would. You seem to wish to do a great number of foolish things," Rilphanifel replied.

Harrier looked at him. "I . . . Wait. The Mages can't be bad. So they must be scary. But can they help Tiercel become a High Mage?"

"Only another High Mage—so the stories go—could truly do that, but much of the High Magick can be gained from the study of books, and that help Greatfather has always meant to provide."

"Books?" Tiercel asked hopefully. "Books that explain the High Magick?"

"Come, and I will show you. It is not far."

RILPHANIFEL led them down through the garden and across the lawn beyond.

"Everyone keeps saying this is a city," Tiercel said as they walked. "But I don't see any buildings."

"Karahelanderialigor is all around you," Rilphanifel said reprovingly. "I have heard that in human lands houses are so close together that you can see all of them at a glance, yet this seems to me a very odd way to live. There are several houses beyond those trees, and the marketplace is just beyond that. Go further in that direction—" he pointed off toward their left"—and you will encounter yet more houses. A day's walk would show you all of the city, and two days would show you the whole of the farms beyond. And now we come to the place which Jermayan has prepared."

They had reached a single-story building that stood all by itself at the edge of the lawn. A few hundred yards beyond, a line of trees began—beyond that must lay more of the houses Rilphanifel had spoken of.

As they approached, Tiercel was relieved to see that the structure seemed perfectly normal, and not like something that might either appear or vanish at a moment's notice. It was a simple building made of smooth brown stone, and some care had been taken to encourage moss to grow over the stone, so that it blended in with its surroundings, but it was unambiguously *there*. Like House Malkirinath, it had a deep porch with a sheltering roof, and the wooden pillars that supported it were carved—very realistically— in the likeness of tree trunks encircled by twining flowering vines.

"This place contains all those items which Jermayan has gathered touching upon the High Magick. It will be yours, do you wish it, for refuge and study, for as long as you remain among us," Rilphanifel said, opening the door.

"Um, I hate to ask, but how long is that going to be? Because aren't we kind of in a hurry?" Harrier asked.

"I do not know," Rilphanifel said simply. "Only Tiercel can say."

"I . . ." Tiercel said. "There was something chasing me. Back in Ysterialpoerin. I don't know what it was."

Rilphanifel actually smiled at Tiercel's words. "Fear it not. The armies of the Shadow at the height of their power did not overset the ancient protections of the Elven Lands, and the land-wards are stronger now than they were in that time."

"OH, that's good," Tiercel said as he followed Rilphanifel into the little bungalow. He sounded vaguely harassed, and Harrier couldn't blame him. They'd both figured that once they got to the Elven Lands the Elves would hear out Tiercel's story and fix things—not tell him he was supposed to be the one solving the problem himself because they were afraid to meddle.

When Harrier got inside, he saw that the room he'd entered

was the same size as the building itself, and looked reassuringly . . . normal. Harrier wasn't sure what it was about the Elven house that struck him as so odd; maybe it was the idea that if he even moved one chair, he'd be messing up somebody's grand design. This looked more like what he thought of as a real building. There was a fireplace along one wall, of the same stone as the exterior of the building, and it was simple and plain and not made up to look like anything else. A stone-topped table at standing height dominated the center of the room, and there was a reading desk in one corner. The walls were lined with bookshelves and closed cabinets.

"Use what is here just as you wish," Rilphanifel said, gesturing around the room. "Jermayan Greatfather gathered them together knowing that someday they would be needed."

"By me?" Tiercel asked.

"He has been gathering them since long before you were born," Rilphanifel answered chidingly. "Some of these items belonged to the High Mage Cilarnen himself, so you will know that Greatfather has been gathering them for a very long time."

"High Mage . . . *High Magistrate* Cilarnen? The first Magistrate of the City? A thousand years ago?" Harrier said, gulping.

"Indeed. And should Tiercel wish to know which items they are, he must say to Jermayan that it pleases him greatly to see the items gathered here, and it would be good to know their history."

"Uh . . . that's it? And he'll tell me?" Tiercel stammered.

"Should he choose to. If he does not, you will not know. To ask a question is to demand that it be answered, which is why civilized people consider it rude," Rilphanifel said blightingly.

"Oh," Tiercel said, "I see. It is good to know that, though I would be very unhappy if I did not find out what I wished to know."

"You are learning," Rilphanifel said, with a small approving smile.

"So now I just stay here and study," Tiercel said, "and hope I can turn myself into a High Mage before the Endarkened come back. Not that one High Mage will be much use, from what I know."

"Indeed, you must do whatever you think you must do," Rilphanifel said.

"But that's just it!" Tiercel burst out. "I don't *know*! The only thing I know is that the Endarkened are coming back—are maybe already here! Somewhere! I might know where, if—if somebody will interpret my visions for me! But what do I do about it?"

Rilphanifel simply looked at him.

"It's not against the rules for you to tell Tyr if the place he's seeing in his head is some place that you recognize, I mean, oh, Light blast it, I can't figure out how to say it except as a question!" Harrier burst out.

"'If Tiercel may tell you what he recollects of his visions, it would be good to hear, of your courtesy, if perhaps the terrain he has seen in those visions is familiar to you,'" Rilphanifel prompted patiently.

"Yeah," Harrier said. "That."

"And this he may certainly do, but I tell you now that the place he dreams of does not lie within the Elven Lands, for we would certainly know of so great a disturbance herein. And all things need not be accomplished today. You have come far, and the weariness of a long journey cannot be erased with a single sleep."

"Could you stop talking about me as if I weren't here?" Tiercel demanded irritably.

He turned his back on both of them and opened one of the cabinets at random. One side was filled with boxes and jars. The other side contained several pieces of wood—from one that looked like the wand that Tiercel had made, and which was probably still back in Ysterialpoerin along with their spare clothes, to something that looked like a quarterstaff. Next to the quarterstaff was a sword that was nearly as big as Tiercel was.

"Very well," Riphanifel said.

"It would be good to know—of your courtesy—if you have any notion of how long it takes to learn the spells of the High Magick," Tiercel said. Though his back was to them, he sounded to Harrier as if he was gritting his teeth.

"Of that I am not certain, but Greatfather has spoken somewhat of Cilarnen High Mage, who faced his own difficulties in mastering his Art. He said to me that upon many occasions Cilarnen said to him that High Mages began their studies in infancy, and labored into old age to master the intricacies of the High Magick."

"In that case, I think we're in trouble," Harrier said.

FOR the next moonturn, Harrier didn't see much of Tiercel. The two of them had been welcomed completely into Jermayan's household, and were treated far more like family than like even the most honored of guests. They were fed and clothed—Harrier actually had more clothes here than he had back in Armethalieh—and everyone in House Malkirinath was happy to do anything at all for them, as far as Harrier could tell, except answer questions. And even that wasn't quite fair, because the Elves were almost always willing to provide information, if Harrier could figure out how to phrase it in a not-a-question way—something he was getting better at as the days passed. He was even given a horse of his own to ride, once Elunyerin had found out he wasn't actually horrible at it. She insisted on giving him riding lessons, too, but he didn't mind too much.

He was bored.

It was okay for Tiercel. Tiercel got up every morning between First and Second Dawn Bells (assuming they'd kept the Bells in the Elven Lands, which of course they didn't), got breakfast from the kitchen, packed a lunch, and went off down to the house at the bottom of the garden to spend the day reading his magic books and probably doing other things as well. He'd come back at dinner time, quiet and irritated, and . . . not talk about what he'd been doing.

Harrier wasn't sure if that was good or bad. He'd known Tiercel all his life, and every time Tiercel started studying something new, he always wanted to talk about it. Not this time, it seemed. The one time Harrier had tried to get him to talk about what he was doing all day, they'd almost gotten into a fight.

So Harrier had to find other ways to amuse himself.

Elunyerin and Rilphanifel had apparently been appointed his unofficial guardians. This meant that he followed them around, or they followed him around, much of the time, at least until Rilphanifel decided that Harrier probably wouldn't insult strangers the first time he opened his mouth. He didn't mind the riding lessons particularly—he could see the point to those—but he drew the line at the fighting lessons.

❦

"COME and watch."

It was the beginning of his second sennight at House Malkirinath, and Harrier had gotten used to seeing very little of Tiercel.

"Watch— Er, it would be good to know what it is I am to watch," he amended hastily.

Elunyerin nodded in approval. The brother and sister were dealing with his lapses from polite speech by simply ignoring everything he said until it was phrased to their satisfaction. This was very annoying, but it meant that Harrier was learning quickly. "If you come and see, then you will know."

Harrier shrugged—a gesture the Elves didn't use, but which didn't precisely count as being rude—and followed the two of them to a room of the house he had never been in before. He hadn't been in every room of House Malkirinath, because despite his immense curiosity and the Elves' great politeness, Harrier knew it was rude to go wandering around somebody's house exploring just for the fun of it, but by now he had a fair idea of the layout of the place. This was a ground-floor room at the far end of the east wing; very private.

And very large. It was larger than the suite of rooms he and Tiercel were staying in, larger than Jermayan's solar, larger than any of the rooms he'd yet seen here. That surprised him, as he'd gotten the idea that the Elves just didn't go in for enormous rooms somehow. The room had no furniture, and a floor of plain stone, though there was a ring of stone in a different color inlaid in the center of the floor. All around the edges of the room stood suits of the most beautiful—and impractical-looking—armor Harrier had ever seen, and the walls were hung with weapons.

"It is not the House of Sword and Shield in Githilnamanaranath, but it will suffice for a dance or two," Rilphanifel said.

Both he and his sister were dressed in extremely simple clothing this morning, nothing more than close-fitting tunics and leggings. Though the Elves often wore what Harrier considered extremely elaborate costumes, fortunately neither he nor Tiercel had been asked to attempt to follow their example.

The room didn't look much like a place where anyone would dance to Harrier, but he didn't bother to think of how to find out just what it was they *were* going to do here. As Elunyerin had said, once he saw, he'd know. There was a bench along one wall, beneath a display of swords that reminded him of the one in Tiercel's cottage. He sat down and waited to see what would happen next.

To his surprise, each of the Elves went to one of the suits of armor along the wall and began removing it from its rack. Elunyerin chose one in a pale peach-gold, while Rilphanifel chose a set of armor that was a deep silvery violet. Once they had armored themselves—there were swords racked beside the suits of armor—they stepped to the edges of the circle.

"Since my sister has seen that you carry a sword, we thought this might be of interest to you," Rilphanifel explained. He raised his helmet and placed it upon his head, concealing his features completely. Then Elunyerin raised her sword—it was very large and very sharp—and attacked her brother.

Harrier watched with a mixture of fascination and horror. He was fairly certain that the two Elves weren't going to kill each other, but the room rang with the sounds of metal on metal, and there didn't seem to be any rules at all to the fight. They didn't just use their swords, they kicked and punched each other, hammered at each other with the sword-pommels, even wrestled. It looked nothing like the decorous mock-battles he'd seen onstage at the Flowering Fairs, and certainly nothing like the formal parades of the City Militia. He had no idea how much time passed before they stopped.

"I know that you will not be familiar with the Elven style, and I will not expect you to have had my years of training in the House of Sword and Shield, any more than you would expect me to know how to go about upon your Armethaliehan docks," Elunyerin said, removing her helmet. "But it would please me greatly did you give me the opportunity to match blades with you. Though the crafting of a suit of armor is a matter of many moonturns, it is a simple matter to use padded suits and wooden blades, and practice forms only."

*Oh, no thanks.* Harrier thought. He might be carrying a sword he didn't have any idea how to use, but Harrier didn't think this was the place to get lessons. Obviously Elves studied swordplay the way High Mages were supposed to study magic—from the cradle. After watching Elunyerin and her brother practice, Harrier didn't think she could teach him anything. Not because she wasn't good enough, but because she was *too* good. His idea of fun wasn't being told he was an idiot over and over again—and after seeing the two of them, the idea that he could ever be a tenth as good as they were even if he studied for even an Elven lifetime was just . . . silly.

"I thank you," he began, fumbling his way through the sentence. "The Wildmage Roneida gave me the sword, and I'm not sure why. I know nothing of the sword, or fighting. My family are merchants, not warriors. I don't think it would be of much use to either you or me if you tried to teach me to use it. But I enjoy watching you."

Elunyerin regarded him for a moment longer, her face unreadable. "Then certainly you must watch, for Rilphanifel and I practice together nearly every day. Those skills which are not honed are lost, even among the Elves."

AND so Harrier had gotten into the habit of watching the two of them practice. It was like watching an extremely violent sort of dancing (something he was much better at than he was willing to admit, even to Tiercel). Sometimes others joined them, all wearing the colorful enameled armor that looked like jewelry, but which could apparently turn the hardest sword-strike. Sometimes they practiced alone. Just as with watching master dancers over a long period of time, Harrier reached the point where he could begin to predict their preferred moves, and also tell whether or not they were fighting at their best. But the idea that he could ever match either of them in skill was foolish. Only Kellen Knight-Mage had ever equaled the Elves in their mastery of the sword. He was satisfied merely to watch.

He did a number of other things, too, since for the first time in his life, his time was entirely his own. In Armethalieh he'd been learning his eventual trade, spending part of every day at the Docks from the time he could walk. Here, Tiercel was the one undergoing the apprenticeship, and there was literally nothing for Harrier to do. His hosts didn't expect him to work, even if there were any tasks he was capable of performing in the Lands Beyond The Veil, and he certainly couldn't study to be a High Mage. And so he went for long rides around and through Karahelanderialigor, finally finding the rest of the city. He met more Elves. He purchased food in the marketplace, and had fascinating conversations there about subjects he *did* understand—prices and trade-routes and what items were wanted in which markets around the Elven Lands. The merchants in the marketplace were patient with his halting attempts to be polite; he thought they were intrigued, just a little, by his tales of other marketplaces in other lands so far away.

He'd even written long—very long—letters to both his parents and to Tiercel's, explaining that they were in the Elven Lands, and safe. Elunyerin had promised to get the letters to Ysterialpoerin, but Harrier knew that it would probably be most of a year before the letters reached Armethalieh.

And he met dragons.

Karahelanderialigor was the Mage City; everyone in the Elven Lands who practiced magic lived here, and every Elven Mage was Bonded to a Dragon. (He'd long since found out that no, Jermayan wasn't King of the Elves, and never had been; a lot of the stories of Ancient Times as they knew them back in the Nine Cities were just flat-out *wrong*.) Among the dragons, the prohibition against asking direct questions did not exist, and—as Harrier discovered immediately—dragons were even more outrageous gossips than sailors.

# Fourteen

# Ithoriosa's Tale

"THERE YOU ARE," Ithoriosa said. "I thought you weren't coming back."

It was the end of Harrier's first moonturn in the Elven Lands, and the idea that he'd just ridden through a forest full of little winged people on his way to talk to a dragon didn't even strike him as strange anymore. Harrier dismounted and walked forward. Reilafar would stay pretty much wherever he was left; that was one of the nice things about Elven horses, he'd discovered.

The enormous gold dragon—the same one he'd seen the first day, as a matter of fact—was sunning herself on one of the terraces that had been built for that purpose. It had taken Harrier a while to find them, but someone in the market had mentioned on his second sennight here that if he wanted to see dragons up close (sounding as if she couldn't imagine why anyone would wish to do such a thing) then he should ride out beyond the edge of the Flower Forest to where the Sunning Terraces had been built. In the late afternoon, Asima had said, the dragons often gathered there to bask in the warmth gathered by the smooth stones.

It had taken Harrier a little while to work up the courage to go, because he didn't actually want to run into Ancaladar again—now that he knew that Ancaladar was actually *the* Ancaladar, he felt pretty embarrassed about the way he'd behaved when they'd first met—but when he finally convinced himself to go—the dragons wouldn't actually eat him, Harrier was pretty sure—Ancaladar wasn't there.

"Of course I came back," Harrier said. "I like talking to you."

"Like listening to me, you mean," Ithoriosa corrected smugly. "You think I'll tell you something the Elves won't. And who knows? I might. I know more than they do."

"I just bet you do," Harrier muttered.

"Dragons' hearing is incredibly sharp," Ithoriosa said. "So, for that matter, is Elves'. If you've been saying nasty things about those pretty little children Elunyerin and Rilphanifel—who, by the way, are older than your grandmother—behind their backs, I assure you, they've heard every word."

"I haven't. Much," Harrier muttered.

"Don't worry, then. They're sure to be polite to you at least until Jermayan dies, and Idalia can certainly keep them in line until *she* dies, and she's no Kindling snowblossom, but I'm sure she has a decade or two of years left to her after Jermayan is hung in the trees."

"I—hey. Wait. What?" Harrier sputtered. Ithoriosa always delivered her gossip in this indirect fashion, but this was the first time it had been about people he actually *knew*.

The great gold dragon sighed gustily. "Jermayan is dying, little human boy. Very fast. If you and Tiercel had come next year, you might not have seen him. If you had come in ten years, you certainly would not. He taught Kellen Knight-Mage to hold a sword, and he was no child then—even *you* must realize how old he is.

And now he is dying, for Elves are not immortal, only Dragons can lay claim to that. And not even we, once we are Bonded. So when Jermayan dies, Ancaladar will die with him, the oldest of the Bonded. I shall miss him."

Harrier regarded her for a long moment, though it was completely impossible to judge a dragon's expression. The long flat scales of her enormous head gleamed like bright metal. Hesitantly, he reached out and touched her face.

"Higher, behind the ridge, where the skin is soft."

He walked back and found the place. The skin there was soft and silky-rough, like the finest quality of suede.

"You've told me this much, you demon bat. Tell me the rest. This is what you meant me to know, isn't it? Not a bunch of stories about people I don't know and probably won't ever meet. And I really don't think you care that much about what goes on in Armethalieh."

"Not even my Bonded calls me such terrible names. Is it a human thing, I wonder? Ancaladar has told me tales of humans, and of the Endarkened. He survived two of Their wars, you know. He helped to win the second one, and without him, all dragonkind would have perished."

"Really? You're not going to distract me, you know. Tell me more about Jermayan."

"I will. But I wish to tell you this, first. Only a Bonded dragon can create more of its kind, since the time of the Great Bargain. In the Great War—the one before the world you know began—many races of the Light perished entirely, and dragonkind was thought to be among them. We were never a numerous race, and there was great need of us in that time. Bonded and Unbonded, dragonkind died on the battlefields of that war, but Ancaladar survived. And though he had hidden himself to escape the Bonding which brings us mortality and death, in the end he could not find it in himself to refuse the greatest joy our kind can know. He accepted the Bond with Jermayan, and the first Elven Mage since the time of Vieliessar Farcarinon was created from that Bonding.

"Then came the Great Flowering, and peace. And Jermayan and Ancaladar searched the land for many years before finding any females of our kind, and it was longer still before they could persuade them to Bond, and then to find them Bondmates. From Ancaladar, Cortiana, and Mebadaene our race was reborn. And now he will die."

"Why?" Harrier asked bluntly. "I thought you said dragons were immortal."

"You must frustrate your teachers terribly. Unbonded dragons are immortal. Bonded dragons are not. Ancaladar has Bonded to Jermayan, and so he must die when Jermayan does. If Ancaladar had found some reason to die first—we are more durable than you soft creatures, but we can be killed—Jermayan would have died instantly as well. But Elves and humans age, and we do not."

It was hard for Harrier to imagine why any dragon would want to Bond, in that case. "So you, um, Bond to, er, breed?"

"Huh. Why bother?" Ithoriosa sounded both amused and uninterested. "If it were only that, we could conduct a lottery; an immortal race does not need that many children. No. The Elven Mages need us for their spells. Some say it is our reason to *be*. And I would never give up my Bonded. She is everything to me. Gladly did I cast off eternity to gaze into her eyes."

"You, er, um, *like* being, um, Bonded?"

Ithoriosa snorted gustily and rolled her head sideways to gaze up at him with one enormous golden eye. "Harrier, have you ever been in love?"

"Light, no!" Harrier said fervently.

"Then you would have no basis for comparison."

"But Jermayan and Ancaladar are going to die—together—

because they're Bonded," he said, wanting to be sure he had what she was saying right.

"Yes. It certainly takes a long time to make you understand things."

"They don't exactly teach Dragonology in Armethalieh Normal School," Harrier answered grumpily. "And Jermayan is going to die soon." *Because he's over a thousand years old.*

"Yes. You seem to have grasped the basics of what I'm telling you. I'm relieved to know that," Ithoriosa said.

"But . . . Can't somebody . . . fix that?"

Ithoriosa lifted her head and looked down at him. The shadow that she cast blotted out the sun.

"Harrier," she said quietly, " 'fixing that' is what—among, perhaps, many other things—caused human Wildmages to take their dragons to fight for the Endarkened during the Great War. The Demons promised them immortality, so that their Bonded would not die at the end of their short human span of years. The Bond is for one, and forever. Nor would I wish to love another were I alive and my Bonded was gone."

Harrier sighed. If it was awful thinking of a dragon dying at the end of an Elf's long lifespan, it was even worse thinking of one dying at the end of a human's short one. "I wish you hadn't told me."

"You would find out eventually," Ithoriosa pointed out reasonably. "And the Elves will not think to tell you until it is too late. They are always certain that 'tomorrow' is soon enough."

WHEN Harrier got back to his rooms, he was surprised to see Tiercel there, though it was still midafternoon. He rarely saw Tiercel until the evening meal. But today Tiercel was sitting in the chair facing the *shamat*-board, rearranging the pieces desultorily. The Elven version was actually called *xaique*, and involved a lot more pieces and different rules. Harrier wasn't sure if he dared ask any of the Elves to teach it to him.

"You're back early. Did you blow up your new schoolhouse?" he asked.

"I need a dragon," Tiercel answered.

Coming on the heels of Harrier's conversation with Ithoriosa, this seemed like an awfully strange thing for Tiercel to say. Had Ithoriosa known Tiercel was going to say it? Harrier didn't quite put anything past dragons, after spending the past sennight talking to one. But he couldn't explain that to Tiercel, because he couldn't actually remember the last time he'd had a real conversation with Tiercel. Maybe back in Ysterialpoerin. Certainly not since he got to the Elven Lands.

"Jermayan and Ancaladar are going to die," he said instead.

"What? When? Why?" Tiercel demanded.

Harrier summarized his afternoon's conversation. He'd had enough time to think about it that he was pretty sure he had all the important details right: Jermayan was really old. He and Ancaladar were Bonded. Bonded dragons died when their Bondmates did.

"Well, I don't think that's fair," Tiercel said.

Harrier laughed. Tiercel never thought anything was fair. "No," he said, "it isn't. But apparently dragons can't breed unless they're Bonded, and Elves can't do magic unless they have dragons, and the dragons like being Bonded to the Elves—Ithoriosa says so, anyway, and since she's a dragon, I guess she'd know. So what do *you* need a dragon for?"

Tiercel just looked stricken. "I've changed my mind," he muttered.

"Oh, okay. So why *did* you need a dragon?" Harrier said long-sufferingly.

❧

TIERCEL sighed. After spending the last moonturn finding out just how unlikely it was he was ever going to be able to do anything more useful with the High Magick than light candles and make MageLight, the last thing he needed was a conversation like this. But a dog with a rat was nothing to Harrier looking for an explanation on the rare occasions when he actually wanted one. It would actually be easier to answer than to explain why he didn't want to talk.

"All spells require power," he said, keeping his explanation very simple. "Like bodies need food, like trees need water, like a ship needs wind."

"Wildmages don't have dragons," Harrier pointed out.

And then again, maybe beating Harrier up would be simpler. Except for the fact that Tiercel had never managed to actually win a fight with Harrier, and after Harrier was sitting on his chest, he'd still be asking questions.

"They get their power from the Gods of the Wild Magic, and from the people involved in their spells. Because everybody has a little of the . . . power . . . that magic needs. But only Mages can use it."

"Okay. That's why you can do some magic already," Harrier said. "Because you have a little power. Like a lamp with just a little oil."

It was always easy to underestimate Harrier, but Harrier wasn't stupid just because he wasn't interested in most of the things Tiercel was interested in. Thinking of the power as lamp-oil was as good a way to imagine it as any.

"Yes. The books I've been reading call it 'innate power.' I do a spell, I use up what I have, and I have to wait for it to renew itself; that's why I can't do much more than light a few candles. In order to do the big spells of the High Magick, I'd have to have a lot more power to use all at once; the power in hundreds—maybe thousands—of people. Or the power of a dragon."

"Just one dragon can do all that?" Harrier asked, sounding impressed.

"Well, apparently they can't actually *do* anything. They just *are*.

But once they Bond, whoever they bond with can draw on the dragon's power to fuel his—or her—spells," Tiercel said.

"Like having a whole barrel of lamp-oil," Harrier said, nodding. "And either you get a dragon, or you have to drag a couple of thousand people around with you all the time and figure out how to get *their* power. Or you can't do any magic at all. And if you did have a dragon, it would die when you did, and . . . you're only sixteen, Tyr, but that still isn't a very long time from a dragon's point of view."

"No," Tiercel said quietly. "It isn't."

"The High Mages didn't have dragons either," Harrier said, after a moment.

Tiercel sighed. *Dog with a rat.* But Harrier was his best friend, and he owed it to him to try to explain. "They all lived in Armethalieh. And they *did* drag a couple of thousand people around with them all the time, in a way. You can harvest the power that people have, like harvesting grain, and store it in talismans and reservoirs until you need it. But it's a complicated process, and, well, you need all those people."

"So you can learn the spells, but you can't do them," Harrier said, nodding.

Tiercel was surprised. He'd explained all he knew about the High Magick for moonturns, but he hadn't thought Harrier was listening. Once he would have given anything to know that he had been. Now he wished he hadn't been, because that just made all of this—given what he knew now—a thousand times harder.

"I can't even learn them properly, because I can't practice them. Remember when I tried to cast MageShield? It would be like that. And that's just half the problem. Even if I had the power to cast the spells, I don't have a High Mage to teach me what isn't in the books—and that's a lot—and even if I did have a High Mage to teach me all that, what I don't have is *time*. It would take me at least twenty years to learn everything I'd need to know. But just imagine that I could, and managed to make myself into a High Mage as good as any there ever was—as good as High Magistrate Cilarnen, even. What use is just one High Mage? As far as I can tell, all the other times it took hundreds of High Mages, Elven Mages, and Wildmages, all working together, to destroy the Endarkened, and every single time they actually failed."

"Fine. That's settled. You can't be a High Mage and it wouldn't do any good even if you could. Let's go home," Harrier said.

"And do what? I haven't had any dreams since I've come here, but I'm sure they'll start again once I leave the Elven Lands, and I haven't forgotten what they're like. Do I just go home, and try to ignore them, and wait until some kind of horrible army shows up at the City gates? The Elves—Jermayan—expect me to figure out a solution."

Harrier shook his head. "Tyr, you can't. I mean, I know you would if you could, but you're not Kellen Knight-Mage. You just *aren't.*"

It was nice to know that Harrier had so little confidence in him, Tiercel thought irritatedly, but he actually knew just how Harrier felt. Kellen Knight-Mage had been a *hero.*

Hadn't he? Tiercel thought about it carefully. For his entire life he'd thought of all of them: Kellen, Jermayan, Idalia, Cilarnen, Ancaladar, Shalkan, as not really being real. As being *different* from the people he'd known all his life: myths, heroes. Even meeting Jermayan, Ancaladar, and Idalia hadn't changed that: he'd somehow kept the people he spoke to and had come to know separate from the wondertale images inside his mind, but they really weren't.

"Well, Kellen Knight-Mage wasn't *Kellen Knight-Mage* when he started out, either, Har," Tiercel said slowly, reasoning his way through the idea even while he was speaking. "All those people in all those stories they tell at Flowering Fair? They were just people. They didn't know they were going to be heroes. They certainly didn't know we were going to turn them into wondertales a thousand years later, and we got a lot of the facts wrong anyway. Jermayan isn't King of the Elves, and remember when we called Ancaladar 'Star Crowned?' I thought he was going to laugh until he choked. So I guess maybe back in the beginning Kellen wasn't a Knight-Mage either, and didn't have any more idea of what to do next than I do."

Harrier sighed and ran a hand through his hair, looking unhappy. "Tyr, you know *exactly* what to do next. You just don't want to do it. Well, neither would I."

Suddenly Tiercel realized what Harrier's harsh words had really been about. It wasn't that he thought Tiercel was either helpless or incompetent. And it wasn't, really, that Harrier thought he should just *give up*, either. Harrier knew as well as he did just how important it was for Tiercel to master the powers of a High Mage. Doing that was the only way to figure out exactly what his visions meant—no, more than that. Tiercel already knew that they meant that the Dark was coming back. But he thought they might also contain information on how to stop it.

"I'm not going to kill a dragon," he said desperately.

"See?" Harrier said inarguably.

IT had been a sennight since his conversation with Harrier, and it was time to face facts: there was no point in sitting around any longer hoping he could become a High Mage in time to avert the disaster that was definitely coming, although the Elves apparently weren't certain whether it was coming tomorrow or a thousand years from now. He couldn't. It was possible that he wasn't even supposed to; maybe Tiercel's entire function was to found the next great school of High Mages, because in a century or two, they could probably figure out how to get the High Magick working again the way it had used to work.

Unfortunately, he really thought that was unlikely.

Not the part about getting the High Magick to work, but the part about what he was supposed to do. If all he was supposed to do was found a new school of magic, he didn't think the visions he'd had would have been quite so . . . urgent.

Tiercel looked down at the page in the spellbook. The ancient vellum glowed brightly in the afternoon light. No magic was involved; just a clear cloudless day and the large windows of what Harrier called his *schoolhouse*—although all he'd really learned here was that he couldn't learn anything. "To See That Which Is Forbidden," the title of the spell said. He turned the page. "To Call Down Lightning From The Sky." Another page. "To Turn Water Into Ice." Page after page of spells, involving hours, even days, of preparations. Each needed to be cast at the right time, with the right tools, after the right prayers, accompanied by the right incenses. And even if he did every single preparation correctly, none of that would matter if he didn't have a source of Harrier's "lampoil." A big one.

Tiercel sighed, closing the useless spellbook, and rested his elbows on the table, staring off into space. He was pretty sure that the Fire Woman and the Lake of Fire in his visions were real things in a real place, and that he was meant to go there. He couldn't really imagine why else he'd kept seeing them. It was the very last place in the entire universe that he wanted to go, but he really couldn't think of anything else to do. He'd already figured out that the Elven sense of time was different from that of humans, and that while the Elves kept saying that this was a matter of "the utmost urgency," that meant that they'd start thinking of doing something more about it than asking him for advice in five or ten years. And there were already Goblins on the Plains and kraken in the oceans.

By the time the Elves decided they needed to stop being cautious and careful, everybody would probably already be dead.

Maybe, at least, if he actually went to the Lake of Fire, that would prod the Wild Magic into doing something a little more useful than almost turning one person into a High Mage. The Wild Magic never did anything for you if you didn't at least try to do something for yourself; he'd been taught that all his life. So Tiercel was going to do anything he could think of, even if he didn't think it would do any good.

Of course, he thought with resignation, the Elves were probably telling themselves the same thing right now.

But to go to the Lake of Fire meant he had to figure out where the Lake of Fire *was*. Rilphanifel had said that it wasn't anywhere inside the Elven Lands, and Tiercel knew by now that the Elves were great Mages. They'd certainly know if there was something Dark within the borders of the Veiled Lands. But if the Lake of Fire wasn't here, the Elves had excellent maps, and should at least be able to give Tiercel some idea of where to look for it.

He'd made the mistake of mentioning something along these lines to Harrier a few days ago. He'd known that Harrier didn't have much to do here, but it hadn't really occurred to him until he'd started talking to Harrier again that Harrier would be spending his time wandering around Karahelanderialigor talking to everyone he met, including dragons. Or that Harrier—who by now knew almost as much about Tiercel's visions as Tiercel did—would be determined to be helpful. Harrier had cheerfully assured Tiercel that he'd find out where they needed to go next—not that Tiercel intended to take Harrier with him—and last night he'd told Tiercel that while not even the dragons recognized the description of the place, the Madiran Desert seemed like the best place to start looking.

For one thing, the Lake of Fire had to be someplace deserted, and there were no people in the Madiran Desert. For another, it had to be someplace where there was nothing that could burn, and

there was nothing but sand in the waterless wasteland of the far
south.

How Tiercel himself was going to survive in a place where there
was no water and no people, he didn't know. That was something
he'd have to figure out later. For now, it was enough to have a plan
and a destination. So he might as well stop sitting around here, pretending he might turn into a High Mage, and go back up to the
house to find somebody to tell.

He was walking up the low hill that concealed the "schoolhouse" from the main house when he looked up and saw that there
was a dragon in the garden—and not just any dragon. Ancaladar. It
was difficult to miss something the size of a full-rigged sailing ship
that glittered like a piece of black glass, and for a moment Tiercel
stopped to admire the sight, though part of him wondered why Ancaladar was here. He hadn't seen Ancaladar since the day they'd
arrived, and he was pretty sure Harrier would have mentioned it if
*he* had.

But admiration quickly gave way to discomfort. Ancaladar was
just going to . . . die. Not because he was old or sick—because apparently dragons didn't get either old or sick—but because Jermayan was dying of old age. For a moment, Tiercel thought about
just going back to the schoolhouse until Ancaladar had left, but he
thought that would be like cheating somehow. As if he were afraid
to meet him. Or ashamed to.

So he kept on walking up the lawn and into the garden, and
only when he'd gone too far to turn back did he realize that Ancaladar wasn't alone. He was talking to someone Tiercel couldn't see.

"I don't even like him," Ancaladar said.

Tiercel stopped. Ancaladar's head was turned away from him,
and whoever he was speaking to was completely concealed by the
bulk of the dragon's body.

"You will grow to love him, Bonded," a familiar voice answered.

*Jermayan!* Tiercel thought. Now would be a really good time to leave. Or hide.

"I won't have time. He'll be dead in less than a century. And so will I," Ancaladar answered.

"Better then than now. And you are needed," Jermayan answered. Though his voice was thin with age, it was still uncompromising.

He'd already heard too much of this. Tiercel turned to retrace his steps, hoping Ancaladar was too involved in his conversation to notice, but he couldn't help hearing Ancaladar's next words as well.

"I won't do it. And whether I consent or not is irrelevant. It can't be done. If it could—" There was a moment of silence. "And here is Tiercel now," Ancaladar added, in a different tone entirely. "You might as well stop trying to slink off. You aren't very good at it."

Tiercel sighed and came back, walking around Ancaladar. One of the large cushioned couches had been brought outdoors, and Jermayan lay upon it with Ancaladar coiled around him.

"I'm sorry," Tiercel said. "I didn't mean to eavesdrop on a private conversation. I was just . . . I've made up my mind what I'm going to do, and I thought I should tell someone, and when I realized that Ancaladar wasn't alone, it was too late to leave."

"It does not matter. And to learn of this decision would make good hearing," Jermayan said. "Ancaladar and I were speaking of decisions just now as well."

"*You* were speaking of decisions, Bonded. *I* was not listening," Ancaladar said.

"I am rebuked," Jermayan said. "Yet if Tiercel wishes to speak, we will both listen."

There didn't really seem to be a lot of way around it.

"I really appreciate all you've done for me," Tiercel began hesitantly. "But I'm not sure that I can do very much more with the material you've gathered for me, and so, well, I really think I need to go find the place I see in my visions. So I guess I should leave."

He'd expected a long argument—certainly he would have gotten one back home—but Jermayan simply nodded.

"A quick decision, but perhaps not a hasty one. It would be good to know the direction in which your search takes you."

"There's a place called the Madiran Desert. It's outside the Elven Lands, but it's on your maps."

"I know it well, though it is far from here. You will need a wagon and supplies for your journey, and they will take perhaps another moonturn to arrange. And now, I fear, my ambitions for the day have exceeded my strength."

"Both always exceeded your wisdom," Ancaladar scolded fondly.

"If, of your courtesy, you would seek out Farabiael and tell her I would rest, she will know what needs to be done," Jermayan added, and Tiercel hurried to obey.

One of the other Elves who'd been with Farabiael—Tiercel was never quite able to decide whether they were all members of Jermayan's family, or servants—was able to tell Tiercel that Harrier was probably down at the stables at this time of day, and Tiercel made that his next stop, since he might as well tell Harrier his plans before Harrier learned them from somebody else. Until they'd left Armethalieh this summer, neither of them had really been much for horses, but they'd both learned a lot of new skills since, and he guessed that Harrier had decided he liked riding.

Tiercel had never actually been in the stables, since he'd walked to Karahelanderialigor, and had gone no farther after that than the workroom at the bottom of the garden. It was an airy building on the eastern side of the house, as large as the stables in the largest inn they'd ever stopped at, and as lavishly-finished as if it were a house, and not a stable. Less than a third of the stalls were filled. As he walked in, he barely smelled horse at all, only flowers, leather, and grass.

"Stay away from the ones at the end," Harrier said as he came in. "Those are Elunyerin and Rilphanifel's horses, and they're war-horses. I suppose they aren't mean, but they have nasty senses of humor. And I'm pretty sure they understand everything you say."

Tiercel walked down the line of stalls, glancing curiously into the ones Harrier mentioned. Two large gleaming animals regarded him placidly, one grey, one roan.

"They look harmless," he said.

"That's what I thought," Harrier answered darkly.

He was currying a cream-colored gelding, working slowly and carefully from the neck back to the tail. The animal turned its head and regarded Tiercel as he walked into the stall.

"Reilafar is perfectly calm, which is why he's mine. If you want to go for a ride, I can find someone to get you a horse."

"No. I've come to tell you that I've decided what I'm going to do."

"We're going to the Madiran Desert? When do we leave?"

"*I'm* going to the Madiran Desert. You should go home. You can be there by winter if you leave now," Tiercel said.

"That's your plan? It's a stupid plan. Have you told anybody else this stupid plan?" Harrier asked in bored tones. He didn't interrupt his even grooming at all.

"I saw Jermayan while I was walking back to the house. He likes my plan. Ancaladar likes it, too," Tiercel said stubbornly. He didn't know why fighting with Harrier seemed like such a good idea right now, except that it did.

"Uh-huh. And you're doing this why?"

"I have to do something."

Harrier stopped, set the currycomb down on an upturned bucket, and turned to look at him. "You know, Tyr, if the Endarkened, or whatever, is this much of a threat—and you know it is— you don't just let it get stronger. You throw everything you can think of at it the moment you notice it. You don't send a kid like you off to wander around hoping he'll think of something useful. Even Kellen Knight-Mage did his wandering around with the whole Elven Army at his back."

"Maybe they're doing what they're doing because they *do* know so much about the problem. Maybe they think this is the only thing that will work. Maybe they've already tried other things—and failed—and won't tell us. We don't know. Anyway, I'm going to be here for a while yet. Jermayan is going to give me a horse and wagon for my journey, and he says it will take a while to get them."

"Well, I think they're idiots," Harrier said simply. "And when you get this horse and wagon they've promised you, we . . ." He sighed, and picked up the brush again without finishing his sentence.

Tiercel knew what Harrier wanted to say. *We should take it and go back to Armethalieh.* But even Harrier couldn't bring himself to say that. Even if the Elves were trying to solve this problem in exactly the wrong way—a frightening thought, considering how much older and wiser they were than either Harrier or Tiercel—the problem itself was real, and not something either of them could bring themselves to just walk away from.

"So we go," Harrier said. "Together. And, oh, Light and Darkness, don't explain to me how much safer I'd be back in Armethalieh trying to explain all this to your mother—and I beg you, don't suggest I stay here, either. I'm sick of Elves. Elf food, and Elf clothes, and Elf manners. Get me out of here before I lose my mind, Tyr."

Tiercel grinned in spite of himself. He supposed he could manage to leave Harrier behind, but only by tying him up and locking him in a dungeon. And even that, he suspected, wouldn't work for very long. "Okay. You want to come see a desert that will probably kill us before any Endarkened creatures get around to it?"

"Sure. You want to go for a ride before dinner?"

"Sounds good."

⊰≈⊱

WITHOUT any need to spend his days studying something he couldn't possibly learn, Tiercel finally got the chance to see more of

Karahelanderialigor. Harrier took a great delight in showing Tiercel a city that had grown familiar to Harrier over the last sennights—the markets, the houses, the fields, even a stream that could be swum in—Harrier said with off-handed smugness that he'd asked the selkies living in it to make sure it was all right first. Despite his constant protests that he found everything in the Lands Beyond the Veil strange and something he was looking forward to leaving as soon as possible—though Harrier never said any such thing except when they were alone, of course—Tiercel thought that Harrier had adjusted to Karahelanderialigor very well.

But the one thing Harrier had most wanted to show off was absent. No matter what time of day they rode out to the Sunning Terraces, there were no dragons anywhere to be seen.

⁓

"I don't know," Harrier said a day or two later. "Something's going on."

"What?" Tiercel asked.

They were staying in today. It had rained once or twice since they'd arrived in Karahelanderialigor, but those had been brief showers in the late afternoon, over quickly. This morning, when they'd awakened, the sky was overcast and the rain was coming down in a steady patter that indicated it intended to rain for quite some time, and neither of them was really interested in riding in the rain. Armed with one of the books from the shelves, Tiercel had suggested they try to learn *xaique*, and Harrier was just bored enough to go along with the idea—but not bored enough to actually concentrate on the game.

"Well," Harrier said, "Elunyerin and Rilphanifel usually practice swordplay in the mornings, and Idalia gardens. We haven't seen any of them at all for the past few days. Not even at meals.

And Ithoriosa hasn't been out on the sunning terraces, which means there isn't anybody I can ask about it."

"Not really," Tiercel admitted. Because when the Elves didn't want to tell you things, they just . . . didn't.

"So what do we do?" Harrier asked. "Because you know I've been thinking, Tyr, it seems like a moonturn is an awfully long time to wait to get a horse and cart, don't you think?"

Tiercel shrugged and frowned down at the book on his knee. "Maybe. I don't know. All we can do is wait for them to tell us, I guess. Or—not."

⌇

BUT the following morning, when the boys came down to breakfast, they found that an enormous dark blue silk canopy had been erected in the lawn beyond the garden, now that the rain had passed. Carpets had been laid down over the grass, and the breakfast table had been carried outside.

"It looks like we're having breakfast with Ancaladar this morning," Tiercel said. From the windows of the now-empty breakfast room they could see that the great black dragon was coiled most of the way around the outside of the blue pavilion.

"I wonder if he's hungry?" Harrier said uneasily.

"You two really should try to get along," Tiercel said, amused. "Come on. I'm sure Farabiael will want us to carry something out."

The table was already set, and by the time they arrived from the kitchen—Harrier with a jug of cider and Tiercel with a basket of still-warm bread—everyone had gathered. Even Jermayan was present, carried out of his rooms on a litter to be set at the head of the table.

There was an air of expectancy over the meal—and not, Tiercel thought, simply because Jermayan was present.

"You will rejoice to know that the King comes to visit, with his

Council and all his court," Idalia said at last, when the platters had gone around and everyone had been served. "Sandalon, King of the Elves, with his dragon Petrivoch, and his daughter Vairindiel, the Heir to the Veiled Lands, will come to Karahelanderialigor to cast a Great Spell, do matters unfold as some here wish. They will arrive within the fortnight."

"Ah, that's . . . nice," Tiercel said uncertainly.

"No it isn't," Ancaladar snapped.

"It is my wish," Jermayan said.

His voice was barely a whisper, and Tiercel realized, with a shock, that Jermayan was weaker than he had ever seen him before. "If you can Bond with a dragon, Tiercel, the power to work the Greater Spells of the High Magick will be yours. And so I wish for Ancaladar's Bond to be transferred to you."

"But hey, I— Wait a minute! Isn't that— You can't— Somebody explain to me why people don't go around saving dragons this way all the time!" Harrier sputtered, dropping the bread he was holding onto his plate.

Ancaladar actually snickered, a peculiar sound from a creature so large. "Yes, Jermayan, do explain to the boy how what you propose is different than the bargains the Endarkened struck with the Wildmages so long ago, for I fear he has been listening to idle gossip."

Idalia put a hand over Jermayan's, and turned toward Harrier. "It is a thing that has never been done, for the cost is high; we shall not conceal that. One Great Spell is given, once in a lifetime, to any Mage who is Bonded to a dragon to cast. The casting of this spell consumes the caster and his dragon utterly. This is the spell Sandalon has come to cast, the spell which, if it works, will transfer Ancaladar's Bond. All that is required is Tiercel's consent."

"So *they'll* die? The—the—other two?" Tiercel said. *"No."*

Idalia sighed. "Tiercel, Sandalon is very old. He and Petrivoch have both agreed to this, and so has Ancaladar. It will gain you the power you need. Without it, I . . . do not think you will survive your coming journey."

Tiercel set down his cup. A moment ago he'd actually had an appetite for breakfast. It would have been nice, he thought, if they could have sprung this on him somewhere a little more private. In addition to Jermayan and Idalia and Elunyerin and Rilphanifel, there were another dozen Elves at the table—all people he knew slightly, all close members of Jermayan's household, perhaps even family, though apparently Elves didn't think it was important to specify exact relationships. He did his best to keep his head. There must be a good reason Jermayan wanted to make this discussion so public.

"You know, don't you?" he said to Idalia. "Whether I'd survive or not?"

The moment after he'd spoken, he realized he'd been unforgivably rude—asking a direct question—but Idalia didn't seem to mind. She only smiled sadly.

"I have looked into the eyes of the Queen of the Endarkened as she ripped the beating heart from my chest," Idalia said quietly. "I do not wish to do so again. Nor do I wish that fate on any other."

Tiercel stood up.

"Do you think this is a good idea?" he asked Ancaladar. "They say you've said 'yes.' "

The black dragon raised his head just enough to be able to stare directly into Tiercel's eyes.

"From my point of view, it isn't going to last very long," Ancaladar snapped sullenly. "I saw the Second Endarkened War start, and I wasn't a young dragon then. Think of yourself. It's going to last for the rest of your life. What little there is of it."

"But you can give me the power I need to do . . . whatever I need to do," Tiercel said. *Whatever that is.*

"Yes," Ancaladar answered, his voice softening. "I can do that. It's what my Bonded wishes, and I will not deny him."

"Then I'll do it," Tiercel said.

"Of course," Ancaladar added, "there's always the possibility it won't work at all. Which would be entertaining for all five of us."

Tiercel opened and closed his mouth several times. He knew there were a lot of things he ought to say right now—polite things, diplomatic things, even things that might somehow get him out of this situation. He couldn't think of a single one.

"Ah, I'm afraid I don't really have much of an appetite this morning. I think—if everyone doesn't mind—I'll just go for a walk instead."

He turned away from the pavilion and walked quickly away. He had no idea where he was going, and right now he didn't care.

⁓

"ARE you crazy?" Harrier asked him almost an hour later.

Harrier had caught up to him a few minutes after Tiercel had left the breakfast table—Tiercel hoped Harrier's apologies to their hosts had been more polite than his had been—and the two of them walked in silence for a while, almost the whole way down to Tiercel's schoolhouse. Eventually, by mutual consent, they'd turned back toward the house, ending up at the stables.

"I guess," Tiercel said. "I mean . . . it's not as if someone's asking me to kill a young dragon by Bonding to it for just a few years—well, my whole life, but it would be just a few years from the dragon's point of view, and . . . Ancaladar's going to die anyway. Soon. At least this way he won't have to die right now."

"You're going to have a dragon. A permanent dragon," Harrier said. "I mean . . . what are you going to feed him?"

"I don't know," Tiercel said, shaking his head. "I guess he'll have to tell me." *If we both live through it.* From what Ancaladar had said, that wasn't certain.

He'd had more time, now, to get used to the idea of having a dragon—being *Bonded* to a dragon. It was still as mind-boggling, really, as it had been almost a moonturn ago when he'd come up with the idea as the solution to the problem of gaining the power to cast the spells of the High Magick. He really had no idea of what it would be like. But at least he could pretend to think about it now.

"I don't like it," Harrier said stubbornly.

"I know." Tiercel sighed and leaned against the wall of the stables. He wasn't even sure how he felt about it, only that it seemed as if this was where he'd been heading from the moment he'd ridden out of Armethalieh. To find out about the High Magick, and then to find a way to use it. If he were Bonded to Ancaladar—he still couldn't quite make himself believe in the idea—he'd have the power he needed to cast the spells. And maybe Jermayan would let him take some of the Spellbooks with him.

"It doesn't change anything. I still have to go find that place."

"Even if you get turned into a High Mage?" Harrier asked.

"Especially then, I guess. You heard what Idalia said. I know they must have sort of been planning to do this even before I made up my mind to go, but I think they guessed I would go—somewhere—eventually. And they figure I can't survive wherever I go without being able to do magic."

Harrier thought about that for a while. "So . . . either it better take us twenty years to get to the Madiran Desert, or you'd better learn how to be a High Mage really fast."

"I guess."

"Okay." Harrier sighed and seemed to relax. It wasn't that he'd come to a decision—Harrier rarely reached decisions quickly—but Tiercel knew that Harrier had known, long before he'd been willing to admit it to himself, that this was the only decision Tiercel could make: Bond with a dragon. And in a way, it was a relief for both of them that Tiercel had accepted his . . . fate.

Tiercel only hoped it was something they could all live with. Literally.

"Do you think there are any leftovers in the kitchen?" Harrier asked. "Because—you know—I missed breakfast."

# Fifteen

# A Necessary Sacrifice

O N THE FOLLOWING day, the Elven Court arrived from Githilnamanaranath on the wings of dragons.

Elunyerin and Rilphanifel had come to waken Tiercel and Harrier early that morning, telling them that there was a sight to see that they would not wish to miss. The boys had dressed and the four of them gone directly to the stables, where their horses had already been saddled and made ready for them.

"Don't worry," Elunyerin had said, noting the look of dismay that Harrier could not completely conceal. "There is breakfast waiting in the saddlebags. But I do not know precisely when they will arrive—there is much to do before tonight—and you will not wish to miss this."

"Tonight," Tiercel said. He hoped it didn't sound too much like a question.

"And, it would be good to know, of your courtesy, what it is that is supposed to happen tonight," Harrier said.

Rilphanifel glanced at Tiercel, then away. "The Great Spell will be cast at moonrise. Greatfather's health is too uncertain to wait."

*Oh.* Tiercel had a sinking feeling in the pit of his stomach. He'd thought he was going to have a little more time to get used to the idea of becoming Ancaladar's new Bondmate, but apparently not.

❧

THEY rode out to the Sunning Terraces, and there, on one of the enormous flat floors of stone, the two Elves spread out a blanket and unpacked the contents of the saddlebags as the sun rose over the field.

*It must be strange knowing exactly when you're going to die*, Tiercel thought. Even though the Elves hadn't told him much—he hadn't seen Jermayan again since the breakfast meal yesterday, and Idalia had been evasive when he'd pressed her for more information later that day—he was pretty sure he knew what was coming. When King Sandalon cast the Great Spell, he and his dragon would die. Jermayan would probably die too, though nobody had said so, but Tiercel couldn't believe that severing the link with Ancaladar would result in anything less.

Two people and a dragon were going to die. And that was just if the spell worked. If it didn't work . . .

"I want— I need— to ask you some questions," he said.

Elunyerin was brewing the water for tea on a small brazier. Tiercel had gotten used to Elven tea in the last several sennights, but he couldn't say he really liked it.

"The time for questions has passed, Tiercel," Rilphanifel said gently.

"No," Tiercel said immediately. "What if— What if— I want to stop this. Now. I can't do this. I can't let all of them die just for me."

Rilphanifel bowed his head for just a moment before he spoke.

"Tiercel, Greatfather is dying, no matter what choice you make. Idalia is a great Healer. It was so in her last life, and it is so in this one. It is her word that he will die before the snows come, and Ancaladar with him. But I think you would speak of Sandalon Elvenking and Petrivoch, who will also die."

"Yes," Tiercel said tightly.

"Sandalon is our king. I think the stories in human lands do not speak of him, but know this: as a child, he saw the Elven Lands ravaged by the Endarkened, and his father, Andoreniel, who was king before him, brought low by the Shadow's Kiss. Along with the other children of the Elven Lands, he flew to the Fortress of the Crowned Horns upon Ancaladar's back to seek what safety there might be, and though he had seen only a few summers, he was an Elven Prince, and he knew full well that he might die there, should the Armies of the Light not defeat the Darkness. He has lived all his years knowing that the peace he reigns over is a gift bought with blood and tears. To attempt to preserve it beyond its time would be to dishonor those who gave it to him. Since the ancient days when the Houses of the Elvenborn sang songs of praise to the Starry Hunt, we have stood against the Shadow when it rose up against the Light, and it is for Sandalon to do all that he can, as Andoreniel King did before him, to save us all from its return. This is his choice, and his gift to you."

It was a long and impressive speech—the longest Tiercel had ever heard Rilphanifel make—and somehow it seemed to make everything worse.

"But . . . But I can't *do* anything!" Tiercel blurted out. It was his greatest fear, and it had only gotten worse in the face of the Elves' calm trust that somehow he would stumble into a solution through nothing more than blind ignorance of the entire problem.

"You do not yet know that. The Wild Magic only asks that you try," Elunyerin said. The water had boiled, and she poured it into the waiting pot. "Now we will eat, and drink tea, and soon you will see the beauty that is one of the Light's great gifts to the world."

Tiercel didn't really feel a lot like either eating or drinking tea, but both the Elves coaxed him, and Harrier simply nagged him, and he ended up eating a great deal more than he intended. It actually made him feel better, and—not for the first time—he wondered if Harrier was right, and a good meal was the answer to most of Life's problems.

As Rilphanifel was packing away the remains of the meal, the horses, which had been placidly grazing up until now, all lifted their heads at once.

"They come," Elunyerin said. "Look."

At first the boys could see nothing in the direction she indicated, then faint specks appeared against the light of the eastern sky. They had to squint against the sun to see, but soon the specks grew larger. It was an entire flock of dragons in all the colors of the rainbow. Even Ancaladar was there.

The flight of dragons was the most beautiful sight Tiercel had ever seen. Red—blue—green—gold—black—the sunlight glittered off iridescent scales and shimmering wings. He kept trying to count them and failing. More than a dozen, anyway. They soared and wheeled through the still morning air like great kites, and their flight was absolutely silent. Soon they were overhead, then beyond, then circling back.

"It is time for us to go," Rilphanifel said, breaking the spell.

"I . . . What?" Harrier said. He sounded as if he'd been hit over the head, and Tiercel could sympathize. He dragged his gaze away from the skyful of dragons with an effort. "I mean—"

"Deshtariel Chamberlain comes now to greet the king and to bring him and his court to House Malkirinath so that they may rest and be refreshed," Rilphanifel said kindly. He gestured, and Tiercel could see where a long column of horses—only a few with riders—and a couple of brightly-decorated wagons moved slowly toward the field. "We shall depart, so that you may greet him later, and properly."

"Come on," Harrier said, sighing as he took a last look at the dragons. They were circling in close formation now, obviously preparing to land. "I guess you'll be seeing a lot of them soon enough, Tyr."

⌒

TIERCEL was a little surprised that he and Harrier were allowed to attend the evening meal at all, since, wouldn't it be a banquet for the King of the Elves? But an hour before their usual dinner time, Farabiael came to their rooms with an armful of clothing—they'd spent most of the day more-or-less hiding out there—and told them to dress themselves and, in the name of Leaf and Star, arrive at the table on time!

When they sorted through what Farabiael had brought, they discovered that they'd been given special clothing for the occasion. And since, compared to the Elves, they dressed very simply, tonight's costumes were elaborate indeed.

Harrier's outfit was in shades of green and violet. He'd almost refused to wear the clothes at all until Tiercel had pointed out that the Elves had picked out blue and pale orange for him, and if Harrier called it "peach" they weren't going to have to worry about the banquet at all, because neither of them would be attending. Aside from the colors—and why did the Elves seem to always want to dress up like flowers?—the outfits were identical: a pair of heavy silk trousers and a long-sleeved tunic over which went a long sleeveless see-through vest that fell to midthigh, closed halfway down its length by a long row of small jeweled buttons. Over the sheer vest went a wide-sleeved robe—equally transparent—that fell to midcalf, and fortunately by now both of them had gotten a great deal of experience with the mysteries of Elven sash-tying, because the robe had no buttons, but was held closed with another of the long wide sashes that the Elves seemed to favor instead of belts. They even had new boots to finish off their new outfits, of brightly-gilded leather that shone like metal.

It took them both a long time to bathe and dress.

❧

HARRIER poked his head in through the door of Tiercel's room. "Whoa," he said, giving Tiercel's finished outfit a startled look. The combination of colors and the translucent layers gave the costume the iridescent look that the Elves favored, though by Elven standards the garb was severely plain: the only ornamentation was on the jeweled buttons of the vest and the metallic embroidery on the belt and along the edge of the robe.

"I don't want to go," Tiercel said, looking at his reflection in the mirror. A stranger stared back, a stranger wearing peculiar clothes much finer than anything he'd ever worn back home. He glanced toward the window. In a few hours the moon would rise. And it would be time for the spell.

"Tough," Harrier said unsympathetically. "If you didn't want to go, you shouldn't have said 'yes' to this stupid idea in the first place. Then I wouldn't have had to get dressed up like a girl."

"Don't you even care that they're going to die?" Tiercel said, looking at Harrier. For all his protests, Harrier looked nothing like a girl. A really dangerous flower, maybe, but not a girl.

"Everybody keeps saying they're going to die anyway, Tyr. And I guess that's supposed to make it better. But no, I don't like it. But I think you're forgetting something."

"I don't think I can be," Tiercel said, staring out at the twilight again.

"Simera died for you, too," Harrier said quietly.

Tiercel turned back, his eyes wide with shock and betrayal. He knew Harrier still grieved for their friend. Thinking about her death hurt so much that he did his best not to think about Simera at all.

"She died so you could get here. So this could happen. And I think this is really stupid, but I also can't think of anything else we can do. We can't go hide."

Tiercel shook his head very slightly.

"And . . . I don't know. You're the one who always knows all the right words, Tyr. I just think the Elves must think this is important."

Tiercel nodded reluctantly. "I don't think I'll be able to eat anything."

Harrier shook his head. "I guess . . . me either."

THERE were few things to mark the meal as different from an ordinary evening meal in House Malkirinath, other than that everybody's clothes were a little more formal than usual and there were a number of strangers present. Because of the extra people, there were two tables laid in the dining room instead of one—some of the furniture had been moved to make room for the second table. Tiercel and Harrier were introduced to Sandalon and Vairindiel—as well as to a number of people who seemed to make up the King's Council, and several people who were apparently Mages—but "Sandalon" and "Vairindiel" were the only names they were really able to remember.

To Tiercel's dismay, he and Harrier were seated at the same table as the King. He was trying not to think about what was going to happen later tonight, and sitting with a man—an Elf, and the King of the Elves, at that—who was cheerfully awaiting what amounted to his own execution would have destroyed his appetite completely, if he'd had any left.

Since Jermayan wasn't there, Sandalon was the oldest person in the room—older even than Idalia, though by only a few years. He teased her as if they were family, and watching the two of them talk quietly together, Tiercel discovered after a moment that they were.

"If this is indeed what is required to cause you to come and visit us, brother, then perhaps I should have sent Ancaladar to steal Tiercel out of his cradle, so you would come to us sooner," Idalia said.

"I am pained to discover that Githilnamanaranath has become such a distant journey for your aged bones, sister, when once you roamed not only the Nine Cities That Were, but all the Wild Lands as well, in not one lifetime, but two."

"Those days are gone, Sandalon, both the good and the bad of them. There are few moments in all my years that I would see undone, for the Wild Magic goes as it wills, and none among us can truly understand its weaving," Idalia answered.

"As always you speak no more or less than the truth, Idalia. I have seen the rebirth of the Flower Forests, and desert turn to meadow. I am content."

Tiercel wasn't sure whether he should be listening to any of this, even though he was seated at Idalia's right hand and the two of them weren't doing anything to keep their voices down. He wasn't quite sure how Idalia could be Sandalon's sister and Kellen's sister both, and he didn't think that was a story she was ever going to tell him even if he could figure out how to ask.

"But I am lacking in courtesy to a guest beneath your roof," Sandalon said, turning his attention to Tiercel. "And you have come from a farther place than any I have ever seen. It would please me greatly to hear of Armethalieh, for many of the friends of my childhood once called it home. I fear, though, that it will have changed much since the days when Kellen and Cilarnen knew it."

Beside Tiercel, Harrier choked on his cup of cider, and Tiercel frantically searched his mind for changes to Armethalieh in the last thousand years that might interest the King of the Elven Lands. For a moment he couldn't think of what to say. *Don't you know you're going to die tonight?* his mind cried.

But of course Sandalon knew that. Rilphanifel had told Tiercel that he'd been alive during the last war, and might even have seen the Endarkened in the flesh. If Tiercel had been willing to leave home and come here to keep something like the Fire Woman from gaining power—and Tiercel had been born after centuries of peace—how much more likely was it that Sandalon was willing to die to destroy her?

*First Simera. Now Sandalon. How many more people are going to have to die hoping I can do something I don't know how to do?*

Tiercel took a deep breath. "Well," he began, "they've taken down the City walls. And they've rebuilt the Great Library. It's bigger now. . . ."

AFTER the meal, everyone gathered outside in the garden. The Elves, the boys had already noticed, decorated nearly everything outdoors with tiny colored lanterns that were lit at dusk, so the garden was as brightly-colored by night as by day.

In Armethalieh, important ceremonies, such as the investiture of a new Magistrate or Light-Priest, or the Parading of the Guard, or the ritual Opening of the City Gates in the moonturn of Seed-time, were conducted with great formality and stateliness. This was obviously the most important thing the Elves could think of to do, but there was an odd casualness about it. People gathered in Jer-mayan and Idalia's garden, and more and more of them showed up, and after a while Jermayan was carried out of the house on a litter, and then they all started to walk down through the garden. All around him Tiercel could hear the Elves talking to each other about the same things people might talk about back home—their gardens, and the weather; horses, and clothes, and people he didn't know. Nobody talked about the Endarkened or magic.

They didn't walk all the way to the Sunning Terraces, as he'd halfway expected, but they walked a good distance past the little house where he had spent so many long and useless hours attempting to learn the High Magick. He suspected now that Jermayan and Idalia had known all along that he'd never be able to master it without Bonding to a dragon, but if they'd suggested a Bonding the moment he and Harrier had shown up, he'd simply have refused. He'd needed to learn for himself that there was no other way.

Now, when he'd thought he'd be most upset, Tiercel felt strangely calm about what was to come. None of the Elves seemed at all upset, and that soothed him a little. He hadn't thought that would be possible, but somehow he couldn't be distressed in the face of Sandalon's cheerful acceptance of his fate. The ancient Elven King might have been going to a dance instead of to his death. He'd sought out the Elves because he trusted their judgment and hoped for their counsel. Now that he'd gotten both, he'd just have to go along with things a little further.

The dragons were already assembled in an enormous circle when they arrived. In the darkness their colors were muted, and they looked almost like enormous gleaming metal statues, until one shifted a wing, or twitched a tail, or blinked. The space that the dragons made with their bodies was large enough to contain two more dragons, and Ancaladar was already waiting in the center, curled up like an enormous unhappy cat.

Jermayan was carried on his litter into the center of the space and set down at Ancaladar's head. He reached up one thin hand to touch the dragon's gleaming nose, and Tiercel angrily blinked away sudden tears. No matter how hard he tried to accept this, he still couldn't feel that separating the two of them was fair!

Idalia followed Jermayan into the circle. She bent low over the litter for a moment, her long pale hair hiding Jermayan's face from sight. When she straightened up, she stroked Ancaladar's brow-ridge gently. When she stepped away from the two of them, all the rest of the Elves began to move into the circle, walking through one of the gaps between the dragons. Rilphanifel was standing directly behind Tiercel, and urged him gently forward into the ring.

Idalia joined the waiting Elves as they arranged themselves in a semicircle around Jermayan. For a moment Tiercel wondered why—since the dragons were in a circle—but then another dragon—a blue one—came forward to crouch beside Ancaladar, furling his wings in tightly.

"I am Petrivoch," the blue dragon said to Tiercel. "I thank you for making it possible for my Bondmate and I to serve the Land beyond our deaths."

Tiercel swallowed hard. Though Rilphanifel had insisted it was true, and he'd been trying to make himself believe it for days, somehow hearing the words from Petrivoch convinced him far more than even Sandalon's calm demeanor had. This was the right thing to do. The price was terribly high—for all of them—even for him and Ancaladar if they survived—but it was right. "I just hope I can," he said shakily.

"Have faith in the goodness of Leaf and Star," Petrivoch said gently.

Now Sandalon entered the circle, leaning heavily on his long carved walking staff. Vairindiel walked beside him. Sandalon reached Tiercel's side and stopped. He set his walking staff carefully down upon the grass and lifted both hands to his head, carefully removing the coronet of green stones and white pearls he wore and placing it on Vairindiel's head. Next he removed a large ring from his finger that was set with a stone of the same pale luminous green, and placed it upon her hand. He kissed her gently upon both cheeks, his hands upon her shoulders.

"Rule wisely and well, child of my House. My father left me a land at peace, but I fear I do not make you the same gift."

"All goes as the Wild Magic wills, Greatfather. So it was in Great Queen Vieliessar Farcarinon's time, and so it shall be in mine," Vairindiel answered steadily.

"Then Petrivoch and I are content," Sandalon said, and Vairindiel stepped back to take her place among the circle of watchers.

Tiercel had thought that Sandalon would speak to him next, that Jermayan would say something, that there'd be a chance to *brace himself*, but the next thing that happened was that Sandalon raised his hands, and suddenly Tiercel couldn't look anywhere but at Ancaladar.

He tried to look away, to find Harrier in the crowd, and he couldn't. *It's happening*, he thought in panic.

He'd thought there'd be bright lights, colors—there always were when *he* did a spell—but there weren't. He could still feel the wind ruffling through his hair, smell the night-blooming flowers, hear the crickets chirping. . . .

He just couldn't see anything but Ancaladar.

Ancaladar was looking at him, too.

And Tiercel realized that it didn't matter if he'd agreed and Ancaladar had agreed—that this was important—he didn't want to be here and neither did Ancaladar. If this was even remotely the right sort of thing to be doing, people would have been doing it for centuries. This was wrong. This was a huge mistake.

Even more than that, he should have stayed home.

Yes, the Darkness was coming back—but slowly. The parts of it that were showing up now were things that people could deal with, and when *those* got bad enough—and maybe they already had—everyone would see that there was a real problem and figure out how to deal with it. There were books in Ysterialpoerin, in Armethalieh. There were Wildmages. Other High Mages were probably being born right this minute: it wasn't a rare Gift, really, it was just that nobody ever did anything with it, and he could go home, he could tell people they needed to start training High Mages again. In fact, he could take all the books Jermayan had gathered, go back to Armethalieh, find those High Mages, and train them himself. That would work out so much better.

*I know.*

Suddenly Tiercel felt as if he was thinking someone else's thoughts, and realized Ancaladar knew exactly how he felt, and understood. Nobody could understand it better. It would be so *comfortable* to run, and hide, and let somebody else deal with all the nasty heroism. It would certainly be better than shouldering the guilt of seeing people die, and knowing that you might have been—probably were—responsible. That you could have stopped it. Or at least not have seen it.

*But if we don't do something, who will?*

Tiercel wasn't sure which of the two of them thought it. All he could see was Ancaladar's eyes, golden and glowing.

*You can still refuse*, the dragon said. *Even now.*

But Ancaladar sounded as if he would be unhappy if Tiercel did, and Tiercel knew, without knowing how he knew, that he would be very lonely. He reached out for Ancaladar in the same way that he reached out to the power behind his spells.

And suddenly Tiercel *felt* the Great Spell complete itself as the new Bond was forced into place. Something they had both consented to, something that had never been meant to be. Yet something neither of them could—now—ever regret.

There was a huff of air, as if the world had turned itself inside out. Tiercel could look away from Ancaladar now, and as he did, he saw that Sandalon and Petrivoch simply . . . weren't there anymore.

And Jermayan . . .

"My Beloved is dead." Ancaladar's voice was soft with grief. "Will you love me now, Tiercel?"

"Forever," Tiercel said. He knew it was true, just as he knew that he now had the power to work any of the spells in any of the books he'd read. He didn't have to think about it. The knowledge was just *there*, something he'd gained as simply as if he'd picked up a book from a table. The Bond between dragon and Mage. But with it came more.

All of Ancaladar's grief and loss abruptly poured through Tiercel as if they were his own, and he flung himself upon Ancaladar's neck, sobbing, as the great black dragon wailed his own grief.

# Sixteen

# A Quest Renewed

ARRIER LEANED AGAINST the wheel of the traveling wagon, trying not to feel angry, jealous, and completely left out.

It was a few hours before sunset, but Elunyerin and Rilphanifel had insisted that they stop early enough to make camp while there was still plenty of light. Their horses were picketed with the two draft horses that pulled the wagon; faintly, in the distance, Harrier could hear the clash of swords as they practiced. The two of them would be turning back to Karahelanderialigor tomorrow morning. This was their last night on the road together; they'd ridden almost a sennight south out of the city with him and Tiercel just to be sure that they were on the right road and that Harrier could handle the team and the wagon.

He'd rather be riding, but somebody had to drive the wagon. It was large, almost a traveling house on wheels; He and Tiercel could sleep inside when the weather was bad, even cook inside. But its main function was to serve as a traveling workroom for Tiercel, now that Tiercel had everything he needed.

Including, apparently, a new best friend.

Harrier hadn't realized, when he had agreed that Tiercel should go ahead with this Bond thing, exactly what it was going to mean. He knew what Ithoriosa had said about Bonding, but frankly, he hadn't paid a lot of attention, because Ithoriosa had said a lot of things that Harrier had suspected at the time were just meant to tease and annoy him. But all that stuff about the Bond being the most important thing in the dragon and its Bonded's life?

Was apparently true.

Sure, Ancaladar missed Jermayan. A lot. And as a result, Tiercel was pretty miserable most of the time lately as well as being all wrapped up in talking to Ancaladar every moment he was awake. They'd stayed in Karahelanderialigor for Jermayan's funeral, and Tiercel had even spoken at it, just as if he were a member of the family, which Harrier would have found creepy if he hadn't been so angry. Back then—ten days ago—he'd just been starting to figure out what this whole Bond thing really meant.

If he'd thought about it at all beforehand, he'd thought that having Ancaladar around would be like having a dog around. Okay, a really big dog. One that was just as smart as a person, and could talk, and fly, and bite Harrier in half if he got really grumpy, but still, in a way, a kind of a tool for Tiercel to use in this magic stuff of his, the way shepherds used flockguards, or the Port Watch used alert dogs. He hadn't thought that Ancaladar would just push him aside and take his place in Tiercel's life.

*But he has. Get used to it.*

He might as well have stayed in Karahelanderialigor. Or gone back to Ysterialpoerin. Or gone *home*. Right now Tiercel was off with Ancaladar—again, the way they were every evening—practicing spells, because Ancaladar had taught Jermayan Dragon-rider to be an Elven Mage, so teaching Tiercel Rolfort to be a High Mage wasn't all that hard.

Harrier saw a flash of light from beyond the trees and sighed. And during the day, Tiercel rode through the sky on Ancaladar's back. For as long as Harrier had known him, Tiercel had been afraid of heights, but apparently being up on the back of a dragon was *completely different.*

Oh, of course Tiercel had offered to take Harrier with him—Ancaladar's saddle was built for two—but there wouldn't be anybody to drive the wagon, then, would there?

It was all he was good for now, Harrier supposed. Driving wagons. He wouldn't have made a very good Portmaster, either.

It wasn't that he disliked Ancaladar. How could you dislike a legend? And he felt sorry for him. He really did. A year was a long time, and Ancaladar had just lost someone who had not only been his friend for a thousand and eight years—maybe more—but his Bondmate, which Harrier had a vague idea was something a lot closer than just "friends" from what Ithoriosa had said.

But that didn't give Ancaladar the right to take Harrier's friend away from him. He sighed heavily. *Well, somebody has to drive the wagons. I bet there were a lot of people in Kellen Knight-Mage's army who did nothing but drive wagons all day long. Nobody remembers their names now. I bet the Elves don't even remember their names. But I bet nobody in the whole army would have gotten a hot dinner or a dry place to sleep if they hadn't been there to drive the wagons.* It made him feel a little better. Not much, but a little.

THAT night it was cool and clear. They'd be heading into the Madiran in winter, which was a good thing. Harrier wondered if deserts had winter at all, and what they were like. He supposed he'd find out soon enough.

All of them slept out under the stars, and Harrier had to admit that the stars here in the Elven Lands were breathtaking. They were brighter than the stars at home: there, the ribbon of stars that they called The Unicorns' Road was only a faint dusting across the sky, while here it was as bright and white as the moon itself. The first time Harrier had seen them, the sight had taken his breath away, and he never got tired of watching them.

They'd still be in the Elven Lands for a long time yet, and for all that time, all their supplies—and feeding Ancaladar, which was apparently no small matter—was taken care of, nor would they have to pay for anything. It was, Idalia had said when they left, a gift from House Malkirinath. Once they left the Elven Lands, they'd have to make other arrangements—and figure out how to deal with traveling with a dragon, since it wasn't as if they could exactly tuck him inside the wagon to hide him if he needed hiding. Neither Rilphanifel nor Elunyerin were certain of what lay beyond the border of the Elven Lands; once more, as in the long ago, the Elves had withdrawn in order to allow Men to go their own way.

Harrier sighed, wishing he could go to sleep and stop thinking about these things. But somebody had to, and Tiercel wasn't going to be that someone. He didn't know whether Ancaladar was that sort of someone or not, and he wasn't going to ask.

"Do you want to talk about it?"

For something the size of a house, Ancaladar could move very silently and gracefully. He'd managed to work his way over to where Harrier was lying without Harrier noticing, and Harrier only barely managed to suppress a yelp at the sudden quiet question. He was getting used to surprises, though. Good ones, bad ones, and just plain weird ones.

"Talk about what?" Harrier asked in a low voice. He looked around, sitting up.

Tiercel was sound asleep—he knew that snore—and Elunyerin and Rilphanifel were *apparently* asleep. Even the horses were asleep. Only he and Ancaladar were awake.

"Whatever it is that is keeping you awake this late at night," the dragon said. "You and I will have to talk sometime, Harrier. I know things have not gone as you wished they would, and for that I am truly sorry."

"What? You mean with monsters coming back? Meeting the Elves? Or my friend getting a dragon for his Naming Day present?" Harrier tried to make a joke out of it, and was dismayed at how bitter his voice sounded.

"It is not what I would have wished for, either," Ancaladar said somberly. "Yet I cannot regret the chance to know Tiercel, however briefly."

"It's going to be for the rest of his life."

Since Ancaladar wasn't going to go away—no matter how little Harrier actually wanted to talk to him—Harrier decided he might as well do his best not to disturb the others. He got out of his bedroll, stuffed his feet quickly into his camp-boots, and walked off. He had to walk for quite a few steps before Ancaladar had to do more than simply turn his head and extend his neck to follow him.

"His life may be short, even by human standards," Ancaladar said.

Harrier stopped and looked at Ancaladar. The dragon himself was nothing more than a big black shape in the darkness, but his golden eyes gleamed as if lit from within. Of all the things about the dragon, Harrier thought that was probably the strangest. *Why* did they glow, even when there wasn't any light around to reflect? They weren't like cat's eyes, or dog's eyes. More like . . . lamps.

"Don't tell me you're going to tell us more than the Elves would," Harrier mocked.

"No," Ancaladar said. "But only because I don't know more. *They* don't know more, not about what you two may face. They—

and I—know a great deal more about the problems of the past, but you see, the Darkness has changed its strategy every time it has faced the Light. Any advice at all may cause Tiercel to consider some solutions and discard others, and in doing so, discard the one that will solve the problem. The Elves believe the Wild Magic will cause him to intuitively know the proper solution."

*That is* still *the stupidest thing I have ever heard.* Harrier thought resentfully.

"We're just kids," Harrier said. "Whatever you think Tiercel is—or can do—he isn't. And can't. Really. If none of this had ever happened, he'd be going off to University right about now. I'd be apprenticed to my father. Someday—if Tyr was very lucky—he'd be clerking for the Magistrate Herself. I'd be a very bad Portmaster."

"Neither of you would be happy in those lives," Ancaladar observed dispassionately.

Harrier shrugged. Whether it was true or not, that hardly mattered now. "You were going to tell me about Tyr's life being short," he pointed out belligerently.

If it had been possible, Harrier was sure Ancaladar would have shrugged in return. "The desert by itself is dangerous to humans, and spells can only protect you if you cast them. If Tiercel finds whatever his visions are showing him as The Lake of Fire—and I have seen the land scoured to desert and grow green again, and what he describes does not sound familiar to me—then there will be more danger. He will need all his friends beside him."

"He's got you now," Harrier pointed out. He wanted to be polite to Ancaladar, and he was *trying*, but he kept thinking about how, even during the worst parts of their journey here, he and Tyr had always been able to rely on each other and the friendship they'd shared since almost before either of them could walk. Harrier had never expected to just be . . . dumped because Tiercel had found a friend he liked better.

"And we will have each other until the end of our lives," Ancaladar agreed. "But this does not mean, nor should it, that Tiercel should renounce all other ties of kin and friendship. I am quite wonderful, but even I have my limitations."

Harrier laughed despite himself. "You? You're Ancaladar Star-Crowned. There isn't anything you can't do."

Ancaladar snorted faintly, amused. "Were he hurt, I could not tend him. I can cast no spells for his protection—I am magic; I am not a Mage. When we come to places where I must hide—and we shall; of that much I am certain—you must aid him, and keep him from rash acts. I do not yet know him as well as I will, but I fear already that there are times that Tiercel is . . . excessively trusting, and it frightens me."

Despite his unhappiness, this was a sobering thought. Harrier had gotten used to thinking of Ancaladar as being someone who'd fought off hordes of Endarkened. A myth. A hero. Not someone with limitations. He thought about it for a moment. Ancaladar was right.

"Huh. If you're scared now, you should hear about some of the things he did on the way here. You'd turn white," Harrier said. It was impossible for him to keep a certain smugness out of his voice. No matter how well Ancaladar came to know Tiercel in the future, Harrier would always be the one who had grown up with him.

"I would like to hear of them," Ancaladar said quietly. "I fear sometimes that my Bonded keeps things from me."

"Oh, he'll do that," Harrier said, grinning now in spite of himself. "He doesn't mean to, but he does. You'll figure him out soon enough. But come on, and I'll tell you about the time we explored the sewers back in Armethalieh when we were little. It was all Tyr's idea, of course. . . ."

⁓

"YOU knew them all," Harrier said. "What were they like?" He leaned back against Ancaladar's chest.

It was several hours later. The two of them had gone to the grove where Tiercel and Ancaladar practiced Magick. Ancaladar had assured Harrier that it was safe—he'd chosen it for privacy, and Tiercel was careful to leave no residue behind from his workings.

Although Ancaladar's scaly hide was slippery, and no part of him—except for the few patches of hide just behind his head—could be considered soft, Harrier found that the black dragon made a very comfortable resting place.

"They were all very much like people," Ancaladar said, sounding as if Harrier's question entertained him greatly. "Except for Shalkan, of course: Shalkan was a unicorn, and . . . well, I suppose you *don't* know what unicorns are like. They tend to be extremely annoying, and they're rarely serious. But the rest of them, well, seemed to me to be very much like other people. This business of being a hero—it is partly in having the opportunity to act, and partly in being remembered for what you did. Certainly when you rescued Tiercel from the end of the dock when you were both children, at the risk of your own life, that was a heroic act."

"You're crazy," Harrier said comfortably. "I just did what anybody would have done."

"And so said Kellen, and Cilarnen, and Petariel, and Vestakia, and hundreds of others whose names you do not know, and which only their families remember," Ancaladar answered.

⁓

IN the morning, Harrier was the last one up for a change, finally being roused from his bed—after only an hour or so of sleep—by Tiercel's determined clattering of cups and plates. He and Ancaladar had talked nearly until dawn. A lot of their conversation had been about Tiercel, but more had been about Armethalieh, a place Ancaladar had seen only briefly very long ago—during the Flowering War itself, in fact. Harrier had originally been surprised that there were places that Ancaladar didn't know about, but Ancaladar had reminded him that the Elves had withdrawn to the East centuries before, and by then he'd had no further interest in traveling.

By the time the noise—and the smell of ham and griddle-cakes—woke him, the other three had already finished their breakfasts, and Tiercel was threatening to throw the rest of the food away.

"I should reconsider such a rash and hasty action, were I you, Tiercel. The Portmaster's son has a fearsome temper, and is quick to anger, especially when he is hungry," Ancaladar said mildly.

Tiercel glanced from Ancaladar to Harrier in surprise.

"Is something going on that I should know about?" he asked slowly.

"No," Harrier and Ancaladar said in unison.

AFTER breakfast, Elunyerin and Rilphanifel at last took their leave.

"I think they're glad to get rid of us," Harrier said, watching the Elves ride away.

"The Elves have always understood Men as little as Men have understood Elves," Ancaladar said. "You have both been a great trial to them, and they are relieved to have discharged the obligations of both duty and hospitality."

"Well, me too," Harrier said. "At least now I don't have to go around watching every word that comes out of my mouth and figuring out how not to ask questions all the time."

Tiercel laughed. "You got pretty good at it, though," he said.

"Elunyerin kept hitting me. Only when Rilphanifel couldn't see her, though," Harrier grumbled. He rubbed his arm in memory.

Tiercel looked from Ancaladar to Harrier. "I was sort of worrying about when they'd leave. I'm glad the two of you . . ."

"I have always known that I would need to seek Harrier's aid in causing you to behave properly, Tiercel. He has told me many disquieting stories of your childhood," Ancaladar said reprovingly.

"We talked all night," Harrier said, smirking.

"Oh, I . . . Blessed Saint Idalia and the Great Flowering," Tiercel groaned.

"Yeah," Harrier said. "Maybe now that you've got a *dragon* to watch your back you'll stop pulling quite so many dumb stunts."

"And to aid you in this endeavor, I believe we might take this opportunity to once more practice the simpler wards and shields. You must not only be able to cast them, Tiercel, but to build them into cantrips, which requires a focus that you yet lack. Only when you have mastered these spells will it be safe to proceed with those which you may need later."

Tiercel looked at Ancaladar and sighed. "I'll go get my wand."

"And your sword," Ancaladar said helpfully.

Tiercel trudged off to the wagon.

"You really do enjoy bullying him, don't you?" Harrier said, once Tiercel was out of earshot.

Ancaladar blinked slowly. "Not so much as he may imagine. But a High Mage is different from an Elven Mage. Were he to attempt spells of storm and lightning now—or even to invoke the Elemental Powers—he would suffer greatly. He must begin with those spells that will protect all of us, should protection be needed."

"It takes years to train a High Mage," Harrier said, because that was something that Tiercel had told him.

"Our Bond speeds many things, Harrier. Perhaps it will be enough," Ancaladar answered.

❧

AFTER Tiercel and Ancaladar had left for their practice, Harrier put the camp to rights, packing up their gear and stowing it in the wagon, and getting out the harness that he'd need to use later. For the first time, as he had watched his friends—*both* his friends, he realized—walk off to the copse of trees where they'd practiced last night, he hadn't felt a sick pang of jealousy at seeing them go off together. And he realized that he was looking forward to this evening, when he could try to have a conversation with Tiercel about what he was learning, and talk to Ancaladar about—well, lots of things. He knew he wouldn't understand any of the High Magick talk, but it might help Tiercel to talk about it.

Getting everything ready didn't take very long, and he knew the two of them would probably be practicing for at least a bell, maybe longer. The day was already getting warm, so he decided to go back down to the stream and maybe get in a swim while he was waiting. It was deep enough for that, and didn't seem to contain any of the Otherfolk that filled the Elven Lands. Brownies, Fauns, and Centaurs were one thing—he'd grown up with those—but every time he ran into something strange here, he was never sure whether it could talk or not. Tiercel was the one who knew about Otherfolk, but Harrier was the one who kept seeing them. It wasn't fair.

HE got down to the edge of the stream—Rilphanifel and Elunyerin always made camp by water if at all possible, and with thirsty horses and a thirsty dragon to tend, it made sense—and walked along it until he found the nice deep slow-running spot where he'd bathed last night. The morning sun was filtering down through the trees, and there were a few birds calling to each other in the distance, and everything was quiet and peaceful. He peered down into the water suspiciously, but nothing outlandish stared back.

He'd pulled off his tunic, and was just about to sit down to remove his boots, when a voice stopped him.

"Well thank goodness. I thought those two would *never* leave.

Elves. Always poking in where they're not wanted. They can be really annoying sometimes, don't you think?"

Harrier yelped and dove for his shirt. He clutched it, staring around himself, but all he saw was forest.

*Just my luck. Now I run into one of the things that's invisible.*

"Er, what?" he said at last.

There was a flicker in the forest on the other side of the stream, as if the sunlight had suddenly gotten brighter, and something stepped through the trees.

It was a unicorn.

Her coat was the pale gold of morning sunlight, except for the white blaze down the center of her face. Her short brushy mane was white as well, as was the lionlike tuft at the end of her tail, and she had four white socks. Her nose was pink, and so were her cloven hooves.

He'd thought all unicorns were white.

As she stepped closer, a shaft of sunlight struck her horn. He'd thought it was just white—it was in the middle of the white blaze in her forehead, after all—but as the light struck it, it flared with color like the inside of a seashell: rose and gold and even blue.

Her eyes were blue, framed by long dark lashes.

Harrier had been startled by many of the things he'd seen in the Elven Lands—the dryads, the selkies. He'd been overawed and impressed by the sheer majesty of the dragons.

Nothing in his life had prepared him for the heart-stopping beauty of a unicorn. She was as fragile, as delicate, as beautiful as a flower. She was grace personified. She was . . .

"I've been following you ever since you left Karahelanderialigor, waiting for a chance to get you alone."

"You're a unicorn," Harrier said.

The unicorn snorted with gentle laughter, tossing her beautiful head. "I've been one all my life. Are you always so obvious? I suppose you've been a human all your life, too."

"Well, yes." Harrier felt a sudden need to apologize for that. For being here at all, even. "You see, I—"

"Oh, don't worry about that now. I've brought you a present. It's in the bag around my neck. Come closer. I won't bite," the unicorn said coaxingly.

Only then did Harrier realize that yes, the unicorn *did* have a bag around her neck. It was more of a small satchel, really, made of red leather and closed with a buckle. The strap around her neck closed with a buckle, too, and in an instant he felt angry. Who could possibly have dared to insult such a wonderful creature by putting a collar on her as if she were a beast of burden?

Without thinking, he walked toward her—only realizing when it was far too late to do anything about it that he'd walked right into the middle of the deepest part of the stream, boots and all.

The unicorn threw back her head and brayed with laughter. Harrier slipped and floundered on the muddy bottom of the stream, sliding completely beneath the water. He lost the hold he had on his tunic. When he surfaced again, he saw it floating downstream, well out of reach.

The unicorn was on her knees, sobbing with laughter. She was shaking her head back and forth. Her tail lashed.

"Oh!" she wailed. "Humans! I had forgotten how funny you all were!" She rolled on her side, kicking out weakly, helpless with mirth.

Harrier stomped his way to the unicorn's side of the stream.

Fragile? Delicate? Beautiful?

He wondered how you went about strangling a unicorn.

"You did that on purpose," he said, standing over her.

She looked up at him soulfully, her sides still heaving.

"Only a little," she said. "There was a log right there. You could have used that, you know."

"And you knew perfectly well I wouldn't," Harrier said. At least he had dry clothes back in the wagon.

The unicorn rolled over and got to her feet, shaking to remove the dirt of the forest floor. Harrier resisted the urge to brush her clean. He didn't think he trusted her.

Standing, they were almost of a height. And her eyes were *very* blue.

"Don't you want your present?" she asked. Her voice was soft and coaxing, as if she were sorry for the nasty trick she'd just played on him, but Harrier could see the sparkle of mischief in her eyes. He wasn't sure he wanted any presents from her.

"Probably not," he said firmly. "Every time people give me presents, it just makes trouble." He thought of his Naming Day party, and the gift from his Uncle Alfrin that had actually started all this. "Especially if it's books. Someone gave me a book as a present once."

"Then you'll know exactly what to do with these. Come on. Don't be shy. You'll hurt my feelings."

"Why am I worried about that?" Harrier demanded. Even though the day was warm, his clammy leggings weren't that comfortable, and his boots were probably ruined. There was also the matter of the lost tunic.

"Because you're much nicer than you want anyone to think. Because it's a present. And because I'm tired of wearing this collar around my neck. I can't exactly hand it to you, you know."

Harrier hadn't actually thought of that. He reached out cautiously. The fur of the unicorn's neck was cool and soft under his fingers. It felt like the softest down imaginable. He got his fingers under the strap and lifted. She lowered her head so he could pull it free.

"Hey!" Harrier said irritably. "Watch the horn!"

"You're very irritable, aren't you?" the unicorn asked pertly.

"I'm very wet," Harrier said. He wiggled his toes. His boots squished.

"Now open it," the unicorn said.

"I ought to just throw it in the stream," Harrier grumbled.

If unicorns could smirk, he would have sworn she did.

"Oh, you could. But really, it wouldn't change anything. If I say

I'm sorry for making you walk into the stream—I'm really not, and you *did* look funny—will you open the pouch? Leaf and star, I'm a unicorn! A creature of the Light! You're supposed to trust me!"

"Hmph," Harrier said. He had to admit that she did have a point, though. She might have a horrible sense of humor, but she couldn't possibly be *evil*.

He unbuckled the pouch.

Inside it were three small slim books.

"It *is* books," he said with a groan. "These aren't for me. You're looking for Tiercel."

"I think I know exactly who I'm looking for and who I'm not looking for," the unicorn snapped, switching her tail in irritation. "Why don't you look at them before making up your mind?"

Grumbling to himself, Harrier pulled out the books. At least they were small; three little books bound in red leather, with some sort of gold decoration on the spine that he didn't examine too closely. There was no title on any of the covers. *Probably can't cause too much trouble,* he thought to himself. He flipped through them quickly. They were all handwritten, and the writing was very small. He closed them again and prepared to stuff them back into their carrying case.

"Why don't you look at the title pages?" the unicorn said, sounding exasperated now. With a sigh, Harrier pulled out a book and leafed through it to the title page.

*The Book of Stars.*

With a terrible sinking feeling, he quickly checked the title pages of the other two books.

*The Book of Moon.*

*The Book of Sun.*

Harrier stared at them for a long moment.

These were the Three Books of the Wild Magic. The Three Books that came—mysteriously, unbidden—into the hands of every person fated to become a Wildmage. Once given, it was possible to renounce them—supposedly—but never to lose them.

"You cannot possibly be serious," he said weakly.

"Why would I want to be serious about something that's just changed your whole life?" the unicorn said, stamping her foot. "And don't even suggest that these would be better off in *Tiercel's* hands. No, Tiercel has other things to do with his life. You, on the other hand, get to protect him. And guess what that makes you?"

"Stupid?" Harrier suggested. "Suicidal?"

"A Knight-Mage!" the unicorn cried cheerfully. "First one born since Kellen Tavadon! See? You don't even have to guess—I'm just going to tell you, and now you can stop being all grumpy and we can be friends. So you don't have to worry too much about casting spells, because you'll never really be very good at it. But you probably should have paid more attention when those silly Elves wanted to give you sword lessons. Oh, well. Too late now. Just read your Three Books and hope for the best. Let's go tell Tiercel and Ancaladar! Oh! And my name is Kareta! I almost forgot to tell you!"

Kareta tossed her head, reared up on her hind legs, and crossed the stream in one fluid bound.

Harrier stared after her clutching the Three Books.

His Three Books.

"Hey!" he shouted after her. "What if I don't want to be a Knight-Mage?"

"You should have thought of that back in Armethalieh!" Kareta called back over her shoulder.

Harrier stared down at the books in his hand for a moment longer before stuffing them back into the bag. He slung it over his shoulder, then walked to the log and began to cross, slowly and carefully. As he reached the other side, a sudden thought struck him.

The Wild Magic never sent gifts without need. If it had just decided to turn him into the first Knight-Mage born since the time of Kellen the Poor Orphan Boy, then things weren't just bad . . .

They were really bad.